ALL WHO WANDER ARE LOST

DESTINATION HORROR STORIES

Gemma Amor

CEMETERY GATES
MEDIA

All Who Wander Are Lost: Destination Horror Stories
Published by Cemetery Gates Media
Binghamton, New York

ISBN: 9798320046402

For more information about this book and other Cemetery Gates publications, visit us at:

cemeterygatesmedia.com
twitter.com/cemeterygatesm
instagram.com/cemeterygatesm

Cover Art: Francesco Giani

CONTENTS

For those, like me, who miss the world entire.

For the travellers, the wanderers, the adventurers, the endlessly curious, the constantly dislocated, the restless and the sleepless, the speakers of many tongues or of none, the seers of many sights, the dreamers who follow their feet, pick stones from between their toes, taste salt on their tongue, feel dust blow hot and hard against their skin, savour the unfamiliar, drink deep of foreign flavours, step where they feared they would never be able to, whether in their minds and their dreams, from their desks, beds, comfy armchairs, cars, or through the pages of a book, in perpetuity.

Wait for me, world: I have an appointment with you.

An ABOMINABLE
Book Club Signed Edition

Gemma Amor

FOREWORD

In case it isn't obvious from the dedication, I started compiling this collection in 2020, during the first of several protracted pandemic lockdowns. The square footage of my house and garden, which I was only supposed to leave once a day for the purposes of government mandated exercise, felt very small indeed. It wasn't. By the standards of many others, I was extremely lucky. I had a garden to sit in. I spent a lot of time there, huddling next to a flowering black sambuca bush, listening to the world as it struggled to cope beyond my fence-panelled kingdom. I remember, mostly, the sounds of life as we'd always known it grinding to a halt. Children crying, dysregulated, out of routine, craving structure and reassurance from agitated parents who valiantly tried to juggle homeschooling obligations with work calls, typing emails with frantic thumbs in the park as footballs flew and dogs barked and bikes and scooters whizzed around their ankles. I remember the bickering of stressed couples out on their daily walks. I unwittingly eavesdropped upon a dozen burgeoning divorces. And I remember the helicopters. I lived near a major hospital at the time. For several dreadful weeks, there was a constantly circling queue of bladed harbingers waiting to land, ferrying in the dangerously sick for urgent treatment. It was bizarre and horrible.

I grew very accustomed to the shape of the sky above my house. To the neighbouring trees and structural idiosyncrasies. Outside the garden, the world, always so full of possibility, felt suddenly dangerous. Inhospitable. People fought in the supermarket for tinned goods and toilet rolls. Death paced the streets. Televised press conferences chaired by untrustworthy types told us stay inside, stay away, stay safe.

It sounds wildly dystopian to recall. Most of us appear to have moved on now. A few lingering signs of the crisis remain. Worn stickers on the pavement telling people to keep their distance from each other. Disposable face masks rotting in parks and ditches. Temporary outdoor dining structures that no longer pretend to be temporary, planning permission be damned. Anti-vax slogans spray-painted onto walls.

That was a dark period. Not the darkest I have seen, but bleak. I lost someone who was everything to me. She caught COVID and died soon after. I was not allowed to travel to see her to say goodbye, which will remain an eternal, bitter regret. I have written about this in other books. Her funeral was a muted, odd affair. We were forbidden from singing hymns in case we spread deadly germs. My days after that as I recall them were hazy. I stayed indoors. I drank a lot and became rather weepy. I mourned and scrolled. I don't regret distancing myself as instructed, but I do regret the time I lost. With family, with the world at large. Those precious things were viewed almost exclusively through the oblong of doom otherwise known as my phone.

It is perhaps no wonder, then, that my imagination ran rampant. I don't think I'd realised until the pandemic quite how fundamental a part of my character it is: the need to roam. I had taken it for granted, as people do.

I first left the UK in my early twenties, to visit Lake Garda in Italy. I remember my first glimpse of the Italian Alps. I don't think I had ever, until that point, seen anything so large, so humbling, as those mountains. It was an obnoxiously transformative moment for this wide-eyed kid from the Fens. We didn't go anywhere we couldn't drive to when I grew up; costs were prohibitive. Beyond money, or lack thereof, I had fear to contend with. To my immediate family, the world at large was deemed a frightening prospect, and I was an odd fish for wanting to experience it.

But standing on the shore of Garda, a stormy charcoal-grey sky above and dazzling turquoise water below, the hulking shadows of mountains beyond, I experienced something very powerful, like electricity. A moment of sheer joy and wonder in which I understood I was a tiny unimportant speck on the face of the earth, whizzing around at lightning speed with millions of other unimportant specks, a miniscule (odd) fish in a massive ocean, and all those things I had previously thought so important no longer were. That first trip made me realise what it was to travel. I soon lost myself in the rhythm and flow of moving about from one place to the next and grew addicted to the mileage. Each destination seemed to take me further away from home, and yet somehow, bring me closer to myself. I understand how achingly, yawningly privileged that sounds, but I was young, I had a good job, and I was responsibility free. I never coveted anything but the ability to go where I pleased. Some of the happiest times of my life occurred when I didn't own much beyond the contents of a large backpack, and I certainly didn't miss what I didn't own.

Later, travel became a key component in my recovery from postnatal depression. It helped me rekindle a hunger for life again. I beetled around the Scottish Highlands in a tiny rented Ford Fiesta, researching my novel *White Pines*, and I can vividly remember standing alone on the shore of Laide beach, looking out at Gruinard Island, thinking *I have so many more stories to tell.*

The world has been through a lot since then. As I type, there is war. Violence rages. Children die, women are murdered, bombs obliterate innocent lives. Hospitals and schools, churches and monuments lie in rubble. Acts of unimaginable cruelty occur daily. My silly little tales are nothing in the face of so much death. I have no direct experience of conflict. I can only watch from afar, broken hearted. Some may think such sentiments have no place in a book like this, but it played on my mind heavily as I edited these so-called 'horror' stories, for the true horrors, as we know, lie out there in the real world. Freedom of movement, which I romanticised in previous paragraphs, will never be a possibility for large portions of humanity. I don't say this to be overly didactic or to beat my breast in performative outrage. I say this because *not* acknowledging world events feels crass. Dishonest. Wilfully ignorant. I remain a powerless, unimportant speck, but this information no longer seems comforting. Words, my entire trade, mean little in the face of colossal tragedy. I suppose one of the only redeeming qualities about doing what I do is that, for anyone looking for some small escapism from the saturation of violent images and reports we are witnessing on such a grand scale, I might be able to provide some small distraction, if only for a short while. Nothing in these pages is particularly courageous, or important, but this collection of what I affectionately call 'destination horror' stories might offer a small reprieve, of sorts. The book you're about to read features tales based on places I've visited and explored, and compiling it brought me enormous comfort during difficult times. I'm fond of these stories. I hope you will be, too.

A further word of caution: as ever, there are some strong themes throughout. Suicide features explicitly in 'The Final Wish Foundation', and there are references to sexual violence in 'Less Exalted Tastes'. Please take care if those things affect you.

It remains for me to say thank you, as ever, to my wonderful, gloriously enthusiastic readers for sticking with me on my journey. *All Who Wander Are Lost* is my twelfth published book, and my fifth book with Cemetery Gates Media, who continue to be fantastic to work with. I feel so very humbled and lucky that I get to write like this, and that my words find homes with you all. It allows me to soar and roam when I am otherwise unable to, and that, I think, is a truly wonderful thing.

-Gemma

THERE'S SOMETHING IN FIRST LANDING
STATE PARK

I am more myself when I travel than at any other time.

This is something my mother cannot understand.

'Why can't you be happy at home?' She complains. I have no easy answer to this.

I could tell her: you only have to turn on the news. It's exhausting living where, and how we do.

But that wouldn't be the reason, and it wouldn't be something she could understand if it were. My mother is rooted firmly into her country of birth. Little I say out loud is going to help clear up the mystery of my wanderlust for her. You can't dig out roots, not after they've sunk deep. Nor can you fight fear, which I suspect lies at the heart of our differences.

Besides, I have a feeling what she really means is: 'Why don't you come and see me more often instead of tripping off all over the place?'

But she knows why. She just doesn't want to admit it. It's hard for me to spend time with a person who fundamentally doesn't understand me, or like the things that I like. It's hard for her, too, which is why we don't meet often. The disparities between us are painful for both parties.

She's been easier on me about all this since the incident, though. I'm grateful for that.

I think about this as I stare out of the tinted aeroplane window next to me. It's not just my mother. In general, I am finding it harder and harder to be around other people. Increasingly, I seek solitude, the peculiar and fulfilling loneliness that accompanies solo travel. Something I would have once been afraid of, until I started to question: why? Alone time, I've come to realise, is a rare and special gift. Other people can crowd in, stop you from experiencing yourself. A nice distraction, but distractions only last so long. You can't run from your own shadow forever.

I mean, you can try, but it's stitched on with sutures of light and dark, so it's a lot better to get acquainted, I think.

I suppose some might say that constantly travelling is a form of running away, especially in my case. *Surely therapy would be better for you,* people say, but I never was that interested in exploring myself with others, which is precisely why therapy hasn't stuck.

Trust me, I've tried.

'But it's not safe for a woman to travel alone!' My mother says. That's why, when this flight lands in Dulles, Washington, I was supposed to be meeting a tour guide, right off the plane. I had thought my original, carefully organised plan airtight: take in the sights on a small, tailor-made, intimate tour, eat good food, drink some cocktails, learn some things about American history and politics.

The guide however cancelled on me a mere half an hour after my flight departed. Flu. Her message popped up on my phone not long after the seatbelt lights pinged off.

So sorry, she said. *Am heartbroken. Full refund.*

I should feel more upset, but I'm strangely okay about it. Any disappointment can be turned into an opportunity, with a little reframing. My mind runs through all my options, suddenly remembering an acquaintance who lives in Virginia Beach, which is not horrendously far from Dulles, I don't think. Maybe I'll go there instead, although how exactly, I'm not sure. Perhaps I'll hire a car. I should probably slow down on the complimentary wine.

Instead, I order another. I have hours left on this flight. Plenty of time to sober up and figure out the details.

I sit back in my narrow chair and sip wine from a plastic glass. My uncle has a saying: 'Drink the free wine, and eat the free food at weddings, especially the meat. Load up on the meat, Melanie. That's the expensive stuff.' I get it. Life is made up of things that cost money (like plane tickets) and things that don't (like memories, and free booze, and meat at weddings). The things that cost money should, in my mind, be experiences, rather than possessions. This is something else my mother, who never leaves the country and replaces her car every year, doesn't understand, so she calls me a 'feckless hippy', but I work, I earn a living, and anyway names are just words, and words only have as much power to harm as you allow them to.

And when it comes down to it, none of this matters much in the end. All that matters is moving forward in the right direction, towards yourself, not away, and making the most of every goddamn moment you've been gifted in this life.

I think a lot of survivors probably feel the same way.

I experience an uncomfortable moment of pride in myself, then force it into a box I've mentally labelled 'good things'.

Because why not? Why not feel pride at the little victories?

A year ago, I could barely go outside.

Now look at me.

*

Moving forward through space and air, but backwards through time, long-distance international travel is a dimensional headfuck if you think about it too much. I can leave a place in the morning and arrive eight hours later only to find it's still the morning in my destination. Is that what they mean when they say time is a flat circle? I never really understood that expression, but then, I've never been too smart.

Outside the oval tinted window, clouds hang thick and level as an iced cake, the consistency of them milky, like inch-thick frosting.

Or, like roiling smoke. The sort that fills your lungs with a foul, acrid residue.

But it's not a good idea to think about that, so I order another wine.

The clouds break up later into small fluffy hummocks that reveal glimpses of the bluest blue far below. It is easy to imagine hopping from clump to clump, as if the clouds are solid things. Easy also to imagine discovering they are not: to visualise falling, suddenly, through the air, plummeting at a thousand miles per second, hurtling towards the vast cold ocean like a brick dropped by God, wind whistling past your ears so violently they feel as if they might tear off and fly away, blue around, all around, sparkling waves racing up to meet you and to greet your fragile form, hitting the surface of the water, bones shattering, piercing your warm wet skin, vertebrae compacting, ribs fracturing, neck snapping in two like a twig underfoot...but at least it's wet and cool, not hot, and smoky, and...

I jolt awake. I have been napping, and my head dips dangerously close to the woman sitting next to me, almost resting on her shoulder. I stiffen and pull away, smiling uncomfortably. She smiles back. Did I have nightmares all over her? Scream in my sleep? I do that a lot. I think she would look more freaked out, though, if I had.

'Was I talking in my sleep?' I ask, self-conscious.

She shakes her head.

I breathe a sigh of relief. I almost crossed a boundary but saved myself just in time.

Then I realise I have tears on my cheeks. I haven't been screaming, or talking in my sleep.

I've been crying instead.

The other woman looks away. I pat my face with a napkin. I will not be embarrassed, I decide. It's not my fault she's uncomfortable.

I should try not to fall asleep on her again, though.

No more wine for me, I think, even as my eyes start to droop once more.

*

The next few hours are hazy. I dip in and out of fitful naps, waking myself up regularly. My neck develops a fierce crick. I get up, move around, do some stretches in the aisle between seats, drawing a few funny looks. I use the bathroom and chat to the air hostess standing nearby. She tells me she used to vacation at Virginia Beach as a child. She tells me about a place near to it called First Landing State Park.

'Between the beaches of Chesapeake Bay and the Cypress Swamps. You like camping?' She asks.

I grin. I do like camping, a lot.

'Well, there's a really nice campsite out there, with facilities,' she says. 'A bathhouse or two, running water. Beach on one side, swamps on the other. Long Creek Trail runs behind it. Nice, easy walking. It won't be busy this time of year. You'll need bug spray.'

She shows me some pictures on her phone: I see huge, old, moss-festooned trees rising up out of dark water, their roots forming distinctive knobbly knee-hummocks in the swamp, and I see long, sandy beaches with placid waves lapping on smooth shores. It excites me. I thank her for the tip.

'No problem,' she says, smiling.

I check the display on the headrest screen in front of me when I sit back down. 37,999 feet up in the air. Outside air temperature: -58 Fahrenheit. Ground speed: 541 miles per hour. 2,651 miles to go. Over the Atlantic Ocean, like a cloud myself, I am skimming the sky. I watch the world inch past the window at snail's pace, knowing we are actually travelling at incredible speed. All things considered, I am calm, content. Hypnotised by the drone of the jet engines. I realise I'll never get tired of looking at the sky. Sky reminds me of water. Water is cool and wet.

I ask my friend- who, it turns out, is excited by my sudden change in travel plans, and changes hers accordingly- if we can take a trip to First Landing State Park, explore a bit once I've gotten over my jetlag.

She thumbs-ups this request, and the plan is set.

Now, if only I could stop thinking about dying, wouldn't that be something?

*

It's a process, I know that. I'm moving towards myself all the time, a good friend once said, back when we still spoke. His attitude towards me changed when it became apparent I was not the same person as before the incident. This hurt, but I couldn't control him, so I let him go. His advice lingers, though.

And I know he's right.
I'll get there, I will.
Might just take me a bit, is all.

*

Another nap. Another jolt awake to check our position. We're over Vermont, now. I am starting to get increasingly sore and uncomfortable, so this is welcome news. I'm bored. I have watched a couple of movies, listened to two episodes of my favourite podcast, jotted copious notes down in my diary. My knees ache. There is not enough room for my legs to rest comfortably, at an angle that's right for my height. I need to pee again (damn you, free wine), but the woman next to me is dozing and I don't want to annoy her any more than I already have. I can hold it for a little longer, but soon, I'll have to clamber over her.

I always liked the word 'Vermont'. It is satisfying to say.

We pass over a huge, white-stepped quarry dusted with snow. The landscape around it is a patchwork quilt of white and black and grey tiles. Very different to the Big Blue of earlier.

A much harder landing, too I imagine.

If one were to fall from the sky.

*

My friend drove from Virginia Beach to Dulles to come pick me up. When she suggested it, I didn't fully realise the distance and effort that entailed. She said she lived 'close by'. In Britain, that would mean a mile, maybe two. In America, it means she drove four hours out of her way like it was nothing so I wouldn't be stranded at the airport. I told her I could hire a car, or get a train, or find a bus, but she wouldn't hear of it. Wouldn't let me pay for gas, either.

She also packed a cool-bag with ice-cold colas, one of which she hands over as soon as my tired rear hits the passenger seat of her truck.

I know then, that she is a keeper.

'Oh my god,' I groan, in relief. I pierce the can with the ring-pull and take a deep long swig before saying anything else. I know it's rude, but I am so dehydrated from the flight and the interminably long queue at passport control that I can barely see straight.

'Hi,' I gasp, eventually lowering the coke can. Gratitude leaks out of my every pore. 'I'm Melanie, and you are a fucking lifesaver.' A small belch escapes my tingling lips.

'Leigh,' she grins, for we've never met in person before, only online. She jabs coordinates into her phone sat nav. 'And don't

15

mention it.' Her voice is calm, easy on the ears and brain. As meetings go, it is low-key, which is about all I can handle.

We pull out of the airport and onto the access road that feeds into the interstate, or at least I think it is the interstate, I don't know what anything is called here. It is a relief to find Leigh isn't someone who needs to talk for the sake of talking. Jet lag is thoroughly kicking my arse. It is mid-afternoon, but nighttime back home. There is some initial awkwardness between us as I struggle with shyness and fatigue, but Leigh is laid-back. It soothes me.

After a short while, we settle into a rhythm: talk, rest, talk, rest. It feels like the right way to get to know someone. Slow and steady, not a violent, frantic exchange of information.

This is my first trip to America, and I cannot get over how fucking *large* everything is. Roads, cars, trucks, horizons, birds, buildings, food portions, gas stations, everything feels inflated and enormous. I am enjoying it. The contrast with home is very welcome. I like how much space there is everywhere. The highways are busy, but not as bumper-to-bumper-steel-and-glass crowded as a major road would be this time of day in Britain. The views are pretty bland: just road and sky, trees, and dozens of signs for rest stops and diners. I realise I need to adjust my definitions of what is a 'long drive.' I get the impression it's not uncommon for people to truck along for eight or nine hours and that still be considered a short journey. I suppose that makes sense when you consider some individual states are bigger than my entire country, but the thought of all that long distance driving makes me wince: my knees are already swollen. I desperately need to lie down, elevate them.

All in good time, though. All in good time.

*

Early on, I fall into the trap of being over-polite to the point of annoyance. 'Thank you,' I keep saying, acutely aware of how much out of her way Leigh has gone. 'I can't tell you how much this means to me. Seriously, thank you. Please let me give you some money.'

'Shut up already,' she says, after the fifth time, before winking and turning on the radio to show there is no bite to the words. Or to shut me up. Either is fine with me. I take the hint but resolve to slip some dollars into the glove compartment when she's not looking. At the very least I'm shouting all her meals from now on.

Turns out, we have a lot in common. She likes to paint; I like to paint. She likes to write fiction, so do I. She grew up with only her mom, just like I did. We both love nature and the outdoors, and have a hatred of crowds and people who try too hard. We're both dog people. We share a fixation with the ocean, too, with water. She likes astronomy, I'm into geology. Our dads are both ex-military. I realise we're going to be fine. We have enough to talk about when we feel like it. The road stretches out and I push my seat back on its track and stretch out along with it: hot, tired, uncomfortable, but I've arrived, and it feels good.

Eventually we hit the outskirts of Virginia Beach. I sit up and look around with interest, almost dead with fatigue but managing to fight it off. There is a large military presence here- naval ships, fighter jets roaring overhead- a lot of water, a lot of birds, and a strip of high-rise hotel blocks lining the beachfront, one of which is mine. Obviously busy during peak season, the place now has a ghostly, preparatory air to it that I like a lot. The streets are quiet, even though it's Friday night. Music, the easy-listening variety, plays at intervals from speakers attached to lamp posts and store-fronts. Playing for who? There is hardly anyone around. I don't mind that, though. It adds to the abandoned theme-park ambience that has settled here like a heady, perfumed melancholy. This is compounded by the haunted house attraction we drive past, tacky-bright lettering and a giant blue fibreglass skull fixed to the outside wall, hands protruding, grasping.

Leigh drops me at my hotel. I am going to take a day to adjust to the local time and sleep as well as I can, before we head off on our little camping adventure. I ask her about First Landing State Park before exiting the car. Leigh goes there all the time. If I'm fine with sharing a tent, we can camp there no problem, she knows the good spots. I can try smores. Maybe we can sneak out for a midnight swim in the ocean.

I say, fuck yeah, and the plan is sealed.

But first, I need to lie down, in a soft bed. Order room service. Find something shitty to watch on the TV. Stay awake as long as humanly possible, so I can adapt. So my eventual sleep is deep and restful, without nightmares. Without dreams of death. Without flickering orange light and a horrible sour burning smell in my nostrils.

Leigh honks as she pulls away from the hotel. I grin and wave, feeling like we've known each other for a hundred years already. I feel good about life, underneath the exhaustion.

Feeling any other way would be ungrateful.

*

It doesn't matter where in the world you go, birds are always an anchoring sight. I watch them wheel above a dawn-stained sea and feel grounded. My plans to adjust to local time have failed miserably: I crashed hard when I got to my room, then woke up at

17

three am. I have been up since. It is mid-morning, back home. Jetlag is one of those things you just have to accept, rather than fight, I am learning. Take the sleep when you can get it, and slowly adapt your schedule where you can.

The remains of my room-service dinner are oddly tempting, at sunrise. I was too tired and out of sync to eat much of it after checking in. Now I find myself picking through cold, soggy fries with gusto. Breakfast here doesn't start for another two and a half hours.

I watch the ocean from my chair by a large sliding window. There is a balcony outside, but it's too high up for me to comfortably sit on. Besides, it's cold and windy out, especially at this height. This armchair is just fine. I have a notebook open on my lap, in which I jot down random thoughts and feelings as I watch the brilliant burnt sienna sun rise slowly over the purple sealine. I feel comfortable yet dislocated. As if I have lived in a thousand places, but none ever completely. Scraping noises from the room above keep me slightly on edge: there is someone moving furniture around up there, but why they are doing it at this hour, I have no idea.

I keep an eye out for any figures strolling along the wide, well-tended beach far down below, but there are none. Too early. Leigh told me dolphins often play close to the shore at dawn, but I am yet to see any. They would be hard to spot from this distance, anyway. That's okay. The sea is enough. It always has been.

A squad of brown pelicans lazily drifts across my line of sight, from left to right. I smile. They are majestic, more like dinosaurs than anything avian. Moving ponderously, they lower themselves in formation, skimming the surface of the ocean before landing and bobbing peacefully on the waves as the sky behind them turns to light, blush pink.

The sun creeps higher, no longer a mere sliver, but a blazing eye, half-closed.

I close my own for a moment, savouring the quiet, the absolute stillness of this sliver of my life. The memory of the sun burns two bright spots into the darkness behind my eyelids.

Eyes inside my eyes, both of us watching each other.

Burning bright spots in my vision, a light so hot it sears, can you feel it on your skin? Can you feel the heat on your face? It only takes a second, they say. A flash in the pan, they call it, only the pan is your body. And that smell, is that your hair, curling, the singed strands scrambling away from the flames? Can you hear the sound of yourself screaming? Can you-

Fuck.

I wish the memories would leave me alone for one fucking single minute, but perhaps that's too much to ask of my brain right now.

I open my eyes again, searching for distraction.

I find it.

A figure now stands in solitude on the beach below.

I frown, trying to fix on it while steadying my breathing, which is suddenly ragged. It's a man, I think, although hard to tell reliably from here. I would need binoculars to be sure, but the longer I look, the more I am convinced. His height, the broadness of his shoulders. He has long arms and legs, really long, or perhaps this is a trick of the growing light, the low angle of the sun.

The man is quite obviously naked. He is one ghostly-pale colour all over. He moves, and I can see the absurd thick white line of his dick, swinging about between his legs. Or am I just making an assumption? The light is so poor, he is barely distinct from the greyish-yellow sand beneath him…

He moves again.

Nope. Definitely dick. No doubt about it.

I laugh out loud.

Not something I'd been expecting to see as part of my 'sunrise over the Atlantic Ocean' experience.

I watch as he stretches as if still waking from a sleep, and then shakes himself, like he is ridding his body of water, dog-fashion. Or is he shedding sand?

Sand, I realise. His hair, which is long, whips about like a stringy nest of snakes. He continues to shake himself as the sun climbs higher, revealing something else.

On the beach by the man's feet, a large shadow stretches out.

I lean forward, squinting.

What *is* that?

It looks like a hole. A body-length hole, like a long burrow.

Has he been sleeping in it?

Buried under the sand instead of sleeping rough under a blanket? Is that why he's shaking himself off?

But if so…where are his clothes? I can't see a pile of garments discarded anywhere on the beach nearby. No bag, no shoes, nothing to indicate he's gotten undressed.

He's just…naked.

Unless the clothes are in the hole.

Either way, it's…

'Weird,' I breathe, out loud.

*

I watch the man closely, feeling like a voyeur, unable to stop myself. I can't decide whether or not to be freaked out by his nakedness. I mean, it *is* early. Maybe naked swimming is a thing here. I'd assumed people would be quite conservative, there are signs on the beach telling people not to swear or curse, right alongside the 'no concealed carry' notices, but...

The man wanders slowly towards the sea. He moves awkwardly, as if hankered by something. Almost like he's not used to walking on land. Like his feet are hobbled, or tender. His gait reminds me of a seal, or a penguin out of the water: ungainly, off-balance, unsure of the solid ground beneath, even if it is only compacted sand.

God, I wish I had binoculars so I could see better.

The man shambles and flip-flops along. Behind him, a trail stretches out from the burrow to the backs of his feet. Darkish in colour, it reflects light in sparkling intervals, so at first I think it must be oil, dense and distinct, but then I realise how stupid that idea is.

He's definitely leaking *something*, though. Some sort of discharge.

Blood? Is he bleeding? Hurt? Is that why he's walking so funny?

Whatever it is, the man doesn't look back to see what he's left behind. Instead, he walks straight into the ocean, transforming suddenly into an elegant shape and disappearing in a gliding, smooth motion not unlike that of a dolphin slipping beneath the waves, streamlined, no resistance.

Mouth open, I wait for him to reappear, but he never does.

Instead, the sun rises fully from its hiding place beneath the waves in a round, furious red ball of promise and mystery. It looks like fire, it *is* fire, but for once, that doesn't upset me.

I push the plate of cold fries to one side.

I wait, and wait.

The man never resurfaces.

Has he drowned?

Or did he swim so far along the shore I can't see him anymore?

But I can see for miles down the beach in both directions from here. And there is no way he can still be underwater. He would have to hold his breath for thirty minutes, for that's how long I've been here, watching.

And as far as I know, no human can do that, not even free-divers.

Can they?

I am so fucking tired.

No point trying to go back to sleep now, though. I still have hours before breakfast.

Time for an early morning stroll, I think.

*

I stand at the edge of the deep hole where the man came from, staring down. Hand-dug, although the finger furrows don't look right. They look too indistinct. Tiny sharp indents surrounded by smudges delineate the sides of the hole: like claw marks that have been wiped over with something softer. I wonder how long it took to excavate this much sand. Also: *where* is the removed sand? There is no pile, just a hole. That strikes me as incredibly improbable. Who would go to all that effort? Why?

Looking up, I can see my balcony from the burrow, a direct line of sight. I am not sure I like this. It feels too coincidental, or perhaps not coincidental enough.

It is a large hole for any one person to have engineered, in my opinion: this long, deep, man-sized depression in the sand, almost like a grave, and wet at the bottom in the way that beaches are wet if you dig deep enough down with your fingers. It is full of strands of seaweed and grass, leaves, stuff that looks like slimy green pond-weed, or algae, furry strands of bedraggled moss, and a rusty coloured sticky residue that is transparent in places, like jelly, like glue. This glue has lumps in it, frogspawnish, and bright, neon-green and orange streaks of shimmery stuff suspended in the murk. I'm reminded of comic-book descriptions of toxic waste, of nuclear residue. Of Swamp Thing. It's like a child has been experimenting with making gloop, colouring it with additives, a mountain-dew and orange Fanta artifice that is one of the weirdest things I've ever seen, in this context.

Leading from the hole, across the breadth of the beach and then stopping at the edge of the sea: more of the sticky stuff. I'm relieved it isn't blood, but fascinated and revolted by the actuality of it. It definitely looks like a discharge or secretion. The way it is laid out, and the scuff marks beneath seem very much as if it came *from* the man, somehow. I have nothing scientific to base that assumption on except for one thing: huge clumps of hair, long strands of it, enmeshed in the gloop. Hair that's fallen out or been dragged out, like wet hair that sticks to your fingers when you're in the shower. The kind you have to plaster to the tiles to get rid of, so it can't clog up your drain pipes. Hair that pisses off your partner or flat mate. It lies in the direction the man walked, adding to the impression of a person or creature actively shedding something, sloughing off a sticky, hairy, gelatinous sheath as he moves.

21

Which begs the question: what the actual fuck?

Strangeness aside, the practicalities of this situation are what bug me the most. Where has he been, or what has he been rolling in? There's a whole lot of this gooey stuff. It smells funny, like dried seaweed, but not quite that. Briny, also eggy, sulphurous. A stagnant pond-water smell. A bit like uncooked meat left too long in the sun. Seafood, on the turn.

Or, like a jellyfish washed up on the beach.

In fact, the residue reminds me of a dead jellyfish a lot. Same texture and density. Glassy and spongy at the same time. Snotty. In a salty, clear porridge sort of way. None of that would make sense if I said it out loud, but it makes sense in my head. Kind of.

I crouch, poke at the slime with a stick. It resists, at first, then sucks at the tip of the wood. I peer as closely as I dare. Can I see things moving around in the goo? Tiny bugs or parasites maybe? The streaks of neon green and orange seem to shift and warp with the light, making patterns in the gloop. I stare harder. There is *definitely* something wiggling around in there. I feel compelled to study it more closely, like I should collect some of the stuff, take it back to my room to look at, but what purpose would that serve? I'm not a biologist or marine expert. Or a doctor. It would only stink the place out, anyway.

I follow the trail right to the edge of the sea, where waves lap at my feet invitingly. The residue floats in small, buoyant clumps on the surf for a little way out before seemingly dispersing. A very faint rainbow-coloured slick of reflective light on the surface of the water is the only other remaining indication that the man has been here recently. Like oil sitting on water. It will eventually disperse too, once the motion of the waves has done its work.

I look for the strange, slime-coated man, who is now, presumably, as clean as a whistle.

But there is nothing out there except for pelicans and other birds, riding the waves.

What am I doing out here? I ask myself, suddenly.

Being an idiot, I realise. Making two and two equal seven. There is no great mystery here, except for why I'm shivering on the beach at sunrise instead of eating pancakes in my safe, warm hotel. Who am I expecting to find, fucking Aquaman? The stranger has been crawling around in some ungodly mess for reasons best kept to himself, is all, maybe he's a drain specialist or works in sewage or landscape gardening or maybe, just maybe, he likes rolling around in unmentionable shit, we all have our kinks, don't we? He took himself out for a little sensory R and R, and then he went for a swim, to clean himself off. That's all.

Just a sticky guy with his dick out, having a good time.

Absolutely none of my business, not one bit.

A guy who likes to sleep buried under the sand? My brain fires back.

A naked guy covered in jelly who likes to sleep in a hole in the beach?

Oh, for fuck's sake.

I give myself a little shake. There's always an explanation, even for the most bizarre of occurrences. Always.

*

As I shiver on the beach, my brain keeps chewing on things. I am a dog with its proverbial bone.

His clothes must be piled somewhere else, I think, *safe from thieves or passers-by, that's all.*

Or maybe he's a naturist.

And so what if he likes to bury himself in the sand? We've all been there.

But the slime...

The discharge...

A pelican takes flight in front of me, slowly lumbering out of the water, moving further out to sea.

It's none of my business, I decide.

I'm tired, and cold.

I should go back.

But the man hasn't surfaced yet.

What if he was drunk? He sure walked like it.

What if he drowned?

Or he could have been unwell. Maybe he wasn't in his right mind, and he didn't know what he was doing.

Or maybe he *did* know what he was doing, and that was why he left nothing behind.

Has he just ended his life, right there in front of me?

What a way to go.

Jesus.

I look at my surroundings properly, fighting against the weird *womp-womp-womp* of my brain grinding along on virtually no sleep. Almost immediately, I see there is a long wooden jetty jutting out from the beach about half a mile away to my right. It has a fishing and tackle shop perched on top of it.

I hadn't spotted the jetty before now. I've been distracted.

My shoulders slump in relief. I feel ridiculous. I can see figures moving around on the jetty, indistinct, but one of them could be the man.

He's swum out in that direction, that's all.

I start laughing to myself.

A prank, I think, *probably some TikTok stunt. He's chilling on the other side of that jetty, tackle-out, enjoying the peace and quiet of the beach before the day starts.*

Waiting for dolphins.

Fishing.

Ejaculating into the surf, feeding the marine life.

Who gives a fuck.

He's fine.

None of it has anything to do with me.

I tell myself this, but I can't quite bring myself to believe any of the plausible explanations, not even two days later, when I leave the beach and head for the swamps.

Turns out, survival instinct is a difficult thing to squash.

Turns out, I should listen to myself more than I do.

You'd think I'd have learned my lesson after last time, wouldn't you?

*

The Cypress swamps of First Landing State Park are everything a person born in a wet, green pastoral country full of reliably deciduous trees wants to see: tropically hot and humid, wild, weird, twisted, and decidedly beautiful. And surprisingly dry in the spaces between the bodies of water. Dead, crisp leaves, moss on the trees, peeling bark...these things stand proud against the damp, heavy air. It is a place of contrast, possessing a certain harshness which appeals to me.

'What's all this wispy shit?' I ask, fascinated by the long, dry, pale green strands that dangle down from the trees all around like an old man's beard, sweeping the floor in many places. I find it enchanting, resisting a sudden urge to drape myself in some of it, wrap a strand of it round my neck like a feather boa.

'Spanish moss,' Leigh replies, smiling. 'You get it a lot where there are cypress trees. It's not really a moss, though.'

'Right. The moss back home...it's more like a green sponge. Wet, and dense, not like this at all.' I finger some of the stuff. It feels scratchy and scaly. Made of long, wiry strands and stems, it grows downwards, reminding me of corroded chainmail draped across a branch.

'It gets greener after it rains. The whole point is that it evolved to store water. So it looks kinda grey at the moment, because it used its water stores up. Been a dry winter this year.'

'Nature is fucking brilliant, isn't it,' I sigh, meandering along a boardwalk that winds through the swamps, taking it all in with wide eyes. I am still jet lagged as all hell. I have moments where the fatigue hits me, and I feel spacey, and displaced, but I move through them quickly and on the whole, find I am energised by my new surroundings. Even if Leigh did catch me napping earlier over my coffee: sitting bolt upright at a table, cup in hand, fast asleep.

'There's probably some turtles around somewhere,' my friend replies. 'This walkway opens out to a viewing platform in a little bit. You can see all sorts of things if you stand quietly for a while.'

She's right. After ten minutes, the boardwalk loops in on itself to form a viewing platform over the largest expanse of rainbow-sheened swamp water in the Park. I'm told this sheen comes from natural oils produced by decomposing matter and bacteria munching on iron deposits in the soil below the surface. Whatever the cause, the iridescent surface is extremely pretty when the sun hits.

It also reminds me of the slime back on Virginia Beach, but of course I don't say this out loud.

We stand quietly looking out over the multicoloured water, listening to alien bird cries and other noises: water speaking, mud burping, insects dancing in the air, other tourists crashing around in the distance. Fighter jets periodically roar overhead. You can't avoid them, even here, but the sound is muted by the trees.

And it is the trees, when all is said and done, that are the stars of the show in First Landing State Park.

They are Bald Cypress trees, Leigh tells me, and I've never seen anything like them. Stretching high and thin, the branches and foliage resemble conifers or pines, with clusters of thin green needles puffing outwards like fur. The bark is thick and scaly, but it is the roots that fascinate me. They don't grow down, like most tree roots. Instead, they grow *up*, thrusting out of the swamp water all around in long, triangular, peaked protuberances, like elongated wooden spikes with fat bottoms.

'Those are so freaky!' I exclaim, fascinated. 'It's delightful. They look like termite mounds, not roots. I saw those in Australia. Same shape, almost. Like, sharply tapered at the top.'

'Yeah, they're called 'knees',' Leigh says. 'I don't know what they do, but they grow real big, some of them. They look like roots, but they must serve another purpose, else why grow like that?'

'Right, because they're growing *up*, not down.' I can't get over it. It is illogical, makes no sense. Roots go down, into the soil, to soak up nutrients. To keep people at home.

Is that my problem? Do my roots grow up? That would make an odd sort of sense.

'They're kind of gross,' I continue. 'Like knobbly old fingers coming out of the water.'

'Ah, look, I told you. Turtle.'

Leigh points. Sitting on a log jutting out of the water at a sharp angle is a gorgeous black turtle, sunning itself, head craned up on a long, wrinkled neck.

'Awww, this is so cool!' I sound like a child. 'It feels so, I don't know...exotic here.'

Leigh laughs. 'Not quite so exotic when the mosquitoes eat you alive.'

I hold my arms out before me, displaying some of the pink shiny burn scars on my skin. 'They can try,' I laugh, 'but they have to like barbeque.'

Leigh blinks. I respect the fact that she's never once asked me, since we met, where my scars come from. I probably will tell her, when I'm ready, but I don't want to ruin the mood.

For now, jokes will do. Introduce the topic lightly, and leave it at that.

Leigh is happy to accommodate.

We fall into an easy silence again, drinking in the atmosphere, until suddenly, a large ripple disturbs the surface of the swamp.

'Did you see that?'

Leigh nods, frowning. 'Yeah, something pretty large in the water.'

'Do you have crocodiles out here?'

She shakes her head. 'Nah. Plenty of snakes. Turtles. Coyotes. I heard rumours of gators over in Great Dismal Swamp, moving up from Florida. But I think that's an urban myth. I'm pretty sure alligators like it warm. Gets too cold here in the spring for gator babies.'

The ripple surges again. We both make surprised noises, pull back from the wooden railing.

'How deep is it?' I ask, meaning the water.

Leigh is puzzled. 'Not very, I don't think. That being said, I haven't been out on this stretch in a boat. I've certainly never swum in it.'

We both watch the water intently, hoping that whatever is making the disturbance will surface fully. We wait for ten minutes. Nothing. Giving up, we cautiously make our way back from the platform and along the boardwalk.

'I bet there are leeches in the water,' I remark.

'You're welcome to go for a swim and see,' Leigh replies. 'I don't think I want to share a tent with you though, if you do.'

'Can we go to the beach instead?' I ask.

'Sure. Little history lesson in it for you, too,' she promises.

Turns out, First Landing State Park is the place where English colonists first landed in 1607 before later settling in Jamestown. I am ashamed I don't already know this. At school I was taught about the industrial revolution, about Pitt and Palmerston and selective parts of the world wars. Not this. It feels like a deliberate and baffling omission to the curriculum, tunnel-vision history.

I can see, on looking around, why a boat would land here: the beach is wide and the shoreline shallow, accommodating. The cypress swamps would have offered water to thirsty sailors, although the thought of drinking that rainbow-bright, oil-slicked liquid makes me shudder. You'd have to be pretty desperate, but then, if you've been at sea for months on end with only weak rum to keep the thirst at bay, it might seem more appealing.

Leigh has brought kayaks, so we drag these along the boat ramp, across the beach, and out into the water. I've not kayaked for a long time, but quickly get the hang of it, even though my arms ache from trying to hold the paddles correctly.

We follow the shoreline for a while, waving periodically at large tankers and ships on the horizon. It's not long before Leigh spots something dark and long and strange, bobbing in the water. She points and scoots over to it skilfully. It takes me more effort to manoeuvre my kayak.

'Shit,' I hear her say, as I gently grab hold of her oar to steady my own rocking.

'Gross.' I grimace and set my paddle down so I can cover my nose with a sleeve.

In the water, belly-up, a dead dolphin floats, fins to the sky, as if offering its soft underside for a tickle, only there *is* no soft underside. The dolphin has been gutted, efficiently, savagely, its insides fully scooped out. I can see its exposed ribcage, and some of its backbone. The sharp, distinctive nose bone protrudes from the waterline, but everything else sags just below it.

The remains are covered in a strange sort of porridge-like glue, streaked with luminous orange and neon green trails. My brain whirs into action as I recognise the gooey stuff. It leaks into the ocean, floating on the surface around the dead animal. The goo is clumped, and where thickest, appears almost like frogspawn, or fish roe. I get a sense of something beyond a mere secretion. I get a sense of purpose or intent, of biological design.

My mind takes me back to my first morning in America, to the man I saw from my high-rise hotel window.

This, I realise, staring at the eviscerated dolphin, is the exact same stuff I found on Virginia Beach. The sticky residue left by the naked guy who dug a hole and then went for a swim.

I try to lean in closer, wondering if I can spot any of the tiny organisms wriggling about in the secretion like before, but I'm too awkward. I do see several long strands of clumped hair caught on a jutting rib, dreadlocked with filth and grease and sand, and that's enough to make me shiver.

Another uncoincidental coincidence, I think.

'Must have washed in from a ways out,' Leigh says, unconvincingly. 'Maybe those gator rumours aren't so ridiculous after all.'

I know better, but keep quiet.

Suddenly my keenness for camping feels rather dulled.

*

Like most fools who don't want to be a nuisance, I keep my worries to myself. I don't know Leigh well enough yet to tell her my wild theories about the hole-digging, long-haired, slimy dick-out dude who disappeared into the sea, and certainly don't want her to think I am a raving lunatic for suggesting the man also gutted, hollowed out and glooped all over a dolphin for some nefarious, no doubt horny and quite possibly biologically improbable, *X-Files* adjacent reason known only to himself.

Neither do I want to suggest, or even think about the idea that the same man was somehow swimming around under the iridescent, knee-pierced waters of the swamp earlier as we cooed over turtles and Spanish moss.

Instead, I do what Brits do very well: I shut up and lean into my finest reserves of idiotic stoicism.

*

We head back to the shore before sunset, so we have time to set up camp. I'm finding the kayak more and more difficult to commandeer as my tiredness grows. This, I have found, is the worst part of the day for jetlag: still daytime, but in reality, nearing bedtime. When I eventually put foot back on the shore, it's a relief. I shoulder my paddle and grab the closest end of the kayak, heaving it out of the sea.

It is then that we both spot a long, man-sized shadow in the sand. It wasn't there when we'd arrived on the beach, meaning, it was created while we were out on the ocean.

We trudge over to the dark patch, but I already know what it is. My heart has a peculiar sinking sensation to it, the sensation you get when you realise things are going wrong.

'Weird,' Leigh comments, looking down.

It's another hole.

From it, another trail of slime, neon-flecked. This time, there are small bones in the discharge that look like fish bones.

'Oh that's nasty,' Leigh says, her mouth drawing down in disgust. I don't realise what she means until I see several piles of faeces in the bottom of the hole, fresh, wet, coiled like plastic joke turds, each of them teeming with wriggling things.

The smell hits us then, and it is not just the eggy, salty smell that comes with the jelly excretion. It's the smell of strange shit, and it is so overpowering, so awful, so revolting, that we both start to gag and back off.

'That's *nasty*,' Leigh repeats, choking back tears. 'There's not even any flies on it, it's so bad!'

I see she's right. Flies love fresh shit, but there isn't a single buzzing pest to be seen.

Plenty of things moving around in the shadow of the hole, though.

'Who digs a six-foot trench to take a dump on a public beach?' Leigh goes on to say, angrily. 'There's a bathroom, like, a five-minute walk away. And...' She grows more thoughtful the longer she stares. 'What's with all the weird slimy shit? It looks like...'

'Frogspawn.'

'Yeah. Look, it's all over the place. I've never seen anything like it.'

I don't answer, because I have a more pressing question.

Why is the same man from Virginia Beach now digging holes in this one?

Because it *is* undoubtedly the same guy, no question about it. Same trench-shaped calling card.

What, exactly, are the purpose of the holes?

I remember reading a news story once, about an elderly man back home who liked digging tunnels beneath his house. He dug so deep and far he hit the water table, opening up multiple sinkholes until the local authorities stepped in and put a stop to it. They called him the Mole Man of Hackney. The old gent said he'd 'developed a taste for it,' which made sense, I guess. When you find joy in something, you keep at it.

This feels different, though. Not digging for digging's sake. This, like the slime, is more purposeful.

I crouch down to peer into the trench from a different angle.

'Look,' I say eventually, squinting and retching as the smell smacks me in waves. 'It's not just a hole, it's a tunnel. It goes way back.' I point to a deep, round exit wound at the far end of the depression. It is pointing in the direction of the swamps, which makes me highly uneasy. A memory of rainbow ripples comes back to me. This guy, whoever he is, can swim, and he can dig, and he can crawl.

And he can gut a dolphin, scoop it out like an ice-cream bowl.

Still no evidence of the displaced sand, though. What is he doing with it all?

The word 'excretion' sticks with me, but I don't know why, exactly.

Leigh crouches and takes out her cell phone, attaches it to a foldable selfie stick she used while kayaking, turns on the flashlight app, and inserts it delicately into the mouth of the hole. The phone illuminates a good three or four feet of smooth-sided, slime-slick excavations, which eventually disappear into blackness. I can see faint dig marks on the walls of the tunnel, the floor of which is coated, predictably, with more of the snotty, jelly-like substance I'm now so familiar with.

'Weird,' she says at last, shaking her head and pulling her phone back. 'Like a rabbit tunnel or burrow, only...'

'Man sized,' I confirm.

*

It's harder dragging the kayaks back up the ramp than down it, and I find, as we leave the beach, that I am starving. My body has no idea what time of day or night it is, so is suppressing my usual hunger signals until I'm running on fumes. It's only when I start to get cold and woozy I realise I haven't eaten anything for nearly seven hours.

The campground at First Landing is as the air hostess described it to me: a well-appointed, tree-covered patch of land with camping plots of various descriptions: some serviced with water and electricity, some that are tent-only. We go for a tent-only plot, as we know this is likely to be the quietest, and Leigh says it is also the best experience. 'When it's super dark out,' she says, 'the stars look incredible.'

I am quietly less concerned about the stars and more concerned about weird slimy men prowling around us in the dark, but Leigh surprises me when she reveals she is carrying a gun. She announces this like it's no big deal:

'Oh, hey, I hope you don't mind, but I'll bring my weapon into the tent if that's cool.'

At first, I don't understand what she means. Weapon? She shows me a box of bullets.

'Just a precaution when I go camping. I've never needed it,' she clarifies.

Reeling a little, I chew on the insides of my cheeks while I momentarily wonder if she's going to murder me in my sleep, but I ultimately decide I'm being stupid. Things are different over here, that's all. Guns are commonplace and having one doesn't necessarily mean the owner is a psychopath bent on death and destruction. It's just a cultural difference, that's all. Like sitting on the floor to eat in India or the tomato throwing festival in Spain.

Besides, something tells me I didn't survive flames and pain only to end up dead years later at the hands of someone who drove four hours out of her way to get me from the airport.

And don't forget the cola, I remind myself.

I take a moment to process how I feel, realise I'm fine with the gun. Mostly. I trust Leigh, and today, I am a lot more worried about other things. Like dead sea creatures, piles of shit so smelly the files won't touch it, wriggling, squirming things, slime, tunnels. I think Leigh is thinking about these things too.

Maybe a gun isn't a bad idea after all.

'Just make sure it stays under your pillow,' I reply eventually, laughing to hide my nerves.

'You got it,' Leigh says, and we speak no more about it.

*

Later that night, when the strangeness of the beach has receded somewhat, we meet a guy called Todd. His tent is a good distance from ours, so we don't encroach on each other's space at all, but he comes over when he sees Leigh working on lighting the kindling.

I am standing well back and off to one side, my body stiff as a board, because fire still terrifies me. I don't know Leigh well enough to tell her why, and she is too fixed on the task to notice my weird posture.

'Can I borrow your light when you're done?' Todd asks, all easy-going affability, 'I dropped mine somewhere, like a dumbass.'

'Sure.' Leigh sparks up a piece of tinder that eventually catches. A bloom of yellow spreads outwards from the kindling.

I begin to sweat.

Come on, Melanie. This is a good challenge for you. Think of it as exposure therapy.

Todd lingers, but he is pleasant, so we let him. He's a tall drink of water with a dry, droll voice and salt and pepper hair, dressed in khaki pants and a thick hoodie with the artwork of a heavy metal band I've never heard of on the front. Leigh seems unphased by his presence. I follow her lead. Back home, if a stranger tried to similarly insert himself into a situation like this without invitation, he'd probably be scowled at or blanked entirely until he backed off, but again, here, things are different. Guns under pillows, no swearing on the beach, would you like a side of friendliness with your burger ma'am?

If only my mother could see me now, I think, shaking my head.

*

We gather round the fire. Beers are uncapped. My uneasiness and fear starts to fade. I convince myself, once again, that I am putting two numbers together and making a word. That people are weird, and gross, but not necessarily dangerous. That slime isn't a crime (I giggle to myself at that one). Hotdogs are consumed. The famous s'mores are made and eaten and are messy and sickly but eminently satisfying.

A bottle of bourbon is drawn forth.

Todd lights up.

I shuffle away from him as surreptitiously as I can, my hands turning slick as the end of his cigarette glows fiercely with each drag. I'm already about as far back from the campfire as I can get without being conspicuous, and the air has taken on a deep chill, meaning I'm shivering where my friends aren't. I think Leigh has finally figured out the source of my discomfort. She's smart, observant, but content to let me work through everything in my own time. I'm grateful for this. I don't want to be patronised.

Casually, I steer the conversation to something that's bothering me more than my recurring trauma: cryptids, and any local lore that might be relevant, given the odd things we've seen. I'm not superstitious, not really, but I am perhaps more accepting of fate and destiny than I was before my accident, and part of believing in destiny is also being willing to accept that things beyond the realms of what I previously considered 'normal' could be possible.

Including, but not limited to, weird man-things who burrow into sand and secrete goo and eat dolphins from the inside out.

'You know, there aren't actually many legends and myths around here specifically,' Todd says, and I can tell this is a subject matter that interests him. 'The Great Dismal Swamp out in Chesapeake and Suffolk has some cool ghost stories, though. And Blackbeard is meant to haunt the sand dunes not far from this campground.'

'Wait, wait...there's a place called The Great Dismal Swamp?' Leigh did tell me this before, but I realise I forgot to comment after the ripples distracted us. 'And we didn't go there.'

I shake my head in mock disappointment.

Leigh grins. 'It's pretty cool, but I didn't know how many swamps you'd actually wanna see on one trip. Besides, it's pretty much more of the same. Water, cypress trees, roots sticking up, wispy shit.'

I nodded. 'Don't forget the alligators.'

Todd snorted. 'There aren't any gators in Virginia. If there are, they are pets people threw out when they got too big. The DEC fetched two outta Whitney Point only a month or so back.'

I frown. 'It's so wild to me that people would want an alligator as a pet. Or any apex predator, for that matter.'

'I guess that's the point,' Todd says, pulling out another cigarette. Now he's started, he can't seem to stop. I twitch as he lights up, but get a handle on it. 'People wanna feel superhuman, right? Superior. Enslaving natural predators is all part of the power trip. Alpha male bullshit.'

I nod. 'I guess so.'

'There aren't many animals other than humans that keep pets. Some capuchin monkeys have been known to adopt other species of monkey and care for them, but that's different.' Todd blows out a column of smoke. 'Although I once read an article about a tarantula that kept a frog as a pet.'

'So what, pet keeping is a...supremacy thing?'

Todd shakes his head. 'With the tarantula, it was more like symbiosis I think? The frog was poisonous, so the spider couldn't eat it, but the frog also ate the ants that preyed on the spider's eggs, so...'

We're getting off point, as fascinating as this segue is. I attempt to reel my campfire mate back in.

'So,' I prompt. 'A few ghosts...anything else?'

'In Virginia beach, there's the Witch of Pungo,' Leigh replied. Her eyes in the light of the fire are intense. 'Grace Sherwood. The last known woman to have been convicted of witchcraft in Virginia. They tied her up and threw her off a boat.'

I shake my head. 'Jesus. Imagine being a woman back then.'

Leigh snorts. 'Imagine being a woman right *now*.'

I raise a weary toast. The others follow.

I'm still not getting what I need.

The silence stretches until I bring it back in once again to what I'm really interested in.

'So...No, um...swamp men myths?'

I feel like a prick, but I have to know.

Leigh flicks me a look. Todd perks up.

'Not a swamp man, exactly...' he says, finishing his cigarette and flicking the dead butt into the fire. I almost fall backwards off my camp stool as the butt arcs over my knees, expecting it to land on me, spark, catch, expecting heat and searing pain, but there is none. The butt sails into the fire, curls, disappears into the flames.

Leigh clocks my overreaction, and her eyes dart briefly to my arms. My burns are hidden now by the sleeves of my jacket. I have mixed feelings about them. After the incident, I was offered plastic surgery to help with the scarring. After that, it was suggested I should have further surgery for cosmetic reasons. Mum said she'd pay for this, but I chose not to take her up on the offer. I didn't like the idea that my new form was something that needed to be cosmetically helped, even though she meant kindly. I think she still struggles with my decision, even if she says she respects it. It can't be easy for her, I know. I was her baby, once. Nobody wants to see their baby damaged so severely.

It was my own dumb fault anyway, I remind her, over and over, but she gets angry whenever I say that.

Todd wears a far-off look.

'But?' I prompt.

'But...I heard a UFO crashed in this swamp, thirty years back. Or a meteorite. It was all over the news when I was a kid. Talk of a government conspiracy, you know how it is. A military cover-up. They said the sky glowed neon green for a whole week over this entire stretch. Mutated frogs and turtles washing up on the footpaths, dead. Real Area 51 shit.'

Leigh snorted. 'Come on, man. I've lived here just as long as you and never once heard anything about that.'

Todd blinks, surprised. 'Really? It was all the local news channels could talk about, for months.'

Leigh shakes her head. 'Nope, not one single word. Don't you think if a flying saucer had crashed into the swamp, it would have been found by now? First Landing isn't the biggest park in Virginia, not by square miles, and its real popular. People all over it for most of the year. Besides, there's at least four military bases within a stone's throw of where we're sitting right this moment. Fort Story, Visser, Mary Graham...fighter jets overhead every two minutes. I think someone would have spotted a UFO if there was one to be seen.'

Todd shrugs. 'Like I said, Area 51. Maybe they *did* find it. Who's to say it isn't in some secret bunker under a lighthouse? Little green man being dissected into salami slices, all in the name of science.'

My friend laughs. 'A small meteor is more likely.' I remember she's an astronomy nerd. 'Earth is hit by debris from space a lot more regularly than we realise. Something like five hundred meteorites a year, if not more. We don't recover a lot because most of 'em fall into the sea.'

Todd sips at his drink. 'You ever read that book where a meteor hits earth and a whole new biosphere starts expanding outwards from the impact site? Strange matter that absorbs everything around it slowly and echoes it back, all mutated and shit. Man, I fuckin *love* that book.'

I smile. Todd is talking my language now.

'I know it very well. It's one of my favourites.' I dig around in my backpack, which is nearby, pull out a neon-pink paperback with a big 'X' on the front cover.

'No shit!' Todd jumps up from his log, goes to his tent, rummages around, and waves at us with his own copy of the same book.

Leigh shakes her head.

'What?' I have a feeling I know.

She reaches behind to where her sleeping bag pokes out the door of our tent. I know what she is going to retrieve before I see it: a paperback book, the exact same as the one Todd and I are holding.

We all laugh, then. It rings out loud and clear across the park.

Maybe that's what attracts it to us.

*

I wake up shrieking.

I've warned Leigh about the possibility of this happening beforehand.

'I might scream,' I tell her, matter of fact. 'I have night terrors. I'll probably toss and turn a bit too. Apologies in advance.'

Leigh shrugs. 'It's cool. I grind my teeth. Between us we'll keep the whole campground awake.'

Despite the warning, I foolishly think I might get away with it for the night, because I'm exhausted, drunk, and, I realise, despite the oddness of certain things, happy. A little on edge but enjoying the ride. There is no overwhelming sense of being in danger. Things feel a bit strange, sure. I'm unsettled, but I don't have any urgent sense of imminent doom.

I might just get through the night, I think, naively. *A full night's sleep, wouldn't that be nice?*

But there is no escape, and I wake up raw-throated, covered in sweat, shaking.

Leigh switches on a small hanging lamp.

'You okay?' It should be a dumb question but isn't.

'Sorry,' I mumble, sheepishly. 'I told you, this happens.'

35

'You don't have to apologise. PTSD?'

And maybe that's what it is, although nobody has ever named it specifically for me before. They use phrases like 'having a difficult time' and 'working through something tricky.'

'Wanna talk about it?' Leigh asks, gently.

I sigh. 'Guess it can't hurt,' I reply.

I give her the nuts and bolts, no embellishments.

*

My arms and chest bore the brunt of the damage, some of my neck too, a portion of one ear, but the rest are mostly brain scars. They are pronounced, and interfere with basic things like memory recall and coordination and multi-tasking, which I used to be very good at. It's not uncommon for me to walk into a room and stand there for some time, lost, unable to remember my purpose for being there. Mornings are worse than afternoons. Getting out of bed can be a struggle, but once I get going, it all slowly starts to fall into place. I am Melanie. I used to smoke heavily, but one night I fell asleep on the couch, drunk, stoned, with a lit cigarette still dangling from my mouth. In seconds, the nylon top I was wearing, a cheap shirt I'd bought from a market stall, which in no way conformed to the usual flammability requirements of clothing, went up in flames.

I remember little about it except waking up as my housemate, returning from the pub, frantically tried to put me out with a wet towel.

Afterwards, there was a lot of pain.

Leigh listens, and pats my hand, just once, in sympathy.

'Have you ever noticed that bad guys in movies have always got scars?' I go on to say. 'Or some deformity- an eye missing, or they're burned. Kind of makes it hard to turn on the TV, sometimes.'

'*What is beautiful is good*,' Leigh replies, quietly. 'There was a study on it, I think. How beautiful people in the media get all the good attributes.'

'You ever watch a Disney movie?' I rub my eyes, tired.

'Only Beauty and the Beast,' she replies, smiling. 'Beast was *way* hotter.'

'I don't feel much like sleeping anymore,' I say, shunting towards the tent door in my sleeping bag. 'I'm just going to sit outside and watch the stars, I think. Jetlag Jenny.'

'You sure?' Leigh croaks, her voice sleep-cranky again. 'I could set up the telescope for ya...I brought it, just in case...'

'No, you're fine. Get some rest. Sorry I woke you.'

'Shut up,' she yawns, flopping back into her sleeping bag. 'You've got nothing to be sorry about. Fuckin' Brits apologizing all the damn time.'

I laughed, but it was a struggle.

*

Leigh is right. The stars look amazing out here, an array of brilliant studs in an almost totally black night.

I doze fitfully, upright on the stool, bundled in my sleeping bag, jacket, thick hoodie over the top, the hood drawn tight around my face. I move my stool so that if I do fall completely asleep, I don't topple sideways and into the embers of the fire that glow on the ground nearby.

In my waking moments I listen keenly, for any sounds that might anchor me better. My ears buzz with a faint exhaustion hum. My anxiety is up, way up after my nightmares. The blackness around feels oppressive, hungry.

Then, as my eyes drift closed for the dozenth time, a terrible scream rings out into the night.

Fuck! I frantically scan the blackness around me with useless eyes.

Who is screaming?

It's usually me, but I'm awake.

Aren't I?

Perhaps not. Perhaps I'm still dreaming. That might be why everything feels so off, so still and menacing.

Another scream rips out across the campground.

No, not me.

If it *isn't* me, and I *am* awake, then it can only be one of two people: Leigh, or Todd.

But Leigh is snoring gently in the tent, and when I shine my flashlight on it, I can see the shadow of her sleeping bag rise and fall with her breaths.

Another cry in the dark.

It's a male voice, and it is terrified.

That means it's...

Todd.

'*Help!*' Todd shrieks, but the word sounds garbled, wet somehow.

Fuck!

I leap up off the stool.

Todd is tall, substantial. Whatever is making him holler like that can't be good.

I throw myself into our tent, shake Leigh.

'Wake up, *wake up!*'

'What the fuck?' Leigh lurches up like a mummy from a tomb in an old black and white monster flick, hinged at the waist, sitting bolt upright, face white and shocked in the glare of my torch beam. 'What's happening?'

'Something is wrong with Todd,' I pant. 'We need your gun. Now!'

'Todd?' Leigh can't make it make sense in her head, scrubs at her hair, blinking. 'Get that light out of my face, damn.'

Another scream.

'Jesus fuck, *help me!*'

Leigh snaps fully awake and into the moment.

'Shit,' she swears, grabbing her gun from beneath her pillow, where she left it, just as I asked.

*

The space between our tent and Todd's is relentlessly black, and terrifying. We have lights, a head torch and a super-strength Maglite, but they barely seem to penetrate the night.

'Todd?' Leigh leads the way across the campground. She's the one holding the gun, after all. 'Talk to me, buddy!'

But there's no answer. I can hear rustling and crackling in the trees not far from us, twigs snapping loudly, and a dragging, heavy sound, but that stops abruptly as we approach.

We reach Todd's tent. There is a huge, ragged hole in one side of it, a hole that goes clean through the flysheet and the layer beneath. Two of the flimsy poles holding it up are snapped like twigs, so the nylon shell sags on one side.

Slime glistens in the beams of our torchlight. A trail of it, leading away from the ruined tent.

I can see what's happened all too clearly. Todd has been yanked clean out of his tent by his ankles, and dragged off somewhere, by something, or someone.

I have a good idea who.

When I move the light away, discharge glows like phosphorescence. Like our beams have charged its luminosity. I cover the end of my Maglite.

'Switch off your headlamp,' I hiss. Leigh does as she's told.

The trail of thick, glow-in-the-dark slime snakes off into the trees, towards the swamp.

Alongside the luminous streaks and smears: distinct, smudgy, dragging footprints.

Whoever took Tood was barefoot, and big.

It's at this point I decide to tell Leigh what I saw that morning on Virginia Beach.

*

The trail leads to the swamp and then into the closest body of water, and after that, goes cold. We stubbornly search for Todd in vain until dawn, calling his name and treading the boardwalks with increasing desperation, until it becomes apparent we're not going to find him. Neither of us can quite believe this is happening. A part of me still suspects I am dreaming, for the lightening sky has that surreal, flat quality to it that dreams often have.

As the sun rises slowly overhead, and the first fighter jets of the day roar past, we admit defeat.

'Now what?' I say, shivering. I'm hungry again, and bone-weary.

'We have to report him missing,' Leigh says, miserably. 'There's usually someone in the small park office hut we passed yesterday. If not, I'll call from my cell, but I have to charge it first. I can do that in my truck.'

My phone is out of charge too: I forgot to plug it into my charge pack. I remember with a jolt that I've left all my belongings back in our tent for anyone to find: my phone, my wallet, my passport. This makes me feel even more panicky than I already do. If someone steals my passport....

I scold myself for thinking so selfishly in the circumstances, but I also know how my brain works: its default defence strategy is to worry about the mundane shit rather than tackle the bigger, scarier problems that seem to have no easy answers.

I chew on my sore lower lip. 'Will there be anyone at the office yet?'

Leigh shakes her head. 'Probably not. Let's go back to camp, call the cops from there.'

But another idea has hit me, and although it's ridiculous, and dangerous, and absurd, I think it's our best way of finding Todd.

'Okay,' I say, mind made up. I square my shoulders, roll my tired head around to work out the kinks. 'You go back to camp, charge your phone, make the call.'

Leigh frowns, realising I've used 'You' instead of 'Let's'.

'And where d'you think you're going?'

'Back to the beach,' I say, and her eyes grow wide.

'Oh,' she replies. 'That's clever.'

*

She flat out refuses to let me go alone. We jog to camp, snatching up our phones and my battery pack (and passport), plugging in Leigh's cell and hoping it regains enough juice by the time we get to the beach for her to call someone before we do what we've newly resolved to do.

Namely, finding the sticky man's freshly dug, shit-filled trench, lowering ourselves into it, and shimmying along the tunnel he's dug to see where it leads.

I have a feeling it'll lead to Todd, with any luck.

Whether he's alive when we get there, or scooped out like the dolphin we found, is another matter.

*

'We don't even know the guy, not really,' Leigh says as we stand on the edge of the man-sized, stinking trough, peering in. Her lip is curled in disgust. The pit smells much worse than it did yesterday, which is saying something. Can excrement ripen with time? My sleeve held over my mouth, I have a flash of inspiration, pulling out a travel facemask I've kept in my hoodie pocket ever since my flight here. It's one of those proper, industrial masks that meet various health regulations. I strap it across my face, and the smell dies down to a more bearable level.

'I know we don't.' My words are muffled by the mask. 'But imagine how fucking scared the poor guy must be. We can't just leave him. It could take hours for the police to even show up. Time is of the essence, surely?'

'We have no idea if this even goes anywhere.'

'I think he...it...whatever- travels like this. Under the sand, under the water. I saw him walking, only once, and it was like...he was awkward, not used to being on land. I think he uses these tunnels to slither around, you know? Like it's faster for him. Makes sense, he can burrow down, stay out of sight. And if that's the case, there might be several of these tunnels, and they might all connect up. Like...' The story of the Mole Man comes back to me. 'Like mole tunnels. You never know. He could have a hideout or something in the middle of them all. A den. Somewhere he might have taken Todd.'

'Like Alien. The Queen's hive. You realise how fucking out of the realm of normal this is, don't you? What you're saying. All of this.'

I nod. 'I do. But if you want be scientific about it, there's evidence, right? We have multiple trenches, we have a missing man and a torn-up tent, we have a dolphin carcass, and the common factor between them all is this gross slime.' I gesture to the hole. 'It's the closest thing we've got to a trail, and I think we should follow it. We can't leave Todd to fend for himself, Leigh.'

She is scared and undecided, staring down at the black mouth in the sand.

'"Bad men need nothing more to compass their ends, than that good men should look on and do nothing." '

'What?'

I shrug. It doesn't matter where the quote is from.

She knows I'm right.

I'm going into the tunnel.

'You don't have to come with me,' I say, not for the first time. 'You can stay up here, wait for the police.'

She shakes her head.

'Not a chance,' she replies.

*

Leigh makes the call while handing me her head torch, which I drag on over my hair. She then passes me the gun, giving me a quick rundown on how it fires. I am terrified I will forget her instructions in the heat of any moment so I make her go over it three times, just to be sure.

'You're probably only going to be able to use it if you're up close, cos aiming long-distance shots is hard,' she says. I agree with her. I'll get close, alright. The memory of the scooped-out dolphin comes back to me. Dolphins are fast. How did he even catch it, let alone gut it so violently?

Doesn't matter, I tell myself, hefting the gun in my hand. Dolphins don't carry. If the freak tries anything with me, I'll blow his brains out, point blank. I run it through in my mind, this scenario, pushing up close, poking the gun into the man's temple, pulling the trigger, replaying these actions so I get comfortable with the outcome, if it comes to it. I have no idea what the gun is, what make, what type, what calibre. Back home, these things barely exist outside of movies or novels. Unless you count farmers, and my granddad, who once owned an air-rifle to scare birds away and nearly shot the neighbour by mistake.

Once upon a time, I would have been terrified by the weight of something so deadly in my grasp, but not today.

I just want to get down there, see what's what.

I can tell Leigh thinks my responses aren't totally normal. I should be more openly afraid. I don't inform her that since the accident, I get scared like anyone else, but a muted, remote kind of scared. Like I'm flat inside, living on a two-dimensional plane,

Edwin A. Abbott style. Old me, before the fire, would never have suggested going down there into the foetid dark.

New me knows how far a brain can go to normalise something terrifying.

The mouth of the tunnel yawns. The mounds of shit before it are faintly steaming.

Still warm, I think.

Even all this time later.

Gross.

I can see organisms thrashing around in the faeces.

Am I really going to get down there in all that?

'Ready, Mulder?' Leigh interrupts my thoughts. She switches on the Maglite and pulls down her sleeves to cover any bare skin she can find.

I don't reply. Best save all my energy for what lies ahead.

*

The tunnel is disgusting. Perhaps even more disgusting than trying to crawl over stinking piles of slimy shit without kneeling in or touching any of it, and failing. Mushy warmth oozes up between my fingers as I put one hand in the wrong place at exactly the wrong time. I don't think I will ever forget this sensation. It will haunt me like the smell of my own burned flesh still haunts me. Sometimes memories come back as pictures, sometimes as scented assaults, sometimes as a feeling or sensation, sometimes all these things at once. My hand is now tainted, forever. When I'm done here, I'm scrubbing it with bleach.

The passage, once I get fully into it, is larger than I first expected. I guess the sticky guy is bigger in person than I realised.

This does not bring me comfort.

The sides of his excavation are coated, like everything else he touches, in the mucoid luminous ooze that glows with iridescence under the beam of our torches, as if we're down in a tunnel painted with toy-shop slime. The secretion reeks. There is little air down here to mitigate its stench. My facemask can no longer fight back the tide. I gag every few moments.

I try to push my disgust and revulsion to the back of my mind.

What the fuck are you doing down here? An inner voice wails. *Go back immediately!*

But going back would entail just as much effort as going forward, if not more. We've been crawling along for a good distance already. I know there can't be too much further to go, because the tunnel is starting to angle upwards, implying it is headed for an exit point.

'It's like every bad smell I ever smelled in my whole life rolled into one,' Leigh moans, from behind. 'I didn't think anything could stink this bad, not ever. Not even in my worst nightmares.'

'Mind the root,' I caution, as a gnarled tree root suddenly protrudes out of the wall ahead of me. I squeeze past it, angling my body to one side.

'I mean, God, Melanie. Oh my god. *God.*' Leigh can't think of anything more eloquent to say. She's overwhelmed, retching frequently, but keeps going, to her credit.

'Todd better buy us a beer after this,' I pant. I am drenched in sweat from head to toe. It is hot down here, suffocatingly so. I wonder what it would be like to die in here, if the ceiling of this man-made construction suddenly caves.

The tunnel angles down once more, so I can let my body slide for a few moments, allowing gravity to do the work. This speeds things up considerably. Leigh bumps into my feet: she was not expecting the dip. Her momentum adds to mine, and for a short period, it feels almost like we're bobsledding down a slope, face first.

Then the tunnel veers upwards again, more sharply this time. Shuffling uphill through slippery gloop when we're this tired and anxious is awful. Leigh hangs onto one of my legs while I use both my hands to grab onto any other tree roots I can find and haul us along. The gun I tuck into the back of my pants, hoping against hope that the safety is still on and it doesn't go off somehow and fire right into the base of my spine, or into Leigh's face.

'Where the fuck is this going?' Leigh says, after ten more minutes of us squirming along. I know what she's thinking. She's thinking the same as me:

Are we going to be stuck down here forever?

Going back the way we've just come would be hard, really hard now, with the rise and fall of the tunnel floor. We'd have to push ourselves backwards uphill the whole way, and that would be tricky.

Tricky, but not insurmountable, I tell myself.

You've survived worse.

But then, the tunnel widens out, and these thoughts become a moot point, for we find, eventually, what I expected and hoped for: daylight.

And, along with it, our first proper look at the thing that took Todd.

*

Swamp Man is the first thing that pops into my head when I emerge from the tunnel and into a huge, freshly dug pit. Just like the comics. I've been ruminating on the idea for a while, but it crystallises when I see where we end up.

When I see him.

His skin has a greenish tinge to it, up close, and his hair is long, matted, stringy with slime. He has adorned himself with dozens of wispy strands of Spanish moss, which are stuck to his lean body with a gummy paste in scattered patches that look deliberate, like a caddisfly larva attaching grains of sand to itself as camouflage. He has a clumsy, slapdash crown of pine needles slimed to his head, and varied types of lichen plastered to his back, along with mud, sand, twigs and dead leaves, seaweed, driftwood, seedpods and fish bones. His arms and legs are extremely long but strong, sinewy, and flexible, like those of a contortionist or gymnast. There is not an ounce of fat anywhere on him, only muscle, slime, and natural flotsam glued on as a disguise. His fingers and toes are webbed, his nails long, deadly and halfway between sharp spades and claws, so he can dig as well as he can swim, I assume. His penis is huge, limb-like, almost down to his knees.

At first, he doesn't see us as we climb out of the tunnel, so we freeze and try to control our breathing while I silently hand the gun back to Leigh. Suddenly, I don't want the responsibility of it. I'll fuck up, I know I will. I want the gun to be with the woman who can actually use it, who can aim straight. Our survival shouldn't rely on my now shaking fingers.

She accepts it without protest, eyes wide as saucers.

My theory was right, I realise, scanning the area. I'm pretending to be a tree, motionless, rigid, fingers spread like branches, because he still hasn't registered our presence, and all I can think of is that dumb quote from that dinosaur movie, *its vision is based on movement*, and that sets me to thinking. If the dude spends as much time underground as he does, and is mostly active in the night or first thing in the morning, then it stands to reason his eyesight might be compromised in daylight. Again, a mole comes to mind. Tiny, glittering eyes that don't work very well out of the dark. He could be nocturnal. I can't be sure, because he still has his back to us.

Either way, it presents an opportunity for me to look around. There have to be other escape routes than the way we've just come.

Swamp Man has made a sizable home for himself on this patch of land between stretches of water. As dens go, it is sophisticated, deep, and his tunnel leads right to it. Tunnels, plural. There are other pits, black-mouthed and waiting. He's given himself multiple access routes to different parts of the park around the den. This is smart, for if one tunnel collapses, he has several others to retreat into. I can see that one heads in the direction of the beach, where we've come from. Others lead into the swamps and still others seem to head out in the direction of the campground. There must have been a concealed entrance trench near our tents, I realise. That's why he was able to get away so quickly.

That's why I couldn't hear Todd screaming after the initial attack.

The scale of the subterranean transit network is mind-bogglingly impressive, especially when I think about the pit and tunnel (the entrance to which I hadn't spotted) back in Virginia Beach. That one must go right under the city itself. If not under the city, then along the entire stretch of coastline, which is vast. A spectacular feat of underground engineering considering it is all hand dug.

It hits me, then, the absolute strangeness of what is unfolding around me. How bizarre and surreal this encounter really is. In the tunnel, things were still unknown, unproved.

Now I'm here, faced with a being I never thought possible, my reality is warping, my perceptions of everything I've encountered so far in my life tumbling down like falling masonry.

*

Swamp Man's circular lair is excavated like a sunflower seed-head with tunnel pit-petals radiating out from it. He has added considerable infrastructure to this large hole, lining it like a nest, only not a den made from twigs and feathers, but more like a wasp or a swallow's nest.

It is immediately obvious where all the excavated mud and sand from the pits and tunnels has gone: here. He has stuck it all over the interior of the pit in hand-sized globules to create a large, bulbous sort of dome that covers one complete half of the lair.

I don't have to wonder how, either, for as we watch, equal parts fascinated, disgusted and horrified, Swamp Man, who crouches on the opposite side of the pit to us, his back still turned, suddenly strains, shudders, makes a guttural, almost orgasmic noise, reaches down between his legs (I can see his member dangling there, shockingly pale and clean compared to the rest of him) and pulls a huge, turgid pile of sandy, soil-laden excrement out of himself that he then expertly applies to the wall of his nest, pasting it on like cement with his large, spade like hands.

Leigh starts gagging again. I punch her lightly on the hip, mouthing *Shut the fuck up!*

I appreciate this is easier said than done. I feel like throwing up, myself, especially when the smell of his fresh shit hits us.

I am fascinated by Swamp Man's hands as he works. Once again I marvel at their build, at the long, broad talons tipping each webbed finger. Streamlined yet adaptable, able to cover a larger surface area when digging. Goldilocks hands, neither too big nor too little for his needs.

Like he's evolved this way.

Swamp Man finishes plastering, then shovels fresh dirt and sand up from the floor of the pit, into his mouth. At least, that's where I assume it goes, for his back remains turned to us. A loud gulping sound fills the lair.

Moments later, he is shuddering and shitting again. More of the stuff goes onto the wall.

He is a completely self-sufficient machine, I realise, equipped with the means to hunt, travel, fight, and build.

So what's the slime for? I am lost in the strangeness of Swamp Man's physique, his anatomy, his biological processes, even as Leigh starts to edge towards the creature.

Maybe it's not for anything. Maybe it's decorative.

But it doesn't feel that way. His body is designed for optimum functionality.

Maybe it adds as a sort of navigational tool. Or a buoyancy device. Or a digestive aid. Or maybe it helps him get around, like a lubricant for the tunnels, or perhaps it protects him from the sun, or from sea water, or...

Leigh has had enough.

'Wait!' I hiss, but she's taken three swift long strides towards him. Her arm comes up. She throws her entire body into the motion and brings the butt of the gun down hard upon the back of Swamp Man's head.

The creature utters an awful, bleating cry, like a goat in pain, and slumps forward, clutching his skull between his enormous hands.

Leigh follows up with two swift kicks to his ribs and spine.

Swamp Man howls, spins around.

Sees us.

His eyes are indeed small and not suited to daylight, bright red in colour, with tiny dot pupils that are lurid green. He has a huge lower jaw, I see, wholly disproportionate to the rest of his face, that juts out like a plough attachment on the front of a train. Again, this is a purposeful design, useful for when he is digging tunnels. Knobbly ridges of bone and cartilage stick out all over this enlarged jawbone like fossilised beard growth. I can see gills behind the jawbones, and it makes me think of a whale shark, swimming around with its mouth open, filtering plankton.

Swamp Man looks from Leigh to me, back to her again.

Leigh hits him square in the middle of the face with the butt of the gun, gibbering in terror.

I know she's trying to stun him rather than hurt him, but I feel sorry for the creature. His cries of pain and confusion are horrible. We're invading his territory, creeping up on him unannounced while he's minding his own business, attacking him from behind...

Todd, I have to remind myself.

Fuck, what is wrong with me?

Todd!

He came in the night and dragged Todd all the way down here.

He doesn't deserve our pity, he is a predator!

Leigh keeps kicking and hitting, but Swamp Man does not seem to want to retaliate. If anything, he just takes the assault, moaning sadly.

'What the fuck do we do?' Leigh yells. She is getting tired, and the creature is showing no signs of injury. 'He won't go down! It's like hitting a tree!'

I mentally wake up, run over. Physically, I know we can't stand up to the strange man, but something about the way his eyeballs swivel wildly in his head makes me think I am right about the whole daylight thing. His pupils are tiny to block out the light, which seems to hurt him.

I grab Leigh's Maglite from where she's thrown it down, make sure my headlamp is on, and shine both torches full into the creature's face.

He lets rip a huge, anguished bellow, rearing back as if burned. I hear anger in the sound. Finally, a reaction. His arms shoot out. He pushes me with immense force. I fly back, hitting the excavation wall hard.

Still howling, Swamp Man turns tail, and dives into one of the tunnels leading out of the pit.

Then, he is gone, but we can hear him shrieking underground for a good while after.

*

I stop feeling sorry for the thing when we find Todd. He's further inside the weird faecal nest structure, hidden by shadow until we venture fully into the dome's gloom.

'What did it *do* to him?' Leigh whispers in disbelief.

47

I survey the carnage that used to be a tall, affable man who only yesterday liked camping and metal and UFO landing theories and cryptids and smoking.

But Leigh wants answers.

'Melanie? What the fuck did he do to Todd?!'

What he has done to Todd is similar to what he did to the dolphin. He's split him open, and scooped out his insides, sticking what remains of Todd's body to the side of his nest with gloop and butt-cement. Why, I do not know. A trophy? Leftovers? Nothing immediately obvious presents itself.

Todd's husk suddenly twitches.

'Oh God, is he still alive?'

Leigh clutches at my arm.

I shake my head slowly, feeling sick.

'He can't be, he has no internal organs left.'

'Then why is he fuckin' twitching?!'

She's reached the limit of what she can reasonably process without having some sort of mental break. I'm impressed she's gotten this far. By all rights, I should be a gibbering wreck too, but I'm keeping it together, hanging by the thinnest of threads.

She asks a good question, though.

I peer as closely as I dare at Todd's hollowed out ribcage, which has been picked clean of flesh. No, that's not right. *Scoured* clean, as if with steel wool, or perhaps some corrosive agent. The bones that remain make a perfect hanging framework for a different kind of excretion. An excretion that moves, the undulating mass giving the impression of life left in Todd where there is none.

There is life *within* him, though, of a different variety.

It's the foamy, gelatinous frogspawn substance. Thicker than the rest of the slime. I stupidly pick a handful of the stuff up, bring it closer to my face so I can see better.

'Don't touch it!' Leigh shrieks. 'You don't know what it is!'

But I do know what it is. Exactly what it is.

These small, dark, suspended larvic blobs quivering in jelly are Swamp Man's children.

They look like tiny frog-people. Miniature webbed feet and webbed hands, greenish in tone, although still translucent, underdeveloped. Embryonic. Very recognisably humanoid in all other respects, that distinctive kidney-bean shape of a human foetus, but with a tail.

It strikes me in an instant that I am not looking at a crime scene. There is no malice or fore-thought in what has taken place here. Todd has not fallen victim to a sadistic predator or maniacal monster.

He has just been used for parts, is all. Insulation.

Like a tuft of hair caught on a branch, woven into a nest. Swampman needed to line his lair. He needed something warm and robust and hospitable enough to support the developing eggs. Apparently Spanish moss is no match for living tissue, for soft organs, for sharp, protective bones.

But why not lay them in the water, like frogs did?

Perhaps…perhaps the carcass nest lining acts as food for when the little ones eventually hatch. There is just enough flesh, sinew, and skin left for this to be feasible. It is only the organs that have been removed. Everything else remains.

Does this make him, and any children he spawns, a cannibal?

But for that to be true, Swamp Man would have to be the same species as myself, as Leigh, Todd. Looking at the mess in front of me, I know that this cannot be true.

Swamp Man is not a cannibal. He is a parent, protecting his young. Building the best home for them he can.

And we came along and invaded his territory.

My stomach lurches.

He'll be back soon enough, once the shock of encountering us has worn off. Back to defend his young.

'We need to get out of here,' I say, voice hoarse. 'Pick a tunnel.'

Leigh shakes her head. 'No,' she replies. 'I'm not going back down there. Ever. We go up and over, out that way. Feels safer.'

I look to where she points. There is a small clearing in the undergrowth at the far end of the nest pit, with protruding tree roots leading up to it, indicating a rise through which we can scramble.

'Let's go.'

Another distant, subterranean roar prompts us to move, and so we do. Fast.

*

We emerge, slimy, scratched, disgusting, by another stretch of rainbow-sheened water studded with cypress knees. Spanish moss tickles our shoulders as we pant and struggle our way towards some sort of path. Several times we meet trenches in the underbrush, half-hidden with twigs and creepers and dead leaves, like booby traps, and have to double back, terrified Swamp Man will erupt out of them and gut us with his scooping spade-hands. Our fear makes us stupid: we get lost quickly, plunging deeper and deeper into the park, searching in vain for trails or boardwalks to get us back on track and failing to find any.

'I think we're in between trails!' Leigh cries, as we stumble on. 'There's several that go in a big loop, all the way right back to North End beaches. We need to try to…'

A group of fighter jets roar overhead, oblivious to the drama unfolding far below them beneath the bald cypress trees.

Leigh clasps her hands together in gratitude. 'Never mind,' she says, reorienting herself by the trails left in the blue above. 'This way, if we-'

She doesn't get to finish the sentence. There is an eruption of movement from a mulchy patch of earth right behind her, which suddenly yawns. Soil and roots burst outwards, as do streamers of goop, hair, and moss. Tiny fish bones fly like darts. There is a huge rush of air as Swamp Man propels himself from his camouflaged trench, grabs Leigh with his lethal hands, and pulls her backwards, back into his hole, dragging her with him into the tunnel as she writhes and screams and lashes out. One of her flailing arms connects with a root, hooks around it desperately. She has moments before her arm is ripped free of her body, Swamp Man is more than strong enough, I know, but all I need is a moment.

I lurch forward, pick up the gun she has dropped, take off the safety, shove it over her shoulder into the darkness, and pull the trigger.

The gun fires. A scream, abominably human in nature, shreds the air. Leigh is released. I grab her and pull, and she emerges like a baby pulled from the womb, red-faced, wailing, coated in gunk.

We scrabble to the trail we made, running for our lives, doubling back on ourselves for safety, reeling from every tiny movement in the trees around us. Swamp Man is not fast on land, I remember, his speed is predicated on being underground or in the water. I cling to the hope that we can outrun him whilst we navigate the dry spots between patches of swamp water, remembering his awkward gait on the beach that first morning in Virginia.

'We pissed him off, didn't we?' Leigh cries, crashing through a wall of Spanish moss and spluttering as it gets in her mouth.

'I think it's more that we found its lair. It doesn't want us to…'

I trip, tumbling forward and landing hard on my knees. Leigh helps me up, and I pick up the pace even though my legs are now screaming at me.

We pound through the trees blindly, calling out for help, but our cries only seem to draw the creature chasing us closer, so we quit yelling. Panic and adrenaline fuel me, despite my exhaustion, but I am sweating buckets. The air is stiflingly hot and sticky. I am finding it increasingly difficult to draw breath when, by a stroke of luck, our feet finally hit a solid boardwalk plank with several loud *thunk-thunks!*

Moments later, a trail marker comes into view, pointing the way back to camp and the main visitor centre.

Relief surges through our bodies. We slow for a mere moment, trying to catch breath, clutching each other for support, desperately gathering enough energy to get us this last small distance back to total safety, shaking and shivering, sweat-slick, filthy, terrified.

A moment is all Swamp Man needs.

Too late, I see the boardwalk crosses a large area of rainbow-sheened swamp I recognize from before. It leads to the viewing platform from which we saw the turtle sunbathing yesterday, and from which I first noticed a large, sinister ripple in the murky waters.

His territory.

Heart sinking, I make this connection without enough time to act on it. Like a fish leaping from a river, a large, slick, strong shape flies through the air, once again grabbing Leigh, this time with both hands, lifting her, hugging her to its form, flipping, and crashing back into the surface of the swamp on the other side of the boardwalk with a colossal splash. Leigh doesn't even have time to scream this time around.

As I watch, a large ripple once again disturbs the water, heading for a cluster of particularly large cypress knees jutting from the swamp, some almost as tall as a person. Knowing I cannot follow, I watch helplessly as Swamp Man once again rears up from the surface, glistening, furious, carrying Leigh as if she weighs no more than a dry twig, and with an ear-splitting roar, proceeds to smash her body down upon the sharp, fanged point of the largest cypress knee, spearing her right through the middle and killing her instantly. Her body sags as life leaves it. Her head lolls to one side, flopping in my direction, sightless eyes gazing at me in accusation.

I scream, but Swamp Man isn't interested in me. He starts to scoop at Leigh's exposed chest with his shovelling, grasping hands.

I cannot watch. I have one chance to survive, and that chance is fleeting, my window of opportunity closing. I take it. I can mourn the loss of my new friend later.

*

The police, when they eventually arrive, find no remains. I lead them to Swamp Man's den, but he has disposed of what is left of Todd's carcass and vacated the massive hollow by the time I manage to muster up any substantial support. I also take the cops to the patch of water near the boardwalk where Leigh died, but there is no corpse to be found. No blood on the cypress knee upon which my friend was speared. A healthy dose of signature slime, but then, as I am told several times, this is a swamp, ma'am.

The beast has cleaned house, has slithered off into his network of tunnels, taking his kills and his gelatinous offspring with him.

Only one small cluster of spawn remains in the den, caught on a jutting rock, abandoned by its father, slowly drying in the building heat of the day without its insulating flesh-jacket to keep the weather off. The police seem wholly disinterested in it. Ants have begun deconstructing it by the time I am led away from First Landing State Park. Parcelling and carrying the little spawn sacks away, one by one, in an industrious little relay that went right past my feet and across the den floor. Nature, doing its thing.

I am under no illusions that Swamp Man will surface anytime soon.

The creature's travel system is likely to be vast, judging by the engineering skills I've already witnessed. He likely has multiple other dens to spawn in, or maybe he's gone back out to sea this time, swum off to a different part of the coast. I show the cops the trenches, both in the swamp, and on the beach, and try to explain about the network he has excavated, where the tunnels lead, and things get chaotic while I'm held in a weird limbo, which is never officially labelled as custody, but the implication is strong. I'm watched closely by several grim-faced uniformed types, some with guns, others without. My fingerprints are taken, my fingernails scraped. My clothes are confiscated. A woman with a camera takes pictures of me from all angles. My version of events is questioned over and over again.

I never once think about asking for a lawyer. I am not afraid of the truth, as improbable as it sounds. I want people to know what happened here, right down to the very last detail.

Later that afternoon, a shark carcass washes up on First Landing beach. It has been gutted, scooped, and adorned with Swamp Man's signature secretion.

Except this time, instead of eggs, the shark holds a different treasure, a more grisly one. Hiding in the cavity where the Shark's liver should have been is a human hand.

Leigh's.

This discovery sets things in motion just as they are slowing down. There is an initial, gratifying surge of interest from all sorts of other, non-police agencies, environmental, government, I don't know who half of them are. One particular group of suited individuals who seem to carry the weight of authority without badges take a very keen interest in my story, and ask me to show them the den and trenches again, but then things go abruptly quiet.

The collective demeanour towards me changes, significantly. My version of events is met with a sudden wall of blank, polite smiles.

I can sense when a secret is being buried. At first I railed against it, wanting Todd and Leigh to get proper justice, wanting their families to have something to lay to rest, and mourn, but forces far bigger and better funded than I can argue with have other ideas. The disappearances at First Landing State Park sink into obscurity faster than a stone dropped into the swamp, and there is nothing I can do about it. I try, believe me. I try to talk about it, until I'm threatened with severe repercussions. My phone is confiscated. I am told, in no uncertain terms, to cease and desist my efforts to broadcast what has happened in the park to a wider audience.

I'm released after four days, no further questions asked. A member of the British embassy escorts me onto a first class, all-extras-paid for flight back home, and I am reminded that all references to the event, public or otherwise, are now explicitly forbidden, and will result in prosecution. I take that to mean exactly what it sounds like: if I blabber anymore about what I've seen, what I've been through, I'll disappear just as definitively as Todd, and Leigh.

They haven't forbidden me from writing about this, though, these mysterious forces. They can't ban me from recording my experience in my own personal diary. So, I have done just that. Think of this as a journal, of sorts. A brain dump of what I saw.

They also don't know that I surreptitiously collected a small sample of Swamp Man's abandoned spawn, while I was initially showing the cops the den. I wiped my hand across the small lingering streak of the stuff on the pit wall, close to where Todd had been pasted and then hastily ripped down, and I scraped what stuck to me into an empty Vaseline tin I'd found in my jeans pocket, a pot I'd been meaning to dispose of, and was very glad I had not.

The spawn lives in a large jar on my windowsill, now, a jar I have populated with twigs, dead leaves, stones, a sunken pit filled with a mix of salt and freshwater, and even some pondweed I collected from a ditch close to my house. I laid a trap in my garden, caught a mouse, popped that into the jar too, arranging the spawn inside the opened animal's chest, which I dissected with a penknife, scooping out the tiny organs with a teaspoon. I wonder if it is substantial enough, this rodent nest, or if I should find something bigger for the young to live off. I have placed a shelf in the jar in case the critter prefers land to water when it hatches. I watch the spawn obsessively as it develops. The process is slow, painfully so. These things do not grow fast. It might take months, perhaps even years before any one of them gets to a size that appreciably resembles an infant Swamp Man. I don't know if what hatches will be male, or female, or how I shall house it, or them, or if I will let any of the things grow to term and reach enough maturity to procreate in turn, or even whether I shall let it live at all when it does eventually hatch from its sticky, gooey shell. I don't know why, in all truthfulness, I collected the spawn in the first place, acting only upon a wild, sudden instinct that came over me when I saw the leftover eggs attached to the earth, abandoned by their father. I don't think I am motivated by revenge, for I still firmly believe the creature acted out of a natural, protective instinct, not, as I said before, a desire to be cruel or to maim or murder for the sake of it.

Perhaps, by observing this creature, I hope to achieve what I have only managed to achieve so far by travel: to understand more about myself, about the world and my role within it. By comparing this anomaly with myself, with my own actions and motivations and behaviours and development, I might unlock something I currently lack. I have been struggling with so many thoughts, since my accident: what it means to be alive, to be human, to experience pain and regrowth, to feel vulnerable, like prey, but also what it means to face death from mere inches away, watch it consume your pink flesh, to survive the wrath of a brainless element, of a natural force with no rationality or purpose beyond combustion, and to remain alive once it has swept what it can away from you. Fire, mother nature: she is perhaps the ultimate apex predator. Now I have looked her in the eye and survived, I don't exactly know where I fit in anymore.

But now I know there are differently evolved forms of man out there, it changes things.

Because there are great mysteries out in the world, mysteries begging to be solved, and I can do nothing but heed the call of my own heart, and attempt to unravel a few, before I run mad with fear, and impotence, and my own, supposed, pathetic place in the grander scheme of things. I can learn, and I can grow, as the sticky little things in my jar grow. Who I shall be when they hatch is anyone's guess.

Perhaps I will be their mother.

THE REUNION

The air smelled of spring.

Tim Lane's wife didn't seem to notice or appreciate this. She had been silent for two hours, almost the entirety of their car journey. This only happened when something was seriously wrong, but Tim knew better than to poke a sleeping snake with a sharp stick. He maintained his own silence, enjoying the sun on his face as he drove. Winter had been too long. He wore a short-sleeved shirt for the first time in months. Sunglasses made the world seem warmer, richer. He arrowed down the motorway with one hand gripping the top of the wheel, the other resting loosely on the gear stick. Air tickled the hairs on his driving arm, which was adorned with a brand-new Tag Heuer bracelet watch, the Carrera model, nine percent off in the sale, although he didn't tell people that. It looked good on him.

He tensed as a sudden anticipatory rash of goosebumps swept along his body. Muscles corded. He allowed himself a quick glance down. He'd been hitting the gym a lot lately. It showed.

All that hard work is paying off, he thought. *That's all it takes. Hard work, to separate the men from the unicorns.*

'Do you know how few people get to live the kind of life you do, Laney?' A friend had once told him. 'You're like a fucking unicorn, I swear. You did the thing. You're living the dream.'

He smiled to himself, thinking about the next day ahead. A chance for this unicorn to prance around a bit, rewrite history. Show off. His moment, at last. It was going to be a good day. He could hardly wait.

His wife sighed. She was thinking about the next day too, for different reasons. He sympathised, but it wasn't his responsibility to go digging for gold. When she could think of a way to start the conversation, she would. Until then, he was going to drive his Audi convertible with the straight-backed joy of a man who had well and truly sorted his shit out. He would show those fuckers at Cresswell High just what success looked like, and, hopefully, erase the memories of everything he used to be when he'd attended as a boy. He hated that a past version of him no longer in existence lived on in the minds of his school peers. A small, weak, affection-starved, repellent kid with no social skills, money, or particular abilities, that had absolutely nothing to do with who and what he was now.

Back then, Tim had been what people generously called an 'all-rounder'. A jack-of-all trades, but master of none. He'd scraped into the prestigious Creswell High school on a scholarship afforded him through an Assisted Place Scheme- an entrance programme designed to allow the less fortunate in society a more exclusive education than they otherwise would have access to.

Of course, he told his wife, whenever they spoke of it, which was often, this had been back in the days when the government cared about poor kids being as well educated as their rich peers.

The scheme had paid tuition fees for under-privileged students displaying enough intelligence to warrant the sponsorship, and Tim knew that, were it not for the programme, he'd still be in his hometown, knee-deep in financial burdens and shattered expectations. Instead, he had this Audi, and he'd built a whole new life in a large new mansion on the outskirts of Winchester, and his kids were the manageable type, easy-going, excellent academic performers, popular, good-looking, somehow unspoiled. Going places. They wouldn't struggle like he had.

He'd married well, too. His wife Jess was a lawyer, a brilliant mother, and a catch by anyone's standards. They had a good thing going on, all of them.

He had 'made it', by any of the definable measurements a person could use to say so.

But still.

The stigma of being the poor kid at a posh school had stuck with Tim throughout his career at Cresswell High and beyond. It had fuelled him onto greater success, arguably, than he might have experienced otherwise, but that wasn't the point. He still remembered vividly how he'd been jeered at and bullied for his second-hand clothes, his thin physique, his small house, his mum's ancient, scrappy car, the fact that he never had the toys and gadgets everyone else did until years after their release, when nobody cared about them anymore, everything. Pop-culture was something other kids had access to, not Tim, for there was no TV in his house (the licence had been too expensive). There were a lot of cruel jokes, he remembered, about how he smelled. These had probably been valid: his mother had strictly controlled how often he showered because she couldn't afford the water bill, and there was only so much a can of Lynx could do when it came to teenage B.O. He'd also been called 'greased lightning,' because his hair had always carried a patina of oil, which in turn had contributed to his horrific acne. All of this had coagulated into what would become his permanent moniker, one that would haunt him for years to come: *Don't sit next to Loser Lane,* people would say. *You'll get nits.*

I'll change all that with the school reunion tomorrow, he thought, pressing his foot down hard.

He was going to shit all over this reunion, or at least, that was the plan. He was going to turn up and dominate. He couldn't fucking wait to see the looks on people's faces when he walked in with Jess on his arm. No more Loser Lane. His friends called him Laney, now. Timothy Lane, Vice President of the country's largest multinational pharmaceutical and vaccine company. And it was a good time to be in the business of vaccines. Tim had done well out of the pandemic. He wouldn't phrase it like that at the reunion, of course not, that would be seen as crass and insensitive, no doubt. Too many people had died, he didn't want to paint himself as a profiteer. He would position himself instead as being a core part of the route to recovery for the nation. Which wasn't exactly true, and wasn't exactly false, either. But he would let others come to their own conclusions. He'd keep talk of assets out of it, obviously. His wife, watch and car would speak for themselves.

Besides, nothing said 'new money' more than a man who couldn't stop talking about it.

He licked suddenly dry lips.

He was nervous, he realised.

He swallowed it down. No need for nerves. He had everything he'd ever wanted in life, didn't he?

Except...

Will she be there?

He kicked that thought away, quickly. His foot pressed down harder on the accelerator. His Audi purred back, delighted.

It doesn't matter if she is, Tim reminded himself sternly, glancing over at Jess, who was pouting at the passing scenery.

I've got everything I need right here.

*

It was a perfect day for the journey; clear, bright, hopeful. The trees were greening up, and the fields had crop growth in them again, breaking the endless monotony of winter mud. Bright yellow fields of flowering rape lay in garish patches all around. It felt fantastic to be driving, just driving, without rain or discomfort. In a way, it was good that Jessica was in the mood she was, and didn't want to talk. It meant he could enjoy this moment better. Prepare himself mentally, too.

Does she still hate me?

What does she look like now?

Tim shook his head as if trying to dislodge a buzzing fly from his ear.

He took the next exit off the motorway and found himself plunged deep into the countryside as suddenly as if he'd flipped a switch. This was a road empty of other cars, which was a relief, for it was one of those narrow, winding roads steeped high on either side with thick hedgerow, so tall it felt as if he were pushing the

Audi along a thin green tunnel. There were passing places at regular intervals along the road, but thorny hedges crowded thickly around each space, which he tried his best to avoid. No scratches on his paintwork, thank you very much. Not until after the reunion, at least.

The satnav lost their position for a moment, recalibrated. It didn't matter much- Laney knew where he was, now. They weren't far from the hotel, a country house affair with a Michelin starred restaurant onsite. He was looking forward to it. He and Jess were going to dress up, drink cocktails, try and remember what it felt like to be romantic, unfettered. They would move onto wine, something French if he had his way, and she would wear a dress and feel elegant again and if oysters were on the menu, he would buy a bucketful. He loved oysters. They tasted like salty snot, but he loved what they represented. A far cry from the supermarket own-brand tinned beans and sausages and stale bread he'd had to eat as a kid. His mum used to cut the blue mould patches off the bread crusts before making toast. *Waste not want not,* she always said, but no matter how many crusts were trimmed, they'd still wanted, for a lot.

Jess sighed again, loudly. Tim found himself getting increasingly irritated by her frequent exhalations. He hoped she wasn't going to spoil things somehow. He hated thinking like that, but Jess did it a lot, these days. Spoiled special moments. It was like she didn't know how to be happy, exactly, which annoyed him. Why was he working so hard, otherwise? Date nights recently had been somewhat nightmarish, there was always something up: the food made her ill, or she got too drunk, or she would choose something particularly problematic about their relationship to try and solve mid-meal, and he would refuse to engage with what he knew would put him on the back foot, and she would get offended by his recalcitrance and drink more and stew in her frustration and eventually cry, and people would look at them, for she did not know how to cry quietly, and he would feel like an arsehole.

Again.

Perhaps I should order room service tonight, instead, he mused. *Stave off any hysterics.*

He immediately admonished himself. *Stop thinking like that. It's a self-fulfilling prophecy otherwise.*

'You should be nicer to your wife,' another friend had told him, a few weeks back. 'It's just a rough patch. Every married couple has them.'

Still, there was a reason she was stewing in silence beside him, and that reason might be at the reunion tomorrow. Her name was Louise.

Jess had never been okay with Tim's convoluted history with his ex. She didn't like how Tim had behaved, for one thing, and felt a lot of second-hand guilt on Louise's behalf; she had told him as much, several times.

She also knew Louise had been his first true love, and for some reason, that still, despite years of marriage and commitment, made her jealous.

Yes, as far as touchy subjects went, his ex-wife Louise was the touchiest. It would be a herculean effort to keep Jess calm for the whole day, he knew.

But tomorrow was important to him, so needs must. That was why he planned on getting her loosened up tonight, with a romantic dinner. He'd ply her with attention, nuzzle the back of her neck the way she liked.

Do whatever it took.

Because everything had to be perfect, no matter what.

But first, there was a conversation to be had.

*

Tim sped up, swerving as a sharp bend hit them out of nowhere. Brakes squealed. Fans of grit spat from under the Audi's tires. Jess hissed in surprise as her arm slid sharply off the door ledge. His burst of speed had irked her, and she overreacted, just as he intended.

If that didn't prompt her out of her funk, nothing would. Tension was there to be diffused, and he'd rather do it now than at the hotel.

'Oww!' She cried, predictably. Then she slapped him on the knee, hard.

'Watch it, boy racer. You scared me.'

'Sorry,' he replied, although he wasn't. She'd been in her head for too long now.

'It's fine,' she said, retracting her hand.

Then she went quiet again, brooding.

Tim kept at it.

'You okay? You've been very quiet.'

Jess knew the jig was up. Her shoulders slumped in defeat.

'Not really,' she replied, cautiously.

'Want to talk about it?'

'I suppose we should,' she said, although she didn't sound very keen.

'No pressure. But it might help, you never know.'

She clammed up again. Tim fought down another surge of irritation.

Softly, softly, catchy fishy, he reminded himself.

'What's up, JJ?' His use of her pet name was calculated, designed to get her to lower some defences.

'Don't call me that,' Jess replied, shaking her head. 'I know what you're doing. I am not butter to be softened up.'

'Oh come on,' Tim cajoled. 'You used to love it when I called you JJ.'

'Do you think she will be there?' Jess said, abruptly changing the subject. She rubbed her arms briskly, refusing to look at him.

Took her long enough, Tim thought. He chose his next words carefully.

'I don't...It isn't...I don't think it's Louise's sort of thing, quite honestly. But how would I know? I haven't spoken to her in twenty years, easily. If not more.'

'It's not your sort of thing either, but we're here,' Jess complained. 'You always swore you would never go to a reunion if you were invited. You always said you hated that school and you didn't like anyone there except for ... her.'

Tim glanced over and thought how tired his wife looked. She was still beautiful, so beautiful, with strong, precise features, but she never smiled enough. She shone when she smiled. Evidence of too many sleepless nights played with the delicate folds of skin about her eyes, and her mouth tugged down as she worked through her feelings. He suddenly felt like giving her a hug.

'I hadn't thought about it," he lied. "Anyway, if she *is* there, it makes no difference to us. Okay? All of that...it was a long time ago. I promise. It'll be fine, Jess. Stop worrying.'

His wife nodded, and went back to staring out of the window in silence.

'Hey,' Tim said, trying to end the conversation on a more positive note. 'How about we drive to France this year for the school holidays? I've always wanted to check out the Dordogne. Eat, drink wine, look at some old shit...what do you say?'

Jess nodded noncommittally. 'Yeah, sure,' she said, her heart not fully in it. 'That could be nice.'

They pulled into the hotel driveway five minutes later, having almost missed the turning. Tim had to yank the Audio into a hard spin at the entrance gates at the last moment. Gravel pummelled the nicely painted wooden sign that was almost completely obscured by exuberant hedgerow, accounting for his almost missing the turning. He would make a point of complaining about that when he checked in. Fancy hotels loved it when their guests complained about stuff, Tim had found. It meant their residents had standards the hotel aspired to meet. It also made his eventual praise hard-won, and therefore more satisfying to receive.

He knew this because that was how he had been raised: praise little, expect lots.

*

The dinner was exemplary. Jess was the best-looking woman in the restaurant, if not the entire hotel. This made Tim happy. The waiting staff bent over backwards for the pair of them, which made him happier still.

After dinner they drank whiskey in an old, wooden-panelled parlour, while oil paintings of long-dead dukes, lords and ladies watched them with egg-shell whitened eyes. Tim was relieved that on this occasion, Jess did not get too drunk, and did not burst into tears. He started to relax and enjoy himself.

The whiskey done, Tim led his wife upstairs to the four-poster bed in their room, where he fucked her three times and fell hard asleep, face down in Egyptian cotton, just the way he had always dreamed of as a young boy, the rise and fall of Jess' perfect tits beside him in the bed sending him deep into dreamland, where he found himself stuck in a recurring nightmare. His old school peers laughed at him as all his teeth and most of his hair fell out, landing in his plate at the dinner table, where he sat naked, and vulnerable, and as he pointed to his brand new Audi parked outside the school to try and redeem himself, he saw a beaten up, rusted old Skoda Octavia instead, a blocky, ugly family car with key marks dragged along each side, a smashed front headlight, and a rear-view mirror dangling from the roof held loosely in place with a strip of gaffer tape. All around, Mercedes and Bentleys and Porsches and Rolls-Royces grinned at him with shiny polished grills, and his wife cried into her bisque beside him, because he had let her down, he had let his kids down, and most importantly, he had let himself down.

Then, Louise appeared next to him at the table. She was cradling the body of their dead son. Twin streams of snot ran down her chin, pooling on the tabletop before him.

After that, his fingernails started to fall out, and his skin began to peel away from his skeleton in long, dry paint strips.

In the morning, he could remember little of the dream beyond the cars and the vague memory of his skin sloughing from his bones. It felt like shedding an old, heavy coat, and he carried that sensation for the rest of the day, never knowing where it had come from, or why.

*

The car park of Creswell High was crammed with vehicles of all kinds, just like in his dream; expensive sports cars, big family estates, small sleek cars, executive cars. The reunion, it seemed, was a popular idea. Tim was amazed by the turn-out. Then his thoughts went to Louise. It was even more likely she might show, if this many of his former classmates had made the effort. He felt excited. He tried to hold onto Jessica's hand to distract himself from the feeling, but she avoided his touch, keeping her arms tightly folded and chewing her lip. She was very nervous.

Printed arrows on bright yellow squares of card led them towards Tim's old assembly hall, which was now twice the size it had been, with a new stage and fancy lighting and bold artwork on the walls. The scale and modernity of the building was a surprise. He'd been expecting everything to appear shrunken and diminished, but the school had, in contrast, outgrown him.

The hall was crowded with half-remembered faces, husbands, wives, old teachers even. In astonishment, Tim pointed out his old Headmaster, an age-stooped man with white hair and a thin moustache who hobbled around with two sticks, greeting anyone who wandered past with the same cheerful declaration:

'I always liked this year best!' He crowed, and everyone laughed indulgently.

'I can't believe he's still alive,' Tim whispered. Jess frowned at him in disapproval.

'Don't be mean,' she said.

'I'm not! He was just old when he taught us, is all. He must be positively ancient now.'

'Well, maybe he takes care of himself,' Jess replied, tiredly.

Tim shrugged, scanned the rest of the crowd. A lot of faces he remembered, many he did not. Some he had forgotten about entirely until he saw them again, upon which, memories would come rushing back. Any time he saw someone who had bullied or crossed him at school, he pointed them out to Jess, describing their crimes in a low, bitter voice. Jess listened and nodded solemnly, but refused to be drawn into conversation about it. Past slights or misdemeanours were just that, she'd told him before they arrived. Things that happened in the past.

'Children are cruel sometimes,' she'd sighed. 'Then they grow up.'

It was no excuse, he maintained, but Jess was not a grudge holder like he was.

A few people approached him, men mostly. It became apparent they were more attracted by Jess than any real desire to bury proverbial hatchets with her husband. Tim didn't mind this. He was proud of how beautiful Jess was and liked showing her off.

He shook hands, introduced his wife, and listened with an amiable smile on his face as a succession of increasingly boring (and boorish) farts hee-hawed on about their fantastic careers, talented children, exalted connections and travels to other continents. He avoided answering questions about his own life; content to just listen. He had a sneaking suspicion half of the people he met had no earthly idea who he was, which made him both annoyed and relieved: Loser Lane and he now lived in two very different realities.

Which was the entire point of this excursion, although Tim did secretly wish for the light of recognition to dawn on more faces than it did.

To her credit, Jess played her part with admirable loyalty, for which he was intensely grateful. She flashed perfect teeth, administered compliments and nodded her head at the roomful of strangers dutifully, knowing, as he did, that the whole thing was a farce. The room fairly reeked of hidden tensions and thinly veiled insecurities, inexpertly covered by loud, boasting laughs and hearty handshakes and the occasional bad joke. Alcohol flowed freely from a long table set up by the stage, and people stood in small, red-faced clusters around it as they waited for the tour of the school. There was a good deal of dick-swinging and showing off, which he knew Jess despised, but Tim found it all rather amusing.

After about an hour, a nervous whisper landed in his ear, followed by a cool hand on his arm.

'Is that her?' Jess asked.

Tim looked to where his wife pointed. A tall woman with a curly cloud of thick blonde hair had entered the hall.

Tim went momentarily cold, then hot.

Then he began to sweat.

Yes, it was her.

Louise had come to the reunion, after all.

*

He was surprised at how visceral an experience it was, seeing her again. He'd suppressed a lot of feelings about his ex-wife in the years since their divorce, but suppression was infinitely easier when the subject matter was out of sight, and out of mind.

Now he was in the same room as her, his body was unexpectedly seized by a force unlike anything he'd ever felt subjected to before. It pummelled him with a series of shocks that felt electric in nature. *Zing!* She had come alone. *Zing!* She was still a hell of a good-looking woman. *Zing!* She was taller than he remembered. *Zing!* She was dressed expensively, meaning she'd done well for herself.

The electric shocks raced along his limbs and thudded viciously into his heart.

Zing!

You fucking left her, you idiot.

'She looks nice,' Jess remarked, in a flat, neutral voice.

Tim found he couldn't reply.

This is guilt, he realised, swallowing hard.

What you're feeling is guilt, you fucking fool.

What did you expect?

Honestly?

That you two would laugh, shake hands, and forget everything that ever happened?

'Don't you think she looks nice?'

Jess was staring at him with fierce eyes. Her tone felt loaded. He had to play this carefully, he knew, or the whole day, week, month would fall off a cliff.

'I guess,' he shrugged, non-committal.

But she does look nice, he admitted to himself, still reeling from the intensity of emotions racing around his brain.

Really, really nice.

In fact, she looks a whole lot better than the last time you saw her, doesn't she?

Tim felt his wife's posture shift. She was growing defiant.

Because the last time you saw her you were both nineteen, and you were saying goodbye, weren't you?

'You guess,' Jess muttered.

You said goodbye, and then you lied, told her you'd be back as soon as you could, didn't you?

Tim squeezed Jess' arm, just once.

'She isn't a patch on you,' he said, sincerely.

He could tell Jess didn't believe him, but she appreciated the amelioration effort. Her expression softened, just a little.

The guilty jellyfish stings to his heart kept on coming, though.

Zing!

You lied, and then you walked out of her life, and left her holding the baby, didn't you?

Zing!

With no money, or reliable source of income.

Zing!

And a mortgage to pay.

Zing!

And a puppy to care for, too.

Zing!

She's seen you.

He sucked in a sharp breath on the last sting.

Louise had spotted him standing across the room from her.

This is it, he thought. *The moment.*

Their eyes, at last, briefly met.

Tim felt giddy, then horribly deflated as his ex-wife's mouth tightened into a hard, hateful line. Her entire body seemed to grow tense, and statue-still.

Zing!

You left them all without a backward glance, didn't you, champ?

She hadn't forgotten any of it, he saw, immediately. She certainly hadn't forgiven, either.

Her gaze locked him in place, and it was pure fury, even after all this time.

Tim felt the room spin. He took an involuntary step back, before bringing himself up short.

He saw now, far too late, that he'd been horribly naive about this reunion.

*

You were young, he told himself once Louise had turned away, and he'd recovered slightly from the shock of seeing her. His ex made no effort to come over and talk to him, choosing instead to mingle with the crowd by the refreshments table.

You were both so young.

A kid, really.

But the thoughts rang hollow. According to his second wife's logic, young people fucked up, and then grew up, but there were fuck-ups, and then there was what he'd done to Louise.

And to Ben. His son.

His first-born.

Tim gulped down a mouthful of warm wine, trying to rinse away the sour taste that filled his cheeks.

He'd been an idiot, back then. He knew this. It was undeniable. He'd been an idiot. Selfish. Scared. He'd fled to Singapore to chase a job offer, to chase a dream salary, and although he'd told her he would be coming back, that everything would be alright, everything would be paid for, he'd lied. He'd had no intention of ever coming back. Or of paying his way. He'd been broke. In over his head. It had been her idea to buy the house. Her idea to get a dog. To have a baby.

Not his.

He'd thought they were too young, and had said so, several times.

Turns out, he'd been right.

But rather than accept this, and do what was necessary, he'd lied, and run away.

He hadn't told Louise his departure was going to be a permanent state of affairs as he'd hauled his suitcase down the tiny, narrow staircase of the terraced cottage he never wanted to buy. He'd been too scared. He'd created an impression of temporary separation, of a grand return and good things to come, even as he'd kissed Ben on the top of his head and hugged his wife half-heartedly. The puppy he'd ignored entirely. It whined and wagged its tail at him nevertheless.

'Call me when you land?' Louise had asked.

Of course, he hadn't.

His foot had been out the door long before the Singapore offer came in, they both knew that, but she'd had hope, he could tell. It had been in her voice, in her eyes.

He had thought it best not to encourage that hope once he landed on the other side of the world.

Tim had little memory of much else from that day, only of how red and swollen Louise had been from crying. Red, swollen and inconsolable, like the baby.

But now, she wasn't sad. He could feel it from across the room. Now, she was angry.

So, so angry.

He couldn't blame her for that. He'd been angry with himself for a while after, too.

Then, he'd buried it.

*

Despite her feelings, Louise was smiling as she worked her small corner of the room. It was a smile that just barely gave away how uncomfortable she felt to be out in public. She'd never liked social gatherings, or crowds, so this reunion had to be something of an effort for her, Tim knew. This mutual lack of social skills had brought them very close when they were kids. At school, she'd felt no real need to make other friends; he was all she'd been interested in. He'd felt the same about her, for a while. They'd been inseparable.

Marriage put an end to that closeness swiftly. As did having a baby.

They'd maintained some loose connection after his move to Singapore, exchanged a few calls on birthdays in the early days. She'd written dozens of letters that he never answered.

But when baby Ben died at eighteen months, just over a year after he left, that was the final nail in the coffin, so to speak, to their connection.

He remembered that call. He remembered it vividly.

Meningitis, she'd said.

It was all over so quickly.

There was no time to say goodbye.

I can't afford a proper funeral, she'd gone on to tell him.

I've lost the house, too.

Both of those things, it was implied, were his fault.

Because he'd sent no money from Singapore.

Not a single penny.

*

Back in the present, Louise did not outwardly acknowledge that Tim was still watching her from across the hall, being too busy with other acquaintances, all of whom seemed happy to see her- which was a turn up for the books considering how much of a loner she'd been at school- and he found himself disappointed that they couldn't share another eyes-meet-across-the-crowded-dancefloor moment.

He had to make do with covertly studying her from a distance whilst pretending not to, for Jess' sake.

And study her he did.

Louise had taken good care of herself over the years, that much was obvious. She had a healthy glow to her skin, and walked around straight-spined, shoulders back, head held high, like a dancer. She was dressed nicely, if conservatively, but Tim knew from experience that these sorts of occasions were difficult to judge, outfit-wise. Louise had erred on the side of caution, something Jess, in her tight-fitting black dress, had not.

A gong sounded out across the hall.

'Ladies and gentlemen, the tours will now begin!'

Tim let himself be steered away. The large crowd was split into smaller groups and taken out of the hall on a series of staggered guided tours of the school grounds.

His group was escorted by two serious sixth formers, who blushed self-consciously, but overcame their nerves after the first ten minutes of the tour. They were obviously very proud of their school, and diligently left no room unvisited on the itinerary. The adults, seeing how enthusiastic their guides were, played along with predictable gasps of approval at how new, big and professional everything looked, along with cries of 'Well, when *we* were here...!' As if none of them could get their heads around the fact that progress was real and inevitable and things, did, in fact, change with time.

The school, Tim saw, was clearly not struggling for funds: the IT room was enormous, the tennis courts had been extended and

67

re-surfaced, and there was now an indoor heated swimming pool and a brand-new library, along with an enormous, light-filled atrium that was sometimes rented out for conferences and other events, at the school's discretion, of course.

The tour took over an hour, which was far too long, in Tim's opinion. As they walked, he could hear Louise behind him in another group, talking and laughing occasionally. It made him feel jumpy, constantly wondering if she was looking at the back of his head. Could she see the small bald patch flowering there, just beyond his crown? He wished suddenly he was wearing a baseball cap, and had to stop himself from touching the balding area more than once.

The tour continued. The more school rooms Tim saw, the more uneasy and uncomfortable he became. Memories of himself at seventeen assaulted him at every turn. The classrooms where he'd sat exams, glared at gloss-painted walls, sulked in detention, detached himself from reality when bullied, dodged board-rubbers hurled at him and surreptitiously cried into his sleeve when he'd failed to make his grades all blurred together to form a single, sterile enclosure of discomfort around his heart. The leisure centre he used to smoke behind in his lunch hour seemed reproachful, somehow, mocking him for all those snatched moments of solitude in the succession of long, difficult days that made up his school career. The bench by the line of redwood trees where he'd kissed Louise so clumsily for the first time looked shabby, uncared for, left out of the expensive renovations that had taken place in the years since his departure.

Jess held onto his hand very tightly as the tour proceeded.

Her grip strengthened until their fingers, intertwined, turned white and red with pressure, and his hand began to cramp.

He knew better than to try and pull it away.

*

After the tour there was dinner. The caterers had been busy in the hall in their absence; there were gold candlesticks and white tablecloths and balloons and banners everywhere, with empty wine glasses standing to attention and a silver service. It felt almost like a wedding feast, without a bride and groom.

As Tim studied the seating plan, held up on a large artist's easel by the main doors, he froze, horrified.

Jess went rigid beside him as she saw, seconds later, what he did.

'I don't believe it,' she hissed in disbelief. 'The *gall!*'

For Louise, they saw, had kept Tim's surname.

68

'What the fuck is she playing at?' Tim muttered, shaking his head in confusion as his guts churned.

They'd been divorced a long time, after all. Plenty of time in which to sort out a name change. Tim had never imagined for one moment that Louise would even *want* to keep his name after everything he'd done. She still hated him, that much was clear.

So why? He asked himself, and then his heart sank as he figured it out.

'Ben,' he murmured, and Jess sucked in her breath.

'Oh, she said, the realisation hitting her, too.

His surname had also been Ben's surname, so Louise had kept it.

Because changing it back would mean having a different name to her son.

It must have been too painful, Tim thought, feeling sick. She didn't want to lose him completely, so she'd kept his name to stay closer to him.

Legally, on paper, she must have a different name, he reasoned, scratching at his bald patch worriedly again. Jess pulled his hand away before he could draw blood from his tender scalp.

Legally, she's probably reverted to her maiden name.

Unless she's remarried, since.

But publicly, a person could call themselves anything they wanted, couldn't they?

And publicly, she'd decided she wanted the same name as her son.

He could hardly berate her for that, not with context applied.

Still, it presented him with a massive headache when it came to the seating arrangements for dinner, for Louise was now placed next to Tim instead of Jess (who had kept her own name after they'd married, rather than take his).

The organisers had- quite understandably, given the circumstances- gotten his wives mixed up.

As a result, Jess was placed on a table at the opposite end of the hall, instead of alongside him where she belonged.

Fucking hell, Tim thought. *What a cock-up, on today, of all days.*

'I'll get it fixed,' he said out loud, as calmly as he knew how, but the damage was done. Jess, overwhelmed by a variety of conflicting emotions, had turned to ice, and was not going to thaw any time soon, he saw. Not until the event was well and truly over.

The opportunity to wow his old peers and bullies and show them how far he'd come had also passed.

Tim found he no longer cared about any of that. A huge wave of exhaustion came crashing down on him, from nowhere.

All he wanted now was to get things over with and leave with as much dignity intact as he could.

Tim collared a server quickly and explained the confusion, irate and embarrassed, his tone brusque. The server looked stricken at the mix-up, but rather than ask either of the wives to swap, which Tim supposed would only lead to more embarrassment, the waiting staff quickly laid an extra place at the table on the other side of Tim, muttering apologies as they shuffled chairs around and scooted the other placements along to accommodate Jess.

This wasn't an ideal solution, but Tim lacked the energy to ask the team to move his ex-wife to another table altogether. He didn't want any more fuss. He was tired, and becoming maudlin.

They were all duly seated side by side.

Three in a row, Tim thought, feeling horrible. *Tim, his wife, and his ex-wife. What larks!*

He recognised no one else at the table.

Rather than waiting to be served, Tim reached across to the wine cooler standing in the centre of the spread and helped himself to a large glass of cold, second-rate Sauvignon Blanc without delay. Jess twitched her fingers in irritation on the tablecloth. She wanted to drink too, but he'd beaten her to it, deliberately. The tacit understanding that she would now be driving back to the hotel passed between them. She was not happy about this, and made her feelings clear on her face. The Audi intimidated her. So did Louise. Both made Jess prickly and insecure.

To his continuing dismay, Louise's body language, Tim found, matched his wife's perfectly: stiff, and belligerent. The two women remained intensely aware of each other as the meal began, so he found himself bookended by animosity while everyone else in the room reminisced and laughed and bragged and caught up. Tim spent the time staring at his napkin fixedly, all his bravado and confidence from yesterday gone.

Louise glared at her own empty wine glass, the stem of which she fiddled with incessantly.

Still not a drinker, but then, she never was, Tim thought.

Meanwhile, Jess moved and kept her right hand prominently on Tim's thigh. It lay heavy on him like a leaden weight. Sometimes her fingers would spasm, gripping his flesh tightly enough to bruise the skin underneath.

As time ticked interminably on, Tim thought about leaving, no, *running* out of the hall and into the nearest pub. But then Louise would maybe consider that to be an admission of guilt, which he was not sure he could cope with, and it would be confirmation to Jess that he was more affected by Louise's presence than he was comfortable admitting to.

He had no choice but to sit there, lodged between wives past and present, and brave it out as best he could.

At least the food was good when it arrived. That was something. Tim ate fast and drank more wine, pretending to listen to the small talk on the table, his mind a million miles away, in another decade, another life.

Should I talk to her? He wondered, more than once. Louise made no effort to speak to him, however, although he wondered if some of that was down to Jess, who was giving her best guard dog impression.

He knew he should follow Louise's cues, but it felt increasingly strange- not to mention rude- to ignore a woman he'd once married, had a child with, bought and furnished a home with, picked up dog shit with.

Walked out on, with no warning.

As the main course wound down, Tim eventually overcame his fear and decided to work up enough wine-courage to say a polite and neutral 'hello' to Louise, because it felt like the right thing to do. He figured it couldn't be any more uncomfortable than the pair of them ignoring each other.

Still, it took him a good five minutes of steeling himself and psyching himself up to the act once he'd decided upon it, and then, unbelievably, he fudged the greeting almost immediately upon opening his mouth, having stupidly not waited to empty his cheeks of food first. The result was that, instead of speaking calmly and conservatively as intended, he inhaled a chunk of roast beef that hadn't been chewed sufficiently, which then got firmly stuck in his throat. Tim then found himself choking and clawing at his airway, convinced he was about to die.

And serve me right, too, he thought wildly as the beef refused to budge.

Jess, who was nearing the limits of her patience, chose that particular moment to abandon him, and take a bathroom break. She thought he was putting it on, seeking attention, for this was something he'd used to do at parties. Pretend to choke, then grin joyously just as someone began to administer the Heimlich. Disgusted with his antics, she rose from her seat and sashayed across the hall to the toilets while he coughed and spluttered all over the table, his shame intensifying as he became dimly aware that everyone in the room was leering at her, watching her walk, with the exception of his ex, who had gone very still.

Probably hoping I'll die, he thought, but after that, thinking got a little difficult.

Tim continued to choke, making an unwelcome spectacle of himself. He received hearty slaps on the back by well-meaning, flushed men in tweed suits who had drunk too much wine and who all, to his watering eyes, looked boorish, and ancient.

When did we all get so fucking old?

Eventually, after much thumping, hacking and slapping, the offending chunk of beef trying its best to kill him came back up, and Tim managed to spit it discreetly into a napkin, instead of onto his plate, folding the disgusting regurgitation away with a sheepish grin.

'Good lad,' someone cried, affectionately. 'It would be awfully bad-mannered to die at the school reunion, right?'

Tim nodded and continued to smile a rictus smile.

'Quite,' he croaked.

Louise remained motionless beside him, almost like she was playing that game they'd all used to play at parties when they were kids. You had to turn around quickly, see who was moving. If you caught so much as a blink or twitch, that person was out.

Louise did neither: blink nor twitch.

Unnerved, but with the meaty obstruction mercifully ejected from his windpipe, Tim did his best to recover, but his heart was racing at a mile a minute, so he just sat there, filled with shame and self-loathing, hearing himself gasp like a heavy smoker, realising he was drenched with sweat, and feeling his embarrassment as total, and complete.

Loser Lane, to the very end, he thought.

Fuck this.

Fuck all of this.

I just want to go home.

Where is Jess?

He sipped at a glass of water, noticing how shaky his hands were. He had a titanic headache brewing, and his throat was now so sore he could barely swallow.

'Are you alright?' Louise asked then.

The question threw him completely off balance.

She almost sounds concerned, he thought.

Almost, but not quite.

Tim had a strange reaction to her voice, which had deepened over the years to something polite, crisp, capable, business-like.

She sounds like Jess, he realised.

He finally raised his head and caught her eye. It was very strange after so long, direct eye-contact, up close. Looking at her

72

like this triggered another barrage of memories, some of them good, lots of them bad.

They were sitting no more than a foot away from each other, but it felt much further.

Tim swallowed a few more times, thanked her, eventually.

'How are you?' He then ventured.

'Fine, thanks.'

Louise was so polite it burned, like dry ice.

What is she thinking?

He felt trapped in her presence, claustrophobic.

Guilty.

He panicked.

'You kept my name,' he blurted, immediately hating himself.

Louise blushed. It sounded like an accusation.

It wasn't.

A horrible silence ensued.

Tim struggled to find words to fill it. Louise stepped in for him.

'She seems very nice.'

'She?'

'Your wife.'

Oh. She was talking about Jess, who had still not returned. Of course she was.

'She is wonderful,' he replied, not knowing what else to say.

'And you have kids?'

He nodded, feeling awful. 'Two. Joel and Nancy. They're both in that awkward teen phase.'

Louise nodded, as if in sympathy.

'I know what you mean,' she said, shaking her head. 'I'm so glad Ben has finally grown out of all that.'

*

Tim froze, staring at his ex-wife with wide, disbelieving eyes.

'I'm sorry,' he stuttered, feeling the colour drain from his face. 'I misheard you. Ben?'

Louise frowned at him as if he was an idiot.

'Ben. Our son? Surely you haven't forgotten your own child's name.'

Tim said nothing.

He couldn't.

He felt freezing cold, and sickness surged again in his gullet.

Louise reached for her handbag under the table, opened it, drew out a photograph.

'You can keep it if you like,' she said, looking away as she thrust it at him.

73

'But...' Tim said, stupidly, not daring to look at the photo. 'But...'

But our son is dead! He wanted to scream.

He died when he was a baby!

You told me!

I sent money for the coffin!

I still have the invitation for the cremation!

The room began to spin once more.

*

'We live in France now,' Louise continued, as if they were having the most mundane of conversations, 'Not far from my parents. They have a place just outside of Carcassonne. It's a nice way to live, actually. The lifestyle there is very relaxed. Ben wants to move back here, though. He says there are more work opportunities. He's probably right.'

A hand on Tim's shoulder signalled the return of Jess, who sat down gracefully beside him, spine ramrod straight.

'What's that?' She asked, pointing to the photograph. She'd been crying. Tim could tell from the puffiness around her eyes, and the catch in her throat as she spoke. She'd applied fresh makeup to try and conceal her feelings, but nothing could conceal the pain in her voice.

Tim, who was having a near out of body experience, looked from his wife to the small, glossy picture loosely balanced on his fingertips.

A young man of about twenty (*twenty-two,* Tim remembered, *June 26th*) stared back at him confidently.

'God. He looks just like you,' Jess said, frowning.

That was enough for Tim.

He stood up, his chair scraping back noisily, and hurled the photo back to Louise.

'That isn't funny,' he said, around a mouthful of bile. 'I don't care what I did to you. There are limits.'

Both Jess and Louise gazed up at him in confusion. Their expressions and mannerisms were so similar, he couldn't bear it.

The other diners at the table smirked into their food, shooting sly glances at each other from beneath their lashes.

Loser Lane, he could hear them all thinking.

Can't get his shit together, even now.

Gossip about this encounter would be all over the gathering within the hour, he knew.

Not the impression he wanted to make at all.

He'd failed.

With that realisation, came an internal collapse. He felt himself subside, like a mudbank assaulted by a flood.

'Damn you,' he said to Louise, hating her violently.

Then he stiffly marched out of the room as fast as his legs could take him, hoping against all hope that he wouldn't vomit his meal up in front of the entire class of '00.

*

He found himself back under the redwood trees. They had grown vast over the years; furry red bark columns stretching high up above him. He felt disorientated, dizzy. His old bench was still there, at the base of the largest tree. He collapsed onto it.

What the fuck was she trying to achieve? He asked himself, over and over. Bringing out that photograph. It was ghoulish. Who even was that kid?

He did resemble Tim, a lot, that much was hard to deny.

A nephew?

A cousin he didn't know about?

Come on, Tim, think clearly.

It couldn't be either of those things, realistically. His family were small. Most of his immediate relatives were elderly. The only surviving cousin he had was called Betty, and she was seventy-three and lived in a retirement home in Basingstoke. Plus, it was extremely unlikely his ex-wife would know about someone he was related to when he didn't. Much less own a photograph of them. As far as Tim knew, Louise wasn't in touch with anyone on his side, not anymore. She'd cut herself off from everyone, after Ben's death, and he had not pursued a connection beyond settling the funeral costs.

A lookalike?

Photoshop?

Some composite, AI bullshit using a picture of him?

It didn't matter. Dropping Ben's name like that in public, at their first meeting in over two decades, was fucked up, fucked up beyond belief.

What did Louise hope to achieve by doing so?

Revenge?

Tim had never had her down as the vengeful type.

Angry, but not vengeful.

You did leave her holding the baby, an internal voice reminded him.

That's pretty fucked up too.

He hung his head between his knees, took several deep breaths. He regretted the wine now. He regretted the whole damn day.

A pair of feet came into view, clad in smart but sensible shoes. Louise.

'Fuck off,' Tim said, refusing to look up at her. He was concentrating hard on not being sick.

Louise ignored his request, sat down on the bench next to him.

'I thought I might find you here,' she said. 'This was our spot, wasn't it?'

'What do you want from me?' Tim replied, exhausted. 'Did you come to assess the damage after your little prank at the table?'

He finally raised his head, stared at her with red-rimmed eyes.

'It wasn't a prank,' Louise said, softly. He realised she was holding the photograph out again.

'What do you mean, it wasn't a prank? It was fucking *cold*, is what it was. I know I treated you abominably, Louise, but come on. Jokes about our dead son? That's the lowest thing I've ever fucking seen or heard.'

Louise sighed.

'We were both very young, Tim. We both made mistakes.'

She tried to hand him the photo.

The implications of her words started to sink in. Something about her resigned tone and the way she still thrust the picture at him was off.

Way off.

'What are you telling me?' He demanded, pushing the photo away angrily. 'Stop trying to give me that, Jesus Christ!'

Louise remained calm, as if talking to a child.

'The photo is real, Tim. The photo is of Ben. Our son. He wants you to have it.'

Tim lurched up, needing to get away from her. Swayed on his feet a bit. Tried to leave.

Turned back.

'Our son is dead,' he said, heavily. 'And I blame myself for it, every day.'

Louise looked at him with big, clear, emotionless eyes.

'No,' she replied, simply.

Tim tried again. 'You billed me for the funeral, remember?'

'It never happened,' she said.

Tim threw his hands up in despair. 'God, what more do you want from me? I've said I'm sorry, I said it over and over! I've spent the rest of my adult life since trying to atone for what I did, trying not to make the same mistakes with...with...' He tailed off.

He couldn't quite bring himself to say the words 'second family' to Louise's face.

Louise grabbed his elbow. Lowered her voice.

'You're not listening to me, Tim,' she insisted. 'Ben is not dead. He's alive.'

Tim shook his head, finding himself laughing.

'How long have you been planning this, you devious bitch? Since before the reunion? It's fucking clever, I'll give you that. Sick, but clever.'

Louise persevered.

'I told you Ben died because you ran out on us. You left us, with no money, no word. You said you were coming back, once you'd gotten your feet under you, once you'd made a living in Singapore, that we'd be a family again...'

'I know what I said! Why can't you just let it be?! It's in the past! I can't fucking go back and change it, can I?'

Louise moved her face, so it was close to his. He could smell her breath, see the pores in her skin. There were lines around her eyes, but not many.

'When it became obvious that you didn't mean any of the things you said...'

She paused, licked her lower lip.

'What are you telling me?' He begged, wanting her to get away from him, but not having the strength to push her off.

'I wanted to hurt you,' she confessed.

Zing!

Tim could not make sense of the words coming out of her mouth.

'What?'

His ears began to buzz with a loud, insistent tinnitus noise.

'I told you our son was dead,' she continued, without any discernible remorse, 'Because I wanted to make you feel how you made *us* feel. More than that...I didn't want you trying to come back into his life at a later date, whenever it suited you. I knew that if you thought he was gone...'

The penny finally dropped in Tim's mind.

Zing!

He felt suddenly as if someone had sucked all the air out of his lungs, then turned him inside out, for good measure.

It took every ounce of strength he had to not punch Louise, then, punch her square in the jaw.

'But...I saw a copy of the death certificate,' he stuttered, scrubbing his face frantically with his hands. 'I saw the fucking invitation to the funeral. I saw the bill for the expenses! Are you telling me all that was, what? Forged?'

Louise's voice went very soft.

'You said you couldn't make the funeral, anyway, remember?'

Zing!

She stared him dead in the eyes, and it was terrifying.

'You had other commitments in Singapore.'

Zing!

The buzzing in Tim's ears grew louder.

The redwood trees seemed to grow taller, leaning over him threateningly.

'Let's say I believe you,' he whispered, eventually. He took a step back to widen the gap between them. 'Why now? Why choose to tell me the truth now?'

Louise chewed on her bottom lip some more. She was thinking.

Could he trust a single word she said, though, when she broke silence?

Tears began to roll down his cheeks. He let them.

'He's asked to see you,' she replied, at last.

'What?'

'Ben has decided he wants to get to know his *father*.' Louise put a sour emphasis on the last word, as if she found the title laughable.

And Tim could control himself no longer.

He bent double and puked all over the exposed roots of the redwood trees.

*

Back on the bench, his head between his knees again, Tim felt awed by the complexity of his feelings and memories. It was all there, swirling in his brain. How intolerant he'd been of Louise as a newlywed husband, how impatient he'd been to move onto the next stage in his life upon realising he was unhappy, how ill-suited he'd felt to domesticity and the quiet, monotonous existence in the ramshackle, tiny house in the countryside that his lack of money and status had doomed them to. He remembered how he'd felt when his son was born: helpless, and afraid. Like he was trapped in a burning car about to drive off a cliff. He remembered the fights and the constant irritations and the mountains of chores and the incessant noise and mess and sniping and passive-aggressive verbal tennis matches. He remembered leaky nipples and blood and endless nappy-changes and the snatched hours of sleep between his son's crying fits. He had not been equipped for marriage at nineteen. For the monotony of fatherhood. For the continued financial hardship. For any of it.

When the job offer had come in from Singapore, it had felt like a lifeline.

Questions followed, while the smell of mown grass and fresh vomit mingled around them.

'What does he know about me?'

'Not much. He knows you're married. He doesn't know you have kids.'

'He knows I walked out on him?'

"Not really. He has never asked about that part of it. I think he just accepted you weren't there. And in my opinion, he was better off without you.'

Louise's jaw was set. She was struggling, Tim realised. This was painful for her, too.

Good, Tim thought. *Fuck you.*

'What is he like?' He asked, out loud.

She flashed angry eyes at him.

'Like you,' she replied, in disappointment. 'Despite all my best efforts. The kid grew up to be exactly like you.'

*

Before she left him sitting on the bench, the photograph gripped tightly in one shaking hand, she laid an envelope on the wood next to him. It was fancy stationery, he saw. Occasional. There was a picture of a castle embossed on the lower left corner of the envelope, a grandiose affair with turrets and battlements.

Invitation, the envelope read, in elegant script.

'He's getting married in a few months,' Louise announced, finally leaving, her mission accomplished. 'For some unfathomable reason, he would like you to be there.'

Tim stared at her retreating form, wondering how much of his life he was going to spend regretting doing the same, to her: walking away.

Walking away when she'd been nothing more than a child herself.

A child holding a child.

He had only himself to blame for this pain, he knew.

*

Later, back in the hotel, Tim got blindly, incoherently, fall-down drunk. Jess had to come down from their room and lever him out of a deep leather armchair in the bar at midnight, on request of the bar manager, who had tactfully called her.

As Tim stumbled foolishly upstairs, leaning on Jess' shoulder heavily when not bouncing off walls and careening off bannisters, he waved the invitation at her. It was crumpled now, smudged with dirty fingerprints.

'What the fuck am I going to do about this?' He moaned, and suddenly, he was crying again.

Jess continued pushing and pulling him up to their room, patient and resigned as ever.

'Well,' she panted, far too philosophically under the circumstances, 'You *did* say you wanted to go to France this year.'

There was, perhaps, a hint of satisfaction in her tone, but Tim was too far gone to detect it.

*

'I'm fucking sick of castles now,' Tim declared, pulling into a dusty carpark and peering up at the forbidding turrets of the Château de Puivert with trepidation. The spaces for parking were always a good half mile walk from the actual site themselves, and he was wearing brand new brogues, unsoftened and shined to be wedding ready. The steep, gravelly path up to the castle looked like it would make short work of his efforts, which made him pre-emptively annoyed, because first appearances were everything, especially in a situation like this, yet his entrance back into his son's life was about to be tarnished with scuffed toes and dust-hemmed suit trousers and sweat-patches under the arms.

Jess, who was sheathed in elegant navy silk, a large hat resting in her lap, checked her makeup in the rearview mirror. She didn't have a bead of sweat on her.

'We have seen a lot,' she admitted, folding a tissue and putting it between her goldfish-pouting lips to blot the lipstick excess that came from applying a fresh coat.

'You can say that again.'

Tim ran a hand over his hair, checking his bald spot was sufficiently covered.

The wedding invitation had given them an opportunity to 'make the most of it', to treat themselves to a little holiday during which they'd explored the whole of Cathar Country, it felt, which sat in the region of Aude, and consisted of at least twenty crumbling, atmospheric castles, forts and hilltop fortifications commonly known as the historic sites of the Pays Cathare (according to the leaflet their hotel had given them). Tim had left his Audi at home in the end, for it had been easy enough to hire a car from Perpignan. He and Jess had spent a good number of days touring the sites, if for no other reason than to distract themselves from the looming awkwardness of the wedding, an occasion Tim knew he did not belong at. He still didn't fully understand why he'd been invited, but had found himself accepting, despite everything in his body telling him it was a bad idea. Louise sure didn't want him there, that much she'd made clear.

Perhaps that's why, in the end, he'd said yes to the invitation.

He felt a dead, cold weight in his heart whenever he recalled the reunion.

He remembered, in vivid detail, the moment she'd told him their son was not, in fact, deceased.

He remembered the excuses she'd given, the look on her face.

Like it was no big deal.

Oh, by the way, Tim, your son was dead, but now he's not.

Hope you're okay with that.

He'd lied about Singapore, and she'd returned the favour.

An eye for an eye, a lie for a lie.

How fucking *dare* she?

Months later, he found he still didn't accept her reasoning behind the stunt. In fact, Tim wholeheartedly rejected it. There was no excuse, none whatsoever, for lying about his infant son's death. Doing so, in his opinion, was an act of evil, pure and simple. Criminal, in fact. He had been victimised against his will, had spent every night since her revelation tossing, and turning, and sweating, and calling out his son's name.

For a while he'd considered reporting Louise's actions to the police, but Jess had persuaded him not to.

'If you want any sort of relationship with your son at all, I would advise against it,' she'd said.

'She sent me a fake funeral invitation,' Tim shot back, furiously. He wasn't flesh and blood anymore, hadn't been since the day of the reunion. He was a man-shaped block of resentment and wrath. 'She made me pay for a funeral that never happened, all the expenses. At the very least, it's fraud.'

'I know,' Jess replied. 'And it was unforgivable. But you can't go back in time and change anything. Fraud might be the only thing you can accuse her of, but at what cost? Lashing out at her now is missing the point. You have your son back. You have a second chance. So now you must make the best of what's ahead of you. Your kid is alive. You get to be his father again. Don't fuck it up before it's started. You owe him that, at least.'

Tim had said nothing, because Jess was right. He *knew* she was right.

And yet, hatred flourished, grew more concentrated every time he thought about his ex-wife.

Fuck her, he'd thought over and over, from that day to this.

Fuck her.

FUCK her.

He would have a hard time keeping his hands by his sides when he saw Louise again.

Thank God Jess was here to keep him in check.

In a bid to stave off pre-wedding angst, they'd planned the driving tour of the region of Aude to be as deliberately hectic as possible. They'd gone at the small adventure with feigned enthusiasm, marking off every single castle on the tourist map, taking little pleasure from any of it. One Château, Tim realised, was much the same as the next. Just blocks of yellowing stone piled up on each other, when all was said and done. Some sites were in better condition than others, and the attractiveness of each location varied enormously. The castles also tended to get very hot, coverage being minimal in castle forecourts, and both Tim and Jess had struggled as the French summer blazed around them. They both sported deep tans, despite trying their best to cover up and use sunblock. Tim didn't like being suntanned. It made him look older than he was, and age was another insecurity he couldn't fight, no matter how hard he tried to convince himself that everybody aged, no matter what, and everybody eventually died.

Except his son, it seemed.

There had been a few highlights to the trip, despite their discomfort. Peyrepertuse had been impressive. The largest and most dramatic of the Cathar Castles, much of the original masonry had remained intact, and the views had been to die for: the castle sat on a stony ridge with sheer drops of up to eight hundred metres on either side. Tim had found himself reluctantly transported as he'd explored. He'd found it easy to imagine, when standing on one of the ramparts, what those men manning the walls hundreds of years ago would have felt and seen- green, rolling, lush countryside worth defending, at any cost.

At Quéribus castle- a small, deserted, degraded site perched on a cliff like a little stony eagle, with more beautiful views all around- Jess and he had snuck in a quick al fresco fuck, which had been strangely invigorating for both of them. They fucked again at Puilaurens. That castle overlooked several villages that nestled in its shadow. It was Jess' favourite: she loved the dramatic approach, where the structure was largely hidden at ground level, but revealed itself slowly, coyly, forcing them to crane their necks so they could just about make out the top of the castle fortifications as they climbed the precipitous path up to it. The vistas at the top were once again more than worth the effort it took to get there. Eroded crenellations on the walls gave the place a staged, story-book feel, extremely photogenic, perfect for a clandestine moment. They'd nearly been caught, that time, but managed to cum together and tuck everything in just before a party of hikers wandered in on them, oblivious.

The Château de Puivert, the wedding venue, was the last stop on their castle tour. Jess made sure to mark it off on the map as they sat in the car, listening to the engine cooling down, mentally preparing for the event ahead. Tim knew they wouldn't be able to hide down here for long. It was searingly hot, and only going to get worse. His car already smelt like hot plastic and metal.

There were a good number of other vehicles in the gravelled patch of land beside them. The wedding party was larger than expected. 'Small, intimate ceremony,' the invitation had stated, but a person's definition of intimate could vary, he supposed.

His own wedding- his first, to Louise- had been truly intimate. Just he, and her, and her parents, and his mother, in a small village church. The only flowers had been in Louise's bouquet. After, they'd gone to the local pub, for ale and chicken. Sung karaoke, drunkenly stumbled home with grease-drenched wrappers of chips. It had been fun, and simple, nothing like the lavish affair he'd laid on when he and Jess had gotten hitched.

He looked at his second wife, and wondered suddenly if she was happy. If he was a good husband, father. If he had made up for his earlier transgressions, displayed sufficient growth.

He suspected the answer was 'no,' but wasn't brave enough to ask and confirm that suspicion. He'd had just about enough of his own failures, to the point where he was completely fatigued with himself.

Even looking in the mirror made him feel faintly ill, these days.

'You know they made that movie with Johnny Depp here,' Jess muttered, flipping through the guidebook she'd bought before stashing it in the glove compartment. '*The Ninth Gate.*'

'Really,' Tim replied, but he wasn't interested. He had gone back to staring up at the mediaeval monument sitting on the ridge above them, which was decked out in white flags and bunting. It was hard, trying to keep his nerves in check.

'Never seen it,' Jess added.

What the fuck am I doing here? Tim asked himself, as sweat trickled down his back.

You're going to meet your adult son, a voice replied, *for the very first time.*

He would have to keep his jacket firmly on.

'Me either,' he replied, on autopilot.

'Do I look okay?' Jess checked her makeup again, patted her hair, scrutinised a tiny mark on her dress.

'You look beautiful,' Tim confirmed.

She took his hand. 'Ready?' She asked, and he could hear the resolve in her voice.

'No,' he replied, but they got out of the car anyway.

*

His son was waiting for him on the other side of the gated portal tower, almost as if he'd known Tim was going to walk through it at that exact moment. Perhaps he had been watching for his car, knowing the other guests were already in attendance. Tim's dust trail would have given him away long before his appearance, given how dry the roads were.

I should have brought the Audi, Tim lamented, immediately hating himself for the thought.

Jess gripped his sweaty hand tight in hers, subtly pulling him along as he slowed at the mouth of the castle. He felt dizzy again, and sick to his stomach.

That feeling evaporated as he emerged into the castle courtyard and saw a tall man, broad shouldered, tanned, dressed in a beautiful suit, with a white rose pinned to his lapel, accompanied by a stunning woman in cream chiffon by his side, and a small, cherubic boy of about two years old, who was balanced comfortably on his hip.

'Oh, god,' Tim said, stopping dead and taking in the scene. He felt as if he'd just walked into a glossy magazine photoshoot, but that wasn't the thing that let the air out of his lungs, made his knees weak so he had to stop walking, before he fell down.

Jess began to cry, unable to help herself.

'Oh god,' she echoed, squeezing his hand harder than ever. 'He looks just like you, Tim.' She dashed away her tears as best she could with her free hand. 'He looks *exactly* like you.'

Any lingering doubt that Louise had been telling the truth evaporated in that moment, leaving Tim a sweating husk of a man with scuffed shoes and a burned scalp.

Ben came forward with his family, sensing his father's distress.

'Hey Dad,' he said, in a rich, mellow voice tinged with a French accent that was brimming with joy. 'Thanks for coming. It means a lot to me that you did.'

Even his voice sounded like Tim's, if you ignored the European twang.

'Extraordinary,' Jess whispered, in shock.

Tim tried to reply, to say 'thank you', but found himself unable to talk.

He looks just like me, he kept thinking, over and over.

He sounds just like me too.

My son really isn't dead.

Ben handed the small boy- who Tim suddenly supposed to be his grandchild- to the woman who was presumably his bride, then stepped close, smiling.

Wordlessly, Tim let go of Jess' hand and embraced his son for the first time in over twenty years. Long arms encircled him, tightly. Tim could feel the other man's solid strength, and warmth, and vitality, and felt himself becoming unmade as they hugged.

'I missed you,' he said stupidly, realising it was partially true. He'd missed this version of his son, certainly.

'I missed you too,' Ben replied, as they stood cheek to cheek.

Unable to hold it in anymore, Tim broke and burst into tears, his entire body shivering and shuddering with pained sobs that came out of him like the barking of a dog, the short, sharp, rough sounds of confusion and longing, of guilt and regret, of relief and shame filling the hot air of the castle courtyard. He cried into his son's shoulder, unable to believe he had ever walked out on this kid, unable to countenance that he'd ever made excuses for himself for doing so. How could he have abandoned him the way he did? What kind of person was he? It was unconscionable. He'd missed out on so much, so much.

Other guests were watching, he knew. He was making a spectacle of himself once more, Loser Lane to the very core, but he couldn't stop.

This was his son, and his son was *alive.*

He had a chance to undo all the mistakes he'd made when he was the same age.

'I'm sorry,' he croaked, after the tears abated, and for a while, nobody else existed but the two of them.

*

Louise, thankfully, was nowhere to be seen amongst the guests, and had not been witness to Tim's reunion with his son. Tim supposed, on recovering some composure, she was keeping out of his way for good reason.

'Come meet my wife,' Ben said, once Tim had wiped his face dry. 'Camille, this is my long-lost father.' The young man said this with no hint of irony or resentment, and Tim felt the deep cut of the shame-blade slice at his soul once again.

The woman in cream chiffon stepped forward, kissed Tim and Jess on both cheeks, French style. Then she introduced the little boy.

'This is Gregory,' she smiled, and the child poked his tongue out, cheekily. 'Your grandson.'

Jess nearly lost it again when she saw the boy, but managed to get a hold of her emotions enough to pinch his cheek and pull a funny face, to which he responded in delight with a loud, rasping guffaw that was easily the most adorable noise Tim had ever heard.

'Now, you must join the party,' Ben said, furnishing Tim and Jess with flutes of champagne from a nearby table. 'I have to make sure I speak to everyone, but I'll return shortly, alright?'

Tim nodded, and chugged back his Moet, immediately craving another.

'In the meantime, mingle!' Ben said, jovially. 'Meet our friends and family. I'll introduce you, now.'

'Introduce us?' Tim blinked. 'Oh you don't have to-'

'But of course!'

Ben turned, held up his arms for an announcement.

'Everyone!' He dinged his champagne glass with a spoon, and shouted in English, repeating himself in French. 'Everyone, meet my long-lost Dad!'

The gathered wedding party cheered in recognition, and raised their glasses to Tim.

He felt his entire body burn with guilt.

Don't toast me, he thought, desperately. *I'm a worthless piece of shit.*

I'm Loser fucking Lane, don't you know anything?!

*

Jess proved a godsend over the next few hours. She spoke French well, and mingled confidently with the other guests, ushering Tim into a conversation only when she was convinced he would be able to handle it, and not before. She even managed to make a few light-hearted jokes about the unusual situation whenever people questioned Tim's relationship with the groom, jokes that softened the bizarreness of his being there and glossed over the years of hurt, pain and deceit preceding the event.

Tim found his energy for socialising came and went, so he dipped in and out of different clusters of guests without staying long enough in any one place to get fully involved. His focus stayed on Ben throughout, although he was content to watch his son from a distance rather than up close. He discovered he had a surprisingly large well of feelings in relation to his son that he didn't seem to feel for either of his other two children, something he would never admit out loud to Jess. Ben had been his first, after all, even if that whole experience had frightened him so much he'd bolted. A part of him knew he didn't have any right to these feelings, which was why he struggled to keep a lid on them. He'd forfeited any sort of familial sentimentality the second he'd left Louise and Ben alone, but still. Seeing the young man grown so tall, so confident, so clearly affluent and comfortable with his place in the world...it had a profound effect on Tim. Like he was watching a better version of himself walk around, a version that had all the kinks ironed out.

A version that had no mistakes in him, and his whole life ahead, still, in which to shine.

Seeing him with his own little boy, who was two, was the final cherry on the icing on the guilt cake.

I'm a long-lost grandfather, as well as a long-lost father.

See what could have been? He ruminated on this as the wedding celebrations unfolded.

See what could have been, had you stayed, you piece of shit.

*

Jess caught Tim looking at Ben and Gregory more than once. She let him have his space, until she could bear it no longer. Detaching herself from a lively conversation about English cuisine, or perceived lack thereof, she came to join Tim on a haybale, bringing with her a fresh flute of champagne, which she handed over without ceremony.

Tim accepted silently, and sipped at the flute, observing Ben as the young man chased Gregory around the castle courtyard, whipping at him playfully with a lightly rolled napkin. The little boy clearly thought this was the most enormous sport, and shrieked and giggled as he stumbled away from his father.

'What age was Ben when you left him?' Jess asked, knowing the answer full well.

'Eighteen months,' Tim replied, heavily. 'Give or take a few days.'

'Did he look like that?' She meant Gregory.

'From memory, yes. A lot like that.'

Jess shook her head. 'So, it's like seeing yourself back then, huh?'

Tim looked at her, irritated.

'What's your point?'

His wife's eyes gleamed. He was in no position to be bad-tempered, and she wanted him to be aware of that.

'I just can't square it,' she replied, and he could tell she'd drunk beyond her limit. Her eyes were not as focused as they usually were, and her smile had become lopsided.

'Square what?'

87

'I can't square it up with the person I know. What you did. I can't believe you would leave them like that. I've always had a problem believing it.'

Tim clamped his lips together, biting back the sarcastic reply he'd almost spat out.

'Me either,' was all he said, in the end.

Jess got up, returned to the party.

*

Ben motioned for Tim to come over and join him several times, but Tim smiled, declined, and kept his distance, albeit politely. There would be enough opportunity for more heartfelt conversations, he hoped, in the future. Today, he wanted his son to enjoy his wedding. Enough money had been spent on the proceedings, if nothing else. It would be a shame to ruin the occasion by being volatile, like he had at the school reunion.

Besides, there was plenty to look at and explore, and more than enough places to retreat to for a breather. That was the good thing about attending a wedding in a castle: lots of hidey holes to run to, like a rat.

The Château, Tim was told, was privately owned, which was why Ben had been able to rent it for the wedding. The wide grassy space within the walls of the Cathar castle was perfect for such an occasion, and had been tastefully decorated with a giant marquee, outdoor games including croquet and a giant chess set, flowers, bunting and streamers, a stage and sound system for a band who were yet to arrive, and artfully arranged bales of hay for people to relax on. A hog roast gave out mouth-watering aromas over to one side, and there was a cognac tasting table set up near it, which was proving very popular.

Above all this, loomed the stone keep, well preserved, forbidding, reaching up over thirty metres into the sky. The tower wasn't usually open to the public, but they had made an exception for the wedding party, which seemed foolish to Tim, given the amount of champagne flowing, but he climbed the structure anyway. He had a sudden desire to get a bird's eye view of things, to distance himself both mentally and physically from the wedding celebrations, and in doing so, perhaps catch his breath a little. Things were airless at ground level. He had a craving for a fresh, moving breeze, and so up he went, champagne be damned.

There were two cool, damp lower levels to the keep, which offered immediate and welcome relief from the dry heat of the day outside as soon as he stepped within their walls. He felt instantly better as he entered the tower and acclimated to the new temperature. The keep smelled damp and musty, but this reassured him somehow. Grounded him more than the aroma of roasting meat had been able to.

A block-cut staircase took him up through each floor. There was no railing to hold onto, which made the experience precarious, but Tim found he quite liked the sensation of almost falling. It was fun to flirt with danger, the higher he climbed, and sobering, too. The afternoon had begun to feel like some sort of fever-dream, but navigating the stairs brought him back to the present with remarkable efficiency.

A third level held a chapel, with a vaulted ceiling and some columns still visible. Tim determined, from the fresh flowers on show, that this was where his son had said the words 'I do,' or whatever the French equivalent of that was. He was momentarily sad he hadn't been there to witness it, but also relieved. He wouldn't have been comfortable in this small room with so many strangers and his ex-wife in close proximity, and the feeling of being an outsider would have been overwhelming.

Thinking of Louise made him wonder again where she'd gotten to. It was strange not to see her in the party below, mingling at her own son's wedding. Tim hoped he'd ruined the occasion for her.

Above the chapel, there was another vaulted room called the 'Minstrels room,' which was self-explanatory.

Finally, above that, blue sky beckoned as the staircase led to the top of the keep structure and opened out onto a platform, once bordered by now disintegrated crenellations. Tim blinked as sunlight once again assaulted him, and exited the stairwell, panting a little, for there had been a lot of stairs to ascend.

He had not gone more than a single step beyond the mouth of the stairwell before realising he was not alone on the platform.

His stomach sank, abruptly.

Speak of the devil, he thought, *and she shall come.*

Standing on the edge of the square space, dressed in floral pink and surveying the proceedings below, was Louise.

They'd had the same idea, he realised. Never comfortable in crowded rooms, always seeking a space to perch.

She registered his presence the precise moment he realised she was there. His heart pounded as she turned to look at him. Her face was twisted with a concentrated hate so fierce and intense, he thought it was a mask, at first, from a pantomime. She appeared almost demonic, her features perverted, and warped.

'You really want to think you're not the bad guy here, don't you?' She spat, without preamble, her eyes ablaze. 'All the damage you did. All the destruction. And they toasted you. Like you're a prodigal fucking hero!'

Tim held up his hands in defeat. 'I don't want to fight. Not today. Not here. Not ever.'

Louise rolled her eyes. 'You never did like arguing. It was easier to run away than to argue, wasn't it?'

'Louise, please. Not today. Let it lie.'

She kicked at a pile of tumbled-down bricks lying on the edge of the platform. Tim worried for a moment that she'd kick one over the edge, where it could crash down on an unsuspecting head.

At this height, anything heavy dropped over the side would undoubtedly kill, on impact.

'You deserve everything you got, Tim,' she decreed, with a resoluteness that chilled him. 'You deserve more.'

Anger flared in his chest.

'You kept me from my son!' He snapped, knowing he shouldn't get sucked in. 'You lied about his death, and kept me from him!'

Louise bent over, picked up one of the bricks. It looked heavy as she hefted it.

Her expression was murderous.

'You deserve everything you never got, Tim,' she replied.

Footsteps echoed up the stairwell behind. Without turning, Tim knew it was Jess. He could tell by the lightness of step, the faint scent of perfume that came to him before she did.

Hands slipped through the crook in his arm.

'Come away from her,' his wife said, calmly. 'No good will result from this.'

Tim did as he was told, backing away rather than turning and exposing himself to risk.

Louise still hefted the brick in her hand, gripping it like a shot-put.

He remembered: she'd been good at athletics, at school.

'Come away,' Jess repeated, and the darkness of the keep swallowed him again. He blinked, unable to see for a few moments as Jess guided him back down the stairs.

He was relieved he'd gotten away from the rooftop unscathed.

Jess had saved him many times in the past, he thought, stumbling down into the dankness.

What was one more rescue, between husband and wife?

*

At the bottom, Jess left him again, without a word. She was beginning to find his presence too much, he could tell, so he let her go, knowing the elastic band of their marriage would pull her back in again when she'd calmed down.

When he was once again alone, Tim took out an emergency cigarette stashed in his left breast pocket, lit it, and sagged against the far wall of the keep, making sure to stay in the shade, out of sight of the main party, sucking away on the cancer stick, as his wife called them, for dear life. He'd quit smoking properly ten years ago, but always kept one about his person, for desperate situations like this. He figured Jess would give him a free pass, given the circumstances. His nerves were shredded by his last encounter with Louise.

He had no idea a person could be so angry, so fixed on one single emotion for so long.

He took another deep toke of the cigarette, then heard a shout.

'Attention!' Someone screamed in French, and without knowing why, Tim reacted, sidestepping away from the base of the keep in one, swift move.

Seconds later, a sound, a rush of air. Movement.

Something dropped, landing heavily in the spot where he'd been standing.

Tim swore, looked down in horror at the patch of earth his feet had been planted upon only a moment before.

A huge yellow brick now sat there, almost innocently.

Tim's eyes widened as he realised it was the same lump of masonry his ex-wife had been holding onto during their final exchange.

He looked up. From his position at the top of the tower, he could see nothing except a thin slice of pink fabric, fluttering in the breeze above the crenellations.

Then, it was gone.

Fucking bitch tried to kill me, he thought, in a daze.

With shaking hands, he finished his cigarette.

Can you blame her? Something inside of him said, and he found that no, he couldn't, no matter how hard he tried.

*

Dusk settled on the party. Fairy lights blinked on. Cheeseboards were brought out, and more cognac. The sun's assault had left people drowsy and affectionate, but hungry. There was palpable relief as the temperature cooled by a few blessed degrees and guests loaded up plates of Morbier, Brie, Sainte-Maure de Touraine and bread.

The band arrived and started to play. It was soft jazz, appropriate for the mood, which was now one of quiet joy, of soft

91

smiles and muted exchanges. Slowly, people began to file onto the dance floor, moving in pairs, children weaving around their legs. The looming keep watched them all, and Tim saw occasional movement on top of the tower, flashes of pink that became harder and harder to identify as darkness fell.

He knew Louise was up there, though. Watching, like some sort of night owl.

He wondered if she would try to kill him again, before the wedding was through.

Let her try, he thought.

I'll be ready.

*

At midnight, the happy couple chose to cut the wedding cake. This felt odd to Tim, who was used to a timelier way of doing things at British weddings, but it seemed to fit the mood out here in the French countryside. It had been too hot to eat something so rich and heavy earlier on as cake, anyway.

Ben and Camille stood proudly behind the tiered confectionary as a small crowd gathered around them, large knife held in their entwined grip. Gregory was asleep now, passed out in a buggy beside his parents, thumb stuck in his mouth, eyelashes resting on his plump cheeks.

Applause broke out as the happy couple levered the blade down through the layers of gateau. The bride and groom then picked up a chunk of sponge each, and smashed it into the other spouse's face, laughing as crumbs and chocolate icing smeared all over their lips, teeth and cheeks, the tips of their noses. In the strange light of midnight, Tim suddenly thought the icing looked like blood, as if he were watching vampires engaged in some lascivious act of foreplay.

Tim felt a growing sense of urgency in his stomach. Things were about to go wrong, somehow, he knew it.

He could feel it coming, like gathering rain clouds.

He looked for Jess, found her right where he thought she'd be: on the dancefloor, moving to the music.

There was no sign of Louise, but she was somewhere. Waiting.

She'd waited a long time, he realised. To see him, to confront him.

He had a growing understanding of some long-concocted plot, some bitterly ruminative scheme that perhaps had not worked out quite the way she'd planned, based on her reaction to him on the tower top. Had she hoped, perhaps, that Tim would be shunned by the wedding party at large? Called out publicly for abandoning his son? That Ben would meet him, and be disappointed in him, and openly embarrass him?

Had she set her son's wedding as a stage upon which to humiliate him?

If so, she had failed. Ben had adopted him as easily as if he hadn't been absent from the man's life at all. As if he were his father, in name and in actuality.

Tim felt uneasy as he thought about his ex, plotting schemes by which to get even with him. Hadn't faking their son's death been enough?

Evidently not.

Tim stood in a line that formed by the dancefloor, dutifully waiting for his slice of cake, watching as Jess whirled about with a sharp-suited old gent who had an incredible sense of rhythm and style. She was having a good time, Tim saw, was now drunk enough to forget some of their cares and worries, and twirled and jittered and turned in time with the old man as best she could, struggling to keep up with his light footwork, her delighted laughter tinkling out across the tops of other dancer's heads. Tim was pleased his wife had found some comfort in such an awkward, fraught setting. This whole thing had been a hell of an ordeal for Jess, and she deserved better.

He was happy to see her happy, and he supposed that was what love was, when it came down to it.

His happiness died when he realised Louise had rejoined the proceedings.

She now stood awkwardly on the edge of the dancefloor, her attention no longer centred on her ex-husband.

Her gaze was fully upon Jess, dancing.

Tim recognised naked, raw, embittered jealousy when he saw it. It made sense. Jess was beautiful, educated, wealthy, a career woman with fine prospects by anyone's standards, and was ostensibly living the life Louise herself should have lived: attending family events with Tim, driving around France with Tim, exploring ruined castles with Tim, raising two children with Tim, from chubby babies to toddlers to skinny, gangly kids right through puberty, and beyond. Tim could see it all in her eyes: the things Louise had lost. The experiences she'd never had. He could tell, from looking at her, that she'd never married. That she'd gone it alone, from that day to this. He could see it all play out on her face as gentle jazz seeped into his ears and he thought then that he'd never seen anything so sad, so pitiable yet contemptible at the same time, except when he was looking in the mirror, and viewing his own reflection.

And in that sense, he realised, he and Louise were one, and the same: consumed by rancour, he for himself, she for the world entire.

Tim watched Louise, and Louise watched Jess, and Jess watched her feet as her dance partner sped up, twirling her round and around and around until Tim thought she must fall down, soon, or puke, for how could anyone stand being spun about like that?

But Jess was having the time of her life, throwing her head back, teeth flashing, hair flying free, and she had never looked more beautiful.

Louise, by contrast, had never looked uglier. She gazed at Jess with bugged-out eyes, as if the other woman were responsible for everything wrong in the world. Tim couldn't bear it. He understood the hatred being directed at him, but Jess was blameless. He hadn't met her until years after Ben's supposed death, when he'd been a different man altogether.

The cake queue shuffled along, and Tim shuffled along robotically with it, pushed gently from behind, and his feelings of unease and fear grew, and grew. The music seemed to get louder, taking on a sharper, more discordant tone.

Jess continued to whirl, and laugh.

Louise, who was somehow closer to the cake table, continued to glare.

Tim had a sudden thought.

Where is the cake knife?

He looked, and found it still stabbed into the wedding cake. Ben and his wife were kissing, now, breaking away from each other's food-smeared faces periodically to catch breath.

'Get a room!' Someone shouted, in English, and the couple laughed.

'We have sixteen in a Château two miles from here,' Ben retorted. 'I only married her for her money, you know!'

Camille slapped him playfully while the crowd laughed.

'Terrible man,' she said, then they went back to kissing, but not before Tim caught an expression on his son's face, an expression tinged with chagrin, and he suspected, suddenly, that Ben had not been lying when he confessed to marrying his new wife for her money.

And Tim had an epiphany, then, while standing in line, watching the couple go at each other with such passion.

It had been a long time coming, a moment that had been building throughout the duration of the day, but seeing Ben there, his face covered in frosting, his hands travelling the length and distance of his new wife's back, shoulders, buttocks, one eye half-open, scanning the crowd as he kissed Camille, his kid asleep despite the noise in the buggy beside them...Tim looked at all this, and realised, in horror, that Louise had been right.

The kid grew up to be exactly like you, she'd said.

She hadn't meant it as a compliment.

He recognised everything he was being shown as stars blinked above, a thin layer of late afternoon haze having covered them until now.

Tim understood the horrible truth, and it crushed him better than any dropped block of stone. His son *had* grown up to be exactly like him, he could tell: successful, attractive, smart, greedy, ambitious, and completely, definitively, wholly lacking of any empathy whatsoever. Tim could see it, see it so clearly it nearly doubled him over with pain. His heart suddenly felt as if someone had slipped a red-hot blade into it.

His son was not his son at all, Tim realised.

His son was a robot man, an automaton, utterly empty inside.

Wired to please.

Going through the motions, even as he kissed the woman he 'loved'.

Driven, no doubt, by a series of pre-programmed commands: secure money, secure sex, secure property, secure social standing.

Once those things were done, once the tick boxes had been checked, replicate the motions, breed, repeat the cycle.

Because he'd grown up poor, like Tim had.

Because he'd struggled, as a fatherless child, just like Tim, and resolved, no doubt at a tender age, that no matter what, he was going to make it.

He was going to succeed.

And here he was, doused in starlight, getting married in a castle to a wealthy, gorgeous woman of status and heritage, and he had no real feelings about any of it.

Tim thought of his other two children back at home with their grandparents, already set on the path he'd predetermined for them. 'I won't have you growing up like I did,' he'd said, over and over, never giving them a chance to develop their own tastes and needs and wants. They were good kids, and didn't want to upset him, so they went along with what he decreed.

He was a disease, he saw, a disease that ruined lives, infected everyone around him. A cryptic lineage of emptiness, and waste. That was his legacy.

Tim moved forward another step in the cake line, feeling the entire bottom of his world crumble away, like old, tired masonry tumbling off the edges of a mediaeval keep.

He understood that Louise didn't need a knife to wound him, not now he knew the truth.

She hadn't needed the brick, either. That had been a playful extra.

Her plan hadn't failed, either.

Tim looked back at his ex-wife, who had moved closer still. She was watching him, now, with huge, dark eyes. She could see the look on his own face, it was hard to hide: a horror so existential in nature that he thought, very seriously, about pushing through the people in the queue ahead of him, grabbing the cake knife himself, and slitting his own throat with it.

He didn't though. He lacked the courage.

This, Tim realised, was Louise's ultimate revenge.

He was not a unicorn, at all.

He was an infection.

Loser Lane to the last.

She had not just killed her son once, but twice, and in doing so, Louise had held a mirror up to Tim's own pathetic, covetous, avaricious existence and shown him what he really was: a cowardly, greedy, pathetic man who had been too afraid and too ambitious to stick around and raise a family. The effects of his behaviour rippled out across the generations like concentric circles in a pond where a stone had been lobbed. Empty ambition, fear of intimacy, shallow connections, love smashing up against inherited glass walls.

Tim died inside, quite abruptly, as the music grew louder and the stars grew brighter, and Louise watched, noticing and relishing the exact moment it happened.

There, her eyes said. *At last. You see?*

You see what you did?

She nodded at him, once. He responded, mesmerised.

A small smile lit up her face, which had been ravaged by shadow and malice only seconds before.

Then, as Jess spun before the band, as the cake was parcelled out and consumed, as a little boy slept, oblivious in his canvas chariot, and a pair of newlyweds went through all the expected, declarative motions of commitment and love, Louise held out her hand, and Tim went to her, followed blindly as she led him off, back into the absolute darkness of the keep, up through the layers of medieval architecture, and out onto the platform.

And after that, she taught him to fall, like the stone that he was.

FIELDS OF ICE

(Published for the first time in the charity anthology REVELATIONS, from Stygian Sky Media, 2022)

In the Northern Reaches of a dying land that was once prosperous, a vast glacier sprawls along the floor of a valley between two distinct mountain ranges. The largest mountains in each range sit on either side of the glacier like guardian sisters. One is called Old White, and the other Old Red, named for the colours that burn on their peaks at sunrise and sunset. Old Red has a distinct geology, one composed mostly of sedimentary Ironstone, the surface of which has oxidised and now glows a brilliant shade of crimson when the sun hits it just so. Old White's peak is perpetually capped with snow. She is taller, and has a more pronounced summit, one that thrusts up into the sky like a dagger jammed between a man's ribs.

Not much is known of the territory that lies beyond the mountains. The barricade of ice that has piled up over centuries between them has prevented the few scientific and geographic teams that have ventured this far north from making much progress in the region.

Those teams did not count Hayder amongst their number.

Hayder does not travel as part of a team. Hayder travels alone. She does not enjoy responsibility. Expeditions that involve more than one person automatically imply an obligation: to protect the well-being and safety of that extra person. This onerous duty interferes heavily with her ability to do her job. Which is, simply, to find things. Hayder is very good at finding things, but only when she is left the fuck alone to do so. She is an archaeologist, one of the few left in the world, and glad for that. Academic scarcity means she is valuable to the Minister, and valuable to the Keep. Being valued as a person in this day and age is not a common conceit.

At this present moment in time, Hayder hangs from two ice picks jammed hard into the side of a steeply curving wall of diamond-white ice, about two miles in on the swooping, ridged surface of the glacier. Her boots are wrapped with leather straps that have wicked metal spikes attached to them: crampons. Her toes are bleeding from the impact of jabbing her spikes into the ice wall over and over again. The thin top layer of the fortification she is scaling is starting to crumble in the midday sun. She must get to the top before the ice becomes too mushy to climb. If she fails, she will spend another cold, miserable night stuck in a deep, cobalt-blue crevasse, and she does not want that. Crevasses are natural traps, and Hayder has heard movement on the glacier at night. She is fairly certain it is a bear, and a hungry one, and she does not wish to present herself as an easy target by spending any more time in the fissure than she has to. Hayder is not enough of an idiot to think that she can fight a fully grown ice-bear and come out of the encounter unscathed.

Hayder adjusts her goggles, grits her teeth, and drags herself higher up the wall. Her foot slips, suddenly, and she finds herself cheek to jowl with the glacier. It is not a gentle dance partner. She hangs there for a moment, too tired to do much else. Her weight is taken by a rope around her waist. The rope is looped through an iron hoop hammered into the ice wall above her head. As she makes progress, she hammers in new hoops and ties the rope off fresh to each one, anchoring herself to the wall. It's a laborious process. Her arms ache. In fact, Hayder's whole body aches, and she feels as if she has been pummeled flat against an anvil by a heavy hammer. She is getting too old for solo expeditions, she knows this. But Hayder is stubborn, and motivated.

Because at the end of all this, there lies a prize. The Minister has given her a commission.

Once she has fulfilled it, she will be free.

As she recovers her breath, something in the ice by her cheek catches her attention, a discoloration in the intense blue that she has not noticed until now. She squints through her goggles, trying to see what it is. It is something stuck in the ice, something huge, and brownish in colour. It is frozen in place about five hand-widths away from her face, embedded into the glacier like an air-bubble in a pane of glass. The frozen mass is too distorted to be visible clearly, but she thinks she can make out legs, insectile, clawed. Lots of legs, in fact, and a blurry, distorted sort of head, or maybe it is a carapace, or maybe just a rock. Whatever it is, or was, alive or dead, it has been stuck in the ice for a long time and therefore doesn't concern her at this present moment. The only thing she is concerned with is getting out of this crevasse and on with her commission. She has many miles of glacier left to cross, and as intriguing as the frozen object is, it is a distraction she cannot afford.

Hayder takes a deep breath, kicks out away from the wall. On the backwards swing, she jams first one foot, and then the other, into the ice, and pushes up. She throws her right arm back, and sharply hammers her ice axe into the wall. She checks to see that the axe has held, steadies herself, and repeats the motion with her left arm, making sure to swing vertically, rather than down. The trick is not to try and dig a hole with the axe, but to drive it in, like it's a nail being driven through wood. Like most things, it's about rhythm. Once a person masters the rhythm, the rest is simple enough. It's also about keeping as close to the wall as possible, to distribute body weight evenly. *Easier said than done*, Hayder thinks, dragging herself higher. She wonders what the Minister would think of her if he could see her now, red-faced and raw, clinging to a slope like a tick on a goat, short hair drenched in sweat beneath her hat, face already bruised from slamming into the ice. He would most likely find it highly amusing, because he seems to find most things about Hayder amusing, indulging her as one would indulge a favourite pet.

Hayder can put up with his indulgence if it keeps her alive.

The Minister summoned Hayder in the early grey hours of one morning three weeks ago, to his private quarters, which Hayder was not too comfortable with. She went anyway, because the Minister was difficult to say 'no' to. She hoped he would not try to seduce her again. The last time he had, both of them had come out of the encounter feeling sickened. She had allowed him to paw her a little, but made it clear that she was not in any way enjoying the encounter. He had continued to paw at her despite this, his small, sweaty hands seeking a confirmation that didn't exist, before eventually giving up, acknowledging that her mind was somewhere else entirely. Afterwards, Hayder had told him, gently, not to be offended.

'I do not find pleasure in other people,' she said, carefully avoiding eye contact. 'Only in my work.'

And her dedication to her work was one of the reasons he kept her around, instead of having her executed. The Minister had a soft spot for Hayder, and probably thought that, in time, she would see sense, and give in to his advances.

Hayder was more realistic. She knew what refusal could do to a man, and she knew the Minister's soft spot could freeze over at any time.

She thought about this as she entered his quarters, situated on the top floor of the Keep. It was with some relief that she found the Minister pacing, fully clothed, back and forth, back and forth, up and down, wringing his hands with impatience, a preoccupied frown upon his lightly powdered face.

'Where were you?' He snapped, when she cleared her throat to make her presence known.

'Sleeping,' she replied, calmly. One had to be calm at all times with the Minister. His temper was legendary, and Hayder was very well acquainted with it. His tantrums could last for days, with devastating consequences. Once, a key report from the Keep's Chief Climatologist had been delayed by an hour, due to a malfunction in one of the four massive solar pillars that cornered and powered the

City. The Minister had executed the Climatologist by locking him in an air-tight glass cabinet he'd had purpose built for such an occasion. He forced the entire staff of the Ministry to watch as the climatologist suffocated, publicly. Then, he hunted down the dead man's family, stripped them naked, and strung them up around the four pillars by their ankles. Hayder would never forget the sight of the climatologist's eight-year-old son, his pale, skinny body twitching and screaming as he hung upside down a thousand feet in the air and tried to fight off a starving carrion-bird as it tore strips of flesh off of him. The bodies hung above the city until the bones were picked clean, and it was at that point that Hayder began to consider, seriously consider, the fragility of her situation.

The Minister grunted, waving away her missing apology. Despite her careful neutrality, not many people spoke to the Minister the way that Hayder did. Most people bowed and scraped, but Hayder had never been one for subjugating herself. While she was in the Keep, she remained courteous and professional, without giving much of herself away. The Minister seemed to respect her for that. It helped that Hayder had made him a lot of money over the years, bringing him the spoils of countless expeditions and excavations without demanding too large a cut for herself. The Minister respected money more than anything on this earth. It was the only thing he thought about, from the moment he awoke to the moment he laid his head upon his fine silk pillow. Money. Riches. Wealth. Resources.

All of which were fast running out. Not just in the City.

Everywhere.

Which, Hayder knew, was why she was here.

She was about to be given a new commission.

And not a moment too soon, Hayder thought. Things in the City were deteriorating rapidly. There were riots. Disease had taken hold of the lower levels. Famine threatened. Political unrest and misinformation was rife. From the Minister's window, she could see thick plumes of smoke coiling into the sky. The smoke came from funeral pyres. Every morning, at first light, the City burned its dead. Mass cremations were becoming problematic, however, acting as a focal point for an already strained population's ire. She could hear the distant cries of assembled protestors jostling around the pyres, beating their drums and chanting angrily as their loved ones burned to ash.

'Rise! Rise! Rise!' They screamed. Hayder knew it was only a matter of time before they did, surging up through the layers of the City like a tide, flooding the streets and eventually swallowing the Keep whole.

In short, Hayder wanted to get out, before the City imploded.

100

'The Pyres will soon become unfeasible,' the Minister said, following Hayder's eyes. 'I do not know what we shall do with our dead then. Our burial grounds are all full.'

Hayder kept quiet. She knew where a good portion of the dead would go: into the Keep's kitchen, or at least, those bodies that tested as disease-free would. This meant the remains of the elderly, the young, and the malnourished would be recycled, for want of a better word. The meat stripped from the bones and dried, the bones ground to make compost for the Keep's arboretum, one half of which was given over now to crop production- but only to feed those who lived inside the Keep. Not for the plenty, the starving masses down in the City. How could the Ministry govern if they were as hungry as their citizens? The Keep's integrity must be protected at all costs, and if that meant cannibalising the wider population for the survival of an exalted few, then so be it.

It was the main reason Hayder had been eating only freeze-dried synthetic protein packs for the past six weeks. It played hell with her digestion, but kept her conscience clean.

Yes, a commission was just the thing. And, once she was out from beneath the delicate, groping hands of the Minister, she had no intention of ever coming back. Soon enough, he would have more important things to think about anyway, such as the collapse of an empire.

Hayder waited, as was her way.

The Minister stopped pacing, and turned to her. His eyes were enormous and haunted in the low morning light. They were the eyes of a zealot. Hayder remembered a different time, when the Minister had thought of things aside from his own fiscal legacy. When the Minister had valued culture, and history, learning and art, and not just his own skin.

'I found it,' the Minister said, interrupting her train of thought.

'You found what, Minister?' She asked, cautiously. But Hyder knew very well what. She just wanted him to say it out loud.

'The Vellum,' he replied, obligingly, and a slow, boyish smile spread across his features.

Hayder reaches the top of the ice wall, drags herself over the lip of it, and rolls onto her back in relief, arms and legs now screaming with exertion. Once she gets her breath back, she sits up, taking off her crampons so that she can stretch out her sore feet. She unties the rope from around her waist and groin, and looks around, working out some kinks in her neck.

Everything is blue and white and brown upon the glacier, and Hayder grudgingly admits that ice is a good deal more interesting than she's given thought to, before. The shapes and colours are extraordinary, and she has to remind herself that, no matter how static the huge stretch of frozen mountain water seems to be, it is in fact in a constant state of movement. Like molten lava pouring down the sides of a volcano, glaciers creep forward constantly. She knows this, but it is hard to comprehend when sitting upon something that feels so solid.

Because this glacier moves quite fast, as glaciers go, it is dirty, much of its surface covered in rock dust and sand that has worn away from the mountains it grinds past. It moves at different speeds in different places, creating ridges and fells, folds and tunnels, caves, crevasses and cliffs. Despite the gravelly top dermis, it is spectacularly beautiful, like an ancient painting Hayder once saw of a melting clock hanging loosely over a naked tree branch: weird, fluid, and improbable. She scans this display with tired, watery eyes, and then freezes. She sees movement to her left, or at least, she thinks she does. It is hard to tell with the way the sun is angled. Hayder frowns. If a clever person was to follow her across this glacier, it would make sense to walk with the sun behind them, so that they could not easily be seen. Hayder's skin prickles. Who would be following her across the ice? Perhaps it is not a person. Perhaps it is the ice-bear she thought she heard before, tracking her through the night.

Hayder discards this idea quickly. Her instincts tell her otherwise.

She removes her goggles, peering through lowered lashes to try and get a clearer look, but the glare is too great. She puts them back on again. Waits, still as a statue.

There! Definitely movement. The sun obligingly vanishes behind a fleeting cloud. Hayder makes out two shapes, dark against the ice. One tall, one small.

Not a bear. Two people. Trekking across the glacier, following the same path she had before falling into the crevasse.

She is being followed. She chews her lip. *Has the Minister sent assassins for me?* She muses. *Has he learned of my plan?*

Hayder is not scared of any would-be death merchants. She has survived four assassination attempts prior to this one. Rivalry and jealousy is rife throughout the Keep, and Hayder's position as one of the Minister's pet academics makes her a target for other people's ambitions.

Hayder is strong and fast, however, and has reasons to live.

She does not think these shadows are assassins. Assassins do not tend to travel in pairs, and they also travel light. The smaller figure seems heavily burdened. Neither of them are particularly nimble upon the ice, nor are they particularly quiet. Hayder can hear clunking and scraping noises as they walk. Assassins do not generally announce themselves quite so noisily.

So who is it? Innocent travellers? Someone from the Keep?

Either way, Hayder does not want to meet them unprepared. She has her ice-axes, but those are only useful for close combat. She much prefers something of a long-range nature.

She crouches, and peers back down over the lip of the crevasse, looking for her pack, which she has left at the bottom. It was too heavy to climb with, so she secured it with a separate rope, meaning to drag it up the slope after her once she'd reached the top.

Hayder clenches her hands, which are sore and bloody from the axes. She starts to haul on the pack rope, pulling the heavy bundle carefully up the wall she has just climbed. Her rifle is in the pack, the barrel of it peeking out of the top flap. It is an antique, like most of the things she owns, but in perfect working order. She learned how to make her own bullets years ago, manufacturing them in her apartment in the Keep as a way of trying to wind down of an evening. She has bags full of cartridges in her pack, and is glad now that she has.

Hayder looks over her shoulder. The couple are much closer now. The weird icy sculptures on the surface of the glacier have warped her distance perspective, making things appear further away than they really are. She curses under her breath, figuring she has maybe five minutes before the couple are close enough to be a threat.

She redoubles her efforts, yanking hard on the pack. Too late, she remembers that she has taken off her crampons. Her feet slip on the ice. Hayder cries out, falling backwards, landing hard on her back and sliding dangerously close to the edge of the crevasse.

Not again! She thinks, frantically, and lets go of the pack rope, not wanting to be pulled back into the deep blue fissure. The pack drops heavily, landing with a thud. Hayder feels her body slip closer to the edge. She tries to sit up, but the sun has melted the ice further in the time that she has been resting on the lip of the crevasse, and everything is now glossy and wet under her feet and hands, which scrabble for purchase, failing to find any. In slow-motion, Hayder feels herself slide inexorably over the edge of the large crack in the glacier, gliding over the ice like a wet fish slipping out of a fisherman's hands. She yells in frustration, twists her body, and grabs the only thing she can in the split second she is given before tumbling back into the crevasse. One of the iron hoops, hammered into the side. Her right hand hooks over it, the sleeve of her jacket catching fast on the hoop's edge, and she is brought up sharp, one arm stretched out fiercely above her head, the other trying to find a hold in the ice wall she is now so reluctantly familiar with.

And this is how Morgan Halligan finds her.

Two faces peer down at Hayder as she hangs uselessly by one hand from the small metal hoop. She is stuck. If she lets go, and slides back down into the crevasse, she will not be able to climb out without her crampons and axes. She is, however, dangling in such an odd way that she cannot lever herself up, even though the top of the crevasse is reasonably close. The situation is not sustainable. Her right hand is quickly growing numb, and her grip is starting to fail. The fabric of her sleeve is similarly unable to take her weight, and very shortly it will rip.

The faces above see this, make surprised noises. They belong to a man and a woman. Hayder realises she knows the man.

'Morgan? What the fuck are you doing here?' She pants, angrily.

The man blinks, and an insufferable smile spreads across his downturned face.

'Saving your life, it would seem.'

His hand reaches down, grasps the back of Hayder's jacket, between her shoulders. Another hand clasps around her snagged wrist. Two more hands seize her free arm, and Hayder is pulled to safety. She collapses in an exhausted pile at the feet of the couple. Before saying anything else, she reaches for her crampons, and straps them back on her feet. She has learned her lesson twice over now: never take off your crampons, not while you're on the ice.

Then she says: 'I would have fallen barely twenty feet, don't flatter yourself.' Her arm aches, having been almost wrenched out of its socket by her fall, and she winces, shrugging and rotating her shoulder in an effort to bring some circulation back. It is a diversionary tactic while she tries to think about what to do next.

Morgan dusts ice crystals off ungloved hands, which look blue from the bitterly cold wind that blows across the surface of the glacier. *Why isn't the idiot wearing gloves?* She thinks. That is just like Morgan: to assume that the rules of play are meant for others, and not for him.

'You're welcome,' he says, dryly.

Hayder considers her situation. It is clear that Morgan has been sent by the Minister to spy on her. Morgan is the City's Chief Geologist, and has crossed paths with Hayder more than a few times throughout her career. They trade barbs frequently in academic council meetings. She considers him a flamboyant arse and a sycophant, but he is also a necessary evil. He, like herself, has the ear of the Minister. It is therefore better to have him on her side than not, in the spirit of keeping friends close, and enemies closer.

Hayder doesn't have friends, anyway.

She swears inwardly. This is not something she has planned for, but she realises that she should have, because the Minister likes nothing better than to pit his employees against each other. Morgan is here because the Minister doubts her loyalty. This is not a good thing. The Geologist has been tasked with keeping an eye on Hayder in case she disappears with the Vellum.

I knew it was too easy, she thinks. She curses her naivety in thinking the Minister would allow her to carry out this expedition alone. He had merely indulged her request to do so in order to persuade her to accept the commission. Not that refusing was ever an option, anyway. Refusal means death. Those terms are hard to argue with.

Hayder takes a good, long look at Morgan's companion while she collects herself. She is an aged, short, stooped woman with a massive pack strapped to her back, although the obvious weight of it does not seem to bother her. Morgan himself carries only a small day-pack. The old woman has bare feet, which on closer inspection are covered with thick, scaly skin, so thick it looks as if she has hooves at the ends of her weathered legs. She does not appear to feel the cold through those rigid soles, and Hayder assumes she is local, a native to the region. One of the elusive Niton tribe, maybe. Or perhaps Clintu. Either way, she is definitely not of the City.

'Who is this?' Hayder asks, rudely. 'A slave? Slavery went out of fashion years ago, Morgan.'

Morgan smiles and shakes his head, unperturbed by Hayder's sarcasm.

'She is not a slave. She has a name. She is called Pamuk, and she is an Ice Sherpa. I hired her to be my guide. She knows this ice field like no-one else. Her family have been crossing it for many generations, guiding the occasional travellers safely along. It is a fine livelihood. Who am I to deny her an opportunity to earn a living?'

'Oh good, a salaried slave,' Hayder says, rolling her eyes. Her hostility comes from one place: anger at herself for being caught out. Hayder hates feeling as if she is standing on the back foot.

Pamuk says nothing, patiently waiting for the foreigners to begin moving again.

'Aren't we all?' Morgan says, smiling.

'You might be,' Hayder replies, squinting. 'I prefer my job title: Archaeologist.'

'Senior Archaeologist.' Morgan makes a dig at Hayder's age. He is younger than her by only five years, but for some reason, in their society, a man is allowed to grow older with considerably less challenge than a woman is. 'Your reputation precedes you, Hayder.'

'Yours doesn't,' Hayder says. 'And I'm not the one asking an old lady to carry my shit around for me.' As if to illustrate this point, she turns to pull her own pack up the slope once more. Morgan and Pamuk wait close by, their intentions clear. They are joining her solo expedition, whether she likes it or not. And, short of murdering the pair, she cannot see a way of saying 'no', especially not if Morgan has been personally tasked by the Minister. Giving up on her would be tantamount to signing his own death warrant, she knows that. This makes her feel as if she is stuck between a rock and a hard place, and Hayder does not like this one little bit.

For now, I will let them follow me, she thinks, watching as the reassuring shape of her rifle's barrel gets closer and closer, along with the pack.

For now.

'I found the Vellum,' the Minister repeated, and Hayder had to forcibly swallow her own excitement.

'Where?' She breathed, eventually, feeling as if fate were suddenly in the room with them.

'I've had a team of archivists working in the Library, renovating the eastern alcoves. A water pipe behind a wall burst several weeks ago. We were at risk of losing over a thousand manuscripts, so I had them remove every single one, dust them off, and re-file once we'd fixed the leak. An intern found it in a box stuffed with absorbent crystals. It's been here in the Keep, all along, Hayder. Imagine that, eh? The irony of it.'

Hayder didn't know or care much about irony, only authenticity. The Minister was educated, but hardly as versed in antiquities as she was.

'How do you know it's really the Vellum?'

'Because of the seal on the box,' the Minister replied, pulling a folded square of paper from a deep pocket in his robes. He handed it to her without further explanation, and Hayder saw a rubbing. Someone had scribbled charcoal across the paper whilst it was pressed to a hard object underneath. It displayed a circle, within which two items were crossed: an old-fashioned telescope, and an ice-axe, the sort used for climbing and mountaineering. Around it were the words, in Old Latin, *Imperium Sine Fine*, which translated to 'Empire without an end', the official motto of the early days of the Keep, several hundred years past.

It was the sigil of an explorer.

Hayder felt a deep thrill race down her spine.

Only one expedition party in the history of the Ministry's exploration records had ever been known to have made it beyond the far reaches of the massive ice-field in the North, some time in the middle of the Oil Age, a little over two hundred years ago. The leader of that expedition was a man called Horatious Hecht, and he came back from his excursion alone, all twenty-five other members of his party having perished, or so the story went. Hecht may have lost his crew, but he did bring back a map, a map that quickly became an object of myth and gossip, and after a time, was referred to as 'The Vellum'. This is not because the map was drawn upon deerskin, or parchment. The Vellum was indeed a map, but the map was coded onto a long-obsolete device a little like an electronic tablet, only smaller, sturdier. 'Vellum' was the rather whimsical name of the operating system the tablet ran on. It was solar-powered, and Hayder had once read somewhere that a rudimentary kind of GPS was built into the device, meaning a course could be plotted that would take the owner of the Vellum across the ice-fields, beyond the mountain ridges that were so hard to scale, and to a distinct location somewhere in the lands that lay beyond.

Legend had it, that location was a seam, a huge, untapped seam of a precious substance known only as Ore.

Before airplanes and helicopters had become an extinct form of travel, this hadn't really mattered to anyone. The Vellum had held little importance to a regime convinced its oil reserves would last.

But now that those reserves had been exhausted, well.

It was a very precious object, indeed.

'Ore is a myth, Minister,' Hayder said, trying not to get carried away. 'There has never been, in the entire history of the Ministry, anything to prove or suggest that Ore deposits are real. Even if they are, we have no certainty that we can exploit it or use it to our advantage, and certainly no indication of whether or not we could convert Ore into any meaningful energy source, even if we could mine it somehow.'

'Pshaw.' The Minister waved her concerns away. 'My Geologist tells me otherwise, Hayder. I know you two rarely see eye-to-eye, but I trust his judgment in matters of this nature. When it comes to digging up the past, there is no-one on this earth who is your equal, Hayder. But I am running out of choices. Our solar pillars are degrading at an alarming rate, down to fifty-five percent of efficiency, and decreasing every day. We can no longer manufacture new panels with any degree of consistency. It is too expensive to fabricate them from silicone, you know this. We have extinguished our cadmium and copper processing capabilities. The last miner's strike lasted twelve months, unless you've forgotten, and we are struggling to return the mines to capacity now that half the workforce has been wiped out by the sickness. This thing...' The Minister tapped the sigil on the piece of paper, and Hyder noticed sweat beading his upper lip. 'This thing could be our salvation,' he said, leaning in towards her, dwarfing her with his fanaticism.

'And you are going to deliver it,' he continued, staring at her mouth.

No pressure, then, she thought, swallowing hard.

It is obvious, after only a few minutes of walking, that Morgan has not been upon ice before. He has no gloves, and is wearing shorts. His long, thin legs are covered in sore slashes from his crampons. Hayder is surprised that his Sherpa has not told him how to clothe himself properly, or how to walk in crampons: toes out, knees bent, one foot pointing up-slope where possible for extra grip. Morgan hobbles along laboriously, every now and then hissing in pain as he catches the insides of his own legs with his metal spikes. Hayder watches this with a clenched jaw. She flicks her gaze across to Pamuk, who keeps her head down. She is fairly certain she can detect a faint hint of enjoyment around the wizened corners of Pamuk's mouth, and this makes Hayder warm to the old woman, if only a little.

Hayder insists that the pair walk ahead of her. She tries to think of how to rid herself of them. Soon, she will have to make camp. She considers leaving in the night while the pair sleep, but knows she will never be able to pack her tent away quietly enough. This means she will have to try and lose them in the day. She will need a diversion, and a way of putting enough distance between them that she cannot be followed easily. She cannot, for the life of her, think of how to do this. If it was Morgan on his own, she would feel confident.

Pamuk is a different kettle of fish altogether.

Hayder shelves the problem for a while. Sometimes, when answers elude her, she lets them sit for a time. Solutions often present themselves in the most unexpected of ways, if she just leaves things alone. Whatever the answer is, she knows what she knows: that she cannot travel as part of a team.

Hayder hasn't always been like this. Hayder had a partner once, a colleague who doubled as a bedfellow, and Hayder had loved him, very much. They had taken many commissions together on behalf of the Minister, found many treasures. They had taken responsibility for each other. Sometimes, while resting during a gruelling excavation, they would sit crossed legged on the floor, back to back, so that they could lean upon each other, balanced perfectly like keystones in a bridge. They would smoke a cheroot, passing it back and forth until only a tiny, soggy nub remained, and then silently get back to work. There hadn't been much in the way of verbal communication between them, and for Hayder, who hated idle conversation, that was just fine.

Hayder's partner died when a large pillar collapsed during an excavation of the lower layer of a Trujillian temple, five years back. Hayder has recurring nightmares about that moment, and probably always will. A grinding, a shifting of balance. A blur of yellow stone. Her partner, frozen in shock as his fate crashed down towards him. Hayder remembers how a ray of sunlight caught in his hair before her view of him was obliterated. She tries hard, every day, not to think of him beneath the stone, flattened and broken. She tries, and fails. She remembers his right hand, protruding from under the massive column. Blood ran out in rivulets beneath it. She fell to her knees, took the hand gently in hers. She held it until it grew cold, and continued to hold it for two more days and nights, sitting, trance-like, cross-legged, only there was no back to lean against hers, this time. No keystone to support her.

It was the worst pain she has ever endured in her life. More pain than she could have dreamed possible.

She has no intention of ever hurting that much again.

Hayder has been alone ever since. She cannot risk more pain, she cannot allow herself the luxury of responsibility for anyone else. Dependency ruins her chances for survival.

And Hayder must survive.

Because there had been a child, six months after the accident.

A child with hair that also caught the sun when it shone.

A child she had not been in a position to love when it was born, a child she had deposited with a long-distant family member when it was only a few weeks old.

A child she fully intends to send for, once she is rid of the Minister.

But first, she has to find a place to call home, far away from the City, and far away from the reach of the Ministry. And what better place than the unchartered territory beyond the ice field? The Minster couldn't follow her across the glacier, not easily. He most likely would, by now, have a full-scale civil war on his hands. Hayder has no interest in Ore seams. All she cares about is her freedom, and if she can get to the end of this ice field, she can secure it.

She has no intention of letting Morgan or Pamuk get in her way.

The three explorers make camp as the sun is setting. Old Red is in fine form, her peak a vivid, glowing torch against an indigo sky full of slowly emerging stars.

Hayder does not make conversation with Morgan or Pamuk as she sets up her one-man tent and a portable biomass burner. Hayder heats up some freeze-dried oats with a lump of ice she chisels from the glacier, and shovels the resulting gruel into her mouth. It is loaded with synthetic nutrients, everything she needs to keep her body running. Hayder misses real food, though. She misses fruit, herbs, cheese. Fuck, how she misses cheese. She eats swiftly, watching Pamuk as she sets up a tent for Morgan. The tall man stands to one side and pretends to occupy himself with a document while the old woman does this. Then Pamuk prepares a meal, boiling up shreds of dried meat with some herbs and a desiccated root of some sort. The smell is incredible. Hayder's stomach clenches in longing. She displays no outward sign of this envy, but she does raise an eyebrow when Pamuk straightens up suddenly, head turned back the way they have come.

She hears it too, Hayder thinks, because the noise is back. It always comes back when dusk falls on the glacier. The ice bear is getting closer, its peculiar shuffles and clicks only just audible. Hayder again trades glances with Pamuk. An understanding passes between them. Be careful.

Something is out there.

Pamuk digs around in the giant bundle she has been carrying, and brings out a tightly coiled spool of razor-thin wire, a bundle of stakes, and a mallet. Wordlessly, she sets up a perimeter around the camp, twisting the two ends of the wire together around a battered looking solar pack. Hayder realises the wire is electrocuted. Pamuk is taking no chances. Hayder approves.

Hayder uses more ice to clean out her pan, and packs everything carefully away, retreating into her tent for the night, pulling her pack and rifle in after her to block the entrance. Morgan watches her do this with a small smile on his lips. Hayder zips her door up, obscuring his smug face, and tries not to think about how flimsy the walls of the tent are.

Once inside, she pulls a box from her pack. She opens the lid, sees a small, rectangular object nestled within on a bed of micro-crystals.

The Vellum.

She presses a finger to the soft rubber power switch embedded into the top of the device, and waits for a second or two. The screen pops into blue, glowing life, and a single word, a word in Old English, materialises on the screen.

Hello, it says.

'Hello,' Hayder whispers back.

It took Hayder four days to reboot the Vellum. Hayder had spent her life studying ancient, obsolete languages and technology. She built her reputation as a young academic not on her prowess as an archaeologist, but her expertise as a forensic antiquities programmer, someone who managed to get computers that were centuries old to boot despite the limited physical life-times of most electronic hardware. She pieced together degraded computer parts like an anthropologist pieces together the human skeleton. What she couldn't coax into life, she cobbled, using junk from the vaults of the Keep and black-market components stockpiled over the years. Her feats of perseverance caught the attention of the Minister, and this rapidly cemented her status as a favourite pet. Because the Minister had fantasised about discovering and exploiting the Vellum since he had first heard about it as a boy. Hayder's impressive skill set represented his best chance at being able to do so if it was ever found. Sometimes, the Minister felt as if a divine intention had been bestowed upon Hayder, as if she had been created for the sole purpose of helping him fulfil his lifelong dream: restoring the Empire to its glory days.

He might not think that if he knew how virulent her hatred of him was.

Hayder wakes. She instantly senses that something is wrong. There is a sound coming in through the walls of her tent. It is the sound she has heard on previous nights, only much, much louder.

Ice bear.

Slowly, carefully, Hayder unwraps herself from her sleeping bag, slides her feet into her crampons. She picks up her rifle, loads it. She takes the Vellum out of its case, and slides it down into a pocket between her breasts, one that also carries the worn image of her partner, and their baby. Then, she slowly unzips the tent door, and pokes her head outside.

The glacier is lit by a million stars, stars which have a chance to shine up here in the north, for the skies are clear, and clean, unlike the murky sky that rests oppressively over the City, thick with smog and pyre smoke.

Hayder clambers out of her tent, and stands up. She knows where Morgan is, because she can hear him snoring like a pig, but she cannot see Pamuk anywhere. She slowly pivots, taking in as much of her surroundings as she can, trying to locate the strange, ticking, scrabbling, snuffling noise that has woken her up. She can see the wire perimeter still glinting in the starlight, so nothing has breached the barrier, not yet.

Hayder calls out, softly.

'Pamuk!'

A wizened hand clamps over her mouth from behind. Hayder pushes back and whirls, sees Pamuk in the glow of the stars. In her free hand, the woman holds a long, wickedly sharp machete, unsheathed, the blade serrated near the tip.

Pamuk raises it above Hayder's head.

Too close! Hayder thinks, frantically. *She's too close for me to use my rifle!*

The sound of a thin electric wire snapping rings out into the night air, followed by the strange ticking, clacking, slippery noises, so loud now they are almost deafening.

Pamuk pushes Hayder violently to one side, swinging down with the machete as something vast and dark slides into the exact spot where Hayder was standing only moments before. Hayder crashes into Morgan's tent, collapsing it on him, and rolls off, barely aware of the man now awake and roaring under the torn nylon.

In front of her, lit up by the bold light of the stars, a scene is playing out like nothing she has seen before in her life.

It is not an ice bear.

The thing is massive, the width and height of a man, only twenty times as long. It is a centipede. Hayder sees twin rows of clawed legs undulating as the creature glides across the ice towards Pamuk, and remembers, with a flash, a brown, blurry, many-legged object embedded in the ice wall she climbed. Not dead, but sleeping. They live in ice burrows, waiting for nightfall. How many of them are down there now, stirring beneath her feet? How many on this glacier?

And what do they eat?

This one seems to want to eat the Sherpa. Pamuk darts away from it as it bears down, raising her machete again and chopping at the beast's head with the deft violence of a seasoned hunter. Her weapon glances off of the thing's heavy armour. Pamuk springs out of the way again, and just in time: rearing up, the centipede slams itself downwards, chittering and screeching as a vicious pair of mandibles snap at her scaly heels.

Coming to her senses, Hayder realises that her best bet is to get far enough away from the scene that she can use her rifle. She scrambles away from the camp, noticing as she does so that Morgan has wrestled free of his collapsed tent, and is standing, blinking, near-naked despite the cold, watching with wide eyes as Pamuk and the centipede dance.

'Morgan, *run!*' Hayder cries, following her own advice as best she can in spiked feet.

Morgan does not run. Morgan screams instead, a high-pitched scream that shreds the night air, and the centipede turns, lightning quick. It glides like silk across the glacier on its thousands of legs, mandibles clicking and clacking, and before Morgan can act, the vast invertebrate is upon him. The snapping, vicious mandibles clamp expertly around Morgan's neck, and with a quick, decisive scissoring motion, Morgan's head is severed from his body with such remarkable efficiency that Hayder stops running for a moment, and stands, stock-still in awe, as the centipede begins to slowly and yet rather delicately stuff the now drooling head of the City's Chief Geologist into its mouth with two of its forelegs.

Fuck, Hayder thinks, and then: *Now's your chance!*

Hayder's trembling hands grip the rifle, and she tries to slow her breathing, so she can get a good aim. She thinks of how Pamuk's machete bounced off the plate armour of the centipede, and refocuses her attention on the thing's eyes, which are large, black, and stuck like blobs of tar to the sides of its ugly head.

She thinks of a baby, who is now a child, growing up somewhere without her.

She thinks of a City, on fire, a place she never wants to return to.

She thinks of a man, leaning warm and solid against her back.

She pulls the trigger.

Hayder can now add centipede-slayer to her impressive resume.

It took more than one shot. She missed on the first try, hit a bullseye- or a bug's eye, she supposes- on the second. The centipede is dead, its body twitching on the ice before her. Pamuk is busy hacking its legs off, to keep as mementos, or food, or for some other purpose.

Morgan is also dead, his blood soaking into the glacier, but Hayder has other, more serious things to worry about, at this moment.

Because the Vellum is smashed, beyond repair. It must have flown out of her breast-pocket when she fell into Morgan's tent. The artifact has been trodden underfoot, pierced by the thick spikes of Hayder's crampons. She has trampled upon the empire's most valuable asset, and didn't even notice.

Hayder sinks to her knees.

What do I do now? She thinks. *I cannot go back. I'll be executed if I return empty-handed, without Morgan, and especially without the Vellum.*

And yet, If I go forward, I will get lost upon this hellscape, she reasons, working through her options. *I've been following the Vellum's GPS signal this whole time, to stay on course. Now, it's gone. I could die of exposure out here. There could be more centipedes. I could run out of food.*

Pamuk stops carving up the centipede, and comes to stand next to Hayder, who, for the first time since her partner died, is crying, letting hot tears slide down her cheeks, unchecked.

Pamuk puts out a finger coated with sticky yellow centipede blood, and catches a tear as it drops off of Hayder's chin.

Then, she spots the smashed artifact in her hands.

She stills, and says something in a language Hayder doesn't understand.

'What?' Hayder replies, dully.

Pamuk pulls her clothes to one side. As she does so, the first signs of dawn creep into the sky. Soon, the peaks of Old White and Old Red will be ablaze.

Hayder gasps. The Sherpa has Hecht's sigil tattooed on her right breast.

Hayder holds out a hand, pleading.

'Show me,' she says. 'Please. I don't want to go back there. I can't. I have a child.' *Can she even understand New English?* Hayder thinks, frantically.

Pamuk smiles, and bows her head.

'I will show you,' she says.

Author note: Hayder and Pamuk will return.

LET SLEEPING GODS LIE

Dearest Elizabeth,

At last I can lift the veil of secrecy surrounding my latest expedition. I write this to you from the mouth of the Faiyum Oasis in Egypt, which is a few days' journey south-west of Cairo. Contrary to any opinion you may have previously held of this country, which I dare say conjures dusty mirages of sand and sky, the Faiyum is a lush, fertile area within a large depression in the desert, situated around a great lake. Mainly, the area is known for its farming activities, and the region is famous for fresh fruit: oranges, lemons, guavas, mangoes, apricots, some delightful treats I have tasted before, and some of which I have never seen in my life. The flavours are alien and astonishing to my palate. The locals also sell sweet, fresh honey, the likes of which I have never enjoyed, nor ever will again, and flowers for perfume making. Fishing is a lucrative business here. In short, despite being surrounded by arid, lifeless desert on all sides, the Faiyum is a type of bounteous paradise, and has been for thousands of years. It does not surprise me that the Pharaohs of old chose to build their edifices here.

I am contracted to explore and excavate within the mortuary complex of a site called Hawara, which is located at the entrance to the Faiyum. I will tell you more of this in the letters to follow. For now, I am weary from travelling, and I can hear the call to prayer, which means the light will be fading shortly. It is a strange and beguiling noise, the *adhan* as I believe they call it, recited from atop a tall tower by a man called the *muezzin* at various points throughout the day, which turns out to be rather convenient for me, as I am too well-known for losing track of time. The call is at once both wild and mournful, not at all like the hymns we sing at church back home, which seem rather staid and prim by comparison. One should not compare gods, or place stock on one particular type of worship above another, as a scholar I think that it is counterintuitive to do so, but I admit I do find the practices of other civilisations fascinating in this regard.

I confess I am heartsick tonight, for I miss you, and the children. How is little Edward progressing with his studies? Tell Bess that I shall endeavour to find her a trinket she may have for a keepsake. Soon enough she will have a collection to rival that of the British Museum! I trust she is taking good care of her treasures, as I trust that you are taking good care of yourself and our dear ones.

Please, as always, I must ask that you maintain as much silence and discretion as possible about my whereabouts. Looters and treasure-hunters abound in these parts, as do agents from other societies and museums, all of them desperate to get their hands on any artefact possible. The Hawara complex has, as yet, escaped the attention of most nefarious treasure-hunter types, and I would like to keep it that way for as long as possible, or at least until I have filed my official report. For now, the site is mine to explore, and anything I discover will belong to the Egyptian Exploration Society as agreed in the terms of my contract and a condition of the renewal of my funding.

As I write this, the dusky air is busy with the sounds of insects and the calls of strange birds I do not recognise. I am both mournful, for I miss you, and excited for what the coming days will bring.

I wish you goodnight, and the dearest of dreams for all of you, sweetlings, as you lay your heads to rest.

Ever yours,

F.P.

*

Journal entry: Flinders Petrie, FRS, FBA
Friday, November 2nd, 1888.
Hawara complex.

The first day of our excavations has gone well. We began by clearing the hard, compact ground in the south-west corner of the mortuary complex, an area that, as yet, has not been explored much. The men in my team, led by a tall, cheerful chap called Hossam, are working well, and are dedicated despite the blazing conditions. I have to remind them to stop, and water, and eat. Hossam and I talk a great deal, about a great many things. He is a gentile and well-educated individual, who speaks excellent English. My grasp of his language is improving at a much slower rate than I am comfortable with, but I do find I can issue forth the essentials, like 'Allah yihanneek', which I believe translates roughly to 'Bon Appetit!' I do not know whether or not it is the exact parlance, for Hossam prefers not to correct me, and the men seem largely ambivalent to my efforts to communicate in their native tongue, clumsy as they undoubtedly are. They keep themselves to themselves, wanting only to be paid on time as each day draws to a close. I sense a strong kinship amongst them, and much affection. The affection is a necessary aid to productivity, I am sure. The heat is interminably fierce here, and although I have grown used to the temperatures in Egypt, they never cease to amaze me in their intensity. The builders and labourers of old must have been made of hardy stuff indeed, to have constructed such wonders under such harsh conditions. I imagine humour and camaraderie carried them a long way. Or perhaps they were whipped, threatened and punished throughout the livelong day, I do not know. Accounts from that period vary. Some say the pyramids and temples of old were built by the enslaved. Others wonder if they were paid labourers. I continue to look for evidence of either as we excavate.

The men's indifference to me is incidental, and does not interfere with their diligent work ethic. No doubt they think I am afflicted by the same treasure-hunting fetish that grips so many of my so-called peers, currently rampaging around Egypt on the hunt for mummies, for golden treasures, for oudja charms, which I hear are all the rage to wear in America. I am told tales of people still consuming mumia, in powder form, a substance procured from ground-up mummified remains (often faked), for medicinal purposes. This is not a new trend, for apothecaries in the twelfth century were recorded administering mumia for a variety of ills, but the recent resurgence in interest (I blame that interminable Shelley and his infernal Ozymandius sonnet) is distasteful to me. I hear of mummy unwrapping parties held in Soho. Sometimes you see men selling ancient, desiccated corpses propped up on the streets of Cairo for this very purpose. It is abhorrent to me. It is not that I consider myself more worthy than those who seek thrills in Egypt's many tombs and chambers, my own place here is funded by a variety of interested parties that make me the least of impartial intruders in these lands, but I must confess I am not driven by glory, only a pure and honest desire to learn. I do not covet anything but understanding. Others, unfortunately, have other objectives, hence my necessity for speed and secrecy as this excavation unfolds.

Once we have finished clearing and preparing the ground, I hope to dig an access trench and locate an entrance into the lower levels of the mortuary complex. From there, I hope to find funeral accessories and, if my suspicions are correct, the entrance to the tomb of a King.

I remain optimistic that I shall be able to furnish the Egyptian Department of Antiquities with some worthy artefacts. For now, my sole achievement of note appears to be the adoption of my person by a rather persistent, albeit handsome, tabby cat that has taken to hanging around my tent when I am working in it. It meows in a piteous voice and rubs up against my ankles as I write, only letting up when I put down my pen, scratch the top of its head, and give it a morsel of my rations. I am happy to do so, for it is too warm for my appetite to flourish, and I find a diet of bread, dates, fresh fruit and water sufficient. My wife will find me much altered upon my return from this expedition, and will no doubt have to send for the tailor to accommodate my reduced waistline.

Cats are sacred in Egypt. I consider my newfound friendship with the tabby an auspicious sign. I am grateful for the company, as well. I have informed the cat that my Arabic is very rusty, but if it can be patient with me, we shall get along just fine.

*

Dearest Elizabeth,

Let me tell you more about the Hawara complex, and my purpose here.

Hawara lies in the Faiyum, as I said before, and consists of one pyramid and one temple, both of which were built by the twelfth dynasty king Amenemhat III.

The pyramid itself, although nearly sixty metres tall and remarkable for its size alone, is made from mud brick, and has been much studied already by my predecessors. I am interested therefore in the complex *around* the pyramid, particularly in what lies to the south: a vast and exciting structure known to Herodotus and other ancient Greek scholars as the 'Labyrinth'.

The Labyrinth covers an area of fifteen acres, and once had twelve covered courts, of which six were aligned to the north and six to the south. Inside, there was a great temple building which covered two floors and three *thousand* rooms, half of which were located above ground, the other half of which were buried beneath the surface.

Herodotus wrote once that he visited this temple complex but was never allowed to visit the underground chambers because they contained the tombs of the Kings who built the labyrinth, and also the tombs of crocodiles, who were much revered and worshipped as deities in the Faiyum, in the same way that cats are still revered today. His account was intoxicating: he wrote of a spectacular, mythical maze of rooms, galleries and courtyards, a wonder of engineering and design. How much of this is hyperbole and how much is based upon truth is unknown, but this is why men such as myself toil away in the fashion that we do: to uncover the absolute truths, and to unpick the embellishments and embroidery that time can bestow upon a site. I am confident that my particular methodology and dating system has yet to be used in Hawara, and I truly feel that for this reason amongst many others, I am the right man for this job.

Today, little of the fabled Labyrinth structure remains above ground, but it is what lies *beneath* the surface that fascinates me, Elizabeth. I want to go below, into the tombs of the kings and the crocodile gods. I want to go where Herodotus could not.

Working conditions continue to be challenging. It is hotter than Hades, and I am plagued by this confounded feral tabby cat that has decided to make my camp her home. I say 'her,' instead of 'it,' for I only discovered the cat was female very recently. She sits in the shade of my tent, licking her paws and watching imperiously as I toil away in the relentless Egyptian sun, and all the while the pyramid looms over me like a great, slumped, sleeping king.

And I too must sleep now, Elizabeth, for I am exhausted in both mind and body. I too will slumber like a mighty king tonight.

Goodnight my darling, and Godspeed to you and the children.

F.P.

*

Dearest Elizabeth,

The cat woke me up last night, when I was in my deepest point of sleep. I was not amused, as sleep is difficult enough out here in the heat, despite my exhaustion.

Upon waking, I thought I heard a strange noise, a noise that could not be attributed to the cat. Whatever it was made the hairs on the back of my neck stand firmly to attention, and rendered the notion of any further sleep almost impossible, such a firm root it took in my imagination. But, imagination is all it must have been, for upon calling out 'What is it? Who is there?' in as firm and angry a voice as possible, only the sound of the cat meowing came back to me from out of the darkness. I cursed myself for a fool. I also cursed the cat for her inconsiderate night-time chorus.

However, upon reflection, I have decided not to remain indisposed towards the cat, for it is company, at least. I reason that if I cannot *rid* myself of the creature, I had better name her. I have therefore chosen Bast, for obvious reasons- Bastet being the name of the ancient Cat god, as you well know. As Egyptian culture reveres the cat so strongly, I shall continue to take her presence at my camp as a good omen, or at least, this is what I tell myself as the silly mog continues to drag her claws along my trouser leg whilst I write.

My faith in the feline as a good luck token is perhaps well placed, as Bast, in an act of gratitude for her newly bestowed and rather grand name, saw fit to leave the shade of my tent today and accompany me on my dig. And, perhaps coincidentally or not, today was the day we found the entrance to the lower levels, right where I predicted it would be, in the southwest quadrant, close to the base of the pyramid. Once the men and I had broken through the stone

119

and found the access tunnel, which was a low stone passageway typical of other mortuary structures of this period, the sun was already beginning its descending arc in the sky. I pushed on, with Hossam's agreement. We lit torches and descended. Within the first few feet of the passage we made some incredible finds, including an antechamber which was sealed tight with carved stone. It was a chamber that was not marked anywhere upon the existing floor plan of the site, and its discovery gave me great hope for what lay beyond.

After great effort, we eventually broke through the huge stone door seal, and found inside a collection of funeral treasures heaped into a haphazard pile in one corner of the chamber, as if thrown in there hastily.

And, Elizabeth, the plot thickens. There was none of the usual care, or ceremony that you see displayed in the tombs of Pharaohs found in the Valley of the Kings. This tomb complex has a feeling of something different. The walls are not decorated with the fine hieroglyphics one would expect. There are riches, gold, jewellery, finely crafted furniture, of course. But, although the quality is indicative of status, the way these things were...well, *thrown* into the chamber...it tells a story I cannot quite decipher, and presents a mystery that is most compelling.

I also found a strange collection of amphora in the room, crafted from alabaster, with a globular body shape, tall necks, two handles, and shallow ring feet at the bottom. Some of the containers even had their alabaster lids still in place, which are very rarely found. I wonder if some of the sealed amphora contain liquids, or oil. I am not comfortable moving them until I know I have a storage case well prepared for their receipt, which I shall do tomorrow.

Lastly, I found several crocodile burials around the mouth of the chamber, just outside the door seal. This confirms my suspicions, first indicated by the descriptions in the annals of Herodotus, that the labyrinth temple was originally dedicated to the crocodile god Sobek.

Tonight, once I have finished documenting these finds, I hope to sleep better. Hossam says I look tired, and I dare say he is correct.

Yours,

F.P.

*

Journal entry: Flinders Petrie, FRS, FBA
Monday, November 5th, 1888.
Hawara complex.

I decided to dismantle the far wall of the antechamber we discovered yesterday and see if there are further chambers beyond. I ordered the men to begin breaking down the wall, which they did with much muttering and nervousness and persuasion from Hossam, who has lost a good deal of his cheeriness since yesterday. Something has shifted in the men's attitude towards me and our excavation these past hours. Where once Hossam's team were diligent, they have now become sullen, withdrawn, and hesitant. They are also extremely reluctant to explore the further reaches of what lies beneath the temple. Progress is slow because of this, and I find I am growing frustrated.

When I asked them what troubled them so, Hossam talked about strange noises in the night. He denies that anyone is driven by superstition and fancy, and firmly holds to the evidence of his own ears, as do the other men. They told me of grunts and groans that have no business being in existence. I have told them to be extra diligent, for I suspect looters scouting the dig site, but they are adamant that these noises are not of human origin. I do not know what to say to this. I do not wish to irritate them further.

I have to admit that my sleep has been greatly disturbed for most of this week, even if I am yet to clearly hear the noises they actually speak of. I had assumed it was the nocturnal activities of the cat Bast keeping me awake at night.

I managed to calm their dissent somewhat with the promise of more money on our return to town, so for now, most have remained with me. Some have left, unwilling to explore further. I do not think it will take much to scare more of them off, which remains a sobering thought.

These struggles notwithstanding, my instinct about the chamber wall paid off, and, as I predicted, we broke through eventually into another chamber beyond, this one much bigger than the first. Inside, we unearthed a black granite statue of the King himself: Amenemhat III. A glorious find! The statue is in almost perfect condition, and is a wonderful example of Egyptian skill in stonecraft. The King has a serious expression upon his face, full cheeks and rather prominent ears. Sometimes, a scholar I knew once speculated, these statues have large ears to indicate that the King hears everything, and rules over us all accordingly. Sometimes, the ears are just perhaps realistic depictions of large ears, the thought of which never fails to charm me. All humour aside, there is a sense of weariness about the King's face, of being tired of the burden of

121

leadership, perhaps. A struggle I can identify with. The peculiar qualities of a double-edged sword, you might say, for it is a privilege to be able to carry out such work as this, but a chore to continue to motivate the men to do as I bid.

More peculiar to me is the damage I found to the bottom of the statue, the part buried furthest into the ground. It took a while to extract from the earth and dust, but once we did, and once the granite had been cleared of debris, I could see...marks. Like great, deep gouge marks, only not made with a blade or other tool that I can make out. These look more like...well, like something has clawed at, or bitten the stone. They are most unusual, unlike anything I have ever seen. I do not know which ancient tool must have made those marks, but it is not one traditionally associated with the craft of stonework.

The men, as I feared they might, looked at the marks and made signs I did not understand, muttering to each other in consternation. I hear them outside my tent now, talking in uneasy Arabic to each other. Their upset has dulled the shine from the day's proceedings considerably.

Bast seems unconcerned by all of this. She is curled up on my lap as I write, purring. Damned cat.

*

Elizabeth,

The men left today.

I woke up, and they had simply vanished into thin air, all except Hossam. They took all the pack mules with them, save for one. They left my equipment in place, and my supplies, my water, my food, my fire lighting tools. They stole nothing, Elizabeth. They just left, quietly, as if they had never been there at all.

Hossam pleaded for me to come with him. I refused and asked him over and over again the reason for the abandonment of the dig. He would not confirm anything beyond the mysterious, frightening noises that have spooked the men. I wonder if he is concealing something from me, if he has more knowledge of what is happening here than he cares to admit, but it is hard to think so when he seems so dreadfully concerned for my wellbeing.

Eventually, we grew angry with each other. I refused to abandon my discoveries, Hossam refused to stay with me and protect them. As our tempers rose, so did our grasp on each other's language, and the conversation became a heated argument in two tongues. I regret this bitterly, for I have become very fond of Hossam. I had thought he had grown fond of me, too. Eventually we broke apart, and Hossam left shortly after. I watched him leave with great sadness and fear. He left behind the little chess set I gifted him, the one whittled from the fallen branches of the English oak in our garden back home. How I miss that tree, that green, secluded space.

I wish I knew what has frightened him so much since we unearthed the statue yesterday. A statue which I will never be able to transport to Cairo by myself, not now.

I considered my options as the morning progressed. I thought briefly about leaving the site and returning to town to recruit more men, but I feel reluctant to go as things are, unguarded. Unfriendly eyes watch me from a distance, I feel it. I cannot let them near. I am so close to something momentous, Elizabeth. So close. I can feel it in the air. Something tangible. Waiting for me to unearth it.

So I shall take the tools down to the chamber and break down the next wall on my own. The stone is soft, and it should be manageable by myself. If I am stubborn and if I can remember to keep myself fed, I should be able to get through the wall within half a day or so. If my assumptions are correct, there will be a series of these chambers to work through before I get to the main burial chamber, as it were. Someone of great stature is sleeping down there in the darkness, waiting for me to set him free. I feel it.

I shall continue to write these letters to you, Elizabeth, despite not being able to send them now that my men have abandoned me and I have no-one to courier them to the city. They shall serve as an accompaniment to my excavation diary, as I have almost filled my journal with notes and drawings. When I return to Cairo I will have them sent, and you and the children can marvel, as I have, at what lies beneath the pyramid.

F.P.

*

Journal entry: Flinders Petrie, FRS, FBA
Tuesday, November 6th, 1888.
Hawara complex.

Dug through the chamber wall on my own. Bast accompanied me as usual. Not a good companion. Lazy. Sat and watched me work whilst licking herself. No help at all.

Still, I must confess, I shall miss the cat when I return to England. Perhaps I can smuggle her home, somehow. The children would love her.

After a long period of labour, I felt colder air coming in to me from behind the stone, always indicative of a larger hidden space beyond. I pressed on, and discovered a sort of lever or mechanism buried deep at the base of the door. I was, however, not careful, and in my clumsy eagerness to finally break through the chamber wall I must have triggered the mechanism. There was a low, grinding noise, and the floor of the passageway where I was digging duly collapsed, falling downwards into a cavernous, hollow space below, and taking me with it.

The speed of the collapse and the force of the fall knocked me quite senseless. I woke to find Bast meowing and pawing at my face. At least, I assumed it was Bast, for I was in complete darkness when I reopened my eyes. I reassured her that I was fine, having perhaps been unconscious for a few moments at most. I was grateful it was not longer. Damned booby traps.

It took me some little time to extricate myself from the rubble and debris, and doing so in total blackness was difficult to say the least, not to mention trying for my nerves, for although I know that I am alone down here, the first man to venture into the bowels of the pyramid for a very, very long time, I could not help but find the darkness aggressive in its totality. I do however keep a strip of matches in my pocket at all times, for this is not my first experience of an underground tomb complex and I have learned a few valuable lessons throughout my time in Egypt. I was able to use the fleeting, weak, flickering light of a struck match to locate my rush-bound torch, which had fallen down into the lower space along with me. I lit it, and looked around.

And what I saw was marvellous.

*

Dearest Elizabeth,

My matches are fast running out, and my torch burns lower and weaker as I progress, for the air is meagre and thin down here, but still, something compels me, spurs me on. I admit I should perhaps be saving the light rather than writing this letter, but somehow, the act of writing makes me feel less alone in the darkness, and as my journal is now completely full, so I shall scratch you this missive upon a scrap of parchment I found in my pocket and hope it shall once again see the light of day, and reach your hands.

I am deep in the labyrinth now. A secondary level into which I fell when I triggered a strange mechanism buried at the base of a wall I was excavating. Be assured I am not injured, only a little bruised in places. The cat, Bast, has followed me down here, and I am very glad she has, for I am in a vast, endless network of corridors, the likes of which you could not even imagine, and it is a comfort to have something else living alongside me as I explore. I feel like I have been down here for days, but I know this cannot be true, else my torch would have burned out completely. Time has, nevertheless, lost all meaning, and my appetite for a return to the surface wars with my desire to map out the extent of the labyrinth, although I am rapidly coming to suspect this is a task too great for one man alone.

When I fell, I was lucky enough to be wearing my utility belt and satchel, so I have all my notes and papers and parchments, my fountain pen, some tools, although no food beyond a few wizened almonds and dates which I have carefully rationed, and my water canteen is almost dry. I do have my pistol, which brings me some small solace, although I could not tell you why, for the only thing down here to shoot at is stone and mortar.

Using chalk, I have been exploring the warren of corridors, marking a trail so that I can find my way back easily. And after only a few hours of steady walking, I found a tomb, Elizabeth. A tomb that has been untouched by human hands for what looks like thousands of years.

The tomb is magnificent, Elizabeth.

It is situated inside a large chamber, a chamber I stumbled into as I seem to stumble everywhere, these days. I knew immediately upon entering it that there was something special about the room, because the walls were smooth and cold like glass, instead of the rough sandy stone of the labyrinth corridor walls.

On closer inspection I found that the entire chamber is carved from a single block of quartzite. One enormous, huge block. It is spectacular, Elizabeth. The light from my torch flickers and echoes around the polished surfaces like spirits dancing in the air.

In the centre of this room is the tomb. It too is vastly superior in craftsmanship and size to anything I have ever discovered before.

Now, at this point, I must confess something to you, darling Elizabeth. I can imagine your face as you read this, I can picture so perfectly the curve of your wry smile, the small shake of your head. But still, it must be said, for I have been a fool, and despite my earlier protestations that I was not injured by my fall into this lower level, I fear that may not be entirely true. I must have hit my head, and hit it quite hard, for I have been in this chamber for an hour or two now, and I am sure that I can hear something, and more specifically, I have become sure that there is a noise coming from the Sarcophagus.

A moaning, scraping sort of noise.

From *inside* the vast tomb.

But as this is quite impossible, I must assume I am, instead, hallucinating, or have started to run quite mad, perhaps through thirst, or hunger, or fatigue. Bast has not stopped meowing in fright since I entered this chamber. Perhaps she is frightened of me, for it is true that I do not feel like my usual good self at all, and I-

*

Elizabeth

I dropped my torch. One scrap of paper left in satchel. I am not mad. There *is* something alive inside the tomb. I know beyond all reasonable doubt that this cannot be, but still. I have my chisel ready. I need to know, Elizabeth. I am not mad. I love you. It calls to me, and I cannot deny the call any longer. If I should not return, tell the children I died in pursuit of greater things, in pursuit of knowledge greater than you or I or them or indeed of mankind at large.

I love you all.

F.P.

*

Dearest Elizabeth,

I made it out, Elizabeth.

Just about.

I feel fortunate to be able to say that. And to think I prided myself on my nous, my survival skills. I am ashamed of the foolhardy idiot I have been. Hossam was right to disown me. I should, if it were possible, disown myself.

To think I ignored so many warnings.

I am once again in Cairo, attempting to recover my strength a little before my ship departs tomorrow. The laudanum has made me drowsy, but I shall try my best to finish this, and hope it is not the last letter I shall ever send.

I do not know how to dress up prettily what I have to recount, so I shall simply forge ahead and state myself as plainly as I know how.

I have had an encounter, Elizabeth. An encounter of such a profound and terrifying nature that I do not know how I shall ever fully recover my faculties.

I am fair convinced, and no man or woman may convince me otherwise: I awoke a god in the chambers beneath Hawara complex, Elizabeth. There is no other way to describe it. A god.

A deity.

A cruel and terrible creature, of such disgusting proportions that I suspect I will never sleep properly again.

And it did not thank me for rousing it from its slumber.

I described to you the noises I heard coming from the Sarcophagus when I broke into it. I wrote it all down, on scraps of paper and in my journal, all of which are now lost, lying somewhere within the vast network of tunnels and corridors beneath the complex.

My memory however remains intact, and that will have to suffice.

At first I assumed I had hit my head during the fall into the lower levels, and that I was perhaps hallucinating, or that the noises I heard down there were mere vivid fancy brought about by hunger and exhaustion. But the longer I stayed in that vast, polished chamber, the longer I grew convinced that I was quite sane. I am still convinced of my own sanity. And, despite the impossibility of such a thing, there was, indeed, something alive *inside* that tomb, Elizabeth. Bast's behaviour only served to reinforce this impression, for Bast has always been a practical, level-headed type of cat, and her distress coupled with her refusal to leave my side finally alerted me to what I had been denying: that there was another presence alive in the chamber with us.

So I took my hammer and chisel to the base of the Sarcophagus, where there existed, already, a small fracture, and I began to chip away at the tomb. Why, you might ask? I wish I had a satisfactory answer. I found myself gripped with a startling type of mania, which led me towards the terrifying anomaly, rather than away from it, as would have been sensible. As I hammered, the strange noises grew louder and more urgent. I wondered madly if perhaps one of the men had come down here after we first uncovered the entrance to the Labyrinth, gotten trapped inside the Sarcophagus somehow, unbeknownst to me, or whether it was another stray animal that had wandered in from another concealed entrance I knew nothing about. I redoubled my efforts, knowing it would take hours given the thickness of the stone and yet also that my torch was on its last tinder, and the thing inside sounded out again.

I cried: 'I'm coming! Oh my God, I'll get you out, don't worry!'

Whereupon the moaning noises turned suddenly to an inhuman growling, snarling, hissing declaration, and I screamed, for the Sarcophagus split apart like a soft boiled egg, showering me with debris, splinters of rare stone embedding themselves in my hands and arms and shins, and the solid lid burst outwards with a roar, further pelting me with lethal fragments of masonry, and all I

127

could do was scream weakly and fall backwards on my rear whilst Bast yowled in my arms, where she had leapt.

After the dust settled, Elizabeth. That is when I came face to face with it. It towered above me, its form scaly beneath a layer of decaying cloth bandages, which it slowly and deliberately raked away from its head with a bony, clawed hand, revealing its true self.

And I cried 'What are you? Oh God! Oh, God! Why do you have my face? *Why do you have my face?'*

The creature, which had mimicked my own features so perfectly as to completely and irrevocably undermine my sense of reality and self, roared at me, a deafening, ear-bursting noise, and it moved one step towards me. It was then that my torch fizzled and sputtered out, and I wheeled about and ran as fast as I could, surging ahead in the refreshed dark, feeling as I went a brilliant, sharp, burning, tearing sensation on my right leg, continuing forward despite this, knowing that at any second I could run straight into a wall and knock myself unconscious, but by some miracle, I managed to escape back through the chamber door and out into a corridor. I felt, rather than heard Bast running alongside me, and together, although I could not say how, we ran and we ran until I eventually saw a sliver of daylight, finding by some miracle of fortune a different section of the Labyrinth where the upper floor ceiling had again collapsed into itself. I was able to clumsily haul myself up the rubble, which formed a sort of ramp, to the first layer and break out on a different side of the pyramid altogether, into the blessed, burning, relentless African sun.

I barely recall what happened after that, and it hardly matters, for Hawara is now behind me.

My leg is in ruins, and I shall be plucking shards of stone from my extremities for many months to come.

Whatever was down there, whatever I unleashed when I broke open that sarcophagus-- it *bit* me, Elizabeth. I felt its foul breath on my skin, felt its teeth sinking into the tender flesh of my thigh, then again on my calf, I felt its hot tongue sliding down my leg. I felt it. It was *real*, and I will forever have the scars to show for it. I can recall its iron jaws perfectly, and I can feel its leathery, scaled skin against mine as I sleep. It was not quite animal, definitely inhuman, but somehow spoke to me with human affectations, in *my* voice, using a language I did not recognise, ancient and terrible. It spoke and I screamed, and my screams linger long in my memory, and probably always will.

I know now why the men ran away in the night. They knew what I did not: that the labyrinth at Hawara was not put there for the purpose of burying Kings, but for imprisoning nightmares. The stone walls and the tunnels and the boobytraps were not designed to keep us from getting in, but from what was buried inside from getting *out*. Perhaps my team had heard these rumours for many generations, and ignored the warnings contained within for as long as they could on the promise of a good wage. Once it became apparent that their fathers, grandfathers, and great grandfathers had not been exaggerating the threat...

But speculation is useless. As useless as regret.

A nightmare, an angry God, a demon, who knows. Whatever it is, I have set it free, into the light. That is my responsibility now. My burden. How I shall bear it, I do not know.

Do you remember my first journey to Egypt, in 1880? I was twenty-six years old, and this country was so exciting, so wondrous to me. I was so green, so naive. Eight years later, I thought I had learned so many lessons. Except one, it seems.

To let sleeping Gods lie.

I love you Elizabeth. I am bringing the cat home with me.

F.P.

THE FINAL WISH FOUNDATION

It was a bright, crisp morning in Venice. The sky, often blue above the island, had a particularly rich quality to it that day. Brilliant sunlight cast shadows so dense they threw the Piazza San Marco into a state of high contrast, where clashing colours were heightened and familiar structures caricatured- particularly the tall red brick shaft of St. Mark's campanile, which thrust itself importantly into the sky like a pointed monolith. The green pyramid-shaped spire tipping the top of the bell tower appeared to brush up against the ripe azure beyond, an effect heightened by small flurries of white doves that flocked around the spire like gathering clouds. The campanile itself dominated the square in which it stood with the immutable confidence endowed upon most man-made structures. False confidence, as it turned out, for the tower had been severely damaged many times over, by lightning, by fire, by storms, earthquakes and poor repairs, to the degree that the entire structure, weakened by centuries of assault, collapsed completely in 1902. The campanile was rebuilt in 1912, to a height of almost ninety-nine metres, and the unwanted debris from the former tower's collapse unceremoniously dumped into the Adriatic.

The woman who sat with an untouched espresso before her at one of the many tables lining the Piazza learned all this from her brand-new guidebook, a book she'd brought solely for the purpose of hiding behind, but which had, despite all her best efforts, managed to suck her in with its many facts and recommendations. The edges of each page were still crisp, and sharp, and would remain so, for she would abandon the book on the table as soon as she'd finished her business in the square, but first, she wanted to learn about the weathervane on top of the bell tower's spire.

A golden weathervane, it was shaped like the archangel Gabriel, and perched like a shining totem, surveying the world beneath at large, for heaven felt close enough perhaps, at some three hundred feet high in the air.

The woman admired the weathervane's glitz and gilt, squinting up into the brightness over the tops of her designer sunglasses. She could, from where she sat, just about make out the golden halo suspended above the angel's head, and see that one hand was pointing to the sky, perhaps in judgement. The other hand clutched a sprig of what looked like lilies. She was sure there was a whole layer of Christian symbolism on display up there that was lost on her ill-educated self, but it didn't matter. The weathervane was pretty, the tower was pretty, the square and basilica behind the tower was pretty.

All in all, it was a very pleasing setting for a killing.

Which was precisely the point. The square was a stage, and she was playing a part upon it.

Like most willing actors, she was dressed for both the task ahead, and the weather: warm, yet stylish, a cashmere overcoat belted around her slim frame, a hint of flesh showing around the neck beneath a thick scarf, sunglasses. It was cold, but she gave off the stubbornly chic air of someone expecting more clement weather any day now, and never shivered once, even though her breath misted in front of her face.

The clothes had taken some getting used to. The outfit had been expensive, but she'd been given a decent budget for it. Wearing it gave her a window into how people with more fortunate lifestyles than her own must live: in comfort. The cashmere coat, in particular, was so well-made and well-tailored she hardly felt she was wearing a coat at all. It felt more like a warm, comforting layer of air had coalesced around her, which she knew sounded fucking absurd, but not when she compared the item to the ancient leather biker jacket she usually wore, the one with rusted buckles and peeling patches on the elbows and cracked sleeves, a jacket that weighed a ton and made her shoulders ache and neck sore, but never seemed to keep her warm.

Perhaps my life would have been different if I'd been able to afford better clothes, she thought, then shook her head. No point in thinking that way. She had a job to do. Self-pity could come later. She was in Venice, after all. She never imagined, in a million, million years, that she'd ever have the opportunity to come here, and being sad about her life up until this point in time was the definition, she felt, of looking the gift horse in the mouth. She didn't know what a gift horse was, but she did know that, for the brief time she had left on this earth, there was finally money in her bank account, and she was sitting under a foreign sky, and that was enough. It had to be enough. Because there wouldn't be any more, and the sun was shining, the piazza bustling with life. Those things were more important and real to her than a lifetime of regrets and what-ifs.

The woman caught the eye of a passing tourist, who smiled. She didn't reciprocate the gesture, instead lowered her gaze, suddenly uncomfortable. She had never liked being looked at. She was beautiful, she supposed, by anyone's standards, and had been told so several times, but never liked to think about it. Beauty had never been an advantage, where she'd come from, only the harbinger of a lot of unwanted attention. How she looked or didn't was nobody's business but hers, she'd always said. Well.

Her business, and the business of the person who had hired her solely on the basis of her photograph.

She was tall, even seated, and slim, which some people were envious of until she pointed out that she'd love to have more flesh on her bones, she just couldn't afford to eat that much, and when she could, she couldn't keep anything down. When people realised her size was down to poverty and illness rather than aesthetic preference they shut their envious mouths pretty fast, which said more about them than her, she knew, but still. It stung, how fashionable her misfortune was in the eyes of others.

She was graceful in the way she moved, displaying a certain fluidity of motion that spoke of a childhood spent climbing trees and clambering over walls and leaping ditches and exploring abandoned industrial units and running around the endless horizons of various maze-like housing estates. There was also something controlled about her, despite the grace. Restrained. As if she could never fully relax, or let go. A predator could drop from the sky at any moment, so she kept an eye to the blue. She worked hard to conceal any outward signs of skittishness, but an observer watching closely might have noticed tiny inconsistencies in the otherwise dignified facade. Tics, nervous ones. Her index finger, for example: poised daintily above the tabletop, it twitched in time to some endless internal rhythm, almost as if there were a piano key beneath her finger tips that she was itching to strike. Tap, tap, went the finger into thin air. An itchy trigger finger, a secret tattoo.

An indication that all was not as it seemed. Like a weathervane swinging to the truth: she was a fake tourist, a fake cashmere-coat wearing socialite, a fake assassin. You just had to look hard to see through the patina, was all.

Still, fraud or otherwise, she was exactly what the client had ordered.

Her eyes were fixed upon him now: a man who sat a few tables away from her, reading a newspaper. She had chosen this seat for this purpose, to surveil him, as instructed. He remained seemingly oblivious to her scrutiny, a theatrical detail that the woman found faintly aggravating, but then, this was not her fantasy. It was his.

He was youngish, late twenties, and thin, very thin. Thinner than she was. He did not have a cashmere coat, and shivered occasionally, setting his paper down carefully and wrapping and re-wrapping his red scarf tighter about his neck. It was obvious without looking too closely that he was not well. Aside from his weight, he had an air of fatigue and suffering that usually accompanied a long period of illness. There were harsh lines on his face, carved deep by pain, and his posture made it seem as if he was consciously trying to hold himself together. The man should not have been sitting out in the frigid air, he should have been tucked up warm and safe in bed, but instead, he shuddered and sipped his cooling coffee, just another face in a merry-go-round of ever-rotating tourists.

The woman watched him rearrange his clothing for the dozenth time, pick his paper back up, turn the page, take a messy gulp of his cappuccino. A few beads of sweat ran down her right temple despite the cold, and she wiped them away, but more tiny droplets sprang up to replace those she dismissed.

Posh fucking coat making me sweat like a pig, she thought, and shifted in her seat uncomfortably.

Again, she wiped the sweat away, and her hand returned to the tabletop to continue its silent staccato in the air.

Sounds began to surge and crescendo around her, a sure sign that her anxiety was building. The Piazza bustled and crackled, bursting with the clip-clop of thousands of busy feet and the clap and flurry of hundreds of beating wings as pigeons surged around in panicky formations, flying too low overhead, bobbing on the floor beneath tables, flustering tourists and generally getting underfoot and being a nuisance. The mid-morning coffee trade had peaked, and each of the cafes that lined the three walls of the square not occupied by religious architecture were crammed with holiday makers drinking overpriced espressos and eating pastries and staring at the gloriously gilded facade of St. Mark's Basilica with wonder or indifference, depending on the person. Selfie sticks battled for space with tour guide placards, artists sold oil paintings and watercolours of the basilica from mobile art stands dotted throughout the square, and lens flares from dozens of pairs of sunglasses glittered and glinted like insects. Again, the woman was conscious of wanting to be able to enjoy all of this, for Venice had long been a dream destination of hers, but now was not the time. Her time would come later. In this moment, she had to get a handle on her anxiety.

It was easier said than done. Two pigeons chose that moment to land on the woman's table, almost knocking over her espresso. She shooed them away angrily, and they took off in a ragged blur of feathers.

She checked her watch for the dozenth time, feeling more stressed as the seconds ticked by. She had been keeping a close eye on the hour, which had created an effect of time slowing down, but she had to let it. She couldn't miss the moment. Doing so would ruin the client's request. All the details had been bought and paid for, and if she fucked any of them up, she would have to refund what she'd earned in advance.

And that would never do. If she lost the money, she lost any chance of securing her own dream. Final wishes didn't come cheap, it turned out.

But they did if you followed the rules.

The watch hands finally clicked to twenty-five past the hour. The bird's intrusion had served as a cue, near enough. The woman dragged in a deep breath of relief and resolution.

Time to go, she thought.

She stood up, downed her cold espresso in one determined gulp, grimaced at its unsweetened bitterness, tightened her coat around her, and walked in a sedate fashion towards the sick man with the newspaper.

He looked up to see her standing over him, smiled tentatively.

'I was wondering when you would arrive.' He seemed relieved, even though he'd known she was there the whole time.

The woman did not reply. It was in her contract not to. Instead, she reached into her coat and pulled out a miniature pistol, which she aimed at the man. The gun was so dainty it was almost engulfed by her long fingers. The matte metal of the barrel gleamed dully against the woman's skin. The man could not see this from where he was sitting, but the words 'TOMCAT-32' were printed on the side of the barrel, which was just over two inches long.

The man stared, mesmerised by the gun, but did not move, could not move. For a moment it seemed as if the two players had been turned to stone. A growing murmur of awareness and confusion rose around them, but they remained in stasis, cardboard cut-out characters on a cardboard stage, until at last the woman licked her lips and spoke. Her voice was deep, hoarse, and unmistakably British.

'You understand it's too late now, don't you, to change your mind?' She blurted this out, knowing it was against the rules, but she wanted to be sure. Murder was murder, even when it was pre-ordered murder, and she had to *know* if this is what he really wanted.

It was the only way she would be able to live with herself until her turn came.

The man opened his mouth to reply, then dissolved into a coughing fit, hacking a wad of yellowish phlegm up into a stained handkerchief that he kept for this purpose: to collect his slow, painful, incremental death-excretions, because it wasn't polite, especially in today's world, to leave them lying around.

The woman suddenly decided that actually, she didn't want to know. She didn't want to take the risk. If he changed his mind, she would be culpable. She had not signed up for guilt or culpability. She had signed up so that she could do some good in this world, before her own time came.

And so she shot him, at point blank range, right in the forehead.

Just like he'd asked.

Once he was slumped over his newspaper, which turned from black and white to red in a few fast moments, she shot him again, in the back of his head, just to make sure. His body jerked a little. Blood flew through the air, squirting delicately onto the paving stones beneath.

The woman stared at her handiwork for a moment or two, the finger on her free hand still tap-tap-tapping away at the air. Then she removed a cigarette carton from her coat pocket, lit a slender cigarillo, readjusted her sunglasses on her face, and walked away from the scene, high stepping through pigeons as the Piazza swallowed her whole.

Behind her, on the table, she left a black, gold-edged business card. An expensive looking thing, it was embossed with three letters: **F.W.F**

The screaming started not long after she left.

*

Two weeks later, a similar business card was found lying next to the body of an elderly woman living in a run-down apartment in Barcelona. The woman had been smothered to death with a pillow, the autopsy found, but not before she had been drugged heavily first. A painless, peaceful end, as deaths go. A clear case of a mercy killing: the woman was old and riddled with cancer, but this is not what interested the police when they discovered the body after neighbours complained of a strong smell in the apartment block and an increase in numbers of flies in the building. What first piqued the interest of the local Guàrdia was the meticulously staged nature of Rosa Cambra's departure. She was seated upright, in a comfy, well-worn chair, facing the window, which was open a touch so that a small breeze could circulate. In her left hand, she clutched an old stuffed bear. Later, this was determined to be her favourite childhood toy. In the background, music softly played from a CD player: an old folk song her mother had used to sing to her when she was little. Her hair was arranged in soft, childish plaits, tied at the ends with ribbons- an identical style to the hairstyle she had worn when she was eight or nine years old, according to old family photograph albums. On her feet, she wore long, snowy white socks and white slippers with little pom-poms attached to them. Someone had pencilled childish freckles across her cheeks, blacked out one of her (false) front teeth to mimic the gap-toothed nature of a child's mouth, and rouged her complexion to make it appear more youthful. On the coffee table next to her, a black and white picture lay- another family photograph. A young Rosa sat front and centre of a gathering of people, a party crown on her head and a small cake in her lap. Surrounded by friends and family, she was radiant, as children often are on their birthdays- the lucky ones, at any rate.

All in all, it was a sad, rather macabre crime scene, one which flies inhabited thickly. In death, the old woman looked like a decaying doll dressed up to resemble a child. It was intentional, it was planned, and Rosa had clearly not done it to herself- she was almost immobile, the Guàrdia later heard. A commode had been put in the room where she sat, presumably because the small bathroom was too far to reach for the old woman. Her bed had not been slept in for years, for Rosa slept in her easy chair instead, finding it more comfortable than lying flat on her sore, scabbed back. The remaining furniture, which was scant in the apartment, was covered in medication bottles, wound pads, IV drip supplies and the various other paraphernalia that accompanies sickness.

So Rosa had been murdered, it was determined, although the words 'mercy' and 'murder' became interchangeable as investigators uncovered more and more about how difficult Rosa's life had become in old age.

Local media outlets, on the other hand, were predictably outraged. Rumours of a sadistic murderer on the loose began to circulate, various names for the perpetrator along with them, but 'Puppeteer' and the 'Doll Maker' won out by an overwhelming majority. Neither the names nor the speculation of sadism were anything close to the truth of the matter, but news pundits are sparing with the truth at the best of times, and it suited them to have a new fear stalking the streets of Barcelona. New fear sold newspapers, it generated clicks and views, it pushed up statistics and figures. Fear was good, a valuable commodity, and so they peddled it, without shame.

Investigations meanwhile turned inwards, to family members, as was usual for murder, even murder cases of such a peculiar nature, but when questioned, Rosa's only surviving son Luca told the police: 'I think the last time she was truly happy was when she was a child,' before providing a rock solid alibi for the approximate time of her death and no further information beyond tears, for he was desperately fond of his mother, that much was plain to see. Flowers were deposited around the entrance to Rosa's apartment block, and the newspapers kept printing stories about it until suddenly, they stopped, for there was a new fear to talk about, as there so often is. The Guàrdia, faced with a distinct lack of any forensic evidence, security camera footage, eye-witnesses or otherwise, chased down a dozen dead ends and then deemed the case unsolved, no longer a priority. Rosa had been old, and she had been dying anyway. Her final moments had been peaceful and non-violent. As crimes went, it was not something that warranted ongoing expenditure, and so investigations wound down, and never fully resumed.

The business card was never traced, and remained sealed in an evidence bag hidden in a storage box for many, many years to come, after which, it mysteriously disappeared, never to be seen again.

*

Another card surfaced in Railay beach, near Krabi, Thailand, four months later. At six-thirty in the evening, a fireball sun crawled slowly down towards the place where the sea met the sky. White sand stretched in a smooth arc between huge limestone karst cliffs. The only way into the bay was via boat, for a hundred Thai baht or thereabouts. This made it an isolated, paradisiacal spot that was popular with tourists and movie executives alike, neither of which could resist the allure of idyllic crystal blue waters, dense jungle foliage and soft, welcoming sand. Hotels hid in the shaded interior of the peninsula beyond the beach, a collection of low, squat buildings with bamboo trimmings, some luxurious, some not, some with designer infinity-type swimming pools and blissfully aggressive air conditioning, essential in the sweltering heat of the day, some with the ubiquitous bunkbeds of a hostel and piles of beaten-up backpacks stacked up against the back wall of the hostel bar. Some with hammocks, some with hot tubs, all with smiling, polite staff who were endlessly professional and accommodating.

The beach itself was crowded, as it always was at sunset. Holidaymakers and sunseekers sat on towels and blankets all across the sand, many with camera phones held out before them, ready and waiting for that all-important money shot as the sunset flexed its muscles and began for real. Behind, lights blinking through the palm trees, a dozen restaurants, where sun-burnished families and holidaymakers sipped on coconut smoothies garnished with bright pink flowers attached to straw stems. Cocktail shakers rattled out beneath varying soundtracks of electronica and chill that softly blepped out from speakers placed at intervals along the beach. Candles in glass holders flickered on tables and upon the sand itself. Laughter bubbled, rose and fell like eddies in the tide, and the air smelled of grilled fish and sea salt and that rich, deep, unique sweet perfume that nightfall brings to such places. The type of jasmine-infused perfume that makes a westerner realise, deep in their soul, that they are not at home anymore.

The type of perfume that does not exist in the suburbs of England, nor in the fells or highlands or lowlands, in cities, estates, castles, forests, marshlands, alleyways, carparks, ditches, coastal paths or mountaintops.

The woman sitting on the beach on a soft, multi coloured towel thought about this as the night crept ever closer. She was dressed in a thin white cotton kaftan and not much else. Her toes were buried comfortably in the sand, and she wriggled them often to feel the silky grains tickle past her skin, re-burying her feet over and over again as she enjoyed the sensation. She had a bright blue cocktail in a highball glass held in one hand, which was scarred and bruised from multiple cannula marks, but in the gathering dusk, nobody else could see this. Her body glowed from too much sun, but that hardly mattered now. Waves lapped ahead of her gently, a rhythmic sound not unlike the sound of a heart beating, and she closed her eyes against the blooming brilliance of the sunset before her, closed her eyes against the pinks and yellows and oranges and purples as bruised as her own skin, and she breathed in deeply, listening only to the ocean, and realised how much she loved to travel, how much she had longed for this moment, to leave England, to smell that tropical night air.

And gradually, as she soaked up all the bounties Railay had to offer, she became aware of another presence, sitting beside her on the beach towel.

She smiled without opening her eyes.

'This is my favourite place in all the world, you know,' she whispered, but the presence beside her said nothing, for it was forbidden. The rules said no conversation, conversation made things tricky. Conversation opened up the possibility for hesitation, and hesitation meant failure. The woman, who was tall and handsome, knew this intimately: she had once been a mysterious, silent presence for another, before her own sickness took control. Except she hadn't been as silent as she should have been, and she had regretted it afterwards, stepping quickly across the bustling chaos of the Piazza San Marco in Venice with her head held high whilst chaos unfolded behind her.

Why did you speak to him? She'd berated herself, slipping quietly into the crowds and long queues directly in front of the basilica. She had escaped only by the skin of her teeth, thanks to a series of items she'd stashed around the city to enable her escape: a wig, a different coat, a change of shoes, a new pair of sunglasses.

It was incredible how easy it had been, really, and she still thought about that, to this day. The ease of death. The ease of murder.

But was it murder?

She still couldn't say.

There was a shuffle, and the woman opened her eyes, reluctantly. A young man, no older than nineteen or twenty, sat beside her. He was hairless, and his eyes were haunted, older than they should have been. It must have taken a great effort to travel all this way, she knew, and this made her feel guilty, but he was here, and for that, the woman was also hugely grateful.

'It's okay,' she said softly, as the sun finally hit the waterline before them. 'I won't make you talk.'

The gathered crowds cheered, clapped and whistled at the demise of daylight, and the young man's hands trembled in his lap as he steeled himself for what he had promised he would do. There was a small bag on the sand next to him: inside, something caught the dying rays of light and gleamed red.

The woman smiled. She knew what he was going through, what he was feeling.

'Really, it's okay. This is what we signed up for, right? Just wait until the sun is gone completely, that's all I ask. Let me have the whole sunset.'

The man nodded, swallowing back tears, and did as she asked. As the sky flared with every colour imaginable, as glasses clinked and camera apps snapped, as laughter crescendoed and the waves lapped ever more urgently, the woman rested her head upon the strange young man's shoulder, her vision filled with brilliant, blood-orange light, and seconds after the last sliver of the sun sank below the waterline, the man drew a wooden-handled weapon out of the open bag. It had a long, thin, pointed blade not unlike a knitting needle in shape and size, only this was wickedly sharp steel, sanitised, unused, and he wrapped one arm around the woman, for all the world as if they were honeymooners at sunset, placed the point of the blade gently into her upturned ear canal as she continued to rest her head upon his shoulder, and then pressed in and *down*, sharply, firmly, a movement he had thought about and practised in his mind a thousand times prior to this point.

There was a crunch, a wet, grinding noise, and the woman stiffened, jerked a little as the needle pierced her brain. He withdrew the blade, and reinserted it, twice more. The woman finally went still, soft, limp, like a ragdoll. The young man continued to hold her, for she was warm and vital, something he himself had not felt for a long time.

He held her until all the colour bled from the sky, until the stars made their presence known one by one, and then he lay her softly on her back on the beach, eyes open to the constellations above, and before he left, he lay a single item upon her chest: a thick black business card, gilt-edged, embossed only with three initials: **F.W.F.** He would be getting his own card soon enough, he knew.

*

In Leverington, a small village in Cambridgeshire in the United Kingdom, an eighty-nine-year-old bachelor called Herbert Smith was found strangled to death in his tidy, well-appointed bungalow one morning in late July. His carer found him upon letting herself in on the Monday after a long weekend. She had come armed with his favourite newspaper and a host of medication, for she had collected his prescriptions for him prior to her visit. Instead of being greeted by his usual cheery *'ho there!'* upon entering the bungalow, she was met only with silence, which raised her hackles, for Herbert liked to start each morning by listening to the news broadcasts on Radio Norfolk at full volume, so loud in fact that she could usually hear it even at some distance from the house. Not that the neighbours ever complained about it: there were elderly couples who were similarly hard of hearing on either side of Herbert, for it was that type of street. Quiet, unassuming, manicured, a little tired around the edges, a street ornamented with cement statues of cherubs and animals, with hanging baskets and bird feeders and planters full of flowers, a street with low curbs and accessibility ramps to make it easier to get wheelchairs in and out, a street lived in by people who had bought their homes when young and full of energy, who had watched their children grow up, leave, make homes and families of their own, who had reverted to an inevitable state of loneliness and routine, content in some cases, acute in others. Herbert had been married once, a long time ago, but that marriage had ended many years back. His children still visited, although not as often as he would have liked, and none of them knew of his diagnosis, which was not good, but Herbert considered himself lucky for having lived such a long and full life, he said.

A life that was now at an end, and what an end it was, indeed.

When the carer, who was called Alison, found Herbert, she stood in total stillness for ten minutes straight as she tried to process the scene of his demise. He lay on his back upon his bed, atop the covers (she never could persuade him to upgrade his cotton coverlet to a duvet, even though blankets and sheets made twice as much work), completely naked. Around his neck, which was mottled blue and a dark, rusty red, a lacy bra had been tied, tight enough to act as a garotte. Each of his wrists was attached to his bed's headboard with handcuffs, only the handcuffs were

140

trimmed with jaunty pink fur, for they were designed to pleasurably restrain, not subjugate. There were lipstick kisses on his chest, face, inner thighs and in other places Alison didn't want to think about, and she considered herself a reasonably unflappable type, all things considered. Across Herbert's body, evidence of whip marks from a bright red leather riding crop which was later found nearby. Draped across his feet, a lacy pair of stained knickers, and dangling from one of his oversized testicles, a small shiny black stiletto, dainty and discarded with the heel firmly embedded in his withered ball sack. The other stiletto was under the bed. Just above his belly button: a dried string of semen. All of these things in themselves were shocking and out of character as far as Alison was aware when later questioned, for Herbert had seemed to be a sweet, mild, rather dull soul who liked tending his begonias and never so much as even drank on the weekend, unless you counted his occasional hot chocolates with the merest dash of rum, the same bottle that he'd been nursing for upwards of two years now. No, it was not the lingerie or the whip marks or the garotte or the shoes or even the strange business card that lay on his chest, a card embossed with the letters **F.W.F** that made Alison stand and stare, and stare, and stare, before rousing herself and calling the ambulance.

No, it was the smile on Herbert's purpled face. A smile of such bliss, of such relief, that Alison never forgot it, not for as long as she lived. Herbert had died happy, which is more, she said later, than could have been said for how he would have died had he continued to go about his daily routine as his insides progressively succumbed to disease.

The business card ended up where all the other cards ended up: bagged evidence in an unsolved murder case, which later became a cold case, one of many, a string of peculiar deaths that were connected somehow, although not one person from a wide range of international agencies or law forces could provide a credible explanation for how.

Nobody could figure out what **F.W.F** stood for, either. Internet searches revealed thousands of acronyms, none of which made sense in the context of the crimes. The dark web brought up nothing of any use, which in and of itself, was almost more suspicious, for anything and everything could be bought and sold upon the dark web, knowledge included, so whatever coordinated murder trend was taking place was evidently exclusive to the extreme. It indicated some sort of word-of-mouth agreement, a covert and clandestine order or movement of some description, but as no digital footprint could be found of any discernible type, black-carded mystery after mystery went unsolved for year after year after year. The closest any investigator got to a lead was when an enterprising young Danish man analysed one of the business cards and found it printed on a type of paper that was unique and in short supply, which only a few manufacturers had access to. After months of searching and cross-referencing order details, a small, exclusive printing press in Copenhagen was eventually determined to be the location where the cards were made, using an old-fashioned, hand operated letterpress from the turn of the century. Upon raiding the press building, however, cops found the entire place abandoned, cleaned out except for the press itself, which had been roundly dismantled. Subsequent examination of the broken device offered no further clues, and neither did looking at the rental agreements for the printing press who had been occupying the now empty building, for there were, simply, incredibly, no details to be found. Not a single paper trail. The building didn't even appear to belong to anyone, which was absurd, and so the Municipality quietly took ownership of it and decided to ask no further questions.

As various investigations ground wearily on, one detail apart from the business cards embossed with **F.W.F** tied the gathering number of deaths together: each victim was in possession of a fatal diagnosis or terrible prognosis of some description. Cancer was the most common affliction, it was discovered, followed in order of numbers by dementia, leukaemia, several neuro-degenerative disorders, cirrhosis of the liver, and heart disease. There was even a case of Fibrodysplasia Ossificans Progressiva, an extremely rare genetic condition rather brutishly known as 'Stone Man Syndrome', in which the afflicted party's muscle and connective tissue had slowly ossified and turned to bone. That particular 'victim' died in an enormous warm bath in Istanbul, surrounded by candles and rose petals, for floating in hot, mineral infused water, one could only assume, relieved the indescribable pressure and pain upon the body, even if by only a small amount. A powerful anaesthetic, it was later discovered, had been administered right before the man had been laid in the bath, and he had drowned there, peacefully.

*

On the Jungfrau Railway line that snakes through Switzerland en route to Europe's highest train station, also known as the 'top of Europe', situated some 11,332 feet above sea level on Jungfrau Mountain, a train tunnelled through a vast snowy panorama, its many shining windows reflecting a world of peaks and valleys, a landscape of extreme blues and whites with occasional patches of emerald green. It was a glorious day, crisp and clear, with high fluffy clouds and bright sunshine, a perfect day for a trip upon one of

Switzerland's most scenic train rides, and the Jungfraubahn service. This service ran regularly, catering mostly to tourists, tickets costing a not inexpensive sum. This particular train had a first-class carriage up front, a curious new addition that was empty except for two passengers, passengers who had paid for the privilege of being alone. It was a luxurious affair, this carriage, with chrome fixtures and fittings, finely upholstered seating, table service and a full al la carte menu, which on this particular day, although the train service was not usually so inclined, included caviar and champagne, if a person was tempted.

Emil, it turned out, *was* tempted, and ordered himself a bottle of Moet, which arrived promptly, beaded with drops of cold. The waiter who brought it, a silver-haired man with a bow tie, stiff collar and a lowered gaze, opened the bottle with a loud *pop!* And skilfully poured out two glasses, no mean feat on a train carriage that rocked and rattled as much as this one did. He filled each glass to the two-thirds mark to give the champagne room to breathe, bucketed the bottle in a chrome ice bucket that was mounted on the carriage wall next to the table, then placed the flutes carefully into little polished chrome holders fixed to the tabletop that were designed to stop drinks from sliding around as the train wound its way across mountainsides towards its final destination.

If anyone had been paying attention to the waiter, they might have seen him surreptitiously shake his sleeve, which was dragged down almost into his palm, over one of the champagne glasses as he mounted them in their holders, and they might have seen a certain amount of suspicious looking powder drop into the glass and dissolve amongst the bubbles, but nobody *was* looking, because the view outside was indescribably beautiful: snowy peaks with dragon's breath rising from the tips, deep valleys and crevasses, huge white plains that looked as if they had been iced like a cake with brilliant white fondant. Sky, blue, clear, high. A burning sun, doing its best to start the spring thaw. The stuff of picture postcards, of dreams, of oil paintings.

The waiter stepped back from the table calmly. The view was lost on him, for all he could feel was the irregular thump of his failing heart in his chest. Sweat gathered on his top lip, but his moustache disguised it, which was a relief. He folded something into the palm of his hand, placed it back into his jacket pocket, and then stood discreetly off to one side, waiting in case he was needed again. It took enormous effort to stand like that, statuesque and firm, but he willed himself into it, because he knew it wouldn't be long until he was no longer required.

Emil thanked the waiter with a tip of his index finger, and they exchanged glances, no words necessary. Contractually, no words allowed.

The waiter's mood matched Emil's as they briefly locked eyes: one of stillness. Of being in control, for the first time in a long time.

Emil picked up his champagne glass and sipped, rolling the fizzy crisp alcohol around his tongue, and wondered how long it would take for the poison to take effect. He wondered if it would hurt much, but pain was not something he was afraid of. Pain was a part of life, an inescapable symptom of being human. Meanwhile, the mountains continued to roll by, and Emil thought, happily, that he had never seen anything so beautiful, not since his son had been born and placed, wriggling and red, into his arms forty-seven years ago.

Emil's son Frederik took his own champagne flute reluctantly. Instead of sipping from it, he stared at the bubbles within miserably, a deeply-drawn frown upon his face. Emil felt bad for his son, for he could see what he was doing to him, but he remained resolute. Besides, the paperwork had been filed, the certificates signed, the emails sent, the contracts sealed. There was no turning back now, he knew. Frederick would have to come to terms with that, sooner or later. Sooner, with any luck, for Emil wanted to enjoy his last moments on this earth, for that was the whole point, wasn't it? Why else go through all this rigmarole?

'It's about choice, Frederik.' Emil spoke even though Frederik had not questioned him. 'It's a *choice*. I choose the way in which I die. I have autonomy over my own exit. I choose how I wish to leave this earth.'

Frederick pulled a face, pushed his glass aggressively back into its holder, chipping a tiny fragment from the base of it in the process. He didn't notice the damage. He was struggling, and he felt abominable for saying so out loud, but if he couldn't be honest with his own father now, face to face, across the table, he knew he would never get another opportunity.

'But *I* don't get to choose!' He cried, feeling his cheeks flush. 'I don't get to choose how to say goodbye to you, do I? Where am I in this decision-making process?'

A tear splattered onto the tabletop between them. Emil looked at it in shock: it was not in his son's nature to cry.

Frederik scrubbed a hand through his hair despairingly, aware of how selfish he sounded.

The old man extended a thin arm and blotted the tear with the tip of his index finger. His son's torment was horrible to see, but he knew it was necessary. Emil was dying anyway. The younger man was in the denial phase of grief, that shadowy, hollow mode of existence that made a person cling to what he had always known, certainties he had always taken for granted, instead of embracing the reality of the situation at hand and making the best of the time left to both of them. This was a process, Emil knew, and for that reason he remained calm and resolute.

'And how do I tell the kids? When your body is found. What should I tell them?'

'You tell them the truth. You tell them Grandpapa died happy, in exactly the way I always dreamed of.'

'Nobody dreams of dying, Dad. Nobody is that morbid.'

Emil sighed. The mountains outside really were spectacular.

'In some cultures,' he said, gently, 'death is nothing more than a beautiful certainty.'

Frederick shook his head. 'Don't lecture me Dad, not now. Fuck.'

Emil persisted. 'Some religions ask you to contemplate your own mortality every single day, to force you to come to terms with it. Some people believe that by thinking about it, your life can have great peace and balance, that fulfilment comes as part of the realisation that we all die in the end. Acknowledging death can be liberating, life changing. I choose to acknowledge mine. Further than this…I choose to direct my own end. Imagine that, Frederick. Complete control, right up until the very last breath. To leave this world, smiling, every single little detail accounted for. Who wouldn't want that? Who wouldn't want that for a loved one?'

Frederick picked up his drink again, calmer after his outburst. He knew the calm was temporary, for his heart was a maelstrom inside, but for now, he could drink the damn champagne, just like Papa wanted.

'So what is this secret, fucked up society, exactly?' He let the cold champagne drizzle down his throat slowly. He pulled a face after his first mouthful: it was sharper than he was used to.

'It is not a society so much as an…exclusive member's club,' Emil replied, sipping his own Moet with renewed gusto. 'Or a foundation, maybe. Yes, that's it. A foundation.'

The waiter, who was listening to everything with attentive ears, flinched as he heard this word.

Careful, he thought. *There are rules.*

The other two men paid no mind to him.

'Meaning you have to be rich to be a part of it?'

'Not at all. The foundation is open to anyone that fits the entry criteria, regardless of birthright or income. Those things are not important, it is only folk who lack belief in themselves who hold things like money and status up as paragons for others to aspire to.'

'But all this...it costs a fortune, surely? Even just logistically, the costs must be huge. How do people afford these grand, performative ends?'

Emil smiled wryly. 'There is a sort of credit process in place. A pay-it-forward form of credit, if you catch my meaning.'

Frederick looked disgusted. 'Like a pay-monthly scheme for your own death? Jesus, Dad, that's depressing. Money makes a difference; I don't care what you say. It shouldn't, but it does. Anyone who says money doesn't buy happiness has never been poor.'

Emil raised an eyebrow. 'You have never been poor either, Frederick. There is an expression, something to do with not looking the gift horse in the mouth, isn't there? You'll be well provided for, when I'm gone. You and the children, and Laurel.'

'That is not what I mean, and you know it. I never asked for your money. I worked for everything I have now on my own merit.'

Emil patted his son's hand to placate him. 'I know you did, darling boy. I know.'

Frederick gulped down more of the champagne, hoping it would take the edge off the conversation.

'Entry criteria?' He said, trying to change the subject.

'Naturally, one has to provide proof of one's diagnosis,' Emil replied, carefully. 'Otherwise, think how the system would be abused. I believe there were a few cases in the past of people forging their own medical records, but there are quite rigorous checks in place now to prevent that happening again.'

'So you're saying the only way you get in is if you're already dying?'

'In a manner of speaking, yes.'

Frederick rubbed his hands over his face, trying to process everything.

'And what else?'

'You do have to be willing to follow certain...rules.'

'The first rule of Death Club is that nobody talks about Death club?'

'Is that a reference to something?'

'Just answer the question, Papa.'

'Secrecy is required, yes. I should not be talking to you about this in quite so much detail, perhaps, but I feel I owe you some explanation.'

'Any other rules?' Frederick's head had begun to swim. The landscape outside suddenly appeared a good deal blurrier than it had before.

'You simply have to be willing to trade your death for another.'

'What?' Frederick stared.

'I told you, it's a credit system. It's simple. You get to dictate the manner of your death, and someone at the Foundation will see it carried out. In exchange, you have to be willing to do the same for another member. That way, we are all responsible, and yet none of us are, in the same breath.'

'You were serious? Like...paying death forward?'

'One good deed deserves another.'

'But...if you are all sick, terminally ill, how do you manage it? The travel? The...all of it?' Frederick put his champagne down, grimacing again.

Emil was still trying to explain how everything worked.

'People sign up for the service at various stages after their prognosis. And the ones that cannot physically be of service can still provide financial support, logistical support, help in other ways. Connections, resources. It's all done by word of mouth, no paper trail to speak of. All eventualities thought about. It's a marvellous thing, really it is, as organisations go. A well-oiled machine. Which the business of one's death should be, I rather think.'

Frederick realised he was sweating, even though he felt suddenly cold. 'I can't...I can't believe I'm having this conversation...' He whispered, running a finger around his shirt collar, which suddenly felt restrictive and tight. 'Is it hot in here? Or cold, I can't seem to...I can't tell.'

Emil frowned, looking at his son, at the glazed look that had come into the younger man's eyes.

Emil's own eyes then travelled down to the champagne glasses, both of which were now empty.

It dawned on him, suddenly: shouldn't the poison have started to take effect, by now? It had been a full five minutes, if not longer.

Shouldn't he be feeling something?

Emil shot a look across at the waiter, who had gone paler than pale. The deal was that Emil died on this train, alone, at peace with his son, and the waiter, who administered the poison, leaving just enough for himself, also got to die doing what he loved best: serving others. Riding the train. Carrying out his duties. Being useful, necessary, in service. A rather pathetic demise, in Emil's opinion, but then, death was uniquely personal, and...

The men locked their gaze, and in that moment, realisation hit.

Emil's stomach lurched.

Frederick, his lips now a distinct shade of purple, had enough time to grip his father's hand with his own, cold fingers, before leaning over and projectile vomiting a heap of bloodied pulp directly onto the floor of the train carriage.

Emil swore, and looked up at the waiter again with an expression of pure rage.

'You idiot!' He roared, anguished. 'You gave him the wrong fucking glass!'

Frederick began to convulse, his hands and head pummelling the tabletop in a frenzied rhythm. Wailing, Emil rushed around the table to hold his son as his body contorted, his face purpling, his eyes popping. This was not the death that had been promised. This was a terrible, undignified end, this was a life cut short with ragged disdain and flagrant ineptitude.

But these sorts of things aren't meant to happen, he thought frantically, as his son convulsed in his arms. *I was clear about the details! I signed forms and waivers!*

The waiter continued to stand stock-still off to one side, watching the grisly scene unfold in sheer horror.

How could he have gotten it wrong?

He'd been given such strict instructions.

He'd rehearsed his part, so many times.

Had anyone ever gotten it wrong before?

There had been that one case, of the woman who had eaten herself, but that had been a question of interpretation. She'd been helped, as was her wish, only she'd not been entirely honest when she'd placed her order, and the delineation between crime and culprit and perpetrator had been muddied, and the rules had been swiftly changed, after that: cannibalism was not allowed, not even of the aided, self-inflicted variety, and...

The waiter began to shake, violently. His pain medication often made him confused, foggy. He must have switched glasses without realising. An honest mistake, a terrible accident.

An honest...

'Shit,' he whispered, his eyes huge saucers in his face. He fumbled for the remainder of the powdered poison, folded in a paper wrap in his pocket. The last measure, his measure. He was only supposed to take it after the old man had passed. Quietly, in one of the train toilets. No fuss.

The waiter fumbled the packet, and dropped it. He fell to his knees, scrabbling for the paper wrap with uncooperative fingers.

Frederick arched his back, strained like a fish on a hook against his father's arms, then collapsing forward onto the table-top, stone dead. Foam and blood leaked from the young man's lips. His eyes bugged, the vessels broken.

Then, there was only the noise of the train's wheels upon the track beneath the carriage. The uncaring mountains outside sped by like implacable gods, the affairs of the tiny humans below them insignificant, transient affairs, like the lives of tiny insects buzzing upon the surface of a faraway lake.

Emil looked at the waiter, his heart broken clean upon his face, which was wet with tears.

'Please,' he begged, pitifully. 'Please, you owe me my death! That was the deal! *Please!'*

The waiter nodded and reached once again for the small wrap of paper. Finally, he got a hold of it, and with great effort rose to his feet, passing the poison to the old man, along with a shiny, crisply cut rectangle of black card from another pocket. As his fingertips brushed against the card, he could feel the slightly raised ridges of lettering, embossed in gold.

'There...there should be enough left,' he croaked, and then, unable to stay any longer, unable to watch, he turned and staggered along the length of the carriage, through the connecting doors, feeling stunned by his own incompetence, moving as fast as his hollow legs would allow, until he reached the very end of the train, where he broke a window using the emergency hammer, climbed through it, and threw himself out of the carriage.

His body was found months later in a deep canyon thousands of metres below, frozen solid, almost unrecognisable from the trauma and impact after his long fall. When an autopsy was performed, it was found that the waiter, whose real name was Jacques, had been terminally ill, a brain tumour the size of a golf ball having attached itself to a part of his anatomy that made any operation and permanent treatment impossible.

Emil unfolded his paper wrap with numb fingers and found, to his desperate relief, a small pile of powder, enough for purpose, he hoped. He tipped it into his champagne glass, topped up his glass as best he could, for the bottle was heavy, swirled the mixture to make sure it was properly dissolved, then gulped the entire concoction down as quickly as he was able.

His death was poor compensation for the one lost to him. He couldn't help but think, as burning fire began to bloom in his chest, that although his mortality was inarguable, and his demise inevitable, it was unfair. Holding his cooling son's body in his arms made him realise that death was a good deal more complicated than he'd given credit to, and with that realisation came shame, for he had been naive and stupid, and his stupidity had ended the life of a wonderful man long before time. Emil realised that he was a murderer's accomplice, when all was said and done, for he had commissioned this scene, the specifics, the scenery, the poison, commissioned it as man commissioned a painting, or a poem, or a hit on another, only the hit was supposed to have been aimed in one direction.

Emil's eyes dropped to the black business card the waiter had thrust at him, the one with the gold lettering, F.W.F, bold and centred. There had been such an air of sophistication about the whole thing, Emil thought sadly, as his organs started shutting down, one by one, under the poison's influence, but the sophistication hadn't been real. What was real was the secretive organisation profiting from the pain and desperation of so many, and masquerading as some sort of social...

Emil didn't get to finish the thought. His eyes blurred. Spittle and blood drooled from his own, now blue lips. His body rolled heavily into the train carriage aisle, where it lay for the remainder of the train's journey through the mountains, until it was eventually discovered when checks were carried out at the final station.

When the train conductor, who had been told to steer clear of the first-class carriage until the very end, entered the luxurious car, he discovered the macabre, chaotic scene, and thought it resembled something from a detective novel from a different era. Two bodies, one seated at the table, face and lips livid with death, another sprawled on the floor, lying atop bloody vomit and broken glass, features contorted.

The conductor drew out his phone. Took pictures, despite knowing he shouldn't.

As he lined up each shot, he spotted something unusual. Pinching the screen of his phone, he zoomed in on the tabletop, then went over to the table itself, where father and son had been seated only an hour before.

And there, the conductor found that Emil, dying, angry, determined to receive some late justice for his son, had scrawled three words in his own crimson spittle.

They read:

FINAL WISH FOUNDATION

A black business card lay face down in a puddle of spilled champagne next to the message.

The gold lettering could no longer be seen, but that hardly mattered.

The conductor *tsk-tsked*, pocketed the soggy card, wiped the spittle lettering away with a napkin from a neighbouring table.

Then, he left the carriage to call for help.

*

The deaths were declared a murder-suicide, perpetrated by Emil. No motive was ever declared, and no real details were ever published, but for several years after, the black business cards were conspicuous by their absence.

Until a body was found under a bridge in Amsterdam, pulverised, skin ruptured and ruined, insides on the outside, a song playing on an old, battery-powered CD player hidden in a bush nearby. It was a sweet song, a song about an ordinary world, and it played over and over on loop, even as the batteries started to drain and the body next to the device also drained itself of fluid, of life, of suffering, until the only thing that remained was a cold corpse clutching a black rectangle of card embossed expensively with three letters: **F.W.F.**

Another card to add to a growing collection, contributed to by many, curated by none. Just an assortment of cards, like an assortment of lives, their purpose fulfilled, now boxed, filed, and forgotten about.

A SONG FOR SAM

I decided to kill my brother on the flight to Norway.

When ideas like that come into a man's head, intrusive, wriggling, nasty-noodly thoughts about murder and death and violence, of digging your thumbs into the soft parts of another man's face, of pulling and poking and tearing and ripping and biting down hard, until flesh squeaks, until eyeballs pop, until things burst under the pressure of quiet denial, of years of bottled rage and subdued resentment, the last thing you want is to be trapped in a flying tin can redolent with other people's farts with minimal legroom and nowhere to go but your own static-stuffed brain for seven hours and fifteen minutes, but circumstances being what they were, I had no choice. I sat in my narrow, uncomfortable seat with the faulty armrests that cut into my forearms next to the woman who stank like burnt toast and the old man who kept sucking on his false teeth and needed to pee every hour, on the hour, and festered in my own hate as the quiet, sibilant voice in the back of my mind told me over and over again that this was it.

The time had come.

It had to be now, on this trip, or never.

My brother had to die.

*

I *had* put up with his shit for long enough, I told myself as the plane prepared for take-off. His end was long overdue. I'd wanted to kill Sean since the day he was born. He should consider himself lucky I'd allowed him to live out this much of his stress-free, silver-spoon existence, really.

And it wouldn't be a bad way to go. In Norway, on top of a mountain, surrounded by the pristine snow, under the glow of the northern lights.

Under the crackle, hiss, and whistle of the aurora.

Not many people know the northern lights give out sound, but they do. There is proof, if you don't believe me. Scientists recorded it in Finland. The strongest auroras actually *sing*. The release of static charge into the atmosphere makes music human ears shouldn't be able to hear, especially as the phenomenon usually dances about sixty miles up in the sky, but Dad always swore to us that he'd heard it, once. He'd heard Aurora's song, in Canada, travelling with Mom when they were young, in a place called Churchill. They'd walked out to watch the lights in the middle of the night and heard them fizzing.

'It was like fireworks, kids,' he'd told us, eyes full of stars. 'Like the best fireworks you've ever seen.'

According to Dad, that was the night I was conceived, under the singing skies as they shifted from green to blue to pink to a deep, dazzling red. I believed the story of my own creation right up until the moment I didn't, when I realised that Dad, as much as I loved him, was full of shit. This was right around the time he swore you could hear the sun sizzling as it went down over the ocean, if you listened really hard, which I later found out was a line he got from a movie. Sean lapped it up, of course, but I saw right through these whimsical musings, these magical tales.

At heart, Dad didn't believe in magic or singing auroras or sizzling sunsets.

At heart, Dad was as broken as I was.

He just wasn't as honest about it as me.

Sean's death would be honest, though. I would make sure of it. I would give him a better death than most people got.

Depending on how easily he went down, that was.

If he fought, it might get messy.

But my baby brother had never been much of a fighter. It wasn't his style.

*

How exactly I was going to murder my brother, I wasn't sure yet. I wasn't a detailed oriented sort of person. I was a more spur-of-the-moment, make-it-up-as-you-go-along sort of person, at least up until the point at which fratricide entered my head.

But in that small window of time in which I was lucid (and there haven't been many of those since), grappling with my seatbelt as it dug into my gut and trying to find somewhere to put my legs- which you wouldn't have thought would be an issue on a brand new Boeing 747, but the airline had prioritised money over comfort and crammed as many of us in as was legal- the intent was enough.

The trick was to make sure the gap between intention and action didn't stretch too wide.

Anyway, before I could touch my dear darling little brother, I reminded myself as the pre-flight safety demonstration started, I had to dispose of Dad.

As per his request.

I struggled to try and keep those two objectives separate in my mind.

Dad first.

Then Sean.

Sean.

Even the sound of his name set my teeth on edge.

Sssseaaaannn.

A snake hiss, impossible to pronounce without a drawl. The name itself sounds entitled, doesn't it? Arrogant.

Too many fucking vowels.

Sounded a whole lot better when you added a couple of words after, though.

Sean Has To Die.

Capitalise the first letter of each word, for dramatic emphasis.

S, for Sssssssssseannn.

S for static, *ssssssss-*

*

The flight was supposed to be my chance to 'bond' with my brother, according to Dad's plan, but Sean apparently had a backlog of air miles, so had himself upgraded to first class, which meant we couldn't sit together.

'Sorry,' he shrugged, when I'd glared at him as we approached the check-in desk at JFK. 'I've just got so much work to do, I need peace and quiet. You don't mind, do you?'

'No,' I lied, because I had gotten good at it. 'Not at all.'

And naturally, because that was how it went with us, I was stuck in the back of the plane, near the toilet cubicles, which stank.

Twenty minutes into our flight, Sean texted me on his complimentary wifi. I had to pay for internet, but I could only afford an hour, and the smug asshole knew that, timing his message very deliberately so as to ensure I'd see it.

How's it going in Economy, cheapskate?

He said.

This was immediately followed by a smug selfie of him wearing a shit-eating grin, legs up in his fancy little cubicle, brandishing a full champagne flute in one hand, and flipping me the bird with his middle finger up against the glass stem.

I didn't answer.

I put the energy into plotting his murder, instead.

*

My resentment for Sean swelled as we roared over the Atlantic Ocean until I thought I would choke on it, until it filled my brain like the white snow you used to get on old TV sets when you couldn't tune into a station. A blizzard of bitterness, envy and hurt, swirling frantically in my aching head. My rancour was heightened by the circumstances surrounding our enforced excursion to Norway.

Namely, my father's death.

Dad had arranged everything before he died, secretly, right down to the last detail, booking flights, hotel rooms, tour guides, hiring a car. How he'd done all that whilst being so sick I do not know, but I suppose impending mortality is as much of a motivator to get shit done as any.

'Take my ashes with you,' his last will and testament had instructed. *'Take them and scatter them beneath the northern lights. Honour me one last time. I love you both so very, very much.'*

Sean had been as pissed about the unexpected trip as I was. He ranted about work and time away from the office and commitments at home, but I knew he wasn't mad about those things, not really. I knew what he was really doing. He was ramming his commitments down my throat, because I didn't have any. I was single, childless, and trapped in a deadbeat job I didn't care about and couldn't wait to get away from.

Thinking about this, and the jar of ashes now bundled up in Sean's backpack- which was, hopefully, safely wedged into his overhead locker in a way that meant it couldn't fall out- made my chest hurt. I clipped and unclipped the buckle of my seatbelt over and over to compensate for the sudden lack of control I felt about my situation, about Dad's final wishes, about the act of killing another man, but it didn't help much. The thoughts eddied and chased each other around like wind-blown snowflakes, and my ears began to ring with a faint buzz I couldn't seem to shake.

I popped a sleeping pill when I realised how obsessive my ruminations and fiddling were getting. Sometimes, sleep was the only way out of the thought loops that kept me spinning like a faulty carousel set to the highest, most nauseating speed. The chemically-induced slumber would take me through the majority of the flight, I hoped.

As I drifted off, the engine drone dragging me down like a drowning man, I had a sudden, violent fantasy of the plane hitting a pocket of turbulence. Of the overhead lockers popping open, of Sean's bag tumbling out, of the stone urn containing our father's mortal remains smashing into pieces, of dark, gritty ash filling the plane's interior. Passengers choked on the dead man's dust, breathing in the remnants of my last, lingering connection to decency, but then thankfully, the pills kicked in properly, and I knew nothing except oblivion until Sean woke me up hours later, at our end destination: Tromsø airport.

'Come on, loser,' he said, smacking my shoulder hard, harder than he needed to. 'Wake up. We're here.'

*

It was snowing in Tromsø. I liked how it felt on my skin as I exited the stuffy, dry air of the plane and crossed the short distance to the terminal. I watched a flake melt on the back of my hand and shuddered involuntarily.

If only thoughts melted as easy, I pondered.

Sean pulled out his phone, began tapping away at his emails once more as we stood in the small customs queue. I watched his thumbs work up and down his screen and it occurred to me that we could have been anywhere in the world, for all my brother cared.

I dug an elbow into his ribcage, hard.

'Dude,' I said, knowing he hated the word 'dude'.

'What? Get off me,' he replied, irritably.

'Did you seriously fly halfway round the world to Norway to check emails? Come on. It's not like you didn't have seven hours on the plane to catch up.'

Sean didn't stop tapping at his screen.

'Look, Norway was Dad's thing, not mine,' he said. 'I'm only here because…'

I folded my arms and glared at my little brother.

'Because what?'

Sean looked up from the email he was composing.

'Fine,' he sighed, pressing 'send' and pocketing his phone. 'It can wait.'

I placed a hand on his shoulder. I hated touching him, it made me want to chew my own arm off from the shoulder down, but I had to lull him into a false sense of security.

Sean was smart, see. He'd be able to sense something was up if I wasn't careful.

Softly, softly, catchy fishy.

'I'm sure the company will survive three days without you.' I forced myself to speak in a kind, patient voice. 'It's not like you take vacations all the time, is it? They can cope.'

Sean smiled a thin, strained smile and subtly shook my hand off. He started tugging on his right ear, hard, a nervous habit he'd picked up more recently.

'I wouldn't call this a vacation. More of a…'

I finished his sentence for him. 'A duty. I know.'

We both looked at the backpack resting between Sean's feet.

The dynamics had changed a lot between us since our Father's death. Sean didn't feel the need to keep up the pretence anymore, of being the good-natured, amenable baby of the family. The golden child. The chosen one. He had stepped over Dad's expectations of him and grown distant, cool. Self-important. He placed himself firmly at the top of the pecking order, appointed himself Most

Important Person in our family. Dad had solidified this ascension by doing two momentous things: handing over the family business to Sean, and then dying.

The King is dead, long live the King.

I hoped this trip would change that.

*

The customs officer who stamped my passport asked me if I was visiting Tromsø for business or pleasure.

I lied and said the latter. There wasn't an option for 'I'm here to scatter our dad's ashes beneath the natural phenomenon known as the aurora borealis and then murder my brother.'

I wouldn't have had the energy to explain further if there had been.

The officer waved me through with a smile. Sean and I made our way across the arrivals lounge, collected suitcases from the luggage belt, and went out into the slushy night to pick up our hire car, which had special metal studs on the tires in readiness for winter.

'I'll drive,' Sean said.

I didn't argue.

I figured, I had been putting on the 'passive big brother' act for forty-three years, I could keep it going a little while longer.

*

Tromsø's roads, we quickly found, went down under a lot of rock, largely because there was a whole-ass mountain separating the airport from downtown Tromsø. Tunnels took us out from the flurries of snow that splattered against the windscreen and plunged us into a brightly lit subterranean highway system complete with roundabouts, parking lots dug out of small caves, and underground garages illuminated with neon lights.

'This is insane,' Sean said, taking a hand off the wheel periodically to tug his ear. The gesture was getting obsessive, like a nervous tic. I could see how red the earlobe was getting, like he'd been tugging at it the whole flight.

Was he nervous about being around me?

Did he suspect?

Probably just stress, I thought, trying to stay calm.

I knew the feeling. The weird buzzing sound in my head was getting louder, harder to ignore. Not exactly static, not exactly white noise either, but something in between the two. I wondered if the

157

flight had damaged my hearing, somehow. Perhaps the pressure in the cabin had been a little off, if such a thing was possible.

'It's like there's a whole other city down here under the surface,' I replied, trying to take my mind off the noise.

'Apocalypse proof,' Sam said, still tugging at his ear.

It was eerie under the mountain, and I realised I was enjoying the ride as we purred along the immaculately maintained tunnels.

I gave myself a little grace to do so.

No reason not to mix business with pleasure, I thought, as rough-cut rock walls sped past.

We followed the signs for SENTRUM and parked in an underground lot that was as close as we could get to our hotel. A narrow set of stairs led back up to the surface. Sean struggled with his bags up the steps, swearing. I let him struggle. He'd always had it too easy, with Dad literally jumping to do anything for him the moment he snapped his fingers. It was satisfying to see him bark his shins against his huge suitcase, and yelp in pain. I'd told him to pack light, but Sean never listened to me.

I did keep a close eye on the backpack containing Dad's ashes, though, ready to catch it if my brother let it slip off his shoulder.

He didn't.

Soon enough we were standing topside in the snow, peering at a map on my phone.

'This way,' I said, confidently, and set off in the direction of main street.

'Do we really have to walk?' Sean moaned, dragging his case behind him. 'Don't they have uber out here?'

'It's like three streets over,' I said, striding ahead. 'Not far at all.'

The city centre was a compact, eclectic mix of historic timber-clad buildings with cute window frames and bright paintwork in shades of mustard, green and blue, nestling up against grim, brutalist concrete structures from the seventies, built with no aesthetic value in mind at all, only practicality. There were hotels and hostels all over, a few cars on the streets but not many, and festive lights strung up around all the trees and lampposts. We passed a tiny wooden hut with a white-crusted pointy roof serving mulled wine and hotdogs out of a small hatch to passersby. With the snow falling, it looked like a scene from a Christmas card: romantic, fanciful, like one of Dad's stories. I'd heard Tromsø referred to as 'the Paris of the north' once, but I didn't know much about that. I had never been to Paris, and probably never would, not now.

Sean had, though.

Sean had proposed to his wife Emma in Paris, beneath the Eiffel tower, a cliched fucking move if ever there was one, not least

158

because proposing to a woman- or, to be precise, proposing to Emma- beneath the Eiffel tower had always been *my* idea.

Ever since I was a kid.

Our mother had been French.

When she died shortly after giving birth to Sean, I made up my mind. I would go to France, eat onion soup, order 'chocolat chaud', kiss a pretty woman beneath the pretty metal tower, then get down on one knee and ask her to marry me. I knew what I wanted right from the moment I lost it, unequivocally. Travel, find a wife, start a family, grow old together. Find acceptance. Find a place I could call home. People I could call home, too. I wanted that white-picket life more than anything, more than money or sex or fame or notoriety.

I wanted the life my dad promised my mom.

I thought I'd found someone I could share all those things with, too.

Until Sean stole Emma clean out from under my nose.

And my proposal.

Because there was nothing original about my sibling, not one thing. He was derivative, genetically, psychologically, emotionally. He was me, with revisions. He had watched me like a hawk since he was old enough to toddle after me, waited and watched as I made mistakes and learned shit the hard way, so he didn't have to, then he went out and did everything I couldn't, because I'd shown him all the multitude of ways a man could fuck up, if he put his mind to it. Sean learned from my errors and used my mistakes like stepping stones to his own future.

He was not stupid, I had to give him that.

Little shit was smart as a razor, but I was smarter.

And more patient.

'No hard feelings, hey, bro?' He'd said, grabbing me in a fake display of affection on his wedding day. Emma, his new wife, my ex, had blushed and ducked out of our clumsy huddle. She knew there were a lot of hard feelings, but ultimately, when it came down to it: my feelings didn't matter, to her, to my brother, or the wider family, who accepted Emma as readily as Sean's wife as they had accepted her as my girlfriend.

And what the family said, went.

I would never get over the feeling of watching her say 'I do,' though.

Like fire ants pouring out of my heart, then consuming me whole.

'No hard feelings,' I'd said, through a grimace.

But there were.

Back in Tromsø, my hands twitched in the cold air, aching to wrap themselves around my brother's throat. The noise was back, too, the weird, staticy *shhhhhhhh* that wouldn't be silenced. It was almost like an alarm, yanking me back to the present, reminding me I had a job to do.

Patience, I thought, as we dragged our suitcases through the snow.

*

Our hotel was clean, modern, soulless. The single large window in our room looked directly out over an expanse of water called the Tromsøysundet strait, over which several massive bridges spanned. Twinkly car lights crawled across them, towards the suburbs of Tromsdalen, another part of the city that lay under the Storheisen mountain on the other side of the straight. The distinctive triangular shape of the Arctic Cathedral squatted over there too, as geometrically pleasing as it was imitative of the mountain behind.

Beyond the cathedral, a cable car station called Fjellheisen lifted tourists to the top of mount Storsteinen, to a Tromsø city viewpoint. There was a restaurant up there too, I'd been told, and several hiking paths that led all over the mountainside. It was the perfect spot to see northern lights from, according to Dad's research. I figured the old man would have liked it up there, with the city lights and river spread out below. He'd always liked being up high.

Sean, on the other hand, hated heights. I was looking forward to seeing his face as he climbed into the cable car and got hoisted up the mountain enormously.

Plus, it was a whole lot easier to lose a body on a mountaintop than anywhere else.

That was for tomorrow, though.

For now, I had to play nice.

If I was going to survive another hour in Sean's company without shooting my load too soon and beating his head in with the bedside table lamp, however, I was going to need a drink.

Maybe even two.

Perhaps that would help me shake off the persistent tinnitus buzz still building in my ears.

*

The Rorbua pub was two buildings along, in the harbourside area.

Inside, it was all wooden walls, shipping memorabilia, candles, music posters, and beer jugs hanging from the ceiling. A giant stuffed polar bear waited to greet us by the door as we walked in. I got up close to the bear, to check it was real, not fake, like Sean insisted. The once magnificent animal was positioned rigidly up on its hind legs, jaws open, teeth bared, paws boxing the air.

'Poor thing,' Sean said, staring at it.

'Hunting is a big part of the history of this place,' I said, shrugging. Dead was dead, in my view. No point in feeling sorry after the event. That was wasted energy. Like grief. Grief was as pointless as remorse, I thought, after mom died. You can't put death back in the bottle after its spilled out. It doesn't work that way.

Although you can, apparently, fuck with the living long after you've died.

As Dad was fucking with me, right now.

He had, it seemed, no compunctions in shamelessly using his inevitable death as an excuse to bridge the gap that had formed between his two warring sons and, by forcing them to travel together to some remote part of the world to dispose of his ashes, he no doubt hoped to engineer some sort of crude truce between us.

A reunion, maybe.

I wondered how he could ever have been so naive as to imagine us hugging, back-slapping, joking around.

As if the past thirty years or so had never happened.

As if Sean hadn't ripped his way through my mother and killed her on his way out of her womb.

As if Emma hadn't been stolen away.

As if the family business hadn't been ripped out of my hands, right when I was starting to get the hang of things. Shareholders, Dad had said, but I knew the real reason. The real reason was Sean, always Sean.

Can't put his particular brand of poison back in the bottle either, not one drop of it.

A man's actions had consequences, Dad always taught us.

I would honour that, if nothing else.

*

I stared at Sean as he ordered beers from the low-ceilinged bar, pointing to an illuminated pump with another polar bear on it.

I didn't think it was possible to hate another human being as much as I hated him, but here we were.

I knew enough about human psychology to understand that my hatred came from jealousy. I'd been jealous of Sean since the day he'd arrived, all pink and bawling and covered in white milky stuff with congealed blood coating his perfect blonde curls. Our mother had held him out to me and told me to give him a kiss, which

I hadn't wanted to do, largely because, at the tender age of ten, I'd thought my brand new baby brother looked more like a weird, malignant tumour than a human child. I'd been so scared of the way his face was all scrunched up and the way his fists were clenched into tight little angry balls that I'd backed up until I hit a wall, shaking my head.

'Where are his eyes?' ten-year-old me had said. 'Why doesn't he have eyes?'

My mother had laughed weakly, attempting to latch the baby onto her breast. This frightened me even more. Why was the baby sucking the life from my mother? Was it a vampire?

My Dad had put a comforting hand on my head. 'Don't be scared, Sam,' I remember him chuckling. 'He has eyes, he just can't use them yet. You were the same when you were born. He'll be cute in a few hours, you'll see.'

I had not believed him, and anyway, it wouldn't matter how much cuter he would get, because I was jealous of the baby, and that jealousy would fester like an untreated wound over the years until decades later, when, on a flight out of New York, as cramp gripped my right leg and my substandard instant coffee slipped off the tray table in front of me, splattering my left leg in boiling brown liquid, I decided, at last, to do something definitive about the cankerous hate in my heart.

Because it was eating me up like the ants, I realised, my teeth now vibrating with the escalating static buzz.

And soon, there would be nothing of me left.

Tomorrow, I told myself firmly.

Tomorrow.

'You would not believe how fucking expensive these beers were.'

Sean returned to our table with two gleaming pints. He set one down in front of me. 'The most expensive fucking beer I've ever bought in my life. You'd better enjoy it.'

'I'm sure you can afford it,' I said, raising the glass and sipping luxuriously. 'How is business doing these days, anyway?'

Sean gave me a look. 'Don't start, okay? Just don't. Dad left me the business for a reason, you know that.'

The beer turned sour on my tongue. I swallowed it down with difficulty.

'Oh I know the reason,' I muttered darkly.

Sean sighed, spoke to me as if speaking to a child.

'You had your shot at it, Sam. Dad left you in charge and you fucked it up. So he gave the company to me. Don't make me feel bad about it. You ran us into massive debt that I'm only now beginning to get a handle on. Not to mention the fuck up with the taxes. You're lucky we didn't get completely screwed by the IRS.'

I said nothing, although it took every ounce of restraint. That was not how things had happened at all, but I couldn't say that, not without causing a scene. Sean had to think I'd moved on past all that.

Still, I couldn't resist one final dig.

'How's Emma?' I asked, in as neutral a tone as I could master.

Sean tugged on his raw right earlobe, hard, and then on his left.

'Don't be a dick, Sam,' he said.

The buzz in my head got a little louder.

*

The beer slid down easily. I managed to guilt Sean into ordering another. A band started playing upstairs: folk music, followed by repurposed rock songs. Tourists and locals sang along as the snow came down thicker outside.

'I hope it clears up by tomorrow,' Sean said, gazing out a window. 'We can't see the lights if it snows.'

'The forecast looks good,' I reassured him, pulling out my phone to prove the point. 'See?'

Sean frowned as he stared at my phone through beer-goggles. He clumsily thumbed the screen to try and get a better look at the forecast results, and accidentally closed the browser window.

My phone background suddenly glared out at him: a picture of Emma and I when we had been together, tiled over with social media apps, a clock, a media player. Emma and I were hugging and smiling at each other happily through the bright, garish icons.

Sean stared at the phone, then at me. He started tugging on both earlobes, simultaneously, not even knowing he was doing it. I saw a small red crack open up on the soft skin around his right ear.

I flipped the phone so it lay face down.

'Never got round to changing it, I guess,' I said, by way of explanation.

Sean said nothing, and went to order another beer.

*

Something odd happened the longer we sat in the pub.

I began to have a change of heart.

The more drunk we got, the less I felt like killing my brother, which was not something I expected after being so determined on the flight. It was like the beer dissolved all my bad feelings. For the first time, I started to see in Sean what everyone else obviously saw.

I got to witness the golden child in all his unrestrained, charming glory. The further down his pint glass he got, the more he relaxed, and as he relaxed, his eyes lit up, and his sense of humour came out. He put all talk of work to one side, and became almost boyish again. We started reminiscing about things that Dad used to say and do, then moved onto tv shows we liked, books we'd read.

As the music swelled louder and glasses clinked harder, I unclenched my own ass a little. I could feel resentment slipping off me like melting snow off a sun warmed roof. Was Dad's plan working? I couldn't ever remember sitting and having a real conversation with my brother like this, not once. The ten-year age gap made that too difficult when we were kids. Now we were adults, I was shocked to discover how much we had in common beyond genetics. Sean told me about his love for Bjork, for the paintings of Van Gogh, for bourbon and trees in autumn. I told him about my fossils, my obsession with impressionist art. We agreed on politics, and agreed to disagree over our taste in films: he was a remake kid, I liked the originals. We laughed. At one point, I found myself sitting with an arm slung over his shoulder in real brotherly affection.

The buzz had subsided in my mind, too.

I realised in horror that I was enjoying myself again.

Just a man on a vacation with his brother, shooting the shit, having fun.

I switched to water as soon as I understood what was happening.

Sean didn't.

He had another two beers, and ordered shots.

And then he had to bring Emma into it.

'It's not like I meant to take her away from you,' he slurred, and I almost took his hand and shook it, to thank him for reminding me of how much of a prick he could be under the veneer of geniality he cultivated so fiercely.

'You sure about that, Sean?' I asked, carefully as I could.

He nodded. 'Sure. I never set out to steal her, or anything. It just…it just happened, y'know? You had that party and I had just broken up with…with…whatever her name was, and I was so fuckin sad, and Emma was just…she was nice to me, Sean. She took care of me.'

'She was my girlfriend. Of course she was nice to you. You were my family.'

Sean gave me a look over the top of his shot glass. 'C'mon, Sam. It wasn't just that. She was attracted to me. I could tell. I can always tell.'

He flexed his arm muscles then, giggling.

I wrapped myself up in freshly laid hate as we staggered back to our hotel after closing time.

It kept me warm as the snow continued to fall.

And the static buzz came back with a vengeance.

*

It wasn't just that Sean was better looking than me, although that was a big part of it. He was taller, fitter, had hit the gym a lot earlier in his development than I had. His arms were twice the size of mine and he never wasted an opportunity to remind me of this whenever we saw each other, rolling up his sleeves or showing up in ridiculously tight-fitting shirts in order to drive the point home.

It wasn't that he had more hair than me, when mine was starting to retreat up my forehead and go grey in places I didn't think possible.

It wasn't even that he'd inherited the business, stolen my wife, and pushed me out of my own life like a baby cuckoo shunts its other nestlings out so it can have all the attention.

It was, I thought the next morning as we ate breakfast, hungover, jetlagged and dehydrated, because he'd killed my mother.

And that was reason enough.

'Have you noticed it's still, like, dark outside?' My brother broke the silence in a gravelly, pained voice.

I nodded. 'It's almost polar night, I think,' I replied. 'The sun kind of hides behind the mountains for three months or something. It's like constant twilight, instead. That's why everything looks kind of blue.'

'How do you know so much about all this shit, anyway,' Sean said, disinterested.

'Because of Dad, I guess,' I said.

'Huh. At least it stopped snowing.' A snow plough drove past the hotel, piling dirty white slush into two mounds on either side of it, as if to prove the point.

'I told you,' I replied, checking my weather app again. 'Everything's going perfectly to plan.'

*

Breakfast helped. So did coffee, a little.

We went back to the room, packed our gear for the mountain. Warm clothes, head torches, dad's urn, collapsible hiking poles, a flask made with powdered hot chocolate from the room. I tried to create the impression that we were both returning to the hotel

165

room, rather than just one of us, but it was hard to keep the deception running when I had a loud, insistent static occupying my brain.

The buzz had swelled during the night to a furious crackling reverb that now filled every part of my head. Bright lights hurt to look at. I had not slept a wink. Sean had slept soundly, drunk as a pig, grunting and spluttering and rolling over and over until dawn. He pulled on his ears all night, so they bled on his pillow. He had to put sticking plaster over each earlobe to stop them leaking down his neck.

Sean wanted to carry the stone jar with dad inside up the mountain in his backpack, but I refused him this time. I had plans for that urn, and needed it firmly in my grasp. It was heavy, and solid, just the right amount of solid to crack a grown man's skull, if wielded correctly.

Little brother was too jaded to argue with me, so I wrapped Dad up in a large sweater and stuffed him in my own backpack, itching to get on with it all.

'Ready?' I asked, patting myself down like Dad used to when he lost his keys.

'No,' Sean said, groggily, but I didn't care if he was or not.

*

'This is really fucking high,' Sean said, as the cable car rose slowly up the mountainside. Not that I could hear him that well. His voice was muffled by the static, and I was learning to lip-read, out of necessity, staring at Sean's lips constantly in case I missed something.

He didn't seem to notice. He had his own distraction, and was pulling on his ears again. Fresh blood leaked through the sticking plaster, staining his fingertips. His skin was pale, with a greyish tinge to it. I couldn't tell if he was still hungover, or if it was something else. He had this weird, far-away look in his eyes, like he could hear something I couldn't, and it was taking all his focus.

Does he have the buzz too? I wondered, suddenly.

That would be just like him, wouldn't it.

Find something unique to me, and commandeer it.

Edit, and revise, nobody will know a thing.

Tromsø spread out below us in miniature, white-dusted and surrounded by mountains and water. Tree tips passed beneath us, leafless and dark against the snow hugging their roots. We passed over cliffside with long icicles dangling from rocky clefts. We had the car to ourselves, which was good, because it meant I didn't have to try and hide the discomfort I was in. Searing pain stabbed my head if I turned it too fast. Even blinking had become painful. My eyes watered constantly. I winced at every jolting movement the car made as it rolled up its cable to the mountain top.

When we got to the upper station, we found a sliver of sun. The sky was a deep, bruised blue. We headed out past the tollbooth, ignored the restaurant, which smelled of cinnamon and coffee, and out to the nearest viewpoint.

'Now what?' Sean, muttered, completely unimpressed by the stunning vista that spread out below.

'Now, we find the trail,' I said, and the buzz became a roar.

*

It was easy enough to find the start of the trail, marked with a waypost, but not so easy to keep on the path, owing to the deep snow that had accumulated on the mountain summit. I ended up walking along the footsteps of others, although there weren't many. The track was supposed to lead along the ridge and eventually back down the mountain again a few miles later, in a loop that came back to the cable car's lower station.

I wouldn't need that long, I reasoned, as the dim light began to fail already.

We walked in silence, trudging through snow that was beginning to freeze hard as an early night fell. When we stopped to rest briefly, for it was hard going in the snow, Sean grabbed at me.

'Can't we do it now?' He asked, his earlobes dripping blood as he yanked on them violently. He'd left little splatters of it on the snow behind him, I saw, like breadcrumbs in a forest. His eyes looked strange, like his pupils were too big.

Did they glow?

I squeezed my eyelids shut momentarily.

The sound was fucking me up, I realised. Messing with all my senses.

'He wouldn't mind,' Sean pleaded. 'I know he wouldn't. We could do it now, just here, look. He'll never know.'

I shook my head, adamant. The motion made me gasp in pain.

'Dad said wait for the northern lights, so let's wait,' I replied, through gritted teeth. I realised my heartbeat was going at a million miles an hour. My hands were sweating through my woollen gloves.

The static rose to its highest level yet.

The sky grew darker, and seemed to lean more heavily on us.

Sean, unable to bear it any longer, went for my backpack.

He had it off my back before I knew what was happening: he was stronger than me, after all. Fitter, taller.

'Hey!' I roared, snatching at the backpack in desperation. 'Give me that! It's mine to do! *Mine!* We have to wait! *Sean!*'

But Sean didn't listen.

A tug of war ensued, with the backpack serving as rope.

It didn't take long for the inevitable to happen.

The bag split apart with a mighty rip, dumping its contents all over the snow.

Dad's urn fell out of its sweater wrapping, bounced on a shard of rock jutting out from beneath the snow, rolled, and landed on another exposed rock, where, finding the mountain harder and more resilient, the urn promptly shattered.

And Dad's ashes plopped out onto the hardening snow around the rock unceremoniously, leaving a dark, large stain on the mountain top.

It wasn't, I thought, staring at the ashen smudge, the least bit magical.

*

For a moment neither of us knew what to do.

Then, my anger boiled over, like jam in a saucepan over high heat.

'You fucking dropped him!' I yelled, shoving Sean hard in the chest.

He lurched back, clutching himself in pain.

'I can't believe you fucking *did* that! What the fuck is wrong with you?!'

My anger and outrage felt genuine, which was odd considering I didn't believe in grief.

Sean's eyes were so large now they looked like someone had drilled two holes into his head.

'It was an accident,' he whimpered. 'Jesus, I didn't mean to! My hands were so fucking cold and...and...'

We both staggered to the shattered urn, fell to our knees and began frantically scraping ashen mush back into the largest urn fragments, but all we ended up doing was making a grey gloop that slopped around like miserable clay.

Realising we were on a hiding to nothing, that we had fucked up beyond repair, I stopped trying to scoop slush-puppie Dad back into the ruined stone jar we'd so carefully transported him all the way to Norway in, and sat back on my heels in the snow.

And saw a large, sharp stone shard lying close to where I knelt, like an offering. A piece of the urn, broken in such a way that it looked like a rudimentary dagger, handle and all. Like something from the stone age, roughly hewn but still deadly.

I took it, held it tight in my hand.

The urn could still serve some of its purpose, if not all.

Sean, meanwhile, was painting his face with Dad's remains. He scooped large handfuls of the goop up from where the urn had smashed, and smeared it all over his cheeks, his forehead, and down his neck.

He was giggling as he painted himself, or at least, I thought he was.

I couldn't hear anything but the static, for the sound was now my only reality.

I turned my face to the sky, which had betrayed us, thus far. I looked for lights, saw nothing. No stars, no moon, no clouds. It was not even a full night, not yet. No daylight, either.

Just interminable in between.

I could feel hot tears on my cheeks.

'I miss him,' I said, softly. 'I miss him a lot.'

And with that, the static buzz suddenly switched off.

The silence that remained was deafening.

*

Sean stopped coating himself in our dead father's ashes, and sat back on his own heels, panting.

'Yeah,' was all he managed.

I felt calm, suddenly. Peaceful. It was nice up here, on the mountain, in the gathering dark.

Cold, but nice.

'I miss the way he would scratch his beard when he laughed, like a cartoon villain, remember that?'

'Yeah,' Sean said, sighing.

'I miss the way he did a dumb little dance back from the mailbox every morning when he collected the mail. I miss the way he always knew exactly when I needed him to call, even though we didn't speak much on the phone, you know? Didn't matter, any time anything went to shit, Dad had this sixth sense, and he would call. Every time, and it would always make things better.'

'I miss the beef cobbler he made. The *smell* of it.' Sean inhaled deeply.

'I miss his stupid-ass jokes. What was that one he always used to tell? At parties.'

'The past, present and future walked into a bar.'

'It was tense.'

Sean laughed.

'Why is Peter Pan always flying?'

'Because he Neverlands.'

I laughed, and tightened my grip on the stone knife.

'Ever had sex while camping?'

'It's fucking in tents.'

We both laughed.

I saw there were tears on Sean's cheeks too.

His eyes were definitely glowing, no two ways about it.

'So fucking dumb,' he said, shaking his head sadly.

Then, something miraculous happened.

I saw movement in the sky.

Without me noticing, night had fully fallen. How long had we been out here? Only an hour, surely?

I looked at my phone, but the cold had sucked the battery flat.

The blackness reflected in the dead screen was intense, suffocating, but it set the perfect stage for what was to come.

Subtle at first, I thought it was a cloud, but as I stared more intently at the rippling, undulating streak in the dark I realised that clouds didn't move that way. Clouds scudded fast, usually from one direction to another, or they boiled up or swirled low, but this...this movement was something else.

Something orchestrated.

Something that seemed almost *alive*.

Like a snake rippling its way across a sand dune. Yes, ripples. That was the best way to describe it. Like the sky had a spine, suddenly, and was stretching its back out.

'Sean,' I hissed, slapping him hard on the arm to get his attention.

'What?' He sounded like he was in a trance. Maybe he was. His eyes glowed a fierce, brilliant blue.

Did my eyes shine the same?

'Look,' I said, pointing up.

Baby brother craned his head back, squinted.

'What am I looking at?'

'There! See it?'

'I see something, but- oh!'

The grey, rippling streak suddenly expanded into a larger, undulating sheet of colour.

'Is that-'

I nodded. 'I think so,' I said, shivering. The temperature had plummeted further.

'But I thought it would be green.' Sean sounded disappointed.

'The aurora colours depend on the wavelength of light they're giving out. The human eye can't process it properly, but...'

'Shh,' Sean replied, dreamily. 'Don't worry. I can see it now. Look!'

A huge green streak of light, like the tail of a comet, blazed across the dark. It was followed by another, in a deeper shade of emerald, and then another, tinged pink with the faintest shade of yellow along the edge.

Aurora was dancing for us, at last.

Sean stared. 'Fuck,' he breathed. 'It's beautiful.'

Then, he cocked his head to one side.

'Can you hear that?'

I listened. 'I hear nothing,' I said, and that frightened me. I wanted to hear. I wanted to hear it so badly.

I missed the static, I realised, missed it hissing into my mind. It had given me purpose, and now that purpose was gone.

Just like my Dad was gone.

And my mom.

'I can hear it,' my little brother said, then. 'Just like Dad said! It's singing! Listen!'

Wonder curdled in my stomach.

I felt my mouth turn down in a grimace of envy.

Of course Sean would be able to hear it, when I could not.

Sean.

Sssssssssseannnnn.

Daddy's favourite.

The stone knife felt warm in my hand suddenly. Warm, and hungry.

'Does my wife like it when you fuck her?' I asked, preparing to strike. 'Does she suck your cock like she sucked mine, all the way to the fucking balls? Huh?'

I brought the knife up, tensing my entire body. I was going to stab my brother right in his smug neck with it, as many times as it took, until he bled out all over the snow.

But Sean had other ideas.

He jumped to his feet, dodged my clumsy lunge, and ran as fast as he could, off into the black.

'I can hear it!' He screamed, his voice lingering even as he disappeared. 'You'll hear it too, soon!'

*

I found him when dawn broke, kneeling in the snow, his back to me.

I trudged around to the front of him wearily, every step sending pain into my skull.

Sean's head, I found, was tilted back, his empty, smoking eye sockets pointed to the sky. He was chewing on an ear like it was a pacifier while he waited for me, having ripped them both off with

171

his bare hands. I could hear the gristly object split under the relentless pressure of his grinding teeth.

He held the other ear out to me in the palm of his hand.

'Here,' he mumbled, rolling his own flesh around on his tongue. He spoke in a voice so soft and childlike I was immediately transported back thirty years. 'Dad said he wanted you to have this. So you can hear.'

I knelt beside my brother, gingerly scooped the ear from his hand.

I held it up to the side of my own head, which was messy with blood from two ragged holes, one on either side, where before, there had been functional organs.

As I did so, the static finally started up again.

Faint at first, then louder and louder, the buzz rushed back in like a high tide, and I started to cry with relief, at first, and then in recognition, and finally, in agony.

It wasn't static at all, I realised, my entire being awash with terrible music.

It was just like Dad said.

It was a song from the sky.

It had always been a song.

My brother opened his mouth wide, screaming silently, then slumped forward into the snow, face down, a small pool of pink spreading beneath him.

I watched his lips move, so I could understand him better as he died.

'I love you, Sam,' he said, and a huge smile spread across his face.

The static pushed everything out, after that, but before I lost my senses completely, I heard the mountains around Tromsø catch the song of the aurora and throw it back to me, soundwaves reflected back like light waves dancing in the sky the night before, only now they only returned my own shame, my own loss, my own failure, and the pain burned, and burned, and burned.

THE ANCIENT RAM INN

'And welcome to the Ancient Ram Inn, contender for the title of Britain's most haunted hotel!' Kirk said, rubbing his hands enthusiastically.

We stood huddled together on the side of a narrow road in a small market town called Wotton-Under-Edge, pronounced *wuh-ton*. It was dark and raining steadily. A thick autumn chill hung in the air. The remains of that year's blackberries lay squashed around our feet, staining the pavement a bruised, purplish-black.

The Inn glared at us from across the street with small, dirty window-eyes. It was a dismal proposition: a squat, sagging collection of rooftops, chimney stacks, timberwork and mullioned, diamond-paned windows. Everything about the place seemed to be in a state of active decay: roof slates hanging lopsidedly by a single nail, a chimney pot about to tumble free, overflowing gutters clinging on for dear life, and the main body of the structure itself slumped inwards like a half-melted snowman, an impression only enhanced by the fact the Inn's walls were painted a dingy yellowish-white in colour. The paint itself was cracked and peeling in multiple places, revealing patches of wounded red brick beneath.

A sign nailed to one end of the building said:

Ancient Ram Inn
10th Century Accommodation
Wotton's oldest house
Haunt of highwaymen

Kirk waggled his eyebrows at us. 'Well?' he said. 'What do you think?'

It was obvious what *he* thought. Kirk was in his element. It was Halloween, after all, and he lived for this shit. I smiled, feeling a sudden resigned affection for him. Dear old Kirk. I didn't share his rampant zeal for the paranormal, but as his friend, I would tolerate it. For one night.

The others weren't quite as accommodating.

'I think it looks like a shithole,' Paul replied, pulling his hoodie up over his head to keep the rain off. 'It's also very 'You'.'

'We have to spend the whole fucking night in that thing?' Martin scratched the back of his neck miserably. His eczema flared up whenever he was stressed. 'I thought we were only here for an hour or something.'

'Well it's not called an overnight ghost hunt for nothing,' Kirk said indignantly. 'Didn't you read the email I sent? The ticket price covers us from nine till dawn.'

'Who actually goes ghost hunting on Halloween, anyway?' Francesca moaned, her small body shaking with cold. 'Fucking Halloween. I swear to god, Kirk, sometimes you are a giant fucking cliché wrapped in a Nike parka jacket.' She sneezed, and wiped her nose with chapped hands. Franny was always sneezing, coughing, or complaining about something. She had Raynaud's, so her fingers were always bone white. I'd bought her six pairs of gloves, and she'd manage to lose every single pair.

'Yeah, when you said we were spending the night at a hotel, this is not really what I had in mind.' Micah rearranged the head-torch he wore like a choker around his neck.

I said nothing, rummaging about in my pocket for my tobacco and papers. I rolled a thin cigarette, using Franny's large red umbrella for shelter.

'That's a disgusting habit, you know,' Paul said, wrinkling his nose. 'It'll kill you in the end.'

I sighed. 'I know, I know. I'm quitting on Monday,' I said.

'You quit every Monday,' Paul replied. I lit the cigarette.

'Well I think it's going to be bloody marvellous,' Kirk said, rubbing his hands again. 'Just look at the place! So atmospheric.'

Nobody replied. Kirk's smile slipped. He wanted our approval.

'I mean it certainly looks…ancient.' Colleen hated hurting people's feelings and was therefore unfailingly polite about everything, but I could tell from the pinching at the corners of her mouth that she was not keen.

'I hate it,' Franny stated, flatly. 'I'll stay for an hour, but that's it.'

'Aggie?' Kirk asked, turning to me. 'What do you think?'

'Is it safe?' I replied, eventually, staring at the building.

'Structurally? I'm sure it's fine!' Kirk smiled a little too hard. 'They do guided ghost hunts here every Halloween, year in, year out, and I'm sure they wouldn't do that if they thought the building was about to collapse or anything.'

'Very reassuring,' I said, noncommittal.

Kirk kept talking, over-explaining as usual. 'As for whether or not it's safe in a spiritual sense, well, that's another matter altogether. The building sits on the intersection of two ancient ley lines that go all the way across to Stonehenge. Legend has it, those ley lines are the cause of the highly concentrated levels of paranormal activity reported here.'

'Such as…?' Micah was reluctantly intrigued.

Kirk took a breath.

'Oh God, where do I start? Commonly reported ghost sightings include a Nun, a Monk- several monks actually- and a roman centurion on horseback, who rides through the walls. There are also rumours of a witch who was burned at the stake on these grounds, oh, and the former innkeeper's daughter, who was found hanged in the attic.'

'Wow.' Colleen laughed uncomfortably. 'That's a lot of ghosts. However do they all fit inside?'

Kirk continued. 'Oh there's more. There have been claims of devil worship on the property, satanic rituals, even rumours of a pagan burial ground sited deep under the foundations.'

'Excellent. Can't fucking wait. I'd much rather be doing this than sitting in an actual pub, getting drunk in the warm and dry.'

'Micah, don't be a dick.'

'LIsten, I had high hopes that I might get laid this evening, okay? Getting laid by a ghost was not quite what I had in mind.'

'Well, actually...' Kirk pursed his lips. 'There is supposed to be a particularly active succubus who has taken up residence here, too.'

'A what?' Colleen frowned.

Paul became more animated. 'A succubus is a sex demon, right?'

Kirk laughed. 'A better definition would be...an entity that feeds off of the sexual energy of others.'

'Right, and they steal semen to impregnate human women, that's what I read.'

Martin raised a hand for attention. 'Isn't anyone going to point out the irony of a sperm-stealing entity being called a succubus?'

We stared at him, uncomprehending.

'A SUCK-ubus,' he repeated.

We all groaned.

'Anyway, the point is, the ghost tours here sell out *incredibly* fast. We're insanely lucky to have gotten a spot. Especially now they only hold them on All Hallows Eve.'

Franny rolled her eyes at Kirk's pronunciation of the last three words.

'Nerd,' she muttered, under her breath.

'I've been on the waiting list for years for these tickets,' Kirk finished, happily.

'Well,' Martin sighed, 'It's almost nine. Shall we get on with it?' He turned and strode across the road on long legs. The rest of us followed arm in arm, talking softly amongst ourselves.

The main entrance was at the rear of the hotel, underneath a ramshackle lean-to that sagged against the bulk of the Inn. The lean-to was piled high with junk: a stack of rusty gas canisters, a mouldy

175

mattress, fluffy clouds of grimy yellow roof insulation, soggy bundles of newspaper, and a wooden dining table with one leg missing. A shabby atmosphere of disrepair and neglect hung thick over the whole scene, which was lit by a crooked street lamp standing nearby.

'It's a fucking fire hazard, all this,' Franny said, wrinkling her nose as she looked around.

I huddled for shelter under Franny's umbrella as I worked on my cigarette. She coughed and waved her hand in front of her face in protest, shooting me an evil look.

'Can you hurry up and finish that thing?' Martin snapped, suddenly.

I took another drag.

'Alright,' I said. 'Calm down.'

'I don't see why the rest of us should have to choke on your cancer-fumes,' he retorted.

I stared at him, and blew smoke out of my nostrils by way of reply.

'Do we just...go in? Or will someone meet us?' Colleen hastily tried to head off an argument.

A voice came out of the gloom of a small doorway to our left.

'Welcome to the Ancient Ram Inn,' it intoned.

'I guess that answers that question,' Colleen said.

A figure emerged from the shadows and moved towards us. I swore, and then stifled a laugh. Kirk went pale.

Micah leaned over and whispered into his ear:

'Something your mum hasn't told you?'

The man who appeared in the doorway was the absolute spitting image of Kirk. So uncannily like him I thought, for a moment, that we were all the butt of a well-orchestrated joke. Height, weight, facial expressions, hair, even the distinctive mole on his left cheek...it was like Kirk's reflection was standing in front of us. Except, when the man shuffled more into the light, I could see that he was older than our friend by a good twenty years. He also didn't have the same liveliness in his eyes that Kirk had. The sparkle was missing, leaving behind a dark, somewhat tired gaze as the man registered our group.

He didn't hold a hand out for us to shake, and for that, we were strangely glad.

'I am your guide,' he said, without any further preamble. 'Please, come inside.'

Kirk hesitated, then followed the guide as directed. 'Ghost tour, here we come!' he said, sounding less certain of himself than before.

The rest of us exchanged pointed looks.

I finished my cigarette with a last, resigned drag, blowing the smoke out into the rain and flicking the glowering butt away into the night without looking to see where it landed. I really did mean to quit, come Monday.

For now, I just had to survive Kirk's special Halloween.

I followed everyone else inside.

*

We entered a low, cold room with a fireplace - the 'Men's Kitchen', our guide informed us in a monotonous voice.

'You will need your flashlights in this building,' he continued. 'The electricity was disconnected some time ago.'

'Yay,' said Paul, throwing his head back. 'I'm having such a fun time.' Colleen poked him in the ribs, a warning to stop ruining the mood.

As a group, we switched on our assortment of headlamps and handheld torches. Seven beams of light stabbed into the thick dark before us, all going off in different directions as we got our bearings. Kirk drew in a sharp breath of satisfaction as the hotel's interior sprang to life. I was considerably less impressed by what I saw.

The inside of the hotel was a hoarder's paradise. Every single available square inch was stuffed with clutter, junk, memorabilia, cheap Halloween decorations, rolled-up movie posters, newspaper clippings, chipped trinkets, mannequins, broken instruments, an old harmonium, stuffed toys, poorly taxidermied animals, clothes, beer mats, tacky ornaments, shells, marbles, pottery, cardboard, pint glasses, leaflets, candles, ashtrays, the lenses of reading glasses and just about anything else you could think of. I had been expecting an old and mostly empty place, with maybe a few fixtures appropriate for the age of the building. Not this mountain of collectible debris and tat.

'The previous owner of the hotel lived here right up until his death a few years ago,' the guide explained. 'He slept on that couch over there.' Our torch beams went to a dark pink velvet sofa crammed into a space in front of the fireplace. Junk loomed all around, threatening to topple down onto the sofa at any moment. For a second, I thought I saw a white, cloudy shape in the air above the couch, but it dissolved as soon as our lights came to bear. I blinked, and blamed Kirk for getting to me with all his paranormal bullshit. I was more suggestible than I'd given myself credit for.

'Much of what you see around you is his personal collection, built up over many years.'

'Interesting,' Colleen said, grimacing politely. Her eye was caught by a smeared glass case fixed to a nearby wall. 'Hey, what's this...ew!' She covered her hand with her mouth. 'Is it...a cat?'

'The mummified remains of a cat, yes.'

We crowded around to get a better look.

Almost perfectly preserved, it lay on its side, head resting lightly on crossed front paws. I could see each of its teeth, white and pristine, bared in an open mouth that seemed frozen mid-yowl. Its ears were crumpled like old leather, its tail wrapped around its hind legs. Were it not for the fact that its eyes were missing and its fur had rotted away, I would have mistaken it, at first glance, for a living cat.

'Why on earth is that even here?' Martin asked. His fingers worked ceaselessly at the skin on the back of his neck, and I could see a nasty red rash gathering under his chin, too. Perhaps the dust was aggravating him, there was certainly enough of it. Franny sneezed, three times in quick succession, as if in agreement.

'How old is that?' She croaked, sniffling and wiping her nose.

'About five hundred years old. It was common to place animals in the walls of buildings in those days, to frighten off evil spirits.'

'Alive?' Colleen was horrified.

The guide barked out a cheerless laugh. 'Alive, I believe so. This was found sealed behind the fireplace.'

'They should have left it there.' Martin's hand travelled around to the front of his neck: scratch, scratch, scratch.

'Stop that,' I whispered, and he glared at me, annoyed. Then, he said something I didn't quite understand, something oddly out of sync with the conversation around us.

'Do you ever get so hot,' he said, fixing me with an intense look, 'That you want to pull your own fucking skin off? Like, just, dig your fingers down real deep, grab a hold, and rip it all off?'

I blinked.

'What?'

'The crispy bits are the tastiest, you know,' he continued, letting out a high-pitched giggle. Then he turned away.

I stared, stunned. My head torch caught his hands, still scratching his neck, scratch, scratch, scratch.

'Martin, what the fuck?' I whispered, but he ignored me.

'Marvellous,' Kirk interjected, grinning, and then he also moved off, having found something else interesting to gawp at.

I glanced back at the mummified cat, irritated by Martin's bizarre behaviour and his incessant scratching in equal measure, and did another double take.

Was it my imagination, or had...?

Not my imagination. The cat's rib cage expanded, as if the dead creature were breathing.

My heart beat a sudden tattoo in my chest, almost in sympathy with the animal. Then, the delicate rib cage collapsed inwards. A small cloud of moisture fogged up the glass near the animal's muzzle. One of its front paws twitched, as if it were dreaming.

I jerked my head back, swallowing, rubbing my eyes. I looked again. The glass was now free of moisture.

Of course it was, because the fucking cat inside the fucking filthy glass case had been dead for five hundred fucking years, and I was just letting anxiety get the better of me. I stared at the thin, small corpse again, extra hard, eyes bugging just to make sure, and confirmed what I knew to be the only possible truth: no movement.

Annoyed with myself, I wheeled about smartly to see where the others had gone.

They were crowded around a two-foot-wide circular patch of bare earth that sat exposed on the floor. It was one of the only clear spaces in the room, and had been kept deliberately so. Someone had placed a plastic skull next to it, and a shovel leaned against the wall nearby, its tip in the earth, as if the patch of dark, damp soil had just this very moment been revealed. A wooden cross was thrust into the soil, which looked compacted, like fresh cement waiting to dry.

'What's that?' I asked, trying to forget the cat.

'An old well,' our guide intoned, and I realised we hadn't even had a chance to ask him his name, we had just launched straight into the tour without preamble. 'Long-since filled in. Also, a burial site.'

'The pagan burial site?' Kirk said, eyes shining. 'It's a bit smaller than I thought it would be.'

'Small, but deep,' our guide confirmed. 'The bones of a woman and a child were found at the bottom, badly burned. Several knives were also uncovered by archaeology students from Bristol university, leading to speculations of ritual sacrifice.'

'That's really sad,' Colleen said, absent-mindedly rubbing her stomach. 'Did they make her watch, do you think?'

Nobody else seemed bothered by her question, but I was. Colleen was not usually so morbid.

'What do you mean, make her watch?' I asked, looking at Martin to see if the two were in league with each other. Martin kept his back turned to me, exposing the redness on his neck.

'I just wondered,' she said, dreamily. 'Did they kill the child first, or the mother? And if it was the child...did they make her mother watch? Did they slit the baby's throat, right in front of her?'

Speechless, I searched for signs that this was some sort of dark joke, or act, but saw no hint of irony, no tell-tale twitch of the mouth

179

that said she was pulling my leg, or even trying to be funny. Her face was sad, and drawn, and she kept rubbing at her stomach.

I felt a bead of sweat work its way down my temple.

'So sad to die so young,' she continued, and then she threw a look of hatred at me that was so pure, so powerful, so concentrated, it took my breath away.

What the fuck?

'They say that if you listen, you can hear the child crying, sometimes. The mother, too,' the guide intoned. 'Something to think about, later.'

We stood in silence, ears angled to the ground, and I half-expected to hear a baby scream, but the only noise that filtered in was the sound of rain lashing on the window panes. The weather outside was getting steadily worse.

'What's next?' Kirk asked, heading for the door that led out of the kitchen.

I followed, not wanting to be near the supposed grave any longer than necessary. It felt sad, somehow. I could imagine bones sitting at the bottom of the well, green and brittle. I didn't like the notion at all.

As I went, I passed the large inglenook fireplace that should have been the centrepiece of the room. I wished there was a fire lit, wondered what it was like when the Ram was still a functioning pub. How many old boys had sat near this hearth, warming themselves and gossiping over flat beer? I envied them, the people of the past. I wanted to feel heat on my skin too, and inhale wood smoke, rich and fragrant.

'Apparently, a man was murdered here,' Kirk said to me suddenly from over his shoulder, interrupting my train of thought. 'His head was thrust into the open fire. Imagine burning alive from the head down! Imagine the *smell*.'

I swallowed. My skin prickled. I said nothing, because that felt like the safest response.

*

'Can you tell us some of the history of the place?' Colleen asked, as we gathered at the foot of a narrow staircase opposite which, a stuffed ram's head hung high up on one wall. My friend was apparently her usual self again, and either feigning interest or trying to distract herself from the grim reality of hours left to go on this dank, cheerless tour.

The guide obliged.

'The Inn was built in 1145, and used to house slaves, carpenters and the stonemasons who built the nearby church. The last pint was pulled in 1968. The landlord has been dead for two years. Have a care on the steps,' he said, and mounted the stairs.

Kirk couldn't help himself. Our tour guide was skimping on the details, and that simply would not do.

'Apparently,' he added, 'Some visitors on previous tours have reportedly been thrown, or shoved up these stairs by unseen hands.' He sniffed the air, like a dog scenting a rabbit. 'Does anyone else smell smoke?' Then he disappeared after our guide.

Several of our group gave me another inexplicably hard stare. It felt orchestrated, this animosity. I was definitely being left out of some recurring joke, some organised prank to shit me up in the haunted house.

I found this to be in extremely poor taste, and decided I wasn't going to play along.

'Pack it in, guys,' I said, feeling weary. 'There's no need, this place is dismal enough.'

My complaint was not registered by a single one of the party. I may as well have been a ghost, tapping at the window.

Colleen turned to Franny, and gripped her wrist tightly. 'Don't you dare let go of me, not even for one moment,' she said. 'I don't like it here. There's an atmosphere, can't you feel it?'

'Do you know what I hate?' Franny replied, her voice suddenly furious. She licked her lips, her breath coming fast. 'Smoking. I hate it. It's a filthy fucking habit, don't you think?'

Then, she started to sob. 'My skin hurts,' she moaned. 'Does your skin hurt too?'

'Guys?' I found myself distraught, confused. Franny *never* cried. 'What's going on? Please, tell me!'

Colleen kissed Franny affectionately on the cheek.

'He doesn't remember,' she whispered.

Franny wiped her eyes. 'He never remembers,' she said, throwing a hurt look at me. The girls then ascended the stairs together.

I stood, stunned at this weird outburst.

'Did I...did I do something?' I called after them, my voice cracking.

Again, I was ignored. The others filed past me on their way up the stairs as I dithered.

I looked back to the room from where we had come, to the empty patch of earth, the shovel, the couch, the glass case with the dead cat inside.

Fuck this, I thought.

'Um, guys...I need some fresh air,' I lied, in a false, bright tone, patting my chest in an act of deceptive pantomime. 'Too much dust in my lungs. I won't be a minute.'

Micah, Martin and Paul stopped dead in the act of climbing the staircase, and turned their heads slowly to look down at me. As one, they mimed the act of smoking, dragging deep breaths in from an imaginary cigarette, and blowing air out in three frosty clouds that hung before them.

Nope, I thought, retracing my steps back the way I had come and trying not to look at any one thing for too long. A whiff of something charred tickled my nostrils as I went. The Inn was getting to me, it was getting under my skin, and the only thing I could think to do was to get outside, quickly, before I completely lost my nerve.

I reached the rear door with a mounting sense of urgency, feeling a thousand pairs of eyes on my back, convinced something sinister was about to emerge from the gloom behind me. But nothing did, and then I had the door handle in my cold, sweaty hand. I breathed a huge sigh of relief, turned the handle and...

Found myself at the top of the staircase, surrounded by my friends, who were all waiting for me.

*

'What the fuck?! I was downstairs!' I cried. The air up here was thin and bitter. Acrid. It left a bad taste in my mouth.

'But your ticket expires at dawn,' our guide said, not unkindly. He was standing next to Kirk in the crowded hallway at the top of the stairs, and they both smiled at me, a syncopated, identikit stretch of the mouth that filled me with absolute horror.

'Dawn,' Kirk confirmed, and then he slowly reached down and slid the guide's hand into his own, interlacing his fingers with his older doppelganger's. They stood like two lovers at the altar, the exact same height and weight, wearing the exact same expression. 'Nobody can leave until the ticket expires.'

I studied these people I called friends with growing bewilderment and fear. Their eyes were cold, and hard. I cringed, feeling disoriented, hurt, scared. I didn't know what was worse: their cruelty and ostracization, or the weird things coming out of their mouths.

'Why are you all looking at me like that?' I asked, pitifully. 'Did I do something?'

Martin slowly began to remove his jacket, then his sweater, and then his shirt, by way of reply. He cocked his head to one side, running his hands over his now bare chest. It looked red, and raw from scratching: his eczema had run rampant.

'Is it hot in here?' he said, and I felt nauseous, because it was hot, blisteringly so.

Behind Martin, the walls of the hallway were plastered with yellowing old newspaper clippings about the hotel. Garish headlines yelled different things at me: *'Ancient Ram Inn at the centre of cash conspiracy,'* one said. Another read: *'Britain's most haunted hotel, terrified guests jumped out of windows.'* Another said: *'Destroyed! Ancient...'*

Paul moved so he blocked that clipping from my view.

I swallowed, frantically looking for some means of escape. I was hemmed in by people. Could I push past them, down the hall? Maybe there was a fire escape I could shimmy down, or...

'What's that room behind you?' Micah asked, looking at Kirk but grabbing hold of my arm with an iron grip as I readied to bolt. I cried out. I noticed Micah's face was covered in sweat. I tried to wriggle my arm free of his hold, but he clung on like a vice.

'Micah,' I said, tears gathering in my eyes. 'Let go, please. I want to leave.'

Micah didn't answer. His fingers dug in tighter the more I struggled.

'Oh this?' Kirk and the guide said, gesturing to a heavy oak door nearby. They spoke in perfect unison, tenderly fingering each other's hands as they stood there side by side. 'This is the Bishop's Room. Shall we go in?'

And with that, the door was opened, and I was ushered inside.

*

The Bishop's Room was awful. I knew as soon as Micha pushed me inside that it was an evil place. Dark oak beams barely supported the ceiling. Thick patterned wallpaper hugged the inwardly-leaning walls. Tattered red velvet lampshades haphazardly set over wrought iron candelabras gave off a sickly amber light. Mismatched bedside lamps stood on either side of an ancient oak bedstead, over which an angry red coverlet was thrown. Around the room, a strange assortment of paintings hung: a bright, artificial print of the battle of Trafalgar, an anatomical diagram of a cow. A cherub upon a cloud. A dead bird, hanging from a nail by a thread tied around its foot. The room gave the impression that it wanted to swallow anyone unlucky enough to try and rest within. It was like a mouth, snapping shut, a gullet constricting, forcing me down. Too much red. Too little space to breathe.

There was a dresser against the far wall. I shook free of Micah and crossed the room, inexplicably drawn to a copy of the bible I could see sitting there, and a statuette of Jesus. I had never been religious before now, but I found myself needing comfort, needing something orthodox to cling to for support.

Martin, who was last in, closed the door firmly behind him with a loud *click*. I glanced across then gasped, unable to help myself. His torso was covered in red welts, blisters and dark, necrotic patches. It no longer looked like eczema, but more like...I didn't know what it looked like. He began idly plucking curling flakes of his own dead skin off, letting them flutter to the carpet. Paul crouched, thoughtfully seized one of the discarded curls of skin, sniffing it thoughtfully, then ate it. He looked up at Martin as he did this, an expression of genuine pleasure on his face.

'You're right,' he said, conversationally. 'The crispy bits are the best.'

I forced my attention back to the dresser. I didn't want to look at Martin or Paul anymore, I didn't want to look at any of them anymore. It upset me too much. I recognised none of them.

A painting above the dresser leered down at me. It was a portrait of an elderly gentleman. He had white hair that sat in a thin circular strip beneath a bald, shining pate. His hooded brown robe gave him away as a Monk, but for some reason, the crucifix attached to the rosary around his neck was upside down.

'I hate this room,' Franny said, in a small, wounded voice.

'Of all the rooms in the Inn, this is our most problematic,' said the guide. 'Many have tried to sleep here, and failed. One guest even jumped out of the window to escape. This room is haunted by the ghost of an excommunicated Monk, and he doesn't take kindly to visitors, I am told.'

'Is that him, over there?' Colleen whispered, pointing.

On the bed, the outline of a large, sleeping body filled the coverlet that had, moments ago, been flat.

As I watched, the outline groaned, shifted, and sat up, slowly. The coverlet peeled back, revealing the old man from the portrait hanging above the dresser. He was naked except for his rosary, and held a long, three-tailed whip in his hand. As I watched, he rose slowly from the bed and stood up, his skinny, ancient form indecently exposed. Then he lifted the whip high above his head, and brought it down smartly across his own back. Wounds opened up on his delicate skin. Blood flooded down his body.

'Penance,' he whispered, taking a step towards me, flagellating himself with great vehemence. 'Penance!'

I threw a silent, horrified appeal to my friends for help as the Monk approached, lashing himself with every jerky, uneven step. Nobody came to my aid. They simply stood, watching me with hollow eyes, and was that...

Was that smoke rising from their bodies?

And that smell. What was that god-awful smell?

The Monk drew closer, his body a latticework of pain and gore, and I remembered the bible behind me. I whipped around to grab a hold of it, only to drop it a second later with a hiss of pain. The bible was white-hot. I gazed at the raw, red patch that now covered my left palm. It looked strangely like the red patches on Martin's chest, and something stirred in my mind, but I was too afraid to pay it any attention. The dragging footsteps of the monk grew ever closer. I looked at the statuette of Christ, hoping for solace there, but the features had melted, in fact the whole statuette was dissolving into a sticky puddle on the dresser top.

I could feel air move behind me as the Monk's whip lashed again, and again, and I realised I had no choice: there was only one escape route left to me. I turned to the bedroom window, panic completely obliterating all rational thought, and threw my entire body through the glittering lead-lined window panes. The window disintegrated under my weight, and I fell, down, down...

Except I wasn't falling down. I was somehow falling up, and up, and up, and I...

I opened my eyes to find myself in a large attic space.

*

I sat up, wiping my face with shaking hands. My head torch wasn't needed up here. A persistent orange glow pierced the gaps between the floorboards of the attic. More junk piled high in complex, precariously arranged mounds. From one of the heavy wooden beams that held the roof up, someone had strung up another cheap Halloween decoration, a half-deflated balloon with a ghost face scribbled onto it, covered in a sheet of thin netting. I waited, terrified, to see if it would turn into anything more sinister. It didn't.

'This is a perfect example of a mediaeval three-bay building,' the guide's voice said from somewhere below me. I realised he was climbing the stairs that connected the first floor to the attic space, because his voice was moving closer.

'The great inglenook fireplace you saw earlier was a Tudor addition to the Inn, as was the dry-stone walling. This building was reportedly the hideout of England's last two highwaymen, who used the Ram to shelter in between raids. Now, mind your head at the top of the stairs, and *PLEASE DISPOSE OF YOUR CIGARETTES CAREFULLY!'*

A figure emerged through the attic doorway, his ruined face ogling me from around the ancient timber door frame. Not the guide. Kirk. But horribly, horribly changed. His eyes ran like milky rivers down the charred contours of his face. His hair was singed and patchy. Brown, cracked teeth worried at skin that hung off him like strips of peeling wallpaper.

'Hello, Aggie!' He said, in a raspy voice. 'Did I tell you that the Innkeeper's daughter was murdered in this roof space in the 1500's? People asleep in the Bishop's Room often hear the sound of something heavy being dragged across the floor over their heads. Did you know that, Aggie, you stupid fucking cunt? Did you?'

The balloon ghost hanging above me began to moan, and choke, and it wasn't a cheap Halloween decoration anymore, but the thin body of a young woman, struggling and swinging from the end of a creaking, thick rope.

'Why can't I leave?' I sobbed, rocking back and forth. 'I keep trying to leave, but I always end up back...here. Did I...did I do something wrong?'

'Oh, Aggie,' Kirk replied, and his ruined face became almost kind for a moment. 'Why do you always forget?'

'Forget what?! I don't understand!'

Kirk shook his head as the rest of my friends trooped into the attic, a ghastly parade of burned, blackened bodies, of crisped, cracking skin, blistered lips, ravaged faces. Behind them, I heard the roar of fire, and the orange glow coming up between the floorboards grew in intensity.

'Please,' I begged, 'No more! I don't want any more! Make it stop, Kirk!'

They shuffled to stand around me in a circle, Kirk, Franny, Micah, Paul, Colleen, and Martin. The guide was nowhere to be seen. Kirk licked his cracked, flaking lips. A thin trail of pus oozed down his chin.

'You should have thought of that,' he said, 'before you ruined my special night.' He leaned forward. He held a newspaper clipping in his hand, and thrust it at me.

Through my tears, I read:

'Destroyed! Ancient Ram Inn, Britain's most haunted hotel, BURNS DOWN on Halloween!'

I remembered, with a sudden rush of desperate shame, how I had flicked my cigarette butt into the night, without a care where it landed. I remembered gas canisters in a pile under a lean-to. I remembered roof insulation and a broken table and piles of newspaper. I looked down. The skin on the backs of my hands began to bubble.

I forced myself to read more.

'The Ram Inn, one of Britain's oldest and most haunted hotels, burned down this Halloween night, thanks to the careless actions of a guest who...' A brown patch suddenly appeared over the paragraph I was reading, widening to become a hole with glowing red edges.

Before it obliterated the clipping entirely, I saw the awful, unforgivable conclusion to the article: *'seven fatalities.'*

'I'm sorry,' I whispered, finally understanding.

My friends no longer cared for my apologies. They closed in on me, slowly, reaching for me with fingers burned down to the bone, and I think I heard Colleen weeping, but it was hard to tell over the sound of fire.

And as the first set of bony claws dug into my skin, gouging a deep furrow in my flesh, and peeling a long strip of it clean off my body, I screamed, because it hurt, oh, *god*, how it hurt, not in my body, but deep in my heart, and then fire rose up all around me.

*

'Welcome to the Ancient Ram Inn,' Kirk said, in a tired, weak voice.

I jolted into myself, breathing hard.

The fire was gone. I was no longer in the attic. Instead, I stood out in the cold, my friends huddled in a group around me on the side of a narrow road, blackberry bushes to one side of us, and a familiar timber and stone structure sitting in a shallow depression before us.

'That wasn't so bad, this time,' Franny breathed. Paul put an arm around her shoulder. 'It's definitely been worse,' he agreed, and they rested their heads together. Their skin was smooth and unblemished. The smell of burning meat had disappeared.

'I hate that Monk,' Colleen said, shivering. 'He's always so...angry.'

'Just be glad it wasn't the Nun, this time,' Martin said, soothingly. No trace of his eczema remained. 'She's worse.'

'Is it nearly dawn?' Micah's shoulders slumped with fatigue.

'I don't understand.' I said, stupidly. 'What...what just happened?'

Kirk's eyes were enormous. I realised that he looked much older than he really was. He reminded me of the guide. Had there ever even been a guide? Or had it been Kirk the whole time?

'They say that on Halloween you can still see the Ancient Ram Inn, standing bold as brass under the moonlight, in all its former glory,' he intoned. 'Only on Halloween, though. The rest of the year...there is nothing left, only a ruin. Because of you. You did a stupid thing, Aggie. We all told you to stop, didn't we?'

'I'm sorry,' I said, bowing my head.

Kirk sighed. 'You always are.'

Then, because I had to know: 'But...what happens now? To us?'

Kirk nodded at something I held in my hands. The newspaper clipping, whole again, no burned patch obscuring the details.

Which meant I could see the date of the article: November the 1st, 2000.

I blinked, began to tremble. 'But this is twenty years old!' I cried. 'We only got here today! We...we only died today!'

As one, my friends laid comforting hands on me. 'You killed us twenty years ago, Aggie,' Colleen said. 'And you did it on All Hallow's Eve.'

'Idiot,' Franny said, but her anger had died down.

'I don't understand,' I repeated.

'You never do,' Micah replied, and they left me, crossing the road, trailing back towards the Inn, which stood waiting for them in the gathering light of dawn.

And then I saw it, as I stood there trying not to regurgitate my broken heart. As the light grew stronger, the outline of the Ancient Ram Inn dissolved, became the shape of a burned out, derelict structure with yawning, smashed windows, a collapsed roof, off-white paint now blackened with streaks of soot, charred roof-timbers jutting out of the debris like a dead man's fingers. A cat wandered sadly amongst the ruins, picking its way delicately over the debris, coming to rest in a clear spot by a ruined inglenook fireplace that seemed to have survived the blaze.

The sound of a baby crying suddenly drifted out into the night. It hurt my ears.

'Are you coming?' Martin called, from across the street.

'But I don't want to go back there!' I cried.

'You don't have a choice,' Kirk replied, calmly. 'This is where we live, now.'

'And what happens when it's no longer Halloween?' I shouted as, one by one, my friends faded into the shadow of the ruins, running from the light.

'It's always Halloween here,' they whispered, until they were no more. 'Always.'

And I thought about that, as a red sun crept slowly higher in the sky. I wondered why I always forgot, even though I had lived and relived the same nine hours, the same Halloween, over and over, for twenty years, on loop. Why did I always forget?

But then, I supposed, staring at the Inn, what did it matter?

We had died in a house already rich with ghosts, a house already crowded with the shadows of lives past.

What was seven more, when it came to it?

I followed.

I despise tourists.

Not, perhaps, as thoroughly as I despise peanuts, pipe smoke, wind, long-haired cats, other people's children, mushrooms, paisley print, bright lights, repetitive noises or the sight of blood or dead bodies, but close.

Dead and mutilated tourists, therefore, represent something of a nightmarish prospect for a lady like me, travelling solo. By and large, one does not expect to countenance such horror during long-distance train journeys, but I suppose I was, on this occasion, rather unlucky. As the saying goes, the best laid plans can oft go awry.

And things went very awry indeed for Frank Hatch, who, sad to say, was about as dead as a person could be.

As a woman of business, a lesson you learn very early on is that whenever catastrophe strikes, a philosophical attitude must be adopted, else everything will quickly fall apart. Things in the world of commerce go wrong so frequently that to upset oneself over every single obstacle would be tantamount to inviting heart failure. Ask my husband, if you don't believe me; except you can't, because he died, of a heart attack, some six years back.

I digress.

A philosophical attitude, as I said before, is an essential ingredient to lasting success.

However.

Even I found it difficult to be philosophical when confronted with the unusual and violent circumstances of Frank's death.

*

Frank, poor dear, was discovered (by me) lying face down in his cabin and wearing what can only be described as a dirty great hole in the back of his skull, a hole with jagged edges and splinters of bone standing proud all around it, a hole that leaked brain matter in rather prodigious quantities all over the small oriental-style rug carpeting his cabin floor.

When I carefully rolled his body over, using my silver-handled walking cane so as not to get any of his mortal fluids upon my hands or clothing, I found his lower jaw had been ripped clean away, as if by tremendous force, leaving behind only a long, red grisly tongue, which flopped listlessly to one side. I remember thinking, even as I cursed (most unbecoming for a lady) and called out for help, that it was apt, really, to give his tongue so much room, for Frank was the talkative kind, or at least he had been in the short time I'd known him while alive.

But I am getting ahead of myself.

First, I should introduce Frank properly, for he was a nice man. He certainly deserved better.

*

When I first met Frank, my chipped pottery bowl of scalding, shivering beef strips suspended in some sort of thin, fatty broth stock was trying its level best, pun firmly intended, to get away from me. It darted about on the tabletop of the dining car booth I was lodged in with infuriating, dextrous avoidance despite the starched linen cloth beneath, put there to prevent that sort of thing from happening. The tablecloth, like my personage, was liberally spattered with greasy spots of broth. This was of no huge consequence, for my travelling-ulster of checked brown and white woollen serge had been tailored to accommodate and disguise any unsightly stains or spillages that occurred whilst in transit- but still, I was frustrated, and when I am frustrated, I like to be left alone. I am not at all fond of eating supper whilst it tries in vain to escape from you, and my patience had worn remarkably thin.

The sweaty gentleman sitting opposite me in the dining car of the Transiberian express train to Mongolia, by way of Yaroslavl, Yekaterinburg, Novosibirsk and Irkutsk, had nevertheless ignored my disagreeable, unapproachable demeanour and subsequent pleas for solace, none of which had been subtle. I tried everything: feigning a headache, direct rudeness, yawning, sighing, staring out of the window, but he would not have it. Apparently, we were to be dining companions, and there was nothing I could do about this but accept and suffer.

My moist new acquaintance appeared to have no trouble pinning down *his* supper, anchoring the steaming hot bowl in one hand and using the other to shovel broth enthusiastically and skilfully into his chattering maw with admirable speed. Clearly, he was both a professional eater and a professional conversationalist: his feasting only interrupted by his exclamations of delight over his food (which was awful), the decor of the restaurant car (funereal), the scenery rolling by outside the window (featureless), the flavour of the local wine (rancid), the hospitality of the staff on board (almost nonexistent), and whatever other happy thought happened to fall into his brain at any given moment. He was incessantly jovial, to an almost pathological degree, and the side-to-side juddering motion of the train passing over its tracks beneath us did not upset him in the slightest.

That Frank found everything so persistently agreeable may have accounted for my intense dislike of the man at first. I had personally nothing to celebrate: the wine he so feverishly praised could (and should) have been used to polish my walnut dresser back home, the heavy, utilitarian decor around us shrieked loudly of state and empire, and the service was quite honestly terrifying, rendering my maid Mrs. Potts positively cherubic, and without sounding crass, she has a face so sour that it can, and I believe has, made grown men cry.

But perhaps I was being what my late husband used to indelicately refer to as 'a snob'. The conditions in Siberia were dreadfully harsh, after all, and one should, when travelling, adjust expectations to suit the locale. It cannot always be cut glass crystal, silk, roses and parfait.

Still.

There is such a thing as silence, and silence can be rather wonderful, but my dining partner had never received such a memorandum, and preferred to try and compensate for my stony recalcitrance with twice as many words as he might have otherwise uttered.

I bore his discourse as patiently as I could, and attempted once more to spoon broth into my mouth whilst mimicking some polite semblance of interest in the man's conversation. He was, I discovered, a holidaying accountant with something of a romantic soul; he boarded the Trans-Siberian in Moscow and was headed to Vladivostok, where he planned to make his way via boat to Shanghai, travel about China, and eventually return home to the no doubt fulfilling and exciting world of accounting and finance, his wanderlust satisfied until the next occasion he should happen to look about his office in Westminster and realise how interminably dull his life really was. His name was Frank Hatch, as I said before, and I suppose for all my humbuggery that he was a pleasant enough individual, if a tad over-familiar and lacking in self-awareness.

My husband often used to tell me that I, by contrast, was too dour and unenthused, so I could, perhaps, have learned a valuable lesson from Frank, if I were also there on my holidays. I might even have found him a more agreeable lunch partner, were I only a tourist like he (highly doubtful).

I am, however, no tourist. I am a businesswoman, a successful one, I like to think, and was on my way to Mongolia, via Irkutsk to explore a potential contract with a fur supplier who specialised in high-quality skins for high-end clients. Whilst there, I intended to keep my wits about me in case any other opportunities should arise. It wouldn't take long for word of my presence to spread, I knew: when you are as tall, ugly, unfriendly and uncompromising as I am, it leaves an impression. Added to this, women did not often travel alone, independently, for such purposes. The fact that I had no visible chaperone would set tongues wagging like nobody's business upon my arrival, and that would bring in the vultures. Local enterprising types who immediately assumed, upon glancing at my skirts, that I was available to be taken advantage of.

Such men, such fools, are the very foundation of my success.

*

Yes, I have learned that the key to becoming a successful woman of commerce is to take advantage of the relentless stupidity of others.

My penultimate destination appeared to be highly accommodating of the opportunistic soul, which was precisely why I was going there. Word had reached England of how Irkutsk was fast becoming an economic nucleus within Russia, largely due to the sudden discovery of gold in the Lena Basin. I had an acquaintance who leapt feet first into the ensuing Gold Rush and made something of a fortune in the process. He set himself up, rather admirably by all accounts, in the city in a fancy new-build house that I intended to make use of, along with his hospitality. He did not know that yet. I found that the element of surprise made those on the receiving end of unexpected visitations more accommodating. Less opportunity for apologetic letters declaring sudden illnesses, or renovation works. If I was unannounced, I discovered, I was less likely to be turned away.

As Frank chattered on before me, my mind ran over the forthcoming meetings I had arranged and whether or not there was anything left in this surge of gold- or whether, as with all gold rushes, it had simply dwindled down to a few rich prospectors who were now steeped in rivalry to see who could spend their amassed wealth first. If I found this to be the case, and Irkutsk held nothing for me, I had a plan to jump back on the tracks and ride on to Ulan Bator, in Mongolia, for I had always had a desire to see the lands once ridden across by Ghengis Khan, but there was more to it than mere whimsy: I heard rumours of liberation from Manchu rule, of independence. I knew from experience that whenever a country changed hands, it invariably changed some of its export rules and relations, and I wanted in on that. Horse trading was becoming increasingly profitable, Mongol horses being hardy, fearless, and much desired, apparently. Hides, skins and silks were also appealing to me, as were the growing rumours of un-mined mineral resources, namely copper, gold and tin, all of which could line a woman's pocket rather nicely, if she were quick and smart enough about it.

But I digress. Again.

As I sat there mulling over all this, something extremely unfortunate happened.

My stomach, delicate at the best of times, made a loud, uncomfortable and embarrassingly audible gurgle of protest.

Something of my dismay at this turn of events must have registered on my face, because Frank actually stopped his jabbering for a few blissful moments, leaning across the table in concern.

'Are you quite alright?' He asked.

I found I could not reply. My stomach churned and rumbled again, like thunder in the distance.

I placed my spoon carefully on the table before me and wiped my mouth with my handkerchief, hoping this action would hide the unmistakable greenness of nausea that had made its presence felt, very acidly, in the back of my mouth.

Mr. Hatch chuckled, and tapped my arm with his spoon. His dirty spoon, I might add.

"Local food not agreeing with you, old thing?"

I despise strangers using familiar terms of endearment such as 'old thing' almost as much as I despise tourists and idle chit-chat. Especially when you ostensibly *are* an 'old thing' in the eyes of society (which I never cared much for). Such monikers tend to grate.

Unable to snap back with a cutting response, my mouth clenched tight as I attempted to keep down whatever foul substance I'd been served during my two day stint on the rattling hotel on wheels called the *Rossiya*, an enormous train comprised of thirteen coaches that ran from third-class to first, with a dining car and a freight car at the rear, I swallowed frantically instead, wondering if it was the parfait, the devilled eggs, or yesterday's capers that had done it. Looking down in horror at my broth as my insides cramped violently, I witnessed shiny droplets of oil quivering on the surface of the stew and realised, with mounting despair, that I was not going to be able to hold whatever was upsetting me down.

Frank Hatch, witnessing my discomfort, did an unexpected and very kind thing. Had I not been feeling so ghastly, I should have felt a pang of guilt at my previously uncharitable opinions of him.

As fate would have it, his kindness went forever unrewarded.

"Here," he said, pushing something papery and crisp into my hand. "Use this. I'll make a distraction."

The gift of a strong, brown paper bag was as welcome to me as water must be to a man lost in the desert. I glanced furtively about the restaurant car. There was, thank goodness, only one other table occupied at the far end, next to the small kitchen tucked away out of sight behind ornate iron fretwork. My dinner mate and I were sitting at the opposite end of the car, next to the door which led to the sleeping carriages, and more importantly, a flushing toilet, which I suspected I would never reach in time.

Frank's choice of table- mine- had irritated me no end when he initially lumbered across with his childlike smile. There had been at least five other empty tables to choose from in the dining car, and I was incredulous when he lowered himself into a chair opposite me.

Now, I silently thanked heaven for him.

Frank winked at me conspiratorially, raised himself from his seat, and made his ponderous way over to the other occupied table, where an elderly lady and her younger companion were sitting staring as excitedly at their watery beef concoction as I was half an hour earlier. There was no waiter in sight; for once, I was relieved about that.

Another rolling wave of sickness hit me.

Here it comes, I thought, mortified to my very core.

I ducked my head down behind the stained-glass and wrought-iron partition that divided each table from its neighbour and heaved as quietly and inoffensively as possible into the paper bag. Hatch's voice reverberated about the dining car as he made idle conversation in that gabbling manner of his, covering for me.

I purged myself once more, and my relief was almost immediate. My stomach ceased its tempest. My temperature dropped, too, from a sudden feverish high to something more temperate.

I took several large breaths, raised my head and shot another glance over to the ladies' table. They appeared engrossed in Frank's patter, although the younger woman had a faint crease between her brows indicating that she, like me, was thinking of other things as politely as she could.

I was overcome with relief. I appeared to have gotten away with it.

I caught Frank's eye, which twinkled with camaraderie, and nodded a solemn thanks.

I now needed to dispose of the evidence of my recent crime.

As I went to fold the lip of the paper bag over, I caught a glimpse of its contents, and frowned. No wonder I had been so ill-disposed, I thought, as a congealed mess of indistinguishable lumps, blobs and textures that looked almost like matted hair, although of course I knew that could not be the case, shivered at the bottom of the bag. The whole mess was surprisingly brown, and turgid, and disgusting.

Frank saw me rise from my table, trying my best to conceal my foetid parcel. He escalated the pitch of his commentary on the state of Siberian hospitality with gusto, allowing me to make a discreet escape, which I did, without further delay.

Before I went, I dropped my business card next to Frank's place setting, along with money for his share of the bill on the table. I made a firm resolution to find his sleeping car later, and offer him my sincere thanks in person. I would also treat him to dinner, should he wish, although on second thoughts, I decided that might not be such a kind gesture until I could be sure my unreliable digestive system would not spoil another meal.

After I ditched the volatile brown paper package, which reeked to high heaven, and cleaned myself to the best of my ability given the unsteady toilet arrangement in my cabin, I changed into pyjamas and climbed into bed. Women aren't supposed to wear pyjamas to bed, I know this, but my late husband's were so comfortable and warm that I just didn't care. Nightgowns are awfully impractical to sleep in, truth be told: too much fabric, too scratchy and restrictive. They get horribly bunched between the knees, making for painfully stiff joints the next morning.

And there are enough inconveniences in this world without unnecessarily sore joints, I find.

*

I planned on starting the next day by wrestling Frank's cabin number from the Prodvinista, who was called Vera. She had a soft spot for me and my money, and was the only member of staff on the train who would countenance a little light bribery in exchange for information. Everyone else employed by the train company had the moral fortitude of a titanium compass.

You must believe me when I say that I fully intended to make more of an effort with Frank Hatch, and to make right on my earlier misjudgement of his character.

I had every intention, until he got himself slaughtered.

Which brings me back to Frank's body.

*

I suppose I shouldn't have barged in on him, but I am an impatient creature, and don't much like being ignored. Thus, when I knocked on the door of Frank's cabin (he was in cabin number seven) at ten in the morning (sharp), and heard no reply, and knocked again, and still received no reply, I decided there was little point hollering at his door like a fishwife until I was blue in the face, and so tried the cabin's handle instead.

Strangely, Frank's door appeared to be unlocked. The handle turned. I pushed until there was a gap around the door several inches wide, then found an unseen obstruction blocking me from opening it further.

Confused, I strained against the wooden surface first with both arms, then with my shoulder, for I am not an insubstantially proportioned woman, as I am sure you've noticed. Neither am I ashamed to admit that I have shouldered more than a few doors in my time, although perhaps we should save the exact circumstances surrounding those occasions for another tale.

But the portal refused to budge, so I put my eye to the gap instead and tried to get a good look at what was blocking my entry.

And that was when I saw the blood, plastered across the only visible strip of the cabin wall.

*

I found I was faced with a choice. Call for help at that moment, or try to ascertain more information, then call. I chose the latter option, deciding that shouting for aid too early would result in my removal from the scene, as the train employees tried to shelter a first-class passenger from any further unpleasantness. I didn't wish to be babied. If something had happened to Frank, I wanted to know *what*, exactly, and how, for several reasons - self-preservation being one of them.

A lady can never be too careful, after all.

I turned around, put my entire back to the door, gripped the doorframe to either side of me, put my legs up against the opposite side of the train carriage where a long brass handrail was mounted, made sure the heels of my boots were securely locked beneath the handrail, hoisted my weight up into the air, and *pushed*, backwards.

The door gave with a loud grind, dismounting from its hinges. I gasped as I was deposited directly into Frank's cabin. *Flimsy*, I thought, staring at the splintered door and its ruined frame. I had expected better engineering on a train like this.

Once I inspected Frank's cabin, however, I promptly and immediately forgot about the door.

For the place was a bloodbath. No other way to describe it.

*

I quickly ruled out any human interference or assault. There was too much blood, too much violence. A man couldn't rip the jaw off another like this, not with his bare hands. There was no evidence of blackening from gunpowder, no sign of entry wounds made by blade or pistol. The damage wrought to Frank's poor, limp remains was clearly animalistic in nature, and extensive. His entire body has been raked with something sharp but also crude, like claws. His pyjamas and silk dressing gown were shredded to tatters. I saw some of his teeth, sprinkled on the carpet like macabre confetti, and clumps of skin and hair (although he hadn't much of that to spare) stuck to the walls.

A bear? I mused, for it was the only creature that came to mind that was large, and vicious enough to wreak such havoc.

But that was ridiculous. A bear on the train was an utterly unfeasible notion. I tried hard to think of an alternative answer, but my mind, dulled with shock, was less than cooperative.

It was only when I clumsily stepped on the ragged stump of a finger and almost fell rear over tip that I came to my senses, screaming blue murder for someone to come, for anyone to help, because I knew, without a shadow of a doubt, that Frank Hatch was beyond any aid from me.

*

After the unfortunate discovery of Frank's body, I spent the entire next day lying down in my sleeping car, nursing my still-aching belly, a burgeoning toothache, and silently cursing all trains and those who served upon them. My grumpiness was well-founded, for I had not felt quite so unwell for years. Thankfully, my car was very comfortable, with a long, firm folding bed anchored to the wall, a sink with running water and polished brass taps and a thick, deep pile rug on the floor. The luggage was stored discreetly in wooden cabinets. This left me plenty of room to move about, which I didn't. I had spent all night dozing in and out of fitful sleep, tonguing something that had lodged itself stubbornly and painfully between my two furthest back left molars, and was utterly exhausted as a result. But that was no fault of the cabin.

It was the fault of whatever had ripped Mr Hatch to shreds only three berths along. Knowing that such a vicious creature was on the loose did not make for a restful night.

Not least because, try as I might, I couldn't make that hypothesis work. It was absurd to even consider the possibility of a bear or a wolf rampaging through first class, unseen, entering Frank's room, committing the terrible deed and then exiting swiftly without witness or detection. Frank's death could not possibly have been the result of an accident, either, so that left only one realistic proposition: Hatch had been murdered by a fellow passenger.

And if that was the case, I was better off in my cabin.

The view from my window, upon waking, was sadly rather spectacular. Even I, who took special pride in being very difficult to please, would happily have admitted to being quite captivated in different circumstances. As it was, I watched the world outside race along with the disinterested gaze of one who was braindead, or hypnotised.

The previous days' bland and unending scrub had gone. We had entered a forest during the night, vast and striking. Thousands upon thousands of slender, luminous birch trees flickered past my window as I lay on my bed. They made me feel quite giddy, especially when the land changed topography. The trees rose and fell gently with the folds of earth forming the foothills of the Urals, which our train was due to pass over, shortly, according to my map and schedule. It was August, so the snow had finally melted. The world had greened. Grass carpeted the countryside thickly, broken by patches of bog, where still water reflected branches and sky in almost perfect mirror symmetry, so I fancied, as I gazed out, as if the entire world were striped and latticed, from floor to ceiling, like a great woven basket inside which I was trapped. A canary in a wicker cage. I did not like the feeling at all.

Occasionally, we passed through a break in the trees and rattled our way through a small town or village where typical ramshackle wooden houses, with their ornate Siberian fretwork, tilted against each other alongside the rail tracks, leaning as if tired. These tiny pockets of civilization seemed to go by in the blink of an eye, whereupon the trees came rushing back, their slender white trunks mesmerising in uniformity. The sun was high and intense already, the sky a deep, optimistic blue.

The scenery, I found, was wild and surprising and not a little intimidating. Russia was a gigantic country and this train ride had given me a newfound appreciation of its enormity. I was on my third day on board. According to the schedule, I still had just under one more day's travel left. The route in its entirety covered more miles than I could count, and made twenty-six stops intermittently en route to Irkutsk.

I suspected, however, that our journey was about to be severely compromised by the discovery of Hatch's shredded corpse, and fully expected our train to pause or even terminate at whichever station had enough infrastructure to summon some sort of investigative authority to come assess the situation.

What I would do in the eventuality of either scenario, I wasn't entirely sure. But the thing about entrepreneurs is that, whenever forced, we adapt. I had wealth, influence and extremely sharp elbows, none of which I have ever been timid in employing.

My suspicions were correct. The train made an unscheduled stop at a station I could not see a name for, owing to the sign being covered in mud that nobody had seen fit to clean. The station we hissed into was nondescript, and I could get no sense of the town that lay beyond it.

I considered disembarking. I desperately wanted to stretch my legs, but found they ached too much. I found I still felt too weak after my food poisoning attack to motivate myself to do anything more strenuous than sit up in bed and wait to see what would happen.

The more energetic passengers duly got off the train and began wandering up and down the platform whilst railway workers changed the bogies under our carriages. Several locals sitting on the platform's solitary bench stared implacably at the English, French, Belgian, Dutch, even American passengers who perambulated along as if it were a sunny afternoon in the park.

Nothing more happened for a long period of time. I assumed that the police, if there were indeed any in this part of the world, were taking their time to arrive.

Bored, I fell into a troubled sleep. My dreams were filled with Frank Hatch's large, beaming face.

When I woke again it was almost dusk outside, and we still had not moved. I saw no evidence of anything resembling a police presence. Nothing to indicate that the matter of Frank's demise was in hand. The train staff were nowhere to be seen either, at least not on the platform, which was now dark and empty. The Rossiya's passengers had all climbed back on board, evidently, for it was dinner time. I could hear chatter in the dining car, and footsteps passing my cabin.

I climbed stiffly out of bed, running my tongue over my teeth, which felt unclean, and furry. To my amazement, I found yet another chunk of something leathery and resistant stuck behind the farthest molar on my right side. I had no memory of eating anything in the last few hours, and was duly puzzled. I had a terrible headache after sleeping so long, and familiar pangs of hunger began to reassert themselves after a long absence. I ignored them. I had no desire to risk another bout of poisoning. I was fully determined to go hungry until Irkutsk if I had to.

I went to wash again in the hand basin in the corner of my cabin.

The water, as it rinsed off my skin, was pink.

I could not make sense of this, so I examined my reflection in the mirror over the sink, and found, to my horror, that I was covered in blood.

I managed to stop myself screaming by sheer force of will alone.

*

The blood was everywhere: on my face, hands, arms, body, bedding, my husband's pyjamas. My walls showed evidence of further staining, with several large, incriminating smears covering the door handle.

Sleepwalking? I wondered, hysteria threatening.

But how? I've never sleep-walked in my life.

And, more importantly, I asked myself as I frantically tried to clean the blood away, just whom, exactly, did all this blood belong to, if it wasn't mine?

*

After an hour of scrubbing, wiping, towelling and cursing, I finally managed to rid myself and my cabin of most of the gore. My bedsheets were beyond saving, as were the pyjamas and the cloth I cleaned up with. I bundled them all up and found, with relief, that little blood had seeped into the mattress on my bunk. I was able to flip it to the clean side. As I did this, the train, which I had not noticed stoking its engine once again, chugged out of the station. I did not know if this was a good thing or not, but took the opportunity, once we were some distance from the mystery station, to open my window, and throw the bloodied sheets out. They landed in amongst the ghostly white birches, and were soon left behind, evidence of a crime I wasn't sure I had committed, but had a nasty suspicion, owing to the foul taste in the back of my mouth, that I somehow had.

*

I tracked down Vera and asked her what our situation was. She told me that nobody had been able to rouse law enforcement at the last station, so the conductor had decided to travel onto the next city, Novosibirsk, and attend to the matter there. She asked me if I wanted to dine in my room, because the restaurant car was full, no doubt with passengers hungry for gossip, rather than food. I declined, but thought I would use the opportunity to check as much of the train as possible, while dinner was being served, for evidence of any indiscretion on my behalf.

It didn't take me long to find the next victim at all.

I did it by process of elimination, starting in first class, where the last killing had taken place. I worked methodically along the car, knocking first at each door, trying the handle when nobody answered. I only had to do this five times before I found another dead body, or rather, a pair.

I recognised them immediately, to my great distress: the elderly woman and her companion who had shared the dining car with us back when I had been afflicted with the collywobbles. Frank had distracted them from my indiscretions with idle chatter, and they had been bemused but polite.

Now, they were nothing at all, only flayed skin, torn hair, smashed bones. Their blood was barely dry on the walls.

I backed out of their cabin slowly, closing the door on the scene and retreating to my own berth, where I sat in silence for a long, long time, worrying at whatever was stuck between my teeth until it became too aggravating to bear.

Whereupon, I used a pair of ivory tweezers from my vanity case to pluck the offending item out of my mouth and held it up to better examine it.

And what I found, pinched between the tongs of the tweezers, part of a set that had been a gift from a Scottish Baron once fond of me, was unmistakable.

It was skin, of the human variety. A great, long strip of it.

I rushed to my sink, thrust my fingers down my throat, forcing myself to vomit. I grabbed the sides of my washbasin and heaved and shuddered, registering distantly, even as I regurgitated a large mass of splintered bone, matted hair and other, unmentionable things, the distinct crack and shatter of porcelain breaking under tremendous force.

*

All I knew after this grim discovery was that I was no longer to be trusted. I had to get off the train before anyone else died, and was eaten. By me.

That I had done these foul deeds, there was no question. I have never been one to dispute irrefutable evidence out of stubbornness or an inability to accept wrongdoing. I did not know how, exactly, any of the awful events unfolding had transpired, but I did know that my cabin basin was filled with half-digested human remains, and there were three fresh bodies on my train missing sizeable cuts of meat that correlated too closely with the contents of my stomach for any other conclusion to be drawn. I decided not to beat my breast about it, and packed a small valise, taking with me only enough essentials to see me through a day or two, whereupon I hoped to be better informed about my bizarre new behaviours.

I waited until long past midnight, having no trouble staying awake now that I knew what I did while the human part of my mind was switched off. When I was sure all the other passengers were asleep or had retired to a further part of the train, I marched resolutely along the length of it until I found a door in a carriage towards the rear, a door that could, with some force (force I now knew I possessed, although from what source it had been bestowed was a mystery), be jemmied open while the train was still in motion.

Then, with the dark night rattling past, and trees blurring all about, I jumped, clutching my valise tight, and the Rossiya raced onwards without me, which was the best thing for everyone on board, all things considered.

*

I wandered for days, and days. I had not considered that the enormity of the Siberian forest, (which I belatedly remembered was called the taiga) and how the sheer volume of trees, from birch to pine, fir to hemlock and spruce, all of which looked identical to me although I knew they were not, would affect me so. I do not, truly, understand how I survived that period of time. I ate berries and tree bark and promptly evicted them before they had a chance to digest. I drank river water, and found it could not sate me. I heard bears and once came across a pack of wolves, whom I fully expected to attack and devour me, but they ran off whimpering as soon as my scent travelled downwind. Mosquitoes, midges and horseflies were not so leery, and plagued my every step. Masses of them gathered on my hands, neck, and face. On the third day, I looked down at myself and saw I had grown a protective layer of thick, dark fur, through which the mosquitoes could not penetrate. I shed my travelling clothes shortly after, for they had become cumbersome, impractical. My appetite swelled with each passing hour, until my hunger was all I could think about. The temperature climbed and plummeted wildly from morning to night, so I was alternatively sweltering or shivering as I shuffled along.

And then, just when I thought the best thing was to lay down quietly on the banks of a stream and wait for death, I stumbled across a small wooden cabin, and there, chopping wood, strong, sinewy arms wielding an axe skillfully and with the repetitive dexterity of a machine, I found you.

To your great credit, you were not put off by my wild appearance. You took me in, draped me in a blanket, and served me a dinner of raw meat, from which animal I do not know. I have not yet decided if I shall let you live or devour you while you sleep, for I have not yet discovered the depths of my own depravity, but in any eventuality, you have proven yourself an excellent listener, and a kind and decent man, especially considering that my fur is now almost a foot long all over my body, and I rather fancy my teeth and fingernails have grown too, although I cannot find a mirror to confirm this fact. Perhaps you are short-sighted, and have not noticed, or perhaps you are just a very accepting individual, a rare find in these harsh, modern times. I know you do not understand a word of my English, just as I do not understand your language, but that hardly matters, under the circumstances.

What matters is whether or not I can keep my last meal down at all.

If not, I shall make for a very poor house guest indeed.

LESS EXALTED TASTES

John Guthrie stood at the end of a long gravel driveway and stared in unadulterated joy at the largest mansion he'd ever seen. In the meagre light of an autumn day, the scrolled corbels, smooth limestone ashlar, and innumerable sash windows of the house shone with promise, a promise picked out in high relief by a fleeting sun that occasionally fought its way through heavy, rain-laden clouds. A storm was coming. The trees around him rustled with a quiet anticipation that he, in his excitable state, could not hear.

All John Guthrie could hear was the sound of money singing.

He wet his lips, looked again at the sales pamphlet he carried. The name of the property was typed out in bold capitals: "THE ROOST". Beneath, a cut-and-paste history lesson. John had skimmed it twice already. Formerly a Bishop's Palace, now privately owned, The Roost was built in 1770, after the great famine. It was sold by the church ten years later to an Anglo-Irish absentee landlord who chose to reside in England, leasing the house to a cruel and entitled plantation owner called Edward Daly, who regularly beat and abused the slaves he brought with him until the master of the house was, in turn, beaten to death one night by the members of a secret peasant society from a nearby village called the "redboys" (owing to the fact they wore red smocks whilst out on nightly raids). These vigilantes had been angry with the extortionate rents Daly's landlord had enforced upon purchasing the estate. Daly was strung up by the neck over the front door of The Roost with his own whip, breeches down around his ankles. The men and women he'd enslaved ran like water down a pane of glass, fleet-footed and full of terror through the shadows of the grounds, silently and swiftly making their bid for a life away from the wants and needs and tempers of a man who had no right to their freedom.

After that, the house fell into disrepair and remained abandoned for decades. Perhaps this is why it escaped the "house burning mania" of 1919, when hundreds of Irish country houses were destroyed during the War of Independence. Not much point burning down something that was already a ruin.

Eventually, the estate was auctioned off to a wealthy family from New York whose descendants still lived there today. As far as John could see, the current generation had not invested in repairs or upkeep of any sort, preferring to exist in a much less exalted state than he would have considered tenable for such famously affluent people.

Not that John Guthrie cared about any of this, even after a third reading. All he knew was the building was well-situated near a major road, and ideally suited to development. He could easily slice The Roost up into at least ten apartments, perhaps more at a squeeze, all of which would make him a pretty pot in monthly rent. City folk would eat them up, he knew it. He'd market the place as luxury living, scrub the controversial stuff from the history of the house with tactful marketing copy.

John blew his cheeks out and wriggled his fingers around the edges of his pamphlet. If he could land this, he was pretty sure he was about to make a fortune.

But first he had an appointment with the owner, a certain Miss Valerie Compton Dubois. John had heard a fair amount of gossip about the current mistress since the house went on the market: Miss Dubois was rarely seen in public, was extraordinarily difficult to get hold of via any of the usual modern communication methods, and seemed to pride herself on being unpredictable and capricious. John figured he knew what was behind her behaviour: shame. Pure and simple. How could it be anything else? All that old money, frittered away. Certainly not spent on maintaining the vast pile of bricks and mortar before him. Miss Dubois had created nothing beyond a legacy of debt and decay, and the beginnings of the end of her dynasty.

John could fairly smell the sad scent of rotting lucre from where he stood, some distance off.

All of which meant he had the advantage, if he could leverage it properly. He could knock the asking price right down. He had no qualms about doing so. It was good business.

He walked up the drive and made notes on the edges of his pamphlet in red biro. *Driveway resurfaced. Tree surgeon. New perimeter wall and fencing. Security gates.*

The Roost, which sat in a tree-choked enclave of giant oaks, seemed in far better condition at a distance than it did up close. The closer he got, the more his heart sank. The west wing of the mansion had subsided considerably. John could see several large structural cracks in the masonry, along with a sagging roof right at the very end of the wing, a sure sign of rotted joists. He wondered how bad the rooms were in that section. The whole place would need gutting, shoring up, stabilising, new foundations dug and re-laid, definitely new roofing, window casement replacements, guttering, a new heating system, wiring, plumbing, sewage cisterns...he started totting up the costs on the back of the pamphlet. As he did so, he felt a spot of rain on the back of his hand. Looking up, he saw birds flying low and quiet, settling in huddled clumps on the chimney stacks of The Roost. He wondered how much bird shit was blocking up the chimneys and added bird-guards and repellents to the itinerary of repairs.

After a moment's pause, one more thing: landscaping. He was referring mostly to the gardens flanking each wing of the house, which were overgrown playgrounds for rampant weeds, brambles, nettles, and bracken. Here and there he could make out the foliage-shrouded forms of statues. Other things lurked in the brambles: a crumbling fountain, an ornamental obelisk with the tip snapped off, a weird, alien-looking plant with giant, purple, globe-shaped seed heads.

He finally reached the front porch, feeling somewhat exposed.

Intimidated by the sheer size of the property up close, John took a moment to gather himself before ringing the doorbell, and in doing so, saw he was not alone. A window cleaner was climbing up a ladder set up to one side of the porch, squinting up glumly at the task he had ahead of him: hundreds of small, lead-lined panes of glass.

John waved 'hello' in a cheery show of false sympathy, thinking to himself: *this is what fucking happens when you don't try hard at school, matey boy. You end up as a window cleaner.* The cleaner did not wave back, having his hands full.

John rang the doorbell. He was not good at waiting, but forced himself to be patient. There were no lights to be seen inside the house despite the gathering darkness of the day. In fact, apart from the window cleaner, there were no visible signs of life anywhere. Doubt pricked him. Was the owner even in? His secretary had written ahead to confirm his appointment, so she'd better fucking be in. Written and posted a letter, with a postage stamp and everything, like it was 1922, instead of a hundred years later.

His bell remained unanswered. Uncertainty and annoyance took a firmer hold of his guts the longer he stood there.

No matter, he told himself, as calmly as he could. Perseverance was the name of the game. His future lay in this house, he could wait right here until fucking nightfall if he had to. He rang the bell again, more insistently this time.

Nothing.

He began to play a game with himself, imagining what he would do with the money he was going to make. What would he buy first? A new car, definitely. Trips to the casino, maybe rent a suite in Monte Carlo and fill it with coke and champagne and women who liked the finer things in life, women who were willing to lick his balls and chase dreams with him: dreams of cold, hard cash. With money it was easier to enjoy beauty, everyone knew that. He would buy a piano or something, fuck girls over it until he got raw.

He abandoned the doorbell and reached for the large knocker mounted upon the door itself. It was painfully cold to the touch, a great brass clapper fashioned into the head of a greyhound with a jagged bone in its jaws. He lifted and dropped it, and it crashed against the door as loud as a gunshot, the hinge nipping his finger. He yelped, sucking at a blob of blood that welled up instantly.

The window cleaner, who was yet to clean any windows, laughed.

"It got me, too!" he called, waving a steaming flask at John.

John scowled.

The man shrugged in a good-natured way, *whatever, pal,* and poured himself a coffee whilst balancing on top of his ladder like a lunatic.

John glared in hate at the still closed door.

Why was no one answering?

Talk about taking the wind out of his sails. He had even planned his opening speech, miming a firm handshake and confident smile in his bathroom mirror this morning. Anger grew within.

"Hey!" he called out to the window man. "Are they even in? Is it worth me looking round back?"

The window man chuckled ruefully. "I wouldn't. Bloody great pack of dogs tied up round there, hiding in the brambles, tried it myself. Nearly got my dick chewed off. Just have to wait, they're a bit slow, but they'll get to you eventually."

John knocked again. The enthusiasm leaked out of him like air from a punctured tyre, but he was not leaving until he got what he came for. What he was owed.

The door opened.

A mere crack. But it opened.

"Ah!" said John, excitedly.

"Yes?"

John gawped. He found himself looking through the crack into the huge dark eyes of a girl who could be no older than fifteen, sixteen at a push. She was unusually tall and extraordinarily beautiful. Unconventional? He couldn't think of the right word, and suddenly felt flustered. She was so young. He had expected...what had he expected? A butler? A housekeeper? Or the owner herself.

The girl regarded him coolly. John felt sweat pop out upon his top lip. He just barely stopped himself from saying "Is your mother home?" and snapped his mouth shut, resisting the urge to push his way inside without introduction.

Behind the girl, an enormous staircase was just visible at the end of a dark entry hall clad with damp-stained velvet wallpaper which curled away from the sodden plaster beneath in long, unappealing strips. Portraits of stern, be-jewelled people stared at him in an unfriendly manner from the shadows. He couldn't be sure but he thought he heard the low rumble of a dog growling from somewhere behind the girl.

Best not go in uninvited, he thought, remembering what the window cleaner had said about the dogs round back.

John fumbled for his card and handed it through the ungenerous gap between the door and his person.

"I have an appointment," he managed.

The teenager took the card and vanished, closing the door in his face.

When she reappeared fifteen minutes later, the girl opened the door properly this time, with a sudden, graceful movement. John fell through it in relief, the gloom of the interior swallowing him hungrily.

He took a moment to adjust to the darkness.

He was inside. Inside!

First mission accomplished. Now, he could finally get a good look at the place.

He craned his head back and stared.

He never thought, after almost three decades of selling properties of all shapes and sizes to people who didn't know what they were being sold, that he would be excited by a building ever again. Over the years it had become increasingly difficult to feel strongly about anything, but the sheer scale of The Roost made him lightheaded. A once-gilded wooden ceiling soared thirty feet, if not higher, over his head. Huge window casements lined the whole floor, letting in weak, filtered light at intervals where the curtains, sagging from their rails and hooks, refused to close properly. The acoustics betrayed how much space John would have to work with, even as his eyes struggled with the unreliable lighting: every tiny movement he made came back to him as an amplified echo. Marble and wood and stained glass and cool granite gave the place a sepulchral air.

But it wasn't just the size of the house that made John feel a little weak at the knees.

It was the decor.

Like the portraits on the walls he'd spotted earlier. Up close, they displayed an assortment of characters who all shared the same high cheekbones, dark eyes, and large build that could have been mistaken for an artist's style choice were it not for the girl who stood before him, looking as if she'd walked fresh out of one of the paintings herself. *Family resemblance,* he thought, trying not to gawp too obviously.

Beyond the physical similarities, there was a thematic approach to the portraits that made John suddenly very uncomfortable.

Because the family, in their various generational iterations, had a rigorous and rather morbid fascination with death. Or, more specifically, with hunting and killing things.

Take the portrait on his immediate left, for example, of a young boy. A blood-soaked frilly lace ruff encircled his neck. In a ring-encrusted hand, he held what looked like a freshly harvested heart, which dripped onto the blue satin of his attire. His face was smeared with blood from nose to chin, and his eyes seemed very dark above the red. He was baring his teeth. John could see blood and gristle caught between the boy's incisors.

In the next painting along, a woman wore a velvet dress, corset open at the front, pale breasts spilling out, one nipple free. She rested a loaded crossbow on her shoulder, and a dead pheasant with a bolt sticking from under its wing was draped across the other. The head of the pheasant was missing. The woman's cheeks bulged, and John realised she was chewing on it like a gobstopper. Her free hand had disappeared beneath her cascading silk skirts. John cleared his throat when he realised why that was.

He started to feel faintly sick. He looked at another painting, hoping to see something more staid, formal, proper. Instead he saw an elderly gentleman with a large floppy cap savagely dicing a hare upon his knee with a ruby-encrusted dagger. The man was smiling happily. In another painting, a young girl, similar in age to the one who stood nearby, cradled a cloth-wrapped bundle to her chest. The cloth had once been white and was now soaked crimson. The girl's face drooped in sadness. Her tongue protruded from between wet lips to capture a single bead of blood that stained her chin.

John blew out his cheeks and shook his head. Then, he noticed the staircase.

It was monstrous, an enormous, carved, polished, twisted leviathan that dominated the entrance hall. The mouth was as wide as John's own dining room, easily. The marble-capped steps that led upwards were a livid grey, and the surrounding wood was walnut, glossy and darkened over the years by generations of hot hands sliding up and down the banister, shaping the wood under constant caresses. John could see birds of prey, game, deer, boar, and hundreds of grimacing greyhounds carved into the bannisters and railings with an astonishing attention to detail. The whole staircase was, in fact, a sculpture, a shockingly realistic hunting scene. Here and there the heads of mauled pheasants hung, necks loose and limp. A rabbit's frantic wooden eye gazed at him, pleading for rescue. A roe deer and its baby ran for their lives, heads craned forward in desperate exertion as they were chased by the hounds. John could almost hear the dogs baying and the deer coughing in terror. At the very bottom of the staircase, the rearing form of a defiant stag formed the foot banister. Its wickedly sharp antlers were chipped and scarred, but deliberately so. This was a fighting stag. Rampant, saliva dripping from slack jaws, it fought like a king for its life, three hounds hanging from it, teeth and claws ripping at tender hide, their collective weight bringing the beast down in agonisingly slow motion. The stag, defiant to the very last, roared at the indignity of its violent death captured permanently in solid wood.

John raised his eyebrows.

He made a small note on his clipboard.

Dismantle and replace staircase.

The house was, surprisingly, much warmer inside than out, and filled with a cloying smell of incense, wood smoke, furniture wax, dried lavender, and the faint underlying odour of damp and wood rot. The back of John's throat tickled. He could use a glass of water but knew better than to ask.

'Impressive,' he said weakly, waving at the staircase and the paintings.

"Mother will see you now," the girl replied, sounding amused. She turned on her heel and disappeared into the interior of the house.

John hurried after her, unwilling to be left alone in the violent hallway. He followed the girl through a long gallery to the left of the staircase, across several once lavishly decorated rooms facing out to the rear of the property. The windows in these rooms were choked with brambles, some of which had forced their way into the house through broken panes of glass. The window cleaner had a hell of a job ahead of him.

John tried hard not to stare as the girl walked in front of him, moving as if she were not made of flesh and blood, but rather smoke and warm air and shadow. The nape of her neck was long and smooth, and shockingly available. His fingers twitched every time he looked at it, and he began to sweat in earnest. She gave off a deep musk as they moved along. Motes of dust hung in the rare shafts of light that crossed his path. He sneezed, violently, feeling as if he was sickening. He'd spent too fucking long hanging about in the cold, outdoors. He needed to go home and to bed. Or have a long, protracted wank. Or both.

First, he had a fortune to make.

They stopped after a convoluted trek up and down and around and along spaces of all types and descriptions: galleries, stairways, halls, alleys, landings, until John found himself in a room decorated entirely in scarlet, a room so completely saturated in red that the woman waiting for them inside melded almost entirely into the walls. The only parts of her immediately visible were her hands and head, for she was wearing red too. Upon realising she was there, John immediately all but lost her again. Searching, his eyes were drawn eventually to two enormous mirrors hanging on opposite sides of the room, which threw backwards and forwards the framed image of a beautiful creature standing in her domain, crushed-berry lips and heavily lidded eyes watching him from further and further away, striking visage vanishing eventually into two tiny specks that he strained to see. There were thousands of her, he realised, and every single one seemed to be judging him with measured, amused intent.

A profoundly beautiful woman of indeterminate age, DuBois wore corseted red satin that trailed behind her like a mediaeval ball gown, and carried herself with the self-same possession, coldness and entitlement that her predecessors on the walls down in the hallway had. Again, the family likeness was clear. John had a sudden vision of her chewing on the mutilated carcass of a pig, sucking on ribs enthusiastically. He felt something strange stir inside him, and cleared his throat aggressively, responding to the woman's scrutiny the way he always did when he was in the presence of true wealth, of class. He became servile, ingratiating, pulling himself into the smaller type of man he knew old money appreciated.

"Good morning." He approached across the deep-pile carpet and held out his hand, not expecting the woman in red to shake it. "We have an appointment. My name is John. I'm the buyer?"

She continued to observe him for a second or two, then smiled radiantly, moving to meet him halfway. Her skirts billowed about her, hissing. She was very tall, towering above him at easily six foot four, five, if not more.

"Of course," she murmured. "My daughter gave me your card."

He swallowed.

Eyes on the prize, John. Eyes on the prize. Do not get distracted. She needs something from you, not the other way around.

She offered him some tea and dispatched her daughter to fetch it.

Silence stretched as the adults faced each other. John, who felt smaller and more hideous by the second, found himself ogling. She didn't seem to mind, tilting her head back, squaring her shoulders. Preening like a purring cat. Her dress was not a costume or style choice, but a genuine antique, thin in places where the fabric had worn through. The lace gathered at her sleeves and neckline was yellowed, ragged, nevertheless highlighting slender, long-nailed hands and full, high breasts between which a gigantic ruby pendant hung. John wondered what it would feel like to have the weight of that ruby on his face as he licked at her chest, then shook himself.

DuBois spoke.

"So, John Guthrie. You want to buy my house."

Her accent gave the simplest of words a ceremonial drawl. It had a strange effect on him. He felt dizzy. He sat heavily upon a low velvet couch nearby. It was as much as he could do to lift his pamphlet to fan himself.

The mistress of the house watched as John struggled for conversation. He realised her right hand was fiddling with the jewel around her neck, occasionally brushing against one or the other of her breasts. She was drawing attention to them, on purpose.

Christ, he thought, frantically trying to get a grip. *Christ.*

The daughter came back with tea, placed it on a table in front of him. It had a bitter taint that lingered, but did the trick. He sobered up somewhat and attempted to bury himself in formalities.

"Miss DuBois. Can I ask..." His collar felt too tight. He pulled on it with a crooked finger. "What exactly were you hoping to make from the place? Pricewise, I mean."

DuBois flashed perfectly white, wide teeth, lowering herself down onto the couch beside him. She reached for his hand, sitting so one warm leg brushed against his through the fabric of her dress. She playfully pulled a pen from the collar of his jacket where he had it clipped, and proceeded to write an eight-figure amount indolently, in flowing script, across his palm with the pen.

Her touch, hot and direct, undid his thin resolve to be professional. He stammered as he looked at the number tattooed into his skin. It felt like foreplay. She wanted so much money. He admired her gall. He found, with horror, that he was nursing the very obvious beginnings of an erection. This discovery made him leap from where he sat and retreat awkwardly to a safer place on the other side of the room. The DuBois musk followed and wrapped around him like a warm scarf. He turned away, subtly rearranging himself whilst feigning interest in the red wallpaper lining the chamber. He forgot, however, about the two giant mirrors that broadcasted his every movement a thousand times over and froze with his hand on his crotch as he realised the women could still see him.

"How many rooms did you say there were?" he asked, high-pitched voice tinged with panic.

The woman and her daughter laughed, compounding his humiliation.

"Would you like a tour?" DuBois countered.

John considered refusing her, but found himself oddly enraptured, once again trailing around the house like a suited, stocky ghost as DuBois pointed out galleries, parlours, bedrooms, bathrooms, dining rooms, a ballroom, a vast kitchen, gables, buttresses, and beams that could squash him in an instant if they ever fell, and more than one looked as if it were about to. Everything mouldered, hung loose, lay broken, stained or scarred. There was art in every corner, upon every surface, but all of it was debased, twisted, the stuff of nightmares. John tried not to see it, tried to focus on the work that needed to be done to the house. The costs mounted up the further he walked, his discomfort intensifying with each step. Every now and then DuBois brushed his hand with hers, or leaned upon his shoulder, or bumped up against him, heightening his anxiety. How desperate she must be, trying to seduce him, undermine him so he wouldn't fuck her over with his low offer. It was so blatant. He could see exactly what she was up to.

As more rooms revealed themselves, as more demented paintings and tapestries and figurines and ornaments burned into his brain, he began to panic in earnest without really knowing why. He should be the one with all the power, here, yet he felt like one of the animals in the portraits downstairs. Prey, soon to be caught and dismembered. He imagined DuBois hacking his ear off at the root with a silver table knife, nibbling at it as she side-eyed the artist from her canvas stage. The sudden vivid imagery terrified and turned him on, which in turn terrified him again.

What the fuck is wrong with me? he thought.

Had there been something in the tea?

DuBois led John to the very top of the mansion and through a tiny gallery, stopping outside an oak door thickly studded with iron bolts, which was initially hidden behind an enormous threadbare tapestry. Stitched into the tapestry: the image of a face, eyes rolled back in their sockets. An embroidered hand extracted brain matter from a pair of nostrils with a hook, just as the Egyptians did with Pharaohs before burying them, only this person was not dead, suffering eternally rendered in millions of tiny, silken stitches.

Ms DuBois swept the tapestry aside and hooked it back. John asked her why the door was hidden. She placed her hot hand over his eyes by way of reply. He did not flinch at her touch.

"Don't look," she whispered. Her fingers pressed into his face, exerting extraordinary pressure. She led him forward through the door. Somewhere in the bowels of the house, dogs began howling and barking, dozens of them. John's feet click-clacked reluctantly across hard, slippery flooring, and he almost slipped several times, but his captor kept him upright.

At last, maybe because she felt tears on her fingers, she stopped, uncovered his eyes.

John gasped.

He stood in a bedroom dominated by two things: a colossal four-poster bed made up with crisp white linen and red velvet pelmet and drapes, and, surrounding the bed, an eerie, silent crowd, formally arranged, a monumental marble audience assembled to watch a show not yet begun.

Statues.

Dozens of them, in a shocking, macabre array of positions and actions. It was like looking at a posed riot, a violent bacchic frieze. He was reminded of the paintings of hell he'd seen in an art book in the school library once.

"What is this?" he was unable to stop staring at the bed, even though, or perhaps because, it was the most innocuous thing in the room.

DuBois let out a long, lingering sigh.

"My passion," she replied. "This is my gallery."

The statues were exquisite and disgusting. They displayed acts of violence so specific that John felt his focus turn inward, attempting to escape. But there was no getting away, because he was unable to close his eyes even as he attempted to shut down his mind.

The sound of baying hounds grew louder. The pack were moving through the house.

None of that mattered when art like this existed.

There were men and women alike, all naked, captured in every horrific pose imaginable. Some looked to be his age, some older, bent with time. DuBois herself featured in these acts many times over, in various different iterations. Sometimes watching, sometimes participating, sometimes fornicating or perpetrating, sometimes...

Feeding.

A cameo player in her own vision, each brilliantly rendered version of her marble-white, impassive, perfectly motionless. Stone hounds frequently accompanied her in her adventures, sometimes as accessories, sometimes as tools.

The combination of sadism and artistry on show in the bedroom was more than John could bear. He tried one last time to move his body, to turn away, but DuBois gripped him by the chin with extraordinary strength and escorted him around the room to survey the statues more closely. John had no choice but to let himself be led.

"This is a particular favourite of mine," the mistress of the house said, stopping by an individual statue set slightly apart from the crowd. John saw a young boy grimacing in disbelief as he hacked the head of another man off with a serrated knife, into a waiting burlap sack. A marble replica of DuBois craned her head over the pair, one palm extended to catch beautifully sculpted, snow-white blood as it spurted from the man's throat. Stone greyhounds licked at the gore pooling on the ground. The statue-boy looked accusingly at John, hating the only warm, pink, innocent man in the room.

"I'd like to leave now," John said, but DuBois continued to hold him tightly in her grip, steering him to another statue.

Here was an elderly woman curled into a ball, arms wrapped about herself. On the floor beneath, her entrails spilled out like pale snakes, coiled and looping across the pedestal the statue was carved upon. A pair of marble scissors rested, abandoned, nearby. Dogs fought over her intestines like they were chew toys, playing tug of war with them. DuBois was nowhere to be seen in this sculpture, but in the next grouping of figures, John saw three bug-eyed men fighting, pulling at hair and skin with nails and teeth, ripping each other apart like...

A pack of hounds set upon a fox.

The baying grew louder.

DuBois' likeness was behind the fighting men, resting on an upturned log, her large skirts hitched, one hand enthusiastically working the exposed slit between her stockinged legs, which she'd torn a hole in. John realised, on peering more closely, that she was not pleasuring herself with her own fingers, but with a bare bone, the same size and shape as a finger bone.

One of the fighting men had an index finger missing, John noted as DuBois led him on with a small, knowing smile. The tips of her two front teeth protruded ever so slightly from her top lip, coming down to poke the soft skin of her chin.

Next, John was shown a marble body kebabbed upon a skewer, horizontally mounted arse to mouth. The body was being rotated by a kind-faced woman who wept as she turned the handle of a spit. Marble flames licked at the human meat above. John wondered, distantly, who carved these statues. They were beautifully rendered, every wrinkle, every fold of skin, every hair life perfect. Some of the figures had been draped with real jewellery, watches, and even a pair of glasses perched upon the sharp polished nose of a man who looked remarkably like his solicitor, although John had never seen his solicitor naked.

He realised he was being led through the statues directly to the bed, where a hummock in the linen became more obvious. He had not seen the lump from a distance, perhaps because the bedding was so white. DuBois undressed herself slowly as they moved through the assembled sculptures, her hand deftly unlacing her own corset with practised ease.

"What's in the bed?" John managed to ask, as his thighs bumped against its side. The hummock was the same size as a person. It moved slightly and made small noises of fear. John could see the linen moving up and down in small, panicked bursts.

"Art is best when derived from reality," DuBois said, stepping out of her dress entirely. Now completely naked, she was magnificent. Her skin was covered in strange red symbols, arcane and indecipherable to John.

"And an artist is happiest when using live models," she continued, smiling at someone over John's shoulder. That musky smell drifted into his nostrils again.

He shuddered as unexpected hands caressed him from behind.

DuBois climbed onto the bed and pulled back the sheets.

The window cleaner, bound, stripped of his overalls, lay terrified beneath. Next to him, a series of instruments. Stone maker's tools.

Standing on the other side of the bed, a large block of marble.

No, make that two.

The women of The Roost came to stand together, tall, impassive, bare skin gleaming, eyes filled with fiery longing. The daughter picked up her tools, and dogs poured into the room, overwhelming the space with their noise and stink as they milled about excitedly.

"What would you have them do, Mother?" the young sculptress asked, and the window cleaner, in full and complete comprehension of his fate, began to scream.

John felt heat rising from around his feet.

The deal, he realised, as sharp, wicked things were placed in his hands, had been done, long before he'd even arrived.

John could no longer hear money singing.

CHRISTMAS IN ANTARCTICA

*S*pend *Christmas in Antarctica!*
The advert said.

Tis the season...to be in Antarctica! Enjoy the ultimate white Christmas on a special celebratory voyage to the southernmost continent!

My eyes skimmed over the glossy travel supplement I was reading at breakfast. I chewed on a lukewarm piece of toast and peanut butter and contemplated how much disposable income you'd need to be able to afford to do something so extravagant. Imagine that, the trip of a lifetime: cruising around the snow and ice of Antarctica on Christmas day. Something rich lucky assholes did, not people like me. I felt a familiar yearning sensation in my heart. Think how incredible it would be, waking up on Christmas morning, peeking bleary-eyed through your cabin porthole, seeing the mysterious white wasteland of the South pole stretching out before you...I needed some adventure. Some excitement. I had barely travelled further than the next town in my relatively short time on earth. There was a world out there, and I wasn't seeing it. This felt wrong, a fundamental error on my behalf.

But what could I do about it? I was flat-out broke. I had a shitty, low-paid role in marketing. I couldn't really afford these travel magazines I kept torturing myself with, let alone book a trip anywhere advertised within their pages. There were bills to pay. A car to fuel and tax. Rent to cover. Every time I let my imagination run away with me, the sad realities and responsibilities of actual life brought me crashing back down to earth with a meaty bump.

'Christmas in Antarctica, yeah, right,' I muttered around another mouthful of toast, rolling my eyes at no-one in particular.

And yet the advert still poked at me.

I tried flipping to a different page, but the marketing spiel was too captivating.

Cruise amongst icebergs in a paradise where the sun never goes down! Land on the continent, take a voyage with penguins, seals, minke whales and humpbacks!

It sounded fucking amazing.

'Ugh, shut *up*,' I said, angrily tossing the magazine as I tried to dismiss the image that had stubbornly lodged in my mind. An icy wonderland, wildlife everywhere. White below, blue above. Me in the middle of it all, bundled, red-cheeked, wide-eyed. Finally experiencing life instead of going through the motions.

My boyfriend looked at me over the top of his steaming cup of coffee, amused at my little outburst.

'What's up?'

I sighed. 'Nothing. Just feeling...you know. The itch.'

'Show me.' He gestured to the magazine.

'There's no point,' I sulked. 'We can't afford it anyway.'

But I retrieved the magazine, flipped to the right page, showed him the advert.

He was silent for a moment, reading. Then he said:

'What you mean is that *you* can't afford it. I can.'

I scoffed. 'Fuck off, Ash. This trip costs...wait...' I scanned the small print, looking for the finer details. 'Ah, there, you see? A thirteen-day luxury cruise to Antarctica is going to set you back twelve thousand dollars per person. Twelve thousand! I'm pretty sure you don't have a spare twelve grand hidden in your underwear drawer.'

'I don't have an underwear drawer, Jen. The floor is my underwear drawer. And as it turns out, I do have some money set aside for a rainy day. Not twelve grand, but I don't think you need to pay that anyway. I have a friend who went to Antarctica. He said all you need to do is go to Ushuaia, the southernmost town in South America, where all the cruises leave from. If you hang around there for a week or so until the various tour agencies release the final, last-minute cabins they haven't been able to fill, you get a discount. A *hefty* discount.'

I shook my head. 'Well. Even if *you* can afford a luxury cruise in the South Pole, *I* can't. I am flat broke.'

'What if I leant you the money?' Ash said, casually.

I spluttered as a mouthful of toast stuck fast in my throat.

He reached over, thumped me on my back until I got a hold of myself.

'What?' I rasped.

Ash chuckled again, then turned serious. 'What if I lent you the money? Don't you think it's about time we got away together, saw a bit of the world? Got away from the daily grind?'

'Are you serious?'

'Of course I'm serious,' he replied.

I shook my head. 'No, I couldn't do that. You know how I feel about borrowing money from you. Anyway, I thought we were saving for our own place?'

'I'm not giving you the money, it's a loan. You'll pay me back. And we can still save for our own place. It might take longer is all, but it will be worth the delay. And I'll put in a ton of overtime when we get back. You won't be stuck in that job forever, Jen, I know you won't. Something better will come along.'

I snorted. 'Will it? Because I feel like I'm going to float from one crappy, demeaning, underpaid job to the next until I can figure out what I actually want to *do* with my life.'

'But that's exactly what I'm saying, Jen.' Ash leaned forward and caught my hands in his. 'Maybe you need to take a step away from it all for a little while, think about what you want from the future. Doing something like this...' He tapped the magazine for emphasis- 'Would give you the chance to see life from a different angle. Help you put things into perspective. It could be life changing for you.'

I gazed at him, wide-eyed, and couldn't think of a response. I could see he was deadly serious. He had the money, god knows where from, and he fully intended to lend it to me so I could get out of this apartment, out of this town, and out of my own head for a few glorious weeks and see something of the world.

He looked back at me, eyes warm and steady, and we sat like that for a moment or two as the implications of our conversation sank in.

There are occasions in your life, rare and precious, when you realise how much you are really cherished. Moments where it feels like you've been smacked upside the head with a large billboard painted with bright red capital letters saying *I LOVE YOU, IDIOT*. I felt my heart beat twice as fast as it usually did. My hands grew hot and sticky with anticipation.

'So, shall we do it? Christmas in Antarctica?' Ash asked me this as if he were talking about a trip to the local supermarket instead of a cruise across the Antarctic circle line.

'I'll think about it,' I replied, smiling.

In my head, I could already see icebergs dancing by.

*

Ushuaia, the gateway to Antarctica, was a small city at the very bottom of Argentina, or 'the end of the world' as the brochures liked to say. It sat under the Tierra del Fuego mountains on the edge of the Beagle channel, and was unlike anywhere I'd ever been before. As a major launch point for cruises to the South Pole, it was a hive of tourist activity. The streets of downtown were crowded with bars, hostels, several expensive hotels, restaurants, Argentinian barbeque joints and steakhouses and of course, outdoor gear shops. I fell in love with it the second I set foot in the place. Rolling snow-capped mountains surrounded the higgledy-piggledy, brightly painted buildings on all sides. It didn't take more than a ten-minute walk from one street to the next to find yourself suddenly confronted by ships, shipping containers, cranes and all the trappings of a well-established port.

The city had a low-key feel to it, despite how busy the streets were. Hardened backpackers rubbed shoulders with wealthy day-tourists, Antarctica expedition crew members, sailors, residents, locals and dock workers. Paint peeled off of buildings in flaky strips, exposed too many times to extreme cold and sea winds. Overhead, tangled bundles of electric cables criss-crossed every street, like vines in a maritime jungle. To a sheltered, been-nowhere girl like me, it was intoxicating. I drank in every sight and sound as we wandered the streets on our first full day after we arrived, jetlagged and a little culture-shocked.

Ash had been right: it turned out to be surprisingly easy to find discounted cabins on cruises to Antarctica. We shortlisted three cruise companies, based on price and departure date. We weighed up the pros and cons of each ship, then made our final decision. I found myself sitting in a little cafe, Ash hunched over his laptop, abusing the free Wi-Fi, credit card in hand, frowning as he waited for the payment to go through on a two-week cruise that left in just three days' time. I pinched myself hard on the back of the hand as he sat back and smiled at me. The payment had gone through. A confirmation email popped up on screen.

'Buckle up, buttercup,' Ash said, taking my hand in his. 'We're going to the South Pole for Christmas, baby!'

I felt sick with excitement. Things like this didn't happen to girls like me.

They just didn't.

The rest of the day was spent shopping for gear that we hadn't been able to buy back home. The travel company's confirmation email had come with a recommended kit list. We worked through it methodically: waterproof trousers, seasickness pills, neck gaiters, super polarised sunglasses, thick woollen 'world's end' socks, thermal underwear, and glove liners- extra nylon gloves that sat inside your snow mittens as a kind of base layer. A few hours later, we had burned through some serious money. I was starting to get twitchy and anxious about it, but Ash seemed relaxed and happy, so I tried to match his mood.

We ended our day in a restaurant called *'Tante Sara'*, exhausted but full of nervous energy which we tried to wash away with tall glasses of Cape Horn beer. When I looked down at the menu, I saw a tagline under a picture of an Albatross.

'Enjoy yourself,' it said, 'It's the End of the World!'

It didn't feel like the end, though.

It felt like the beginning.

'Shit, we overslept, Jen!!' Ash woke me in a panic. It was the morning of our departure.

And we'd overslept.

'Oh, *fuck!*' I swore as I realised what the time was. 'Why didn't you set the alarm, Ash?!'

'I did, but my stupid phone has run out of power! It didn't charge! The cable must be broken or bent or something. *Shit!*'

'Fucccckkkkkkkkk!' I stumbled out of bed, tripping over my backpack and barking my shin against a chair as I did so. 'We're going to miss it! We're going to miss the goddamn boat!'

By the time we checked out of our hostel, which was a little ways out of town, we were in shitty moods with each other, bickering back and forth like couples do when they're stressed. A cab arrived to take us to the dock. We got in, asking the driver to step on it, convinced we were about to miss the boat. When we bundled out of the taxi in a panic, we were informed by a dockworker that departure had been delayed for an hour, so we had plenty of time. Passengers were still boarding. We almost collapsed on the floor with relief on hearing this, then looked ruefully at each other, regretting the mean words we'd exchanged while stressed.

'Shall we start over?' Ash said, holding out his arm for me to slip a hand under.

'Let's start over,' I agreed. We took a slow, calm walk together to find our ship.

And when we found her, what a ship she was. She lay peacefully in the dock before us, white, long, sleek bow designed to break through ice. She was boxy and functional in the middle- I didn't know what parts of ships are called, but I was pretty sure 'middle' wasn't it- and there was a crane mounted on the back, near the stern. A collection of smaller boats were secured on the rear deck, near the crane. I later found out these were called Zodiacs- inflatable boats used to ferry passengers from the ship to the mainland during expeditions.

The ship had two observation decks: one at the aft, and one at the fore. Her name was painted on her side in Cyrillic text, for she was a Russian ship. I couldn't read the text, but I didn't need to. I knew what she was called: *The Akademik Ioffe.*

I was enchanted from the second I saw her.

The Akademik Ioffe was originally a hydrographic research vessel built in Finland for the Russians, we discovered. Now she was an expedition ship, and spent her days taking tourists on cruises to Antarctica and the Arctic, depending on the season. Tourists like me. I felt a surge of adrenaline and joy race through my veins as I realised I was going to be sleeping, eating, breathing, *living* on board for the next few weeks.

Ash read off the spiel from the travel literature we'd been sent.

'Forty-eight suites and cabins, ninety-six passenger capacity, ten zodiacs on board- zodiacs are those small boats you can see, look- a bar, a dining room, a lounge, a library, a gym, a sauna, top deck and observatory, massage room and the mud room.'

I said nothing, quietly observing the white, beautiful thing in the water in front of me.

'Happy?' Ash asked, draping an arm around my shoulders. A seagull landed on the railing next to us, and started screeching a mournful, ugly song across the water. I ignored it, nodding, my heart fit to bursting.

'Happy,' I whispered.

It was not to last.

*

Walking up the gangplank of the Ioffe was the most surreal experience of my life, up until that point. We filed in near the back of a long queue of people, some of whom looked a little familiar- I must have seen them around town or at our hostel. One girl about the same age as me turned, caught my eye and smiled.

'Hi,' she grinned, sticking a hand out.

'Hi,' I responded, warmly, doing the same. She had a firm grip.

'Sarah,' she said.

'Jen.'

'What cabin are you in?'

I scrambled for the piece of paper with our details on. 'Cabin 401,' I said, scanning the email we'd been sent.

'Cool,' Sarah replied. 'I'm in cabin 402! Hi, neighbour!'

I grinned. *This* is what travel was all about. Not just the things you were here to see. It was the people you met along the way. They formed part of the journey. Part of the destination.

Our passports were taken from us for customs. We were told we could have them back at the end of the cruise once we'd paid our bar bill. We laughed at this, and went off to explore. Sarah waved at me as she disappeared into her room, which was indeed next to ours. She shared it with a tall, confident British woman called Mary. I listened to them moving around, unpacking and chattering from behind the thin dividing wall. I smiled at Ash.

'I like her,' I said.

Ash rolled his eyes. 'Uh-oh,' he replied, shaking his head.

Our cabin was sparse and functional: two bunks, a wardrobe, desk, and a small sofa. There was a big window through which cold, pale light spilled. Ash looked at it and laughed.

'Perfect size for barfing out when the weather gets bad,' he said, and I tried not to think about that. To get to the Antarctic peninsula, you first have to cross the Drake Passage, a notorious stretch of ocean known for its terrible conditions. We would either get lucky and have a smooth crossing, referred to as the 'Drake Lake', or a terrible one, otherwise known as the 'Drake Shake.' I was nervous about the latter. I wasn't used to boats, I wasn't used to the sea, and I certainly wasn't used to twenty-foot waves and all the fun that came with them.

Ash saw my worried expression, rubbed my back soothingly. 'It'll be fine, babe,' he said, his voice gentle. 'Trust me.'

I frowned out of the window. I was a ball of nerves and excitement and expectation, and I couldn't wait for the ship to set sail so I could relax a little. Once we were at sea, it was all out of my hands. The longer we remained docked, the more I thought about all the things that could go wrong.

At last, when we were thoroughly settled in our cabin, I got my wish. The ship backed out of the harbour slowly. Ushuaia retreated, shrinking in size until it looked like a toy town. The ship, once it was far enough out, turned, pirouetting in the water with her thrusters, and let fly one loud, long blast from her horn.

Then, we were on our way.

On our way to Antarctica.

*

There was a lifeboat drill before dinner, where every passenger was instructed to don their lifejacket and queue in an orderly fashion ready to be taken onto the zodiacs in the event of a crisis. The zodiacs carried emergency supplies and rations as standard, in case the ship got grounded, hit a rock, or anything else sinister happened.

We were timed as we assembled. Instead of the six minutes we were supposed to be gathered within, we did it in twelve. The expedition leaders shook their heads and made jokes at our expense but I could see they were faintly exasperated with us. Next time, we needed to be quicker. I realised, with a moment of unpleasant clarity, that this was because ships sink fast. The difference between six minutes and twelve minutes could be the difference between life and death. The knowledge sobered me up somewhat.

After the drill, we were called for dinner, held in a large dining room with Christmas decorations hanging from the ceiling. I blinked when I saw them. In all the excitement, I had completely forgotten about Christmas. It seemed absurd to be thinking about Santa and stockings and sleigh bells in the setting of this ship. I thought about the gift I had bought for Ash, stashed away in the bottom of my rucksack. I hoped he would like it. I could never tell, with him. He was so self-sufficient, he rarely needed anything. I'd drawn a portrait of him in charcoal, rather than buy another gadget he didn't need with money I didn't have. Whether or not he liked it was something of a moot point, as I didn't have a back-up gift. He hadn't left my side since we'd flown out to Ushuaia, and I hadn't found enough time to go shopping before.

In the end, the portrait was lost anyway, and is probably slowly decomposing under the briny, freezing ocean somewhere, reduced to a tiny, floating scrap nibbled at by fishes, a vestigial smudge of black all that is left of my labour.

Perhaps. But it's not good to think about those sorts of things, not if I want to stay sane.

The dining room hummed with conversation and laughter. I could see, now all the passengers were assembled, there were about a hundred of us on board, give or take. We were introduced to a dizzying number of passengers from all over the world: Dutch, Australian, Russian, German, American, English, Irish, Spanish, Italian, Norwegian, Japanese...I felt breathless with the weight of new information thrown at me as I shook hands with person after person over a three-course meal served by a smartly dressed chef in a white hat. I knew, given time, I would get to know some of them, and I was looking forward to that. But for now, I felt overwhelmed. I was a long, long way from home and about to sail off into the Southern Ocean for the adventure of a lifetime. Networking and socialising was suddenly proving a little difficult.

I excused myself from dessert, told Ash I needed a minute, and went to find a quiet spot to sit by myself. My head ached and I felt too warm. I decided I wanted to go up on deck, get some fresh air. I slipped on a jacket and hat and climbed outside to the forward observation deck. It was peaceful out, if cold. The ship moved at a steady pace, the engine a comforting throb underneath me. I shivered and watched the islands of the Beagle Channel diminish as birds flew overhead, screaming in that wild, lonely way seabirds have. I realised we were now almost to the open ocean. A thrill went through me.

I became aware, then, of a presence beside me.

I turned, thinking Ash had joined me on the deck. It wasn't Ash.

It was a tall, thin man with hair so blonde it was almost white. He had waxy skin, and the palest eyes I had ever seen on a person. His nose was curiously long and pointed, his cheeks hollowed, and he didn't seem at all bothered by the cold, even dressed only in a light shirt and pants.

He stood uncomfortably close. I pulled away. Who the fuck was this guy? Didn't they have personal space where he came from?

'Hi,' I said, apologetically, even though he was invading my privacy. My default setting was always a polite 'beg-pardon,' and I didn't seem to know how to change it.

'I'm Jen,' I continued, sticking out my hand. Why, I couldn't tell you. Ingrained good manners, I suppose.

He stared at it with those peculiar eyes, and slowly slid his thin hand into mine. His palm was cold, shockingly so. Why was he out here without a coat on, the stupid man?

His fingers gripped me tightly, and I winced. He had long fingernails, and they dug into my skin. I felt a sudden, irrational fear shoot through me. There was something really off about this guy. He gave out an air of violence, somehow. Of being dangerous. His eyes were bright, artificial, and betrayed no hint of emotion. He seemed flat and cold and uncaring, like glass.

No. Like ice.

He didn't introduce himself, but I saw a word written in biro on a label on his shirt. We had all been told to write our names down on labels for the first night, so we could get to know each other.

His read, simply, 'Jack.'

'Nice to meet you, Jack,' I lied, trying to extricate myself from his grip.

He kept a hold on my hand. My pulse quickened.

'Please let go,' I asked, as calmly as I knew how. I was painfully aware I was alone with him on this deck. Most of the crew and passengers were still indoors, eating.

Jack didn't let go. His hand stayed tightly gripped around mine. I began to sweat.

'Please let go,' I said again, wondering desperately if maybe it was a language thing, he didn't understand me, or speak English. I could feel something wet on my hand, now. Thinking it was sweat, I glanced down, and saw with shock that his long, pale fingernails were so deeply dug into my skin they were drawing blood.

There was red all over my hand. *Fuck!*

I panicked, pulling hard to try and get free of him.

'Please,' I begged, one final time. 'You're hurting me. Let go!'

He didn't. I yanked backwards again, but remained stuck.

Then, to my immense relief, a voice called out from behind me, raised above the noise of the engine and the ocean brushing against the ship.

'Everything okay, Jen?'

I nearly wept as Sarah came to stand beside me. She frowned as she took in the scene: the strange, silent man, squeezing my hand so hard it was turning purple, blood dripping onto the deck.

'Hey!' She cried, outraged. 'Get off of her!'

Sarah placed a hand on the man's chest, and shoved him backwards, angrily.

Jack held onto me a moment longer, searching my face with his terrifying, blank blue gaze. Then, he let go. I sagged against Sarah in relief, my hand now numb. As the blood flowed back into it after his crushing grip loosened, agonising pins and needles flared. I bit my lip, determined not to cry in front of him.

'What the fuck, dude?' Sarah shouted furiously. She was about to launch into a full-blown tirade when Jack did something that made me sick to my stomach.

He lifted the hand that had gripped mine, studied the crimson blood that now painted his fingernails. *My* blood. Then, he slowly and deliberately sucked on the fingertip of his index finger, licking the blood off with a slow, exaggerated pleasure that horrified me to my core. He repeated this with every other finger on his hand, and when he had finished, Sarah and I just stood there, fixed with disgust and disbelief, while he smiled. He had large, thin teeth, too many almost for his crowded mouth, and I had never seen a smile so devoid of anything remotely human.

Then, he turned and walked away, and the ship swallowed him.

*

Once I'd recovered, Sarah and I went to tell someone about creepy Jack. We collared the first expedition leader we could find: a garrulous red-haired man called Duncan. We found him in the ship's bar, which was crowded. It was happy hour, two-for-one on cocktails. The barman, an affable man called Carlos, was busy pouring shots for a group of young passengers who chattered and laughed excitedly nearby.

Sarah and I cornered Duncan, herded him to a quieter corner of the bar. He kept half an eye on the room as we talked to him in low, urgent voices, and then gave us his full attention when I showed him my hand, which was now coming out in a deep, livid bruise. The small bloody crescents where Jack had dug his fingernails in were raw and painful, and I tried not to think about bacteria and diseases and tetanus as I stammered through the rest of my story.

Duncan's face had lost all jollity by the time I finished my tale.

'What did you say he looked like?' He asked, quietly.

I told him. 'Tall, really pale, really skinny, kind of weird-looking, white blonde hair. Really distinctive blue eyes.'

Duncan thought for a moment, then patted me on the shoulder. 'Okay, look,' he said. 'Here's what we'll do. Get yourself to the ship's doctor to check that hand. I'll look for this guy, and question him. I don't remember him from check-in, but it's always hectic, so maybe he arrived when I was elsewhere. Doesn't matter. We can keep him confined to his cabin while the Captain figures out what he wants to do. If he's going to be a problem, we could, in theory, turn the ship around, if we have to. We aren't too far from the port.'

I blinked. I hadn't thought of that. 'Turn the ship around?'

'In the worst case scenario. Might piss off a lot of people, but...'

I backtracked a little. 'I don't think you should do that. Not on my account. It would be such a shame. But I do think he is dangerous. Maybe if...maybe you could just...'

I trailed off as Duncan moved past us, tapping another expedition leader called Patrick who was also in the bar on the shoulder as he did so. 'We'll take care of it,' he said, as they left. 'Don't worry about it.'

I watched them go, jumping when Sarah touched my arm gently.

'Why don't we get a drink to calm those nerves before you see the Doc?' she said.

I reluctantly agreed.

We didn't make it to the Doctor at all. The pain in my hand subsided, so I figured it could wait. Sarah and I ended up around a table playing cards with a group of backpackers and Mary, Sarah's cabin mate, who knew all the rules. The group had a great time pointing and shouting *'shithead!!'* at the person left holding all the cards, which was often me. I struggled to keep up with my injured hand, but found, after a while, that I relaxed, with the help of alcohol. A little.

The ship's crew will take care of Jack, I told myself. As much as I didn't want them to turn the ship around, neither did I want to be stuck at sea with a crazy, creepy grabby-hands guy. But maybe we wouldn't have to turn around. Maybe Duncan could talk to him, warn him off. Let him know he was being watched. And if he couldn't be reasoned with, we weren't far from port. Surely a police boat could come and take him off the ship, if necessary?

I felt better once I'd worked through it all in my head.

Ash found me a little later. He came over to our table and stood there, frowning.

'Are you okay?' He sounded annoyed. I couldn't blame him. I'd disappeared during dinner and hadn't come back, and now here I was, drinking in the bar and playing cards. Guilt pinched at me.

'I'm fine,' I said, avoiding eye-contact. 'Just making friends. Come, sit down. We're playing shit-head.'

He squeezed in next to me, and immediately noticed my purple, swollen hand. 'Hey! What did you do to yourself?'

Sarah piped up, covering for me. 'She slammed it in one of the ship's doors,' she lied. 'They're so heavy, once they decide to swing shut there's no stopping them. She didn't move out of the way quickly enough.'

Ash tutted and cooed over me. I brushed it off, thanking my lucky stars that Sarah was on board. Sure, the night had taken a momentary bad turn, but if nothing else, I'd made a good friend.

The booze flowed, cards flew. The Akademic Ioffe made speed for the Drake Passage. Duncan didn't return. My hand throbbed dully, and in the back of my mind, I knew Jack was somewhere on board, lurking, my blood on his lips.

But I was damned if I was going to let him ruin the best Christmas of my entire life.

*

We found a British guy called Keith face down asleep on a table in the dining room the next day when we came in for breakfast. I poked him in the ribs to wake him up.

'Gerroff,' he muttered. I poked him again.

He rolled off the table, grumbling. 'I think you should eat something, Keith,' I laughed. He was clearly still drunk.

'Nah,' he mumbled, sloping off to his cabin. 'Eating is cheating!'

There were quite a few sore heads on board that morning. A big, booming Norwegian man called Trond who shared a cabin with Keith came and slumped down next to Ash and I with a groan. His eyes stared at two different horizons, and he ate nothing, just sat there with his head in his hands staring listlessly at his coffee.

'Good morning,' I said gently.

'My fucking head hurts,' he replied, miserably.

I was glad I hadn't drunk quite as much as everyone else, because it was a far rockier day at sea. A six-metre swell made breakfast hard to eat and keep down. So far, the sea sickness hadn't been too difficult to deal with. I had found that if I went outside as often as possible, or sat by a window I could stare out of, and took a pill when it got really bad, it was manageable. But the weather was changing fast, the 'Drake Lake' threatening to become the 'Drake Shake'. I could see green gills everywhere onboard. Not from the staff and crew, obviously. They had sea legs. But everyone else looked pale and tired as they tried to adapt.

The day's agenda had been planned with this in mind. To distract the passengers from feeling nauseous, the expedition team arranged a ship's tour. As the Ioffe was a hydrographic survey ship, Ash was beside himself with excitement, nerding out over the prospect of the science equipment and getting into the parts of the ship we'd not yet been allowed access to.

Breakfast was done, I left him talking to a quiet American called Rahul and ducked away to track down Duncan, who I found in the ship's library, going over a schedule for the day. He looked worried as I approached.

'Well?' I said, crossing my arms and wincing as I caught my injured hand. I could tell from his face I wasn't going to like what he said.

'Listen,' he replied, lowering his voice. 'I did a thorough door-to-door of each cabin, looking for this guy, okay? I had to talk to him before we took any further action, so I took Patrick and went with your description. White, blonde hair, pale blue eyes, extremely tall, thin, kind of weird looking. Hooked nose.'

I nodded.

Duncan took a deep breath. 'We went to every single cabin. Couldn't find a single person on board, not even a crew member, who fitted that description.'

I stared at him. 'But-'

He cut across me. 'What's more, I went through the passenger list with a fine-tooth comb again this morning. Not one single person called Jack on this ship, I'm afraid.'

'But...but...' I didn't know what else to say.

'Look,' Duncan continued. 'It's not that I don't believe you. You had a witness, and I saw your hand. I don't imagine for one second that you would make up something like that for attention.'

I bristled. Despite his words, the implication was obvious.

'So you believe me...but won't do anything about it?'

He sighed. 'If I can't find the guy, I can't talk to him, can I?'

'But where did he go? You can't just *lose* a passenger, right?'

'I am sure he'll show up again. In the meantime, be vigilant, and stay close to your partner. Ash, is it?'

Disappointment flooded through me. Why was he so blase about this? This was my personal safety onboard. He seemed so unphased, I started to question myself.

Was I overreacting? Had it really happened the way I remembered?

229

The ship took a sudden roll as it hit a large wave. I gripped onto a pillar, feeling sick. Duncan glanced at his watch, aware that the tightly scheduled day was slipping by.

I went back to my cabin and locked the door, upset. I did not come out for the rest of the day.

*

The next day I woke feeling more refreshed, and determined not to let anything further spoil my trip. Although the sea was still rocking and rolling under the ship, I felt more used to it now. I was getting my sea legs.

Ash and I went up to the bridge, a glass-encased observation point that housed all the navigation equipment. There was a bank of screens up there with all sorts of digital readouts and displays that I didn't understand. Ash drifted over to the equipment and started questioning the Captain, who stood surveying the sea from his position on the bridge. Bored, I looked around, spotted a door to one side of the bridge. Outside this door was a small metal platform, like a balcony. I felt a sudden yearning to be outside.

I shrugged into my coat and glove layers, dragged my hat down over my ears, and went out to the platform.

And there I stood, gripping onto a metal railing as the thunderous sound of the ocean filled my ears. The ship rose and fell as it cut through huge waves. It was like riding on the back of a giant horse. Feeling such a large, heavy object move beneath me with the force of the sea was exhilarating and a little terrifying as we listed from one side to the other. An Albatross appeared to my right. It swooped low over the waves, enormous wings coming to a sharp, aerodynamic point at each tip, eyes fixed forward. It banked and wheeled, rose up on an eddy of cold, southerly wind, and dipped back down again, tilting its body to one side so that a single wing-tip dragged through the water. Then the bird righted itself. I watched it soar, watched it keep pace with the ship, and I had never in my life until that point felt so alive.

And then, I saw it.

My first iceberg.

It loomed from the grey, at first an indistinct, white blob on the horizon. As we drew closer I saw it was maybe the size of our ship, which I thought was huge at the time. I would discover later that this was small fry as far as icebergs went.

It grew larger and larger. I found it so hard to believe this floating, fortress-like object was made from ice, not marble. It was so white, so pristine, it looked utterly man-made. The berg was accompanied by a flurry of tiny, wet snowflakes that landed on my face and eyelashes. The temperature dropped considerably. We were no longer just at sea, we were at sea at the ends of the earth, coursing through the Southern Ocean like a greyhound on a track.

I whooped in excitement. The wind snatched the sound and threw it away before anyone could hear, even me.

The ship skirted by the iceberg, far enough away to be safe, but close enough to get a good view. I saw some dark, fat blobs sitting on the lower end. Weddel seals. Their podgy, furry faces lifted lazily to watch as we sailed by. There were four of them. They reminded me of dogs, four tubby labradors lounging by a fire.

A great wave suddenly rose and smashed into the berg, and I thought then that I saw something else, something *within* the wave, something dark and big and sinuous. It was hard to determine in the black-grey seawater and churning spray, but I was almost sure of it.

A whale? I thought, excitedly, but another flurry of snow and sea spray doused my eyes. I blinked, trying to wipe them clear with heavily gloved hands.

When I could see again, there was one less seal on the berg, and no sign of anything in the water at all. I realised the wave must have knocked the seal off its perch, but hard as I tried, I couldn't see it swimming anywhere.

The berg soon retreated behind us. More followed as we headed further south, and they grew more surreal in shape and form. Sometimes, the water had eaten portholes and archways into the ice, giving the appearance of massive, carved monuments. The holes and crevices that ran through the bergs were always the deepest, brightest blue in colour.

Almost the same colour blue as Jack's eyes, I thought.

Eventually, I grew too cold to stay outside. I went back into the bridge, and slowly peeled layers of gloves from my freezing hands, feeling my face tingle and sting as warmth replaced the bitter chill. I couldn't see Ash anywhere on the bridge, and realised that an hour had passed, which was why I was so cold. He must have gone back to the cabin. I shook myself out of my coat, then froze.

Jack stood opposite me on the bridge, still and rigidly upright on the spot, unmoving despite the swell. His eyes were fixed hard upon me. I had the impression he had been watching me for some time. I felt the blood drain from my face. His whole body was held tight, as if he were clenching hard against something. I was reminded of a cat preparing to pounce. There was something different about his eyes this time. Before, they had seemed unnaturally blue. Now they were a pale, faint grey, so light his irises almost disappeared into the whites. It was like looking at an iceberg again. Was he...was he wearing contacts? I frowned, and blinked. I felt strange.

A woman walked past him, seemingly unaware of his presence, which was absurd, for Jack was easily over six foot and odd-looking. His angular frame and bright white locks were hard to miss, yet the woman didn't even throw him a glance.

Not even when, as she passed, Jack's hand lashed out lightning quick and grabbed a handful of her hair, and with a disgusting tearing, ripping sound, yanked a great clump of it out of her head, all the while maintaining eye contact with me.

I stifled a scream. The woman did not react, did not seem to notice there was now a shiny, bleeding bald patch on the side of her head. She rubbed at it absent-mindedly, and exited the bridge.

It was as if she couldn't see Jack at all. Not like I could.

As if he wasn't really there.

Duncan's words echoed in my mind: *'Not one single person called Jack on this ship, I'm afraid.'*

Jack lifted the hair up to his toothy mouth, and very slowly and deliberately stuffed it in, chewing on the fibrous clump as if it were a great delicacy. He swallowed, then leaned over to a nearby window, breathing heavily onto the glass.

I saw the window frost over with a glittering film of ice. Using a long finger, he wrote a solitary word into the frost, nails squealing painfully across the cold glass as he did so.

CHAOS, it said.

I bolted from the bridge, not wanting to see any more.

But I could feel those eyes on me as I ran.

*

I should have told Ash about it. I didn't. It was obvious he was having the time of his life on this cruise. So he hadn't noticed that I was a bit quieter than usual. So he hadn't noticed that I jumped more than I should, that I cradled my aching hand against my chest, that I didn't like to be left alone anymore. There was such beauty all around us, such sights to be seen! Earlier in the day he'd spotted a minke whale in the distance. He told me about it with a face shining with joy before we went to bed. I couldn't ruin the trip for him with my crazy, nightmare delusions. Even if they somehow turned out *not* to be delusions. Not after he had paid so much money for us to be here.

I kept my mouth shut. Thought about knocking on Sarah's door, talking to her about my visions, but it was quiet in the cabin next to us. She and Mary were probably sleeping. Besides, I didn't want to burden anyone with things that might not be real. Lying in my bunk, I replayed the oblivious woman's hair tearing loose a million times, until exhaustion rocked me to sleep.

My dreams were full of terrible, dark things.

*

The next day was Christmas Eve. Ash scrambled out of bed. I was slower to my feet, having slept like shit because of nightmares and the roll of the ship during the night.

We ran to breakfast, stuffed pastries and coffee down our necks, layered up and went out to the front observation deck. By nine a.m. we were supposed to be crossing the Antarctic circle line, and neither of us wanted to miss that. Ash because this was a life goal of his, and me…

Well, I just didn't want to be left alone anymore.

I scanned the deck when we got there for any sign of Jack, and found nothing, to my immense relief. The weather was worse than it had been the day before. Frozen rain hit us hard in the face, the deck rolled and pitched and we were drenched in moments.

A small crowd of us gathered as more icebergs floated past. We braced ourselves and hung on to each other in a little huddled group as the ship listed sharply. I suddenly felt very small and insignificant in the face of nature.

And where was Jack? I thought I could feel him watching, but could not see him. It made me frightened and breathless. Where was he?

Was he even real, or a figment of my imagination? Surely not- Sarah had seen him too. I clung to that as tightly as I clung to Ash while the waves tried their best to knock me off my feet.

And then, at nine-seventeen am that morning, we crossed the Antarctic Circle line. Sixty-six degrees and thirty-three minutes South, to be precise.

Someone rang a brass bell hung on deck to signal our crossing. The bell pealed out across the deck and a great cry went up from the assembled passengers, followed by delighted applause and cheering. The ship's fog horn let out a loud, blasting screech and we all jumped.

Trond brought out a bottle of Laphroaig he had hidden inside his jacket. We stood in a circle and toasted the icebergs that loomed at us out of the thickening fog and gloom.

I gazed up at Ash as the whiskey hit our cheeks and turned them red.

'It's going to be hard to go back to normal life after this, hey?' he said, gazing down at me, fondly.

I laid my head on his chest, too overcome to speak.

233

It really was. For lots of different reasons.

*

The weather cleared later that morning, as if welcoming us to the South Pole. The fog and clouds lifted, and brilliant, deep blue skies spread high over our heads.

Just like the brochure, I thought, and suddenly, Jack's spectre seemed less of a problem.

The Ioffe, having navigated the turbulent Drake crossing, now approached the Antarctic peninsula on waters as still as a millpond. We could see land: mountains, deep grey in colour and plastered with thick, brilliant white snow. Glaciers, ridged and cracked like dried mud, which tumbled into the sea. Icebergs, drifting everywhere, glowing a delicate, ethereal blue. There was not a man-made structure in sight. Not another boat, or building, or vehicle, or anything. It was incredible.

The whole ship came out on deck as we entered into a beautiful narrow passageway between the mountains called the Lemaire Channel. A hush descended as the ship glided on through. The channel was only a few miles wide, but there was a world of beauty contained within. We saw snow-capped peaks, glaciers, black granite spires and floating sea ice that bumped and ground against the ship as we passed. It was so stunning I almost forgot about Jack completely.

Almost.

Someone tapped my shoulder as I leaned over a railing. I turned to see a smiling couple holding out a camera to me. The guy, who introduced himself as Mark, smiled. 'Mind taking our photo?' He asked, with a thick Australian accent.

I took the camera and nodded. His girlfriend was called Flick. She grinned at me and threw her arms around Mark's neck. 'You're a sweetheart!' she said, then kissed her boyfriend on the cheek.

I snapped the picture, making sure to frame them with the Lemaire Channel stretching out behind. Ash looked on as this played out, his face a picture of contentment.

I handed the camera back and the couple thanked me, then went back to leaning against the bow, gazing at the view.

It was as I turned away that I glimpsed a bright, white shock of hair. A feeling of dread punched me in the gut.

I whipped back, lightning fast. Jack had materialised out of nowhere, which was impossible, but somehow not. He now stood next to the couple, on Flick's side. They both seemed completely unaware of him, wrapped up as they were in each other. I watched with a sick, sinking feeling as the pale man leaned in and whispered something in Flick's ear. I saw a white, frosty breath mist out onto her face. Crystals stuck to her cheek like diamonds. Her expression changed as Jack's words pierced her ear. She frowned, and her mouth turned downwards. Her cheeks flushed. She was *angry*, all of a sudden.

She turned to Mark. The unsuspecting man reared back upon seeing her face, which was a rage-filled mask.

'Babe?' he said, uncertainly. 'What's up?'

Flick didn't reply. She just shoved him, hard. She was tall, and strong, and she took Mark by surprise.

There was a second or two when he tried to get his balance, but couldn't, because Flick then rammed into him with her shoulder, grunting with effort, determined to flip him overboard.

'Stop!' I cried, but no-one seemed to hear me or notice what was happening right in front of their eyes. Ash stood contentedly beside me, gazing out at sea with a blank, stupefied smile on his lips.

'Ash!' I shrieked, shaking his arm desperately. 'Ash, she's going to push him overboard!'

'Hmmm?' He replied, absent-mindedly. 'That's nice, babe.'

Mark grappled with Flick, pleading with her to stop. His pleas fell on deaf ears. She reared back, then rugby tackled him, heaving him up and over the side of the ship. It all happened very fast. One minute he was standing there, the next, he was tumbling overboard.

I rushed to the side and peered down. Mark's body lay not in the water, but on an iceberg ten feet below. His head had connected with the ice hard. A bright puddle of blood now haloed around him. He was still alive, but twitching. I didn't think it would be long before he died unless treated.

I staggered across to where Duncan and Patrick stood chatting nearby. Before I could open my mouth, however, Jack's thin, long, waxy face pushed through the gap between them. Their expressions became slack, emotionless. Jack put his arms around the men and grinned at me. Without a word, the expedition leaders turned and walked away.

Jack put a long finger to his lips.

'Shhhh,' he said.

I heard a cry, and then a splash. I closed my eyes. I didn't have to look to know what had happened. Flick had thrown herself overboard, after Mark.

I looked anyway.

And saw nothing but a large ripple in the water, and bright, red drag marks on the surface of the iceberg.

The ship sailed on out of the channel without two of its passengers. I understood that I was trapped. There was no way for me to escape. Jack controlled the ship and had everyone on it under some weird sort of suggestive spell, Ash included.

Well, everyone except possibly Sarah and myself, for she had seen him too, but what good would that do me? Even if we could somehow get off the ship, steal a zodiac, figure out the crane and lower it into the water, where would we go? It was the South Pole, for fuck's sake.

The Ioffe moored in a bay sometime that evening. I waited for sunset, then remembered the sun did not go down in Antarctica during winter. The sky remained a pale sort of beige that somehow made me feel even more hopeless than ever as midnight approached, and I lay wide awake in my cabin, terrified and half-mad with worry.

*

The next day was Christmas day.

'Christmas in Antarctica!' Ash boomed as we woke, mimicking the marketing spiel from the advert I'd read weeks ago.

I tried and failed to raise a smile for him.

'Aren't you excited, babe?' Ash said, his enthusiasm waning as he saw my pale, worried face.

'I just...' I swallowed. 'I just don't feel too well, that's all.' I knew there was no point explaining our plight to him. He wouldn't be able to understand what he couldn't physically see, hear or feel, which I supposed I couldn't blame him for. I wasn't entirely sure I believed it myself. I didn't know what was worse, that Jack was real, or that I was hallucinating violent incidents around the ship for no discernible reason. Brain tumour? Concussion? Some sort of inflammatory thing?

I was too tired to do much more than wait the cruise out, and hope for the best.

Concerned, Ash hugged me. 'But you can't be sick, not on Christmas day!' His disappointment was obvious. He had been anticipating this occasion for weeks, and I was spoiling it.

I faked a smile for him, and wondered at what point that day I was going to die.

Christmas lunch was laid out on the front observation deck. As a special treat, four long trestle tables were spread out side by side, with plastic chairs all tightly crammed around them. There were paper hats tucked under the cutlery, party poppers on the plates and Christmas crackers at each setting. Behind all this, the spectacular wintry landscape of the peninsula spread out like a painting on a Christmas card, everything white and blue and crisp and cold.

We sat at a table with Sarah, Mary, Trond and Keith. Sarah and I looked listlessly at each other over the noise of crackers being pulled. Her eyes were hollow, with dark circles underneath. She had seen things too, I realised, unmentionable, nasty things. Jack had been working his chaos everywhere, and not just when I was watching.

'Kiss me,' Ash said, trying to get my attention. He had managed to get hold of a sprig of plastic mistletoe, which he dangled over my head.

With a dull feeling in the pit of my belly, I did as he asked.

Ash reached into his pocket mid-kiss, and placed something on my plate.

I looked down and saw a small jewellery box tied up with a large, cherry-red bow.

A box the right size for an engagement ring.

I took in a breath.

Not now, I thought, fighting back tears. *Oh God, not now.*

'Merry Christmas, babe,' Ash said.

With numb hands, I untied the bow, looking around furtively for any sign of Jack. Surely, if he was going to appear at any time, it would be now. Ruining this moment would be extremely characteristic of him, but I saw nothing. No trace.

A diamond ring glinted at me from within the box. I felt dizzy. Was this really happening? Or was this another nightmare?

Ash took the ring out of its box, and knelt down on the deck. Behind him, festive lights twinkled gently against a backdrop of snow-plastered mountains and that same rich, blue sky that had greeted us yesterday. The sound of people chattering happily died down to a low murmur, as the other passengers nudged each other and pointed at us.

'Awww,' said Mary, in a soft, teary voice. 'How lovely! He's proposing!'

I felt a hot tear slide down my cold cheek.

'So?' Ash held the ring up in front of him. The diamond on it caught the light and bounced it back to me, and I thought about all the things that the ring should have promised for the future.

Should.

But, I honestly couldn't see us surviving the day. Jack had designs on the ship, and its passengers. He was an agent of chaos, pure and simple. And he wanted us dead, I knew it.

I just didn't know why.

Ash stared at me with puppy dog eyes.

I swallowed, and nodded.

'Yes,' I whispered, too afraid to do anything else. Ash and I kissed. I threw my arms around him, crying. He mistook it for joy. The other passengers erupted into cheers and happy applause.

'We're engaged!' Ash crowed. I held him tighter. I was so afraid of what was going to happen I could barely breathe. I caught sight of Sarah over Ash's shoulder. She was white as a sheet.

And then, from the corner of my eye, I saw someone tall and blonde push back his chair. It screeched on the deck as he stood up with a ceremonial flourish of hands.

Jack.

He seemed taller and thinner than ever, hair so bright it outshone the snow. Unlike the rest of us, wrapped in our layers, he was still dressed in a thin shirt and pants, for the cold couldn't touch him. He looked down at me from his place further along the table, and a wicked, crooked smile lit up his face.

My heart turned to ice in my chest.

He raised his arms up, and started to clap. A slow, deliberate clap that mocked our happiness. The other diners carried on celebrating. They couldn't see him. Only Sarah and I could...

'Huh,' said Keith, frowning. 'Who the fuck is that guy? I swear I've never seen him before.'

I gaped, grabbing Keith's sleeve. 'You can see him? You're sure?' I shook him in my desperation.

'Well, yeah. Looks like a right prick,' he replied, and Ash grunted. I turned to look at my boyfriend- no, my fiancé.

'Can you see him, too?' I whispered.

Ash nodded, his face suddenly grim. He had an odd expression on his face, as if he was waking up from an unpleasant dream, the details of which he could only half-remember.

'Oh, thank fuck,' I said, my relief immense, as Sarah rose to her feet and joined us. 'I thought I was going mad. We have to get out of here, Ash, he isn't- that man, he isn't...he's not...'

I struggled for the words.

Jack stopped clapping.

He flexed a long-fingered hand instead, and snapped his fingers.

A single, sharp, staccato sound boomed into the silence his laughter had left behind.

And that's when Mary started screaming.

A long, angry, howling scream, a demented scream, the kind of scream animals make when they are fighting or just plain out of their minds with the unbridled rage only wild things are afflicted with- survival rage. Primal, base, uncontrollable. The kill, or be killed kind of screaming.

In a daze, I tore my eyes away from Jack and fixed them on the shrieking woman. Mary sat at the table, muffled by her outdoor gear, only a small section of her face visible through the layers of her jacket and her neck warmer and absurd green paper hat, but that was enough.

Enough to see that she was bright red, and completely, batshit-crazy out of it.

She screamed an endless, shrieking *'Ahhhhhhhhhhhhhh!'* that only stopped when she ran out of breath, then started up again after she took large gulps of air to help fuel her noise, and I couldn't see what had started her off, I couldn't see anything that would warrant that much fear and anger and volume and distress, so I assumed Jack had crawled into her head, put images in there she could not escape from.

Before any of us could react further, Mary picked up her fork, lightning fast, turned to Trond, who sat beside her, and sank the piece of cutlery deep into the Norwegian's left eye.

'ARGHHHH!' he roared, and clamped a hand to his face, howling in pain. I saw a fork handle sticking out of his eyeball. Blood gouted down his cheek and splattered onto the tablecloth below. He instinctively went to yank the fork out, then realised if he did that, he'd probably pull the eyeball out right along with it. So he just went on gripping the side of his face and howling, and Mary, who was also still screaming that idiot, mindless cry, looked down, saw more untouched cutlery by her plate, and went for her butter knife.

'What the fuck?' I heard Ash yell from behind me, and it was such a relief that at last, at long, *long* last, he could see what was happening. So could everyone else, it seemed, for passengers were suddenly hollering and scrambling over themselves to get away from Mary and her cutlery.

I snapped out of my daze, and screamed 'Stop her! The knife!'

There was a blur of movement. Patrick rushed into view. He launched himself at Mary, who flung herself in turn at Trond, brandishing the knife like she wanted to scalp him with it, still making her hideous racket. The expedition leader wrestled her backwards and onto the ground, evading her gnashing teeth and frantic limbs. The pair struggled, but Pat was younger, fitter, stronger. He yanked the utensil out of Mary's clenched hand and there was a moment were they looked at each other, panting. A second of stasis. Patrick knelt astride Mary, pinning her to the desk, his blue expedition fleece now splattered with blood. Trond still wailed in pain at the table, clutching his face with one hand and banging the tabletop repeatedly with his other, over and over, *bang,* he went, *bang, bang, BANG!* A member of the ship's crew was trying to get to him with a first aid kit, but couldn't move around the other passengers who were panicking all over the crowded deck.

Patrick lifted the knife carefully away from Mary, a slow deliberate movement that was designed not to trigger any further violence.

As he did so, Mary snarled and made unintelligible, feral noises beneath him.

And then Jack appeared, a slow, cold nightmare man.

He squatted down on his haunches next to the pair. White patches of ice began to spread across the deck from under his feet. Mary whimpered like a dog about to be beaten. Patrick, who could finally see the bizarre stranger, tried to push Jack away.

'Who the fuck are you?' He cried. 'What the fuck is your problem!'

Jack just smiled, and raised his hand.

Snap!

The sound once more boomed out across the ship. Pat went still.

So did everybody else.

Well, not quite everybody. The small group of us unaffected by whatever power Jack held in those long fingers huddled together, frightened, watching, knowing shit was about to get wild.

The finger snap lingered in the air. It was a signal. A harbinger.

And then, it died.

Chaos ensued.

Patrick lifted the confiscated knife high above his head, and plunged it down as hard as he could into Mary's open mouth, pushing it up into her brain. Mary gargled and shuddered, then went limp. Jack chuckled. He fondled Pat's hair, which immediately turned white, and stiff. I watched, rooted to the spot as the expedition leader's skin crusted over with ice. His heaving chest froze mid-breath. When the man was completely rigid, Jack pushed him over, casually.

Patrick fell hard onto the deck and smashed into a thousand glittering pieces.

And the passengers of the Akedemic Ioffe began killing each other.

With a roar, Trond stood up, flipping the table. There was an almighty crash as everything slid off onto the deck. He picked up a chair, the fork still sticking out of his mangled eye, and brandished it like a demented farmer scything corn. I saw the chair connect with an old man who was too slow to escape. His face crumpled under the impact of the hard plastic, and he dropped like a stone. A sweet Japanese lady in her seventies began to bludgeon her neighbour to death with her heavy, expensive digital camera, ululating as she did so. Brain matter and blood fountained as she swung, again and again and again. Another woman in an expensive fur hat clawed at her husband's face with crabbed, bare hands. He smashed a plate over her head, then pushed her down hard onto the edge of one of the trestle tables. She crashed to the ground and he stamped on her until there was not much left that was recognisably human, then, he turned and looked for someone else to attack.

The deck became a bloody, brutal battlefield around us. The air fizzed with violence and pain.

'Run!' I shouted at Ash.

I did not have to tell him twice.

We fled to the rear of the ship, joined by Sarah, Keith and Duncan, who yelled at us as we dodged flying chairs and fists.

'What the fuck is happening!'

'It's Jack!' I panted, jumping over a young couple who were grappling on the floor. One of the pair was trying to throttle the other with a noose made from a scarf.

Keith narrowly avoided a meat cleaver to the collarbone, wielded by the once smartly-clad and now blood splattered chef. 'Pack it in, mate!' He yelled, shoving the chef hard to clear his path. Chef went overboard, screaming and thrashing the meat-cleaver about in the air as he fell.

'Where are we even going?' Sarah panted, tears streaming down her face.

'Zodiacs! Rear deck!' Ash shot back, skidding on a puddle of blood and grabbing me to stop himself from going down.

'But we need a crane to get them in the water! We don't know how to operate that!!'

'There's a zodiac in the water already!' Duncan cried. He'd managed to get up ahead of us, barging people out of the way with rugby-player shoulders. An angry German man ran at him with a full magnum of champagne clutched in his hand like a club. Duncan punched him in the face before he could bring the bottle down, and shoved him to one side. 'We kept it afloat in case we needed it,' he continued. 'That's our best shot. But we don't have time to lower the gang plank, understand? You're going to need to jump.'

'From the deck?' I tried to remember how far down it was from the deck to the surface of the bay.

'From the deck. It's not far.'

Ash pulled me along. 'We don't have a choice. We need to go now!'

We reached the rear deck and looked over the side. There in the water sat the zodiac, just as Duncan said. We positioned ourselves above it, looking around all the while for Jack. I swung a leg up and over the side of the ship, and then the other, perching precariously on the side, gripping the cold railings for dear life.

I looked back at Ash for reassurance.

'It'll be okay, babe,' he said. 'I'll be right behind you.'

I jumped, and landed square in the Zodiac, my legs folding painfully beneath me. I scrambled over to the engine, realised it was a simple outboard motor. I fired it up, knowing that the bowline would stop me from zooming away until we were ready, and looked up at the ship, waiting for the others to drop into the boat beside me.

I saw Jack, then, up on the front observation deck, his arms raised up to the sky. He was drenched in blood from head to toe, smiling in ecstasy. Bodies littered the deck around him, and every now and then one would tumble from the ship, smash into the sea. Blood streamed down the prow and sides of the ship like rusty tears. Mangled Christmas lights dangled like broken vines across the bow.

It was, as he'd decreed, chaos.

And then something huge erupted from the water behind the ship, propelled by two massive legs. It was completely white, a vast, glaring shape in the vague form of a man, with two great arms dangling by its sides, only they were not arms, but tentacles capped with massive, webbed fingers that clutched something: a whale. A dead whale. Or at least half of one: only the end of its body remained, the dorsal fin and tail flukes. The head and the front half of the creature were missing.

It didn't take a genius to figure out where the rest had gone.

My eyes travelled up the leviathan's head, which was vast, a round, pale skull covered in glossy, milky skin. There were no features on the head except for a huge, yawning hole in the centre. A mouth. Inside, rows of teeth, each one the size and length of a man, needle sharp and pointing backwards, like barbs in the mouth of an eel. Row upon row of these teeth marched down the beast's neck, and into the dark oblivion of its gullet.

I looked for Ash. I saw him reach over blindly and grip Duncan on the shoulder. I couldn't hear what he said, but I could see his face, slack with fear.

I gasped as one of the colossal tentacled arms reared above the ship, rocking the zodiac wildly beneath me and almost tipping me into the freezing ocean. I had a sudden understanding of what had transpired. Jack, whatever he was, whoever he was, had summoned this thing from the deep with his blood sacrifice. We had been offerings to an old, ancient sea god, or demon, or something else entirely. My mind teetered on the edge of sanity as I heard the roar of the ocean erupting skyward. Another tentacle loomed, then wrapped itself around the Ioffe. This one protruded from beneath the surface of the ocean, and I realised the thing was not propelled by legs, but more tentacles, similar to those that functioned as arms.

The sea god dropped the whale carcass and reached down to the observation deck of the Ioffe, where Jack stood, arms opened in rapture to the strange creature he had summoned from the sea. With a deft flick, the mute skinny man was plucked from the deck, brought up to the level of the creature's mouth. The tentacle flattened out like a palm so Jack could kneel as if praying before an altar.

A long, grey tongue snaked out of the monster's cavernous mouth, pointed and thin, the same colour as shark skin. It quested the air, exploring the now tiny figure in its grip. The tongue dragged itself along Jack's back, tasting him, assessing. There was a moment of complete stillness, as Jack knelt in reverence, and the beast tried to judge his worth.

Then, a noise that I knew instinctively to be displeasure rumbled out from the thing's open mouth. Halfway between a roar and a shriek, the inhuman sound ripped through the cold southern air and tore up everything in its path. Snow and rock fell from the mountains all around, crashing down in thunderous discord. A huge chunk of ice calved away from a nearby glacier, and smashed into the ocean. Birds in the distance changed their flight paths, screaming in fear. The sea shivered and shook beneath us. I clung to one of the handles on the zodiac, bleating in agony as the noise assaulted my eardrums.

I had a moment, an awful, forever-moment when I saw Ash's face, and Sarah, Duncan, and Keith. They looked down on me with utter desperation from the railing of the rear deck.

Then, they began to scramble over the side.

'JUMP!!' I screamed, and they did, just as the sea god crushed Jack with one strong, slippery motion, hurling his mangled, flattened form away from itself in disgust. Then, with a furious, almost disappointed roar, it lifted the Ioffe clean out of the water. The bowline holding the zodiac to the ship snapped. I throttled the engine, getting as clear from the drop zone as I could, scanning the water desperately for signs of Ash and the others.

But there was no time to save them. With a colossal, grinding screech, the ship crumpled in the monster's sticky coils like paper. Then, the mangled mass of iron and steel was thrown back down into the bay.

I had a second to realise a tidal wave was coming at me from the vicinity of the ship. It was a second in which I thought I felt a frosty breath upon my cheek, when I thought I glimpsed a shock of white hair behind me in the little boat.

Then, the wave hit. I was thrown backwards. My head connected with the engine.

The world went dark.

*

My zodiac was discovered the next day by another cruise ship, drifting near an old, abandoned whaling station further round the peninsula. Ash and Sarah, the strongest swimmers, had somehow managed to find the zodiac amongst the chaos as the Ioffe sank down beneath the sea. They had hauled themselves aboard, near-dead from hypothermia, to find me lying unconscious inside, and jetted away as fast as the outboard motor would take them. Emergency supplies stored on the zodiac kept us warm and fed for a short while. Of Duncan and Keith, there was no trace.

Nor was there any substantial trace left of the Akademic Ioffe, despite many different organisation's best efforts to recover the wreckage in subsequent weeks. A sudden, freakish dip in temperature refroze the thawing waters of the bay solid for several months when sea ice was usually retreating, for it tended to peak in September and fall back by February. The fresh and unseasonable freeze scuppered all immediate recovery efforts and confounded meteorologists everywhere. By the time divers and boats were able to get out to the site again, the chances of recovering much of use had long passed, for it was assumed the Ioffe had sunk to depths unnavigable, or at least, this much was reported in the limited news coverage the disaster garnered. And by limited, I mean, the story was everywhere for a few weeks until it became apparent that the mystery had no clear resolution. Then, the headlines moved onto other things. This was a pattern I saw time and again in the years to come, with missing planes, with other anomalies. People forgot tragedy as quickly as they mourned it. Like a melted snowflake, the story of the sunken tourist ship largely vanished from view, leaving behind only rumours and ripples, and those smoothed out eventually too.

Forty-eight suites and cabins, ninety-six passengers, a bar, dining room, lounge, library, gym, sauna, top deck and observatory, massage room and mudroom. All gone, to the bottom of the ocean. Dragged there by god knows what, summoned from the depths by god knows who. A sprite? A demon? Something else? Not human, that much I knew. And why had he chosen us? Why our ship, our cruise?

I would never know. Nor would I ever see the terrifying, pale man ever again. I did not believe that he was dead, despite the sea god's disdain. I did not believe Jack knew how to die. He was elemental, almost, something of the same ilk as the thing that lived deep beneath the ocean in the frozen south. The same ilk, but perhaps not the same status.

Either way, I can still remember the feel of his icy breath on my cheek. I feel it every time I close my eyes and try to sleep. The only way I can sleep now, is if Ash is wrapped around me, warm, solid, reliable. It's the only way he can sleep too. We anchor each other.

'Spend Christmas in Antarctica!' The advert in the magazine had said.

I don't buy travel magazines anymore.

Gemma Amor is a Bram Stoker and British Fantasy Award nominated author, voice actor and illustrator based in Bristol, in the UK. She self-published her debut short story collection *CRUEL WORKS OF NATURE* in 2018, and went on to release *DEAR LAURA, GRIEF IS A FALSE GOD, WHITE PINES, GIRL ON FIRE, THESE WOUNDS WE MAKE, WE ARE WOLVES* and *SIX ROOMS* before signing her first traditional publishing deal for her novel *FULL IMMERSION*, published by Angry Robot books in 2022. This was followed by *THE ONCE YELLOW HOUSE, CHRISTMAS AT WHEELDALE INN* and *THE FOLLY* in 2023. *ALL WHO WANDER ARE LOST* is her twelfth published book, and her fifth for Cemetery Gates Media. Her next scheduled release is an anthology of ancestral horror for Titan Books called *ROOTS OF MY FEARS*, as Editor.

Gemma is the co-creator of horror-comedy podcast *Calling Darkness*, starring Kate Siegel, and her stories feature many times on popular horror anthology shows *The NoSleep Podcast* (including a six part adaptation of *DEAR LAURA*), *Shadows at the Door, Creepy* and the *Grey Rooms*. She also appears in a number of print anthologies and had made numerous podcast appearances to date. A short film she co-wrote called HIDDEN MOTHER (2021) was well received at multiple film festivals and she is currently working on her first feature length screenplay.

Gemma illustrates her own works and also provides original, hand-painted artwork for book covers on commission. She narrates audiobooks too, including *THE POSSESSION OF NATALIE GLASGOW* by Hailey Piper, in 2020, and *FULL IMMERSION* in 2022.

Other books by Gemma Amor:

CRUEL WORKS OF NATURE
DEAR LAURA
GRIEF IS A FALSE GOD
THESE WOUNDS WE MAKE
WHITE PINES
GIRL ON FIRE
SIX ROOMS
FULL IMMERSION
CHRISTMAS AT WHEELDALE INN
THE ONCE YELLOW HOUSE
THE FOLLY

Forthcoming:

ROOTS OF MY FEARS (as Editor)

Short stories:

IT SEES YOU WHEN YOU'RE SLEEPING
FERAL